no good deed…

Craig Sherman

IMPORTANT NOTICES

ISBN   9781734108446

Library of Congress Control Number: 2022904464

Cover Design and Creative Direction by Brandi Sea Heft-Kniffin.
Created with photos courtesy of Alice Triquet, Philipp Berndt, Tiard Schulz, Oliver Needham, Ryan Loughlin, and Timothy L. Brock on Unsplash.

First edition

Edited and published with assistance from ABLiA Media LLC in the USA

TO

Helena, the joy in my life.

Contents

PREFACE.. i

A Quick Question... 1

Oy! What to Do?.. 8

I Wish I Could Do It 13

A Gnawing Feeling.. 22

Hello, Dear Boy.. 26

I Made My Decision 36

Take The Ball... 45

I'll Make Them Say Yes 54

Moses Didn't Want to Lead.. 59

Next Rung on the Ladder 65

A Broken Heart.. 69

The Right Decision 75

I'll Have the Usual.. 81

Stones Never Die 87

Loud Whisperers... 99

Falling Down Drunk 114

It was an Innocent Kiss 122

Finally, the Day has Come 127

Financial Secrets... 136

It's the Rabbi's Decision 147

Table the Discussion 156

You Aren't My Type 160

It's None of Your Business 172

I'll do it, I'm the President 183

Unhealthy Relationship... 191

What Are You Trying to Say?... 197

That's Not the Way Boys Behave... 203

A Fait Accompli 211

A Break from the Synagogue 220

It's Almost Over...223

I Don't Know What I'll Do 228

Dead Silence..232

The Truth 242

Angel Hair...247

GLOSSARY..258

ACKNOWLEDGMENTS...263

ABOUT THE AUTHOR 265

PREFACE

When I was a young boy there were two things I loved—music and the New York Mets. In second grade, my teacher gave me an assignment to write about anything I wanted. I wrote about my beloved Mets and remember scribbling furiously in my notebook with the words flowing as easily as my dreams of being a professional baseball player. In my mind's eye, I still see the large A+, a yellow smiley face, and "Great Work!" my teacher brashly marked on my one-page paper.

Those kudos implanted in my brain and heart the dream of being a published author.

As a student, my grades were at best, unremarkable. I was fraught with undiagnosed learning disabilities such as dyslexia, auditory processing disorder (APD), and attention-deficit/hyperactivity disorder (ADHD). My parents and teachers attributed my academic struggles to laziness and lack of effort. If I had a dollar for every time I was told how smart I was if only I applied myself…well, you know that story.

Fortunately, the H in ADHD was not applicable, therefore I was never a behavioral problem, nor was I pushed medications such as Ritalin. As I matured, my academic studies improved, especially in college, as I innately learned how to work around my disabilities using common strategies employed by students today with similar learning challenges.

Throughout my high school years at Rutgers Preparatory School, I enjoyed English classes and loved reading terrific classics like *The Great Gatsby* and *Pride and Prejudice*. Although, I struggled to get through them in the allotted time. Where were audio books when I needed them?

Wonderful teachers inspired me. There was the sharp-tongued Mrs. Howell from Dallas who imprinted in my brain the difference between the words "may" and "can" each time I told her nature was calling. I remember how, like a Jedi Master, she told me, "Mr. Sherman, you will be taking my Women's Writers course this semester." There was also Mrs. Lange whose appearance was of a schoolmarm but who taught masterfully with the wit, sense of humor, and compassion of a good friend. I will always appreciate her patience with me as one of the "boys" in the back of the class giggling as she taught us to conjugate the verb "lay." Also, I fondly remember the gregarious thespian, Mrs. Hertzberg, who made reading Shakespeare surprisingly pleasurable.

At Temple University, I studied Economics and Finance but still loved writing. Therefore, instead of opting for basket weaving or pottery for my electives, I took literature and writing courses. I also volunteered time proofreading articles for the school's literary magazine, The Journal of Modern Literature. It was during this period I began taking my writing seriously and worked to fiercely battle fear of the dreaded "blank page."

However, after my academic career, family and work life did not afford me time or energy to write. I put down my proverbial pen and focused on a career in technology and raising two wonderful boys.

Years later, when I became president of my synagogue and was required to write monthly articles for the synagogue newsletter, my love for writing was invigorated. It was truly the highlight of my volunteer experience. It inspired me to write again and motivated me to submit and have published several articles and short stories.

In 2016, as an employee of a Fortune 500 company and a volunteer in its Mindfulness Program, I wrote an article about wellness author and speaker, Kirsi Bhasin, who spoke at a company event. I shared my piece with her, and she enjoyed it thoroughly. She shared it with Arianna Huffington. Not long after, I was invited to contribute as a blogger for the Huffington Post. I thoroughly enjoyed conveying a range of topics such as mindfulness, politics, sports, and music.

I began writing this novel seven years ago with a renewed resolution to complete it in 2021 during the COVID-19 pandemic. However, I've been writing this book my entire life. It has been a lifelong dream of mine to write a novel.

What you read and experience on these pages is the culmination of the life and dream of a young boy who put down on paper a story about the thing he loved most.

In so doing, I discovered a lifelong passion for writing.

no good deed…

no good deed...

A Quick Question

No man is an island, entire of itself; every man is a piece of the continent.
John Donne

One moment changed everything.

Perhaps it had been triggered by a thousand other moments, but this one, this one, transformed him into the person he didn't know existed.

They all told him, "Dan, don't do it." They all said, "You'll regret it." They all added, "No good deed goes unpunished."

However, despite the glut of warnings and the anxiety that entangled him, he pushed aside his fears like Sisyphus rolling his over-sized boulder uphill. He jumped in with the enthusiasm of a little boy playing baseball on a bright spring morning. What's more, he never imagined they would ask him to do it, let alone his immediate response wouldn't be a resounding, "No way!"

Yet, on that Friday evening in February, like the cold bitter night air hitting his round cheeks, he would be shocked out of the warmth of his comforting complacency.

Dan and his family drive down the tree-lined street in his compact blue hybrid Honda as the pastel-colored small Levittown homes rush past, reminiscent of an era gone by. Six statuesque green pine trees grow larger as the car approaches the end of the street. Only the whispers of their tires can be heard as the car makes a sharp and sudden right turn, thrusting its passengers into the parking lot of their destination.

One did not stumble by accident into this place. Only those seeking it ventured past the bright yellow diamond-shaped dead-end sign. Dan zooms through the parking lot until he finally maneuvers his car into a tight spot. The fifty-five foot tall, oblong brick building that stands before him marks the official departure from the mundane routines of work, school, and everyday life. He and his family are about to enter the warm and loving place of community he describes as his Shambhala.

Congregation Beth Emet. A welcoming egalitarian Conservative synagogue in the heart of West Huntington, New Jersey, an hour outside of New York City—just as the glossy brochure promises. The membership of three hundred and fifty-five families is a modest size for the area. As modest as many of its members' incomes and the tight budget, which keeps the building's lights on. The façade of the outside white stone structure displays the community's name with reddish brown copper metal—just six small Hebrew letters shared among two words.

On this evening, the bright round moon shines light on a stone depiction of the ten commandments that hangs just below the synagogue's name. These are the only ornaments that decorate the sacred gathering space that one might consider prosaic compared to the more lavish houses of worship in neighboring communities.

Dan, his wife Joy, and their young boys, Max and Jake, snake through the parking lot toward the large glass doors that welcome them into their home away from home. He is by no means religiously observant, as his propensity toward cheeseburgers can attest to, but his community provides him with a sense of belonging that makes his weekly attendance feel more like a social gathering rather than a religious obligation. Besides, as a boy, he had always attended services in the well-known Jewish community of Lakewood, in Central Jersey. It was there, among those with numbers branded on their arms and scars in their memories, he learned the importance of Judaism and the necessity of belonging to a synagogue.

However, growing up, Dan's family switched synagogues as often as switching gym memberships. His parents chose the more liberal Reform temple when Dan and his twin brother Evan were toddlers. Disappointed in the lack of tradition at their eldest son Alan's bar-mitzvah, they moved the family to the more traditional Conservative synagogue in time for their other son Steven's bar mitzvah. Finally, when the failing public schools necessitated the twin boys attend the local Jewish Day school, the family landed at the more stringent Orthodox synagogue up the street from their previous two synagogues.

Even then, their affiliation was driven more by community and tradition rather than fervent religious conviction.

Perhaps those same forces compelled him to agree to serve on the synagogue's board of trustees.

2

Joy enters the building first; the boys follow, scattering into the modern yet understated house of worship like shooed away pigeons in a city park, presumably running off to join their friends. Dan enters and glances over his right shoulder to look at the 120-year-old tarnished brass plaque that was once mounted on the cornerstone of the original foundation and now hangs on the wall by the doorway. When he turns his head back, he flinches, startled by an enthusiastic "Shabbat Shalom!"

"Shabbat Shalom!" Dan responds.

The well-dressed man moves toward him like a tiger pouncing on its prey. He looks down at Dan as Dan looks up, a maneuver made necessary by their differing statures. The man forces Dan's limp hand into a hardy handshake while he grabs his shoulder with his left hand.

"Listen, I need to talk to you about something extremely important. Ya got a sec?"

Rob is the President of Beth Emet, but by day is Vice President and head of risk management at a well-regarded Wall Street firm. He wears his occupation with pride and gratification as well as he does his expensive Armani suits. It was commonplace for them to talk about temple issues even during what is supposed to be time away. Dan greets him with a diffident smile while he squeezes back at his sturdy handshake.

"Well, ah Rob, I'm running late, and I really have to join my family. Also, it's Shabbat, and I don't think I should work on the synagogue's computers tonight…"

"No, no, nothing like that. Listen, I hate taking you away from your family, but it should only take a minute."

"Okay. Sure, not a problem." Dan draws satisfaction from his work with the computers despite it being the purview of a paid professional staff member rather than a member of the board of trustees. Dan chuckles inwardly, remembering when Rob asked him to take on the job, referring to it as Dan's "portfolio of responsibility."

Rob releases his grip as his eyes peer down the hallway.

"Listen, I gotta go talk to the Rabbi first, but let's meet inside the social hall in a few minutes." Rob races off, leaving Dan alone in the bustling foyer with Joy and the kids long gone and engulfed by the community somewhere inside.

Dan hurries past the sanctuary and down the hallway and enters the modest Maurice Silverman Social Hall where the nostalgic smell of traditional Friday night fare of baked chicken, green beans, and potatoes greet him. His mouth salivates as he places his hand on his stomach to muffle the rumbling.

The family was delayed because of Jake's late-afternoon basketball practice. That and Rob's diversion meant only a few small chicken wings lay languishing in a pool of what his grandmother referred to as *schmaltz* at the bottom of an aluminum tray. The hall is clamoring with ninety congregants on this typical Friday night in a room that can barely squeeze 150 for a special synagogue event.

He watches as the usual volunteers dance about the room cleaning up the detritus of paper plates, plastic cups, and half-eaten meals left by kids more interested in playing than eating. They roll up the paper tablecloths into oversized balls and hurl them into the large plastic garbage bins, leaving behind near-empty wine bottles on the naked wooden tables. Perhaps a bowl of cereal will have to suffice when he arrives home later that evening.

Dan glimpses Joy through the bottles of wine amassed at their usual table, where she sits with their friends. Next to them, a group of congregants sing, pounding fists on their own table to keep the lively beat. At a neighboring one, Mr. Chasen, surrounded by his usual cohorts, pounds his fist also, but not to the song; presumably, making some nuanced point about some archaic Jewish law. There is a loud din of conversation mingled with laughter that floats through the room.

Dan stands amid the beautiful chaos and feels a serene smile. When he finishes breathing in the intoxicating excitement, he makes his way over to Rick.

Dan and Rick are on the synagogue's board and have become good friends in the course of volunteering. During board meetings, they often share the same viewpoints, which don't always coincide with more senior members such as Rob. They both will nod in agreement from afar at opposite corners of the oversized crude table arrangement devised by the Rabbi, whereby four long rectangular tables form one large square one.

To prepare for the monthly board meeting, the Rabbi always oversees the custodial staff as they arrange the tables and place three chairs on one side of the square for the Rabbi, the President, and the

Recording Secretary. The remaining fifteen chairs are positioned on the other sides of the square, facing the three chairs at the head. The empty square space that forms in the middle of this formal configuration acts as a barrier that proves fortuitous on those nights when controversial topics are on the agenda.

Dan and Joy have been members for over seven years. Rick had grown up in the synagogue and yet until their time together on the Board they had only greeted each other at services. Dan had served on the board three years while Rick two; and even during that time their discussions centered on synagogue business.

Then, by chance, they sat next to each other at an annual gala. The event honored three of the more generous families; Rob and his wife, Jill, were one honoree. They talked all night, sharing views on politics, music, men's fashion, and religion. They even talked about relationships and Rick's recent breakup with a woman he had been dating for several months.

Dan joins Rick at the far west corner of the social hall where the other men of the congregation gather. He stands and turns to face the center of the hall as he looks over at Joy and smiles. She is still at their table but surrounded by her two closest friends she dubs, "the girls."

Joy and Beth met at Beth's senior prom. Despite having grown up in different states, they've become lifelong friends. Joy was raised in Havertown, a suburb of Philadelphia and Beth in Oceanside on Long Island. Joy's date for the prom was Beth's friend Rich, who she met at sleep-away camp. Beth took her Rabbi's son.

Hope, who grew up in West Huntington and went to Beth Emet her entire life, joined the duo when the three took a Mommy and Me class together.

Although an egalitarian Conservative synagogue, Beth Emet's members often partition themselves, without intention, by gender, which can suggest to those unfamiliar with the community a more Orthodox congregation.

As an errant young boy pushes open the double doors of the social hall, Dan glimpses Max and Jake in the hallway with the other kids playing some sort of game resembling baseball, using a wrinkled old yarmulke as a makeshift ball. Despite being accustomed to high-tech video games, and since it was Shabbat, when one is prohibited from operating electronic devices, the kids manage to find amusement within the constraints of the temple walls.

The myriad of sounds in the social hall seem to get louder as empty wine glasses are refilled and emptied again. Kids laugh, friends joke, and intellectuals philosophize.

"Rick, I like the tie you're wearing," Dan says.

"Thanks."

"How do you find such trendy, colorful ties that match your shirts and suits perfectly?"

"Well, this guy in the city near my office tailors my suits, and he always provides a selection of shirts and ties to choose from."

"I couldn't get away with wearing that stuff. Besides, the cost of your ties probably equal what I spend on my entire wardrobe."

"Nonsense, you dress impeccably. You always look good, Dan."

"Thanks," he says with a touch of 'aw shucks.'

"By the way, speaking of your office. How's work going?"

Rick is the Sr. Executive Director of Food & Beverages at JB Witherspoon in New York City. He and his team focus on convincing consumers to purchase an array of snacks and beverages, including pretzels, potato chips and pinot noir.

"Works busy, but going well. Thanks for asking. How about you?"

"Oh, the same, going well. It's been hectic for me too. I'm working on the launch of Scribner's new website."

"That sounds fascinating..."

"Probably not as interesting as being an ad man in the big city."

"I don't know about that..."

The men stand close to each other with their hands in their pockets, each scanning the open crowded area. Dan rocks back and forth on the heels of his black scuffed shoes; a habit picked up from years of rocking Max and Jake to sleep when they were both infants.

"Besides, some of us have to dress this way out of necessity. A few of us are still trying to attract the right person."

Rick then glances over toward the table where Joy is sitting and lifts the wineglass he has been coddling as if to make a toast.

Dan follows Rick's lead.

Oblivious she is the subject of the two men's conversation, Joy sits unaware, facing Hope. Their boisterous laughter tries to break through the noisy commotion.

"You're a lucky man, Dan," Rick says. Even from the far corner of the hall, Dan can see Joy's radiant face and her hazel-brown eyes glistening from the bright lights.

"Yeah, I am," he whispers.

Rob startles Dan as he jumps in between the two men.

"Hey guys, what's up? Dan, can we talk now?"

"Sure. What would you like to talk about?"

"I have a quick question; it won't take long."

Uh oh, Dan thinks, *What could this be?*

Oy! What to Do?

I refuse to join any club that would have me as a member.
Groucho Marx

Rob grabs two chairs and drags them into the center onto the faux-oak floor where the community dances the traditional *hora* during simchas. Dan follows, glancing back at Rick with an expression something akin to a condemned man looking for his sentence to be commuted. Rob places the chairs in front of each other and then turns one around and straddles it. Dan sits straight up in the other chair with his arms at his side.

He scours his brain, trying to discover the question Rob is about to ask, hoping to be prepared for a suitable response. *What could it be?* Dan thinks. *Maybe he wants me to recruit some new member to the board?* Then, remembering his time on the board would soon end, he thinks, Rob's relentless efforts to keep current members on the board might be it. *Is that it?* Dan had been considering taking a hiatus despite enjoying his time volunteering.

"You know, Rob, there are many other things I'd like to do at the synagogue…"

"I'm glad to hear that."

"…and while I've enjoyed my time on the board…"

"How are you? How are Joy and the kids?"

He looks at Rob. "Joy and the kids? Well…you know, Joy has a new job managing clinical trials for KAEA Pharma…" Rob produces a smile and nods. Dan continues to ramble on like a schoolboy called on in class without an answer. "…and Jake has been struggling at school…"

He rummages through the possibilities in his head, doubting his original theory about what Rob is going to ask him. *Perhaps he wants him to get some guys together to clean out the musty old shed at the back of the synagogue? No one wants to do that.*

"Oh, and the dentist thinks Max is probably going to need braces…"

"Yea, you know that's great, Dan." Rob's voice drops an octave and his speech becomes more deliberate.

8

"Listen, I've an important question to ask you, and I don't want you to give me an answer tonight."

"Joy and I've already discussed it and while it may be a stretch for us, we're going to increase our annual donation to the synagogue this year…"

Rob leans forward and puts his hands on both Dan's knees to stop him from talking.

"I want you to be executive vice president," Rob says in a loud whisper.

"Yea—right,"

"Don't laugh! What do you think?"

"What do I…What do I think? That would mean in two years I would become synagogue president!" He stated aloud a well-known fact he, Rob, and most congregants know. According to their constitution, no one is asked to be synagogue president; they are simply asked to be the executive vice president, a role that in two years' time miraculously transforms into president. Probably a tactic devised long ago by some shrewd past president who believed recruiting a credulous and unsuspecting person to vice president would somehow be easier than recruiting them to synagogue president.

"Rob…" he took a deep breath, "…are you asking me to be synagogue president?

"Yes, and I think you'd make a great one and many others agree. The Rabbi says he can't imagine anyone else in the position."

"Um…I don't know what to say."

"Again, I want you to think about it. No answer tonight, I insist."

"But I don't think I can. I really am not good at…"

"It's really not difficult. You run a few meetings, give a few speeches, write your article for the monthly newsletter, and everything else runs itself."

Dan dreads running meetings at work, and he never feels comfortable with public speaking. He used to write when he was younger and had dreams of being published, but that ended a long time ago with a family and a busy work schedule. And well, he probably wouldn't find the time to write something people would find interesting.

No way, Dan thinks. *Unequivocally and without doubt, I will not be executive vice president and subsequently president of the synagogue.*

9

"Well, um…I don't know…"

"Think it over, talk to Joy. Speak to the Rabbi and any of the past presidents. I insist you at least do that before deciding. Let them tell you how great it is to be synagogue president."

Rob scoots his chair closer and puts his arm around him. He looks over the sizeable crowd and smiles as he waves his arm gracefully, like a model showcasing what's behind door number one. He stares past the sea of congregants and speaks about the hope and promise of Dan in the role of president.

Dan listens with amazement as Rob weaves the beautiful and magical story.

"You know, during the High Holidays everyone wants to shake your hand. People look at you differently—with more respect."

He touts the benefits the prestigious position will afford him. With minimal effort and just a few hours a week, Dan can place on his resume the significant experience of running a non-profit organization with a two-million-dollar budget. No one would have to know the synagogue virtually runs itself and Dan's important role is effortless. And for all of this, Dan can have at his disposal a prime parking spot and a soft and luxurious throne-like seat on the *bima* right next to the Rabbi.

Dan winces when Rob elbows him in the stomach and says, "The ladies love a man in power."

As Rob continues, Dan's mind races in all directions, with Rob's voice changing into something resembling Charlie Brown's teacher. Dan trembles as he thinks of speaking in front of hundreds of people during the High Holy Days and dealing with disgruntled members. He remembers the nervous and painful sorrow he felt when a congregant called him, unable to reach the Rabbi or Rob or anyone else on the board, to inform him of the tragic death of her son-in-law. Dan struggled to get out the words of condolence to help ease her pain.

Rob's voice becomes clearer as Dan's thinking pauses for a moment out of sheer exhaustion.

"You know too, mostly people pay their dues on time, and our bookkeeper follows up on any issues."

Dan remembers the passionate discussion he had the previous year at a board meeting when Rob proposed a policy that would require congregants to leave a credit card on file to ensure timely payments of dues. Dan and Rick both argued the case that a synagogue membership was not a gym membership. Dan pleaded with those present. His voice trembled and his hands shook as he made his case.

"Sure, there are those who don't prioritize their dues and choose to pay them late…but many late payments are a function of these difficult financial times. This is exactly when our members need us most."

Passionate, astute arguments made by both Dan and Rick proved fruitless. They would later discover, from someone who had overheard Rob boasting, "I secured the votes to pass the motion long before I pounded the gavel on the table." He smirked and leaned over to whisper something in the Rabbi's ear. Apparently, it was not an accident Rob called the vote on the matter the night of the local high school parent-teacher conferences. With the minimum eleven members needed to form a quorum, it took only six yes votes to pass the motion.

Six months later, Dan and Rick found some solace when members refused to comply with the policy and threatened to leave en masse. The policy, with no strategy to cope with such a backlash, was rendered feckless.

"You know, it's not that much more work than what you already do."

"Rob, the amount of effort isn't really my primary concern. I was fine with adding the computer support work to my portfolio of responsibility…"

"You know, I really enjoy talking to the congregation from the bima and I bet you will too once you become comfortable. Dan, just be yourself and you'll do great…"

Dan remembers standing in front of the congregation when asked to speak at a friend's son's bar mitzvah. Tongue-tied, he stood behind the old podium at the center of the bima in front of the entire congregation. His mouth was dry and his palms sweaty. He tried to spit out a few words of congratulations.

Oh God. He suddenly feels nauseated. *No, absolutely not!*

"…and that is why you should seriously consider being synagogue president," Rob concludes.

"Um…you know I don't…"

Rob stands up and offers Dan his hand.

"I know you will make a great president. Let's talk in two weeks."

11

He returns a lukewarm handshake.

"Sure, I will give it serious consideration."

Dan sits alone in the middle of the room with the turned around chair in front of him as he devises the perfect plan on how, in two weeks, he will release himself from Rob's clutches.

There is one slight problem with his perfect plan.

He slumps in the chair.

Out loud he cries, "Oy! What am I going to do?"

I Wish I Could Do It

You've left it for somebody other than you to be the one to care.
Jackson Browne

Dan grabs his favorite large blue ceramic bowl from the cabinet, the one Joy had made for him on the evening of *Pinot and Pottery* with "the girls." After fishing for a spoon from the kitchen drawer, he snatches a box of the boys' favorite sugary cereal, opens the refrigerator, and balances a carton of milk on his chest as he kicks the door closed. He hops onto the stool at the island in the kitchen, pours the cereal and the milk, and eats his Friday night dinner, alone.

He places the cereal box in front of him when Jackson, the family's fluffy, almost white colored golden retriever, scurries over, sniffing at his pants leg. He pets the dog's head and whispers as if talking to an infant. "That's a good boy. Do you think daddy would be a good president?"

The dog responds. He pants, wags his tail, and looks up at Dan with his big brown eyes.

"Yeah, I guess you think I can do anything." Dan returns to his bowl and devours his dinner. The sound of Jackson's tail smacking the tile floor accompanies his crunching, filling the otherwise silent room with a symphony of noise. As he places another overflowing spoonful dripping with milk into his mouth, Joy enters the kitchen and informs him the boys are getting ready for bed. From behind his cereal box comes a sound somewhere between a crunch and a grunt.

Joy walks over to the dishwasher, lowers its door and empties it, removing one plate at a time and placing it in the cabinet above. With each dish landing on top of the other, a blaring clang echoes in the room. He does not flinch or shudder with the clatter. It's as if, wrapped in an impenetrable cone of silence, he is protected in his own citadel. He finds comfort behind the cereal box and in the paltry dinner he is relegated to eat because of the frenzied evening, which gave him both an empty stomach and a heavy crucible.

Joy's upturned face looks toward him, her gaze fixed while she continues unloading the dishwasher with the precision of a circus juggler. When she finishes her task, she putters around the kitchen, wiping the countertop and closing cabinet doors, all the while focusing on Dan. She yields to the silence.

"You're awfully quiet tonight. Are you still ruminating over your talk with Rob?"

"You know, I wish I could do it."

"Well, you c-aaa-n!…" she says, drawing the word out like Max's annoying habit of stretching out his chewing gum. "…if you want to."

"I don't know about that."

"If you don't want to do it, then don't do it. But you certainly can do it."

"I wish I were as confident as you are…"

"Did you tell Rick?"

"No, but of course I'm going to tell him."

"He will help you figure this out…"

"Well, I'm not positive he'll understand why I don't want to do it. Rick has all the confidence in the world. He would be a great president. Besides, there is nothing to figure out. I'm not doing it."

Dan goes back to his cereal, finishing up the last few bits at the bottom of the bowl, raising it to his lips, and slurping down the last ounce of milk. He pushes the empty bowl aside and grabs the soft, well-worn leather briefcase on the floor leaning against the wall. Joy gave it to him as a gift when he joined the board and received his promotion at work. As a software developer for a large publishing house in New York City, he liked his job, although he exchanged his dream of being an author years ago for a consistent and ample paycheck. Being near books and writers gives him some satisfaction. He takes the briefcase with him everywhere. It contains both his office and synagogue papers, along with a few assorted items like a pack of gum, a small bottle of ibuprofen, and sunglasses.

He pulls out a beat-up blue notebook, its cover partially ripped from the sharp spirals, and drops it on the counter in front of him. He flips through its pages like one of those old flipbooks when viewed in a quick motion animates still images. The pages, filled with notes, scribbles, doodles, and lists, overflow. Some have yellow stickies; others have folded papers hidden behind them. He stops on one page and mumbles a few sentences. Then, as if she had been listening to his incoherent thoughts, he continues, clearly and out loud.

"Remember this, Joy? Mr. Stein asked me to talk to the Rabbi. He wanted me to get the Rabbi to explain, from the pulpit and during services, some prayer rituals. You know, like a teaching moment."

"I thought that was a good idea," Joy says.

"Mr. Stein said he hadn't grown up going to temple and wanted to know what's with all the standing, sitting, and bending.

"Hey, I've been going to temple for years and I still don't know what all that means."

Dan chuckles, "I remember Mr. Stein saying, 'Oy! I get more exercise on Saturdays than I do when I go to the gym.'"

Dan rummages through the notebook as if searching for something. With each turn of a page, he seems more animated. He shakes his head several times and blurts out a few unintelligible words, then taps several times on a certain page as if sending out morse code.

"Oh, and here." His booming voice startles Jackson, who leaps up from his curled and quiet position at Dan's feet.

"Mrs. Kupferberg wanted me to talk with the Rabbi because of her son, who had just come out. He felt unwelcomed at the synagogue."

He continues to rattle off a few more incidents where people had reached out to him or confided in him rather than going directly to Rob or the Rabbi.

Suddenly, a large, folded document falls out of his notebook and lands on the tile floor next to Jackson, who jumps back and crouches down in front of it and begins sniffing. Dan pats his head as he picks up the papers and unfolds it to its original form, then flips through the glossy colored pages. It was a PowerPoint presentation he had presented to the Board and the Rabbi on how to make improvements based on his conversations with members. He raises the sheets over his head.

"Remember this presentation I gave to the Board?"

"The Rabbi and the Board members were impressed with the effort you put into that, Dan."

"Yeah, and the Rabbi said..." he then spoke in a gravelly and severe voice, '...these are extraordinarily complex issues with subtle nuances.'"

"People always feel as if you listen to them."

"Yes, but I don't seem to get anything done!"

15

"But you listen. Sometimes people just want to be heard. Besides, you get things done."

"Like what?"

"What about what you did for Ms. Moskowitz?"

Dan shrugs and presses his lips together. He lowers his head and places the document back in the notebook. Joy looks at him with a sigh and shakes her head.

"Anyway, it doesn't matter. It's not like you're going to be president."

He continues to leaf through the worn notebook, either not hearing her comment or simply ignoring it. She can see his breathing becoming deliberate as the corners of his mouth lower a touch, causing his bottom lip to protrude, accentuating the clef in his chin. Joy walks over, pushes the notebook aside, and turns his body and the stool he is sitting on toward her. She wraps her arms around his waist, kisses his lips, bows his head, and places her lips on his forehead.

Dan puts his arms around her, rests his head on her chest, and returns her firm embrace. Jackson jumps up, trying to insert himself between them and licks his face. The two welcome Jackson into their arms.

"Dan, I love you and I think you can be the best president Beth Emet has ever had."

"You have to say that. You're my wife."

"Don't be silly and don't drive yourself crazy. If you don't want to be president, don't do it, but you are more than capable. C'mon, let's go up to bed. You have tomorrow to drive yourself nuts."

The two make their way upstairs, holding each other's hands. Max and Jake are in bed already when they enter the boys' room. Jackson enters too and jumps back and forth on each boy's bed until finally settling on top of Max's. Joy joins Jackson while Dan sits on Jake's bed.

"Jake, I almost forgot. How did the big math test go today?" Dan says.

"I did okay."

"What do you mean, okay, honey?"

"Mom, you know I always do good on my math tests."

"Yes, Jake, I'm sure you did well on your math test." Dan says.

"We know you are bright, honey."

16

"I'm not that smart, Mom. Math is just easy. I'm dumb when it comes to English."

"Jake, you're not dumb in English and just because you find math easy, it doesn't mean it is," Dan says.

"Many people find math hard, including me," Joy interjects.

"I think if you could find the same confidence you have in math with your English, it might surprise you at how well you do in it," Dan says.

"We are proud of both of you, and it's been a long day for all of us. Let's all get some sleep," Joy says.

Dan and Joy kiss each of them goodnight and walk toward the door as Jackson flies off and sprints past them out the room. Dan follows as Joy whispers, "Good night boys" and turns the light off, pulling the door behind her, leaving it ajar, allowing the hallway light to seep in.

Dan and Joy make their way to their bedroom, where Jackson has already entered. They perform their nightly rituals. Jackson jumps up onto the end of the bed and curls into a ball. Joy turns off the lights as they both get under the covers.

"Joy, I think I'm going to read a little. I don't think I can sleep, anyway."

"Sure, just make sure you turn off the lights before you do and try not to stay up too late."

Joy kisses Dan on the lips, rolls over, and closes her eyes. Dan turns and tugs at the pull-chain on the small lamp on the table beside his bed. He picks up the book next to the lamp, sits up, and opens it to where he had left off. He places the synagogue brochure that is his bookmark on the bed next to him. He props up his pillow, makes himself comfortable, and enters the realm of the story, leaving behind the frantic night without effort.

The small lamp illuminates the dark room enough to see the words. His eyes move from left to right as he reads. The pace speeds up and soon he devours the words like the cereal he had finished a short time ago. Dan is not reading a mystery, or a thriller, or a classic romance novel, which usually lay on his nightstand. This time, a biography, a genre he usually avoids.

"I'm not interested in reading the minutiae of someone's fabricated version of their life," he would say to Joy.

It is Barack Obama's book, *The Audacity of Hope*. The Senator's speech at the Democratic National Convention the previous year had inspired him. One Sunday afternoon, perusing the table of bestsellers at the local chain bookstore amid lattes and croissants, the title, along with the senator's smiling face, caught his attention. This prompted him to disregard his aversion to biographies and purchase it on a whim.

The two other sleeping occupants in the room do not notice the ferocity with which he turns each page, and the crashing sounds it makes. Joy continues breathing in a manner that borders on a light snore. Jackson whimpers and flaps his paws in mid-air occasionally, no doubt dreaming about playing fetch with the boys in the backyard.

When he finishes the chapter titled, "Values," he notices the faint glow from the small electric clock on the shelf near the side of the bed. Before beginning the next chapter, he listens for a moment to the sound of the second hand making its way around the face of the old-fashioned clock decorated with yellow dandelions. It had been his Grandmother's and had fallen into his possession. It seems rather superfluous surrounded by cell phones and the digital white numbers on the cable box, perched underneath the TV.

Dan directs his attention back to the book and continues to read. After five pages, his eyelids become as heavy as the decision his reading distracts him from. He perseveres, always liking to finish a chapter before he turns out the lights. He whispers aloud the words on the page to keep himself from falling asleep, a strategy he often employs.

"If enough of us took that risk, not only the country's politics but the country's policies would change for the better," he whispers. The sentence reminds him of another quote the Senator had made two weeks earlier during a speech he gave on Super Tuesday.

He cannot remember the exact phrase, but it too was about change, and the spirit of it evokes something in him. The sentiment of the quote had simmered and percolated since the moment he'd heard it. The day after the speech, he picked up the New York Times and reread its entire transcript. He cut out the article, highlighted the quote, and saved it in his box of keepsakes stowed away at the bottom of his closet.

"Change can't happen…No, that's not it! For change to happen, we must…No, that's not it either."

Dan goes through several iterations in his head, finally landing on. "Ah, change is good, mon…" spoken in a Jamaican accent mimicking Rafiki from The Lion King, one of the boys' favorite movies. He must have watched it with them a thousand times. He remembers whispering to Rick about the quote during the last Board meeting while Rob droned on about the details of the new rider in the synagogue's insurance policy. He snickered noticeably when Rick responded, "...the only change I'm interested in is the change in this topic."

"Damn! What is that quote?" Dan says in a loud voice, forgetting that not only is he tired, but that Joy sleeps beside him.

He turns his head in a quick motion toward her and sees she's still asleep. He looks over at Jackson, whose head pops up from being startled by his outburst. Jackson looks at Dan, bleary-eyed and with faint interest. Dan flashes him a smile. Jackson drops his head back down on the bed and goes back to dream what big dogs dream.

"Now, what was that quote? Something like change comes from others."

"I know the darn thing, but I'll never get to sleep if I don't remember."

Dan puts the synagogue brochure back into the book, closes it, and places it on the bedside table. He throws off his blanket, leaps out of the covers, and creeps one step at a time toward the closet. He turns the doorknob and opens the door with apprehension, as if expecting some apparition or psychopath from a horror film to be hiding inside. He looks over his shoulder to make sure all is quiet behind him as the door creaks. "I'll have to oil the hinges."

He steps inside the dark closet and closes the door behind him by pushing the back of it with both his hands in a snail-like deliberate motion until he hears the dead bolt click. Inside, he gropes for the light switch like a blind man, then sits cross-legged, facing his side. He grabs the large cardboard box in front of him and pulls it toward him, out from under the dangling pants, shirts, and suit jackets. He opens the overstuffed box, and it greets him with an acrid smell of stale cologne and old newspapers.

Inside resides a treasure trove of memories. There are greeting cards, photos, letters and notes from past lovers, including a bunch secured in a rubber band that Joy had sent him when they first dated. An assortment of sandwich-sized plastic bags is filled with tickets from concerts, sporting events, shows, and movies he had attended. Each bag has the year of the events written on it.

However, two larger bags burst with ticket stubs. One is labeled JB and the other NY Mets. Two dozen alone to Jackson Browne concerts in the one marked JB. He loved Browne's music ever since he was a little kid at summer camp, which was the year the artist's self-titled first album was released. There wasn't a life situation he couldn't relate to one of his song lyrics. Joy and the boys love Jackson Browne too, but often tease him about his borderline obsessive adoration for the singer-songwriter. They even affectionately call the troubadour, whose sorrowful and heavy lyrics with music written in minor keys, Jackson "boring."

He then pulls a ticket out of the bag marked NY Mets. He holds it in his cupped hands like a delicate flower. The ticket is from his first baseball game; July 8, 1972, The New York Mets vs. the Los Angeles Dodgers. On it, in a little boy's handwriting, are the words, "We won 4-1!"

A closed-mouthed smile appears on his face. The image of the big round baseball head of Mr. Met on the ticket seems to return the gesture. He puts it back in the bag and resumes his hunt for Obama's quote.

Dan digs deeper into the box, as if searching for a prize buried inside a Cracker Jack box. He shoves a bunch of items up against one side, discovers a manila envelope and opens it. He pours out forty or more snippets of paper that had quotes printed on them. Some pieces look like they had come from humongous fortune cookies. They bear a variety of quotes from famous people such as Martin Luther King Jr., Albert Einstein, and the Dalai Lama. He notices a headline from a folded newspaper at the bottom of the box that reads, "Beatle John Lennon Slain."

"It can't be over here. I just placed it in the box only a few weeks ago." He pushes aside the items on the other side of the box and discovers a large faded black-and-white photo of him and his Little League team. A shorter young Dan sat cross-legged on the bottom row in the center, surrounded by a bunch of smiling young boys. He wore a giant grin that took up his entire face. A baseball cap tilted to the left sat on top of his bushy brown hair as he clutched a sign that read 'Lakewood Little League Braves 1974.' On the photo, just above his head, was the signature of Del Unser who had scribbled his name on when he appeared as a guest of honor at Dan's Little League awards dinner.

"Ah, here it is!" he proclaims in a loud whisper as he lays aside his beloved photo. The newspaper he had been searching for had been obscured by several dozen baseball cards, which includes one of those lenticular cards where the ball player's picture changes depending on the observer's perspective. It is a Mike Schmidt all-star card he had unearthed from the bottom of a Wheaties cereal box. He raises the printed object that is his Holy Grail toward the light and grips the sides as if to read it at the morning breakfast table. He scans the pages and finds the sentences he had underlined. He snaps the newspaper to straighten it out and moves closer to the words in the dimly lit closet.

He reads aloud in a soft yet vociferous voice, cognizant Joy and Jackson are sleeping. He begins at the first sentence in the paragraph right before the underlined ones. He wants a jumping off point to provide the proper effect, despite being alone with no one present to hear.

"You see, the challenges we face will not be solved with one meeting in one night."

"You can say that again, Barack," he mumbles.

"Now for the pièce de résistance."

"Change will not come if we wait for some other person or some other time. We are the one we've been waiting for. We are the change that we seek."

"That's it! That's the quote."

He notices he had drawn an arrow from the passage down the right margin to the bottom of the page. There, he had scrawled, "You've left it for somebody other than you to be the one to care— Jackson Browne."

"That's it!" he repeats. "Yes, now I can go to sleep."

He sits for a moment in the silence. He feels flush all over his head and face. He takes in a sizeable amount of air through his nose, shakes his head back and forth.

"Oh no, that *is* it. Now I've got the two of them telling me I should do it."

A Gnawing Feeling

There is nothing either good or bad, but thinking makes it so.
William Shakespeare

Dan wakes to darkness, eyes shut as the ticking sound of his grandmother's clock emerges into awareness.

tick tock, tick tock, tick tock...

His eyes open and focus on the timepiece like the camera lens of a photographer targeting a wild cat on the African plains. It is only six. Face to face with it, he lies warm and protected under the covers, somnolent and half-asleep, with no justifiable reason to get out of bed on a Sunday morning. But an unknown force urges him to start his day.

Instead, Dan yields to his utter exhaustion and closes his eyes, listening again to the tick tock sound until his mind and body fade back to sleep. As the morning progresses, rays from the sun peek through the blinds of the bay window next to the bed, throwing vertical lines of sunlight onto the dark blue comforter, keeping him warm.

This time the gnawing feeling at the pit of his stomach prevails, and he sits up. The bright digital clock perched underneath the TV in front of him reads 11:11 a.m. He rubs his eyes and stretches his arms while groaning. Joy stands on the other side of the bed, fully dressed.

"Why'd you let me sleep late?"

"You obviously needed to, and you've gotten little in the last week."

She pulls clean laundry and folds them from a basket that sits at the foot of the bed.

"It's been two weeks since Rob asked me to be president."

"And...?"

"I don't know." He grabs his cellphone from the side of his bed and runs his thumb up and over the face.

"He's going to call today...he's going to want an answer."

"Well, you've had plenty of time to sleep on it."

"Haha. I wouldn't exactly say I've been sleeping...except maybe this morning. I just wish I had more time."

"What do you think you'll learn with more time?" She continues folding the laundry while he sinks back under the covers into the safety of his warm and cozy blue blanket.

"Dan, why are you driving yourself crazy?"

His muffled voice emanates from under the covers, "I don't know. I'm just afraid I'll commit to it and then realize I can't do it."

"You know that's nonsense. You need to focus if you want this."

"I don't know if I want to do it! What if people get pissed off at me? What if I screw up? Damn, I slept way too late."

"Dan, it's Sunday. What do you have to do today?"

He throws off the covers and hits his grandmother's clock with the comforter as he jumps out. He catches the clock just before it reaches the floor and places it back on the side table. He leaps into sweatpants and a t-shirt and dashes through the double doors that connect the bedroom to the bathroom, leaving Joy alone with her chore.

"Ya know, maybe I don't wanna know what goes on behind closed doors," he calls out.

He turns the faucet on and squeezes out some toothpaste onto his toothbrush and scrubs his teeth hard.

He gurgles the question, "...so, what do you think?" A small amount of saliva-mixed toothpaste dribbles down his chin and onto his t-shirt. Brush, brush, brush. "Should I do it?"

"What?" Joy shouts from the bedroom. He gives his teeth two more quick swipes and then spits out the toothpaste and turns off the faucet. He pokes his head from behind the double doors like he did as a little boy, eavesdropping on his parents discussing his poor grades in school.

"Really, what should I do?"

"You need to make this decision on your own, Dan."

"I know, but what do you think I should do?"

"Dan, we've been discussing this for two weeks. I can't decide this for you. Only you can—no one else..."

"But what do you think? I need your opinion."

"You are scared. I get it. It's an enormous responsibility, but you can do it. But if you are that stressed about it, why don't you just tell Rob no?"

"Because I feel like I should do it!"

23

"Uh uh, Dan! No way, you're not pulling that card. You tell the boys all the time, 'Only use the word 'should' for moral and ethical obligations…'"

"I know, but I feel…"

"You've no obligation to do it. I know people trust you and look to you for answers, but you shouldn't take on this responsibility unless it's something you want."

"I know—you're right."

"Why don't you meet with the Rabbi and the past presidents as Rob suggested, maybe then you'll finally realize you can do it and then determine if you even want to try?"

"I don't know…Rob said he wanted an answer in two weeks."

"Then ask him for more time."

"I guess I could. Hmm…You know talking to the Rabbi and a few past presidents might make me feel better; at least I'd feel like I've done my due diligence."

"Exactly, just meet with them soon. I'm not sure I can take another week of this."

"Okay, I'll call Rob right now."

He dashes back to his side of the bed, picks up his cellphone, taps on the display, then enters Rob's name on the screen. The phone rings four times until he hears a voice at the other end.

"Rob here."

"Oh, um, Rob, hey, this is Dan. "

"What's up?"

"I wanted to get back to you on your question. I know I had promised to give you an answer in two weeks."

"Great, are you in?"

"I want to take your advice and talk to the Rabbi and past presidents. So, I'm going to need a little more time."

"No problem. I'm glad you are taking this seriously. That's what I admire about you, Dan. You've always been thoughtful in your decisions."

"Thanks."

"I think this is a good thing. I think this'll make you feel much better about being president."

"I…I didn't say I would do it. I just said I wanted more time to explore the possibility."

"Of course, I know, I'm just glad you're at least considering it—listen can you just take care of that for me? I don't have the time to…."

"What?—Rob?"

"Oh, sorry I was talking to Jill. I'll setup a meeting with a few of the past presidents and one with the Rabbi for next Sunday. I'll meet you in the chapel after you drop your kids off at Hebrew school."

"Okay then, I'll see you next Sunday."

The screen on his cell phone shows, "call ended." He puts it down on his bedside table and sits there. The gnawing feeling in his stomach seems to subside. His older brother Steven, a real estate agent, once told him, "If a potential buyer is negotiating the appliances, they've most likely decided to buy the house."

He gets back under the covers.

"How'd it go?"

"Well, I bought myself more time."

"That's good. Do you feel better?"

"Yeah, I think so."

Hello, Dear Boy

The only thing complaining does is convince other people
that you are not in control.
Anonymous

The week flies by with work and the usual routines occupying his time. Monday, he works late on the launch of Scribner's new website. Tuesday is game night and Wednesday Joy and he are up late helping Jake with a school essay on the American revolution. These distractions, along with the promise of meeting with the past presidents and the Rabbi, and the week-long deferment seem to provide a much-needed respite.

They only discuss the pending decision twice. Once, after the boys had gone to sleep while he was responding to an email. A congregant upset about the synagogue's lack of acknowledgement for their generous donation reached out to him. Then again, while watching the news together where talking heads were discussing the upcoming presidential election.

However, the calm before the storm ends on the following Sunday when the welcoming large glass doors at the entrance of the synagogue swing open with an unabashed exuberance as if to announce some prominent person. A gust of chilly March air propels Max and Jake through the double doors and into the swarm of parents and kids bustling in the lobby. Dan, a few steps behind, catches one door swinging back into his face as he strides inside.

The boys wave to him and in unison roar, "Bye, Dad!" as they weave and disappear into the crowd.

Warm smiles and bright eyes greet him as he makes his way through the lobby and down the hallway. It is the usual scene on a Sunday morning at Beth Emet. Kids are being dropped off for Hebrew school, teachers scurry getting ready for class, and volunteers mingle, waiting for meetings to begin.

He strolls down the hall and gazes into the enormous glass windows that offer a voyeur's view into the chapel where he is to meet Rob and the presidents. A dozen familiar faces dart about the room gathering their belongings, preparing to move on with their day after the morning service. The scene reminds him of the large shark tank at the Camden Aquarium where he and the family enjoy visiting.

The chapel, although primarily used for weekday and Sunday services, also doubles as a meeting space for committees and adult classes with the Rabbi when twenty-five or less take part. As the chapel empties, his breathing speeds up. The muscles in his jaw tighten and he rubs his neck, trying to release some tension. He knows within the next hour and amid the watchful eyes of passersby his fate is to be sealed. Either the illustrious group will provide words of encouragement that will inspire him to disregard his insecurities and take on the exciting opportunity, or they will feed into his fears, dissuade him from assuming the presidency, and release him from the immense responsibility.

At the far left of the hallway, on the opposite side of the chapel, he glimpses Jackie Goldin's bright red hair. Occasionally, he and Mrs. Goldin exchange pleasantries such as a courteous "Hello, how are you?" or a warm "Shabbat Shalom." However, their interactions are as perfunctory as nods shared by two strangers in an empty elevator. He often wonders why it is this way, since they are both active in the synagogue. Mrs. Goldin often plays an advisory role on matters of great importance, but she never serves on the Board or on any committee. He assumes it is pure circumstance and chance that prevents a more meaningful relationship.

There are always rumors and mysteries swirling around her. Her husband Norman, a wealthy concert promoter, is several years her senior. The story goes she had been a groupie with the Grateful Dead and followed them around the country, which is how the two met. If anyone asks Jackie about these tales, she winks and says, "Ah, what a long, strange trip it's been..."

Born and raised in Dallas, Texas, her family was one of only a few Jewish families in her neighborhood. Her background had molded her disposition into something more resembling a streetwise New Yorker rather than a genteel southern belle. He enjoys listening to her beautiful melodic singing voice during services. There was something intriguing about the combination of her sultry tones and her Texas twang that softens the guttural Hebrew words of the prayers.

She leans beside the modest storefront of the synagogue's gift shop dressed in a short skirt and a low-cut, loose-fitting blouse, which seem excessive for a Sunday morning at Beth Emet. The ensemble is perhaps more suited for someone years younger and a size or two smaller. She reminds him of one of those models showcasing a shiny new sports car at an auto show.

The store's window display beside her features both a Philadelphia Phillies and New York Yankees yarmulke surrounded by baseball pennants. There are old baseball cards, a beat-up Yankees cap, and a well-worn old-style baseball glove that is tiny compared to the oversized gloves of today. This relic on the window display, cradling a scuffed baseball in its worn webbing. Popcorn and peanuts are strewn throughout the bottom of the case, lined with fake bright green turf.

No doubt this is some clever marketing device devised by some well-meaning volunteer hoping to fill the synagogue's coffers by enticing a young fan to persuade his parent to purchase him a yarmulke.

Despite the crude presentation, Dan stands transfixed. He can almost smell the rich and earthy scent of the cowhide and feel the soft, supple leather on his hand. As he moves closer to the gift shop, he feels an impalpable force drawing him into the storefront window, urging him to put on the glove and pick up the ball and throw it. He imagines the little boy who had once owned this vestige of a time long past fantasizing that he is the hero making the last out to win his team the World Series.

"Hello there, dear boy. Do you see something you like?"

Dan, hypnotized by the display, is not aware that he is nearly standing on top of Jackie Goldin. Startled by her greeting, he drops his notebook and bends over to pick up the detritus of papers that have fallen out. While on the floor, he notices her red high-heeled shoes.

As he stands up, he replies, "Um, oh, Mrs. Goldin, I was just noticing that there isn't a Mets yarmulke in the window."

"Well, I'm sure if you go inside the store, you can get whatever you want."

Her soft southern drawl, bright green eyes, and enormous smile, which reveals unnaturally white teeth, distracts one from the crow's feet and laugh lines on her face.

"How are you doing, Dan?"

"Just fine Mrs. Goldin."

"Oh, dear boy, please call me Jackie."

"Oh, okay—Jackie."

"After all, I'll be taking you out to dinner and you don't want to be calling me Mrs. Goldin all night."

"Excuse me?

"It's my custom you see. I take out all the new presidents to Blanche's where we discuss your goals and plans and what you'd like to accomplish when you become president."

"Well, I don't know…I mean, I have to…"

"Now don't be frightened dear boy. I'm old enough to be your mother."

"Well, what I mean to say is, I haven't decided if I'm going to be president."

"Of course you will, and you will be a damn good one. Now get along. It seems June is in the chapel by herself, and Rob'll be along soon with some of my other previous dinner guests."

He stands silently in front of Mrs. Goldin and the display. He doesn't know if he wants to stare more at it, talk to her, or walk out and go home. He arranges the papers in his hands and smiles.

"Mrs. Goldin…I mean Jackie...can I ask you a question?"

"Sure, anything deary."

"Did you really travel with the Grateful Dead?"

"Sure did. That was one of the best times of my life. Are you a Dead Head, Dan?"

He is not sure why he asked such a personal question or why she's so forthright, but the words flew out of his mouth and he couldn't rein them in.

"Well, I wouldn't call myself a Dead Head, but I love their music."

"Yeah, I remember seeing Jerry sing, "Friend of the Devil" for the first time in 1970. Norm and I drove our VW all the way up to Port Chester that night."

"Very cool, Mrs. Goldin. That must be a great story. You must promise to tell me more when I have time."

She flashes a bewitching and mischievous grin, "Sure, dear boy. How about we talk about it over dinner at Blanche's?"

Blanche's is a diner about a mile and a half from the synagogue on Route 22. Although, calling it a diner is misleading as it has been transformed into an upscale dining experience. Established several decades back by its namesake as a simple family restaurant, home cooking was its mainstay. It was the most popular spot in West Huntington until falling into hard times. Blanche sold it to a young, ambitious, and well-known chef from New York City. After her husband committed suicide, she spent all the money she earned from its sale on booze and gambling and died penniless two years later.

Those acquainted with the affairs at the synagogue often refer to it as "the satellite office of Beth Emet." It's an ideal spot to go if one wants to be seen. Select meetings of synagogue business take place at one of the many tables out in the huge and expansive floor plan. The jovial atmosphere is ideal for recruiting volunteers and the public setting prevents sensitive conversations from getting out of hand. However, there are also tables squeezed into nooks and corners where high-backed booths provide privacy for indiscreet encounters.

He smiles back at Mrs. Goldin, crosses the hallway, and enters the chapel through the glass door. The room is now empty except for June who sits at the far end of a long rectangular table in the back of the room. He takes a seat.

"Good morning, Dan!"

"Hi June, thank you. I appreciate your coming today and helping me figure this thing out."

"It's my pleasure. I'm thrilled to hear you're considering becoming president."

"Thank you."

"You know, I remember when you and Joy first joined the synagogue."

"You gave us a tour and told us all about this place."

"Yes, I believe I was immediate past president at the time, and it was a pleasure meeting young folks like yourselves instead of dealing with budget issues for a change."

"Well, we still remember your kindness."

At that moment, two men burst in, laughing. They each take a seat at the table on opposite sides. One of them sits on its long side next to Dan.

"Hello," they say in unison.

The man next to Dan is about six and a half feet tall and towers over Dan even seated. The other man has a full head of flowing white hair and a white beard to match. He reminds Dan of Charlton Heston in *The Ten Commandments*. Dan knows them both but is not acquainted with either. They had served as presidents long before he and Joy joined.

30

The bearded man turns to Dan and says, "Okay, you want to be president. What's your motivation? You want your own reserved parking spot?"

"Excuse me?"

The tall man laughs and says, "You know it'd be a lot easier to bid for the parking spot at the next big fundraiser."

"I'm not looking for a parking spot. I'd just like to make some positive changes."

The bearded man clears his throat, sits up straight, and assumes his pontificating posture as he is known to do,

"You know there are three types of people at a synagogue: prayers, players, and payers. I see you as a prayer kind of guy. Am I right?"

"Well, if you want to be a player, you're going to need a lot of prayers," says the tall man, which sparks a burst of laughter from the two men.

Just then an older man strolls into the room wearing a beat-up old Brooklyn Dodgers cap and donning a cardigan sweater. He sits next to the man with the white hair across from Dan.

"What? No coffee? When I was president, I always made sure there was plenty of coffee at every meeting." The question is a declaration and not directed toward anyone particular. He sits down and looks at his watch.

"What time is this supposed to start?"

The white-haired man says, "Ten o'clock and you're late, Sid."

"I'm allowed to be late; with age comes privileges. Where's our illustrious leader?"

"Sid, I see you're in rare form today," says June.

"June, you know it's always a pleasure to see you."

The banter continues while the group waits for the rest of the attendees. Dan looks around and takes in the musty smell lingering in the air. The chapel contains a large old wooden ark, and a table used for reading the Torah, the top of which is slanted like an architect's worktable. Numerous scratches and dents adorn its top and a tarnished gold menorah stands out embossed on the front. He imagines the stories these flaws might tell if they could speak. Perhaps, when it stood in the old sanctuary, the synagogue's first Rabbi inadvertently scratches it when he lays a Torah on it. That Rabbi, now long gone, can't see the scratches that still serve as evidence of that seemingly inconsequential moment in time.

31

A memorial plaque hangs on the wall beside the ark with names commemorating fallen soldiers from World War I. The raised letters on its surface, worn down by time, makes it difficult to make out the names. These remnants of the original synagogue are relegated to the small chapel after having once been the epicenter of the congregation's religious life from 1910 to the late 1970s. Then the synagogue moved from the old building in the center of town to the current five-story modern location.

He glances out the large windows into the hallway and sees Jackie smiling, still posing outside the storefront. A small crowd of people appear in his field of vision, obstructing his full view. At the center of the group is the Rabbi and four or five individuals vying for his attention. He is scurrying by with Mrs. Winthrop, the synagogue's administrative assistant, in tow. When the Rabbi and his entourage exit the scene being played out in the window, the spot where Jackie had been standing is vacant.

Dan looks to see where Jackie had gone when Rob rushes into the room from the other side of the hallway. The others in the room don't seem to notice him and continue with their conversations. Rob sits at the head spot facing June and places a pile of papers and a travel coffee mug down in front of him.

"Okay, let's get started. Dan here is considering becoming our next synagogue president, and he's asked you as past presidents to allay his concerns."

"You sure you want to know how the soup is made in your favorite restaurant?" Sid blurts out.

"Well…"

"Will the Rabbi be joining us?" asks the white-haired man.

"He's never on time," Sid complains.

"What are your concerns, Dan?" asks June.

"Are you afraid people won't be happy with your decisions?" says the tall man.

"Well…"

"I remember when the urinal in the men's bathroom broke. I had a new one installed, and some complained it was mounted too high. Jeez! People!"

"Actually…"

"Yeah, that comes with the territory," the white-haired man chimes.

"I wouldn't worry about the congregants. It's that vixen Jackie Goldin you must watch out for," says Sid.

"Gentlemen, we're here to encourage Dan, not discourage him. Jackie is a lovely woman and was nothing but helpful when I was president," says June. "I for one found being president a rewarding experience that allowed me to really make a difference in my community. I also think Dan would be a wonderful president."

"That is if he kowtows to the Rabbi's wishes," says the white-haired man.

"How do you know? When you were president, the Rabbi was wearing diapers," says Sid.

"Well, I've seen how he works."

The group discusses the merits and disadvantage of what June refers to as "the Rabbi's assertive leadership style."

The tall man then turns to Dan and says, "Listen, for the most part, I found the experience rewarding, too. Not that hard. I enjoyed my time as president. There are plenty of people around you prepared to do most of the work. You can pretty much do as little or as much as you want."

"Yeah, and you did as little as you wanted," laughs his friend from across the table.

"Why don't you tell the group your concerns, Dan?" Rob says.

"I know the synagogue has been having some financial difficulties. Tell me about the budget process. I've never managed such a large budget."

"That's one of the easier parts," says the tall man. "Every year Jackie and Norm donate the salary of our bookkeeper and she takes care of everything,"

"Don't you still have to worry about where the money goes?"

"Nah, between the bookkeeper, the Rabbi, and Mrs. Winthrop all the numbers seem to add up at the end of the year. Yeah, we go through some issues during the year with cash flow, but it all works out in the end."

"Hasn't the preschool been floundering?"

"Dan, I think this is where you can make a difference. I think with your help, you might revitalize the school. I know you have great ideas," says June. "I know the Rabbi, as our preschool director, would really appreciate your input.

"What else ya got?" says Rob.

33

"Well, I'm afraid I'm not an eloquent public speaker and it terrifies me."

"Dan, I've heard you speak in public, and you are more than capable. I'm sure if it comes from the heart you'll deliver delightful speeches, and with time, you'll overcome your apprehension of talking in front of the congregation," chimes in June.

"Just imagine everyone in the front row in their underwear," says one man.

"Have you seen the old ladies that sit in the front?"

"Sid, is that really necessary?" says June.

"The good news is you get a break from your family because you won't be seeing them for a while," says the tall man. "After I finished my term, it was like a second honeymoon for me and Gladys."

"You know I've taken up too much of all your time. I think I've gotten a good idea of what to expect."

"Well, you need to speak to the Rabbi," says Rob. "Maybe we can go see if he's in his office."

"No, I don't think that'll be necessary."

"Oh, you're going to chicken out?" says Sid.

"Well, you guys haven't made the position sound enticing."

"What? You don't like your own parking spot?"

"What's with the parking spot?"

"Dan, don't listen to these old curmudgeons. They don't know what they're talking about. This is really a great opportunity," says June.

At that moment, Mrs. Winthrop pops her head into the door and announces, "The Rabbi cannot attend the meeting. Something unavoidable has come up."

"You know, I just think this isn't for me. I appreciate all of your help, but I'm going to have to pass."

He stands up from the table, pushes his chair back, and gathers his papers. He looks at each man at the table and then at June. Her face conveys an expression of disappointment and resignation. She knows there is nothing she can say or do that is going to change his mind. What is worse is that she can't blame him for his decision. He looks into her eyes as if to say I am sorry and at that moment has an epiphany.

He sees in her the reflection of his own disappointment. He discovers for the first time since this whole thing started that he

34

really wanted to be president. He wanted to make the difference that June, Rick, and Joy believed he could make. But most of all he wanted to be the person he never imagined he could be. But he knows that is not possible now.

"I've got to get out of here anyway," says Sid. "I need a cup of coffee."

"I really think talking to the Rabbi would help," says Rob.

"Well, thank you all, but…"

Rob asks. "Listen, can you at least not tell anyone you said no until I find another suitable candidate? In the meantime, talk to the Rabbi. He'll want to at least know why you said no."

"I'm pretty sure I'm not going to change my mind."

"I hear you, but at least give him the courtesy of meeting with him. He'll be disappointed and will want to talk with you."

"Um…okay, I guess I can do that, but make sure he understands. I've made up my mind."

I Made My Decision

Things are never quite as scary when you've got a best friend.
Bill Watterson

The family attends services on the following Saturday and sits in their usual spot, seven rows from the bima in pews on the left. Dan always settles on the aisle seat. Everyone knows it is his spot and if anyone is sitting there when he arrives the occupant gets up and moves along as if they've been keeping the seat warm.

He never asks anyone to move, nor does anyone offer to relocate; it just happens as a matter of course. It's like being in a classroom where everyone knows and takes the same seat day after day.

Occasionally, when a synagogue newcomer or guest finds their way to his spot, he shimmies past them into the row and finds an available seat without complaint.

On this Saturday morning, like most, Rick waits for him and Joy. He stands up to let Joy and the boys into the aisle. Dan drops his *tallis* bag on the aisle seat next to Rick. The bag is a gift from his mother who needle-pointed it the year Max was born just in time for High Holidays. The bag portrays the scene of Daniel in the lion's den with his Hebrew name stitched in an arc across the top.

He unzips the bag and pulls out the colorful wool tallis and puts it over his head and wraps himself like a caterpillar inside a cocoon. He mumbles the blessing for donning the prayer shawl, emerges from the tallis, places it on his shoulders, and drops himself into his seat next to Rick.

During services, Dan and Rick stand when the Rabbi asks the congregation to rise and sit back down when he tells them to. They bow their heads and bend their knees when the rituals require it and sing aloud the rich and soulful prayers. They recite the text from the prayer book in unison with other worshippers in response to the Rabbi's liturgical reading, then they sit quietly and pray in silence during individual prayer meditations.

But, most of all, the two men talk during the service.

The volume of their voices rises and falls with the sounds of the service and the voices of their fellow parishioners. Talking is common in the pews at Beth Emet. Although some turn to them and stare daggers when their conversation becomes incessant. They cover a vast array of subjects on this Saturday—sans the matter of Dan not becoming president.

"Hey Rick, you wanna come over to the house on Sunday? Maybe we can watch the Devils game?"

"Sure, why not."

At the conclusion of the prayer for removing the Torah from the ark, the two get up from their seats along with the rest of the congregation as the Rabbi leads a procession of parishioners off the bima.

"Well, the Rabbi will work the crowd now. We get a break. You know, like the first intermission during the Devils' game," Rick says.

Dan can see there is a short gray-haired man displaying a proud and ecstatic grin standing next to the Rabbi at the head of the line. The man, who has been granted a much sought-after honor, carries the Torah in an embrace one might give to an old friend not seen in many years. As the man walks, the ornaments hanging on the shiny silver crown at the top make a clanging sound, which breaks through the chattering of the people in the sanctuary.

The Rabbi personally greets every person he passes, sometimes stretching his hand down an aisle of people just to reach a doting worshiper who wants to wish him a "Shabbat Shalom." Congregants, as is tradition, kiss the revered Torah by putting their lips on their prayerbook or the fringe of their tallis and then graze them against the Torah as it passes.

Halfway down the far-right aisle the Rabbi stops to chat with a congregant to ask them about a sick relative or wish them *mazel tov* on the engagement of their child, or perhaps the birth of a grandchild. These maneuvers, which cause a bottleneck of congregants behind him, often frustrates some of the regular attendees who want an expeditious service and who want to eliminate what they view as an unnecessary and arduous practice.

During this break from prayer and formality, the congregation loosely sits and chats with their neighbors. Some get up and stroll around the room to mingle. The sound of the congregants talking and laughing grows louder and Dan hears Mrs. Nusbaum, seated two rows in front of him and to the right.

"Rita, I can't believe how cold it is in here. Why do they have the air conditioner on high blast? I can barely feel my toes."

37

"I know. I keep asking Murray to lower the air conditioner. I think he just walks over to the thermostat and pretends he's doing something," says her neighbor.

The Rabbi is now at the back of the room with a crowd of people around him. He turns right onto the aisle on the far left where he begins the last leg of his trek back to the bima.

"Hey, listen Dan, I'll be right back."

"Sure."

Rick walks toward the front of the sanctuary and goes over to talk to a crowd of people who have gathered in front of the bima. Dan walks back into his row and turns toward Joy.

"Hey, honey. I invited Rick over on Sunday afternoon to watch the Devils game."

"Just remember, you're picking the boys up from Hebrew school."

"Yes, I know. I should be home in time for the puck drop. By the way, where are the boys?"

"Out in the hallway with their friends."

"Oh, okay, I guess we should be glad they're at least in the building."

"Well, they don't have much of a choice."

At the other end of their aisle a heavy-set bearded man calls out to Dan in a voice competing with the boisterous crowd in the sanctuary.

"Hey Dan, I hear you're going to be synagogue president."

"Hi Harold. Well, we'll see."

"You gotta be crazy to take on the thankless job. They couldn't pay me enough."

He wanted to tell him he wasn't crazy, which is why he wasn't going to take the position, but he promised Rob not to tell anyone yet. Harold's wife, standing next to him, says, "Harold, it's an important job and there are a lot of things which have to be taken care of at the synagogue and Dan will be a great president."

"Well, better you than me, pal. I got enough problems being co-president of the men's club, which, by the way, we're going to need some new barbeque equipment for the *Lag BaOmer* picnic this year...I'm expecting you to help make it happen."

"Yeah, well, let's see if I become president first."

"Good luck...sucker!

Harold laughs out loud. He belts out the jovial sound from the bottom of his corpulent stomach. His eyes squint and his pudgy round face is beet red as the bristles of his salt and pepper beard stick out like a porcupine protecting its territory. His wife smacks him on the shoulder and says in a contemptuous voice, "Don't be such an idiot."

"I'm only kidding. You know that Dan. Right?"

Harold continues to laugh while Dan waves a dismissive hand and turns back toward the aisle seat. By this time, the Rabbi had passed his row and is stopped two rows in front, talking to Mrs. Nusbaum, no doubt about the frigid air in the sanctuary. Rick is making his way back to Dan via a circuitous route. He goes down the middle aisle to the back of the room and then follows the Rabbi's path up the aisle on the far left and squeezes his way past the congestion. He scoots his way back into the seventh row, where he stands next to Dan.

"What's going on Dan? The 'It's too cold in the sanctuary brigade' at it again?"

"Yep."

The two stand there and watch the exchange between Mrs. Nusbaum and the Rabbi. Rick turns to Dan and places his arm over his shoulder.

"I know you said you would not be president, but you've always wanted to make some changes—God knows we could use some."

"Shh...quiet. Someone will hear you. Besides, fixing the air conditioner isn't exactly the monumental change I was looking to make."

The crowd quiets down and sits in their seats as the service continues. Conversations remain, but now in softer tones. Dan settles in to enjoy his favorite part of the service. It reminds him of going to *shul* with his father when he was a young boy. Although his father wouldn't use that Yiddish term for synagogue. Instead, he would use the rhyming slang, "John Bull" a remnant of his days as a child growing up in Northern England. As congregants' voices grow louder, he can hear his father sing the familiar melody and smell his clean and musky shaving cream, a scent which accompanied his scratchy five o'clock shadow.

It's about noon and the sun shines into the sanctuary through the stained-glass windows which look down upon the congregation from either side of the room. The dispersed colors from the windows illuminate the pews and the congregants seated in the first few rows. Dan notices rays of cobalt blue from a menorah on one window shining down several rows in front of him onto Jackie Goldin's bright red wild curls, giving them a purplish hue.

As the service continues, Dan scans the room, drinking in the faces of his community. He watches as the scene plays out before him with the melody of the prayers serving as the soundtrack. Andy Gross reads to his daughter from a child's book while she sits on his lap playing with the fringes at the end of his tallis.

A small group of teenagers play cards in the last row of pews. Their neighbors do not seem to notice the malaprop game taking place; likewise, the youngsters aren't disturbed at all by the voices of prayer around them. He can see Mr. and Mrs. Fineman at the other end of his row, holding hands and whispering.

Warmth envelops his body, which he thinks capable of even breaking the chill of Mrs. Nusbaum's complaints.

He notices two empty seats in a section on the right side of the sanctuary. Rob and Jill are not in attendance, which means he won't have to contend with Rob trying to convince him to change his mind and go speak with the Rabbi. He enjoys his respite from the hurried week and the decision which had been weighing on him. But he no longer needs to worry about it since his decision is final.

After the service, Dan, Joy, and Rick make their way out of the sanctuary, where they join in the mass exodus.

"We're extremely excited you're going to be synagogue president," Sylvia Goldstein says with a warm bright smile which radiates from her face, as her husband nods agreement.

"You'll be a wonderful president, Dan."

He shakes their hands, wishes them both a "Shabbat Shalom," and thanks them, explaining he has not yet decided if he is going to take on the position. He hates lying to the sweet lady, but is grateful Rob swore him to secrecy because he just doesn't have the heart to tell her he will not be president.

Dan and Joy merge into the crowd amassing in the hallway just outside the sanctuary doors. The mob carries them forward toward the front of the synagogue and the glass doors, which functions as both entrance and exit. Rick chooses the opposite direction, fighting the current of congregants like a salmon swimming upstream. Dan and Joy catch up with the boys who are already in the middle of the large foyer. The family is squeezed into the throng of people where a chorus of "excuse me's" and "sorry's" can be heard.

As they inch their way closer to the exit, they greet the Cohens, the Rothbergs, the Milsteins, and several other families. Mrs. Nusbaum asks him if he thought it was too cold in the sanctuary and if there is something he can do about it.

"Of course. I promise to investigate it."

The movement of the mass seems to stop. The culprit of the bottleneck is a group lined up waiting for an audience with the Rabbi for a quick exchange and a "Shabbat Shalom." A friend of Max's forces his way through the crowd and over to the family. The boy tugs at Max's coat sleeve and the two exchange, "Heys!"

The boy then turns to Dan.

"Hey, Mr. Barkan, I hear ya gonna be president. That's pretty cool."

"Well, I haven't decided yet, Jason."

"Why wouldn't you? You get to be in charge and everything."

"Well, it's not that simple, Jason."

His mom calls him over and before he runs off, the boy says, "See ya tomorrow at Hebrew school Max, bye!"

In time, the line of parishioners' funnels into the parking lot and the family moves closer to the Rabbi who is perched under the exit sign shaking hands like a politician on the campaign trail.

Rick emerges from the mass as the horde separates to give him room to get to Dan.

"Hey buddy, you mind if I cut."

"Why, you afraid you won't get whatever they're giving away at the front?"

"No, I'm supposed to have a hot blind date tonight and I wanna get outta here to get ready. "

"Oh yeah? Who're you going out with tonight?"

"Someone from Greenblatt's office. By the way, Greenblatt asked me if I'm going to be your vice president."

"What did you tell him?"

"I told him you haven't decided yet."

"Listen, I'm sorry I've been nuts lately. Just…this whole thing was driving me crazy. But now it's over and I can get back to normal."

Rick reaches over and kisses Joy on the cheek and shakes the boys' hands, wishing them each a Shabbat Shalom.

"Hey, Jake, was Rachel Schoenfeld smiling at you during services today? I think she likes you." Jake blushes and flashes an enormous grin as he punches him in the arm. Rick feigns injury and then turns back to Dan.

"Was the meeting really that bad you just got up and said no?"

"Yeah, it was awful. They were all obnoxious except for June. It was painful. And Sid spent the whole time complaining."

"I'm not surprised. He's always complaining. I'm not sure why you want their opinions, anyway."

"Of course, June was the only one who said anything which made me even consider it."

"Rob must have been pissed about it."

"He actually said little, he just kept saying I should talk to the Rabbi."

"You know I would've been more than happy to be your VP. You know we could've gotten a lot done, or at least had fun trying..."

"You would've done that for me? Anyway, it's a good thing we don't have to worry about it anymore."

"If it meant you would've been less stressed about this whole thing, I would've done it."

"Thanks! That means a lot."

"Well, it probably worked out for the best because there is no way they would've wanted me as your vice president."

"Why not?"

"You know they have their reasons...but, if possible, I would've done it for you. I've great confidence in you Dan Barkan." They embrace and pat each other on the backs.

By this time, they have reached the front of the line and stand in front of the Rabbi who is still saying goodbye to a couple on his right. The Rabbi glances over at the two men hugging and then returns to the couple to finish his goodbyes. The men release each other from their embrace. Dan adjusts his tie and straightens his jacket and stands in front of the Rabbi waiting for him to recognize him as Joy and the boys stand behind him talking to Rick.

The Rabbi is dressed in a well-tailored dark blue suit and a red power tie, perfectly knotted. The pleasant smell of his cologne often lingers on one's hands long after a handshake and the sunset after shabbat. Draped over him is a traditional cotton black and white prayer shawl with an embroidered design of Moses leading the children of Israel to the Promised Land. His Hebrew name is spelled out in a golden thread resting on the collar. He always grasps the fringes at the corners of his tallis and covers his hands with the garment when he shakes congregant's hands. This technique, Dan later learns, he employs as a precaution from contracting any unwanted germs. Despite this safeguard, Dan can still see his gold monogrammed cufflinks, that reflect the fluorescent lights in the synagogue hallway.

The Rabbi always wears French cuffs and except for major Jewish Holidays dons the same gold cufflinks with his initials embossed on them in a cursive font. Rabbi Ben Stern has been the spiritual leader of congregation Beth Emet for over twenty years. It is the only synagogue he has ever led.

"Dan, Shabbat Shalom, nice to see you. "

"Thank you, Rabbi. I enjoyed your thought-provoking sermon today."

"Thank you. I hear your meeting with our past presidents didn't go as well as I had hoped."

"Yes, well, I realized this wasn't the right time. I think I'm better serving rather than leading."

"Don't underestimate yourself. Dan, you have the potential to be an outstanding leader. You know I'd still like an opportunity to meet with you. How about eight pm on Thursday, in my office?"

"You know, I appreciate it, but it won't be necessary. I know you're busy."

"Nonsense. I can always find time for you. Regardless of what you decide, we should catch up."

"Well, I'm confident this is the right decision."

"Of course, you are. Listen, I want to hear how everything is going with you and the family. By the way, how are your parents doing? Tell them we look forward to seeing them again."

"They're doing okay; you know my Dad; he forgets a lot, but he's blissfully unaware."

"Yes, it's a difficult situation for you and your family. Please send them my regards."

"I will Rabbi, thank you."

The Rabbi places his right hand in Dan's and gives it a slight squeeze. He places his left hand on Dan's shoulder and looks him straight in the eyes."

"Wonderful, then we're set for eight pm Thursday in my office. I won't take no for an answer. Okay?"

43

"Sure, Rabbi but remember I've made my decision."

"Of course, I respect it."

The Rabbi releases Dan's hand and then kisses Joy on the cheek and wishes her a Shabbat Shalom. He then turns to Max and Jake and grabs their limp hands and shakes them both.

"Hey Max, you heard my Phillies got Dan Stevenson? They're going to be a powerhouse this year!"

As the family exits the synagogue with the rest of the mass to make their way home, Max calls back to the Rabbi, "We still have Miguel Padre! We're going to beat your Phillies!"

The Rabbi waves and responds with, "We will see…"

Take The Ball

You miss 100% of the shots you don't take.
Wayne Gretzky

When the family arrives home from synagogue, Dan races up the front porch steps, jumps over the folded newspaper on the welcome mat laying at the door, turns back, and quick picks it up and reads the headline *Obama Rejects Idea of Back Seat on Ticket.* He reads the first few sentences.

I don't blame him. He should stay in and fight. Why settle for second place when it isn't over yet, he thinks.

He unlocks the blue door and pushes it open to be greeted by Jackson who twirls around him with excitement. Dan takes the stairs two at a time to change out of his suit, while Jackson follows on his heels as he makes his way to the top of the stairs.

"Honey, I'm going to go take Jackson for a walk in the park,"

"Sure, I think it's a good idea. You need to get outside and relax a bit. It'll do you both some good."

A few minutes later Dan returns dressed in shorts and a t-shirt. Jackson circles as he attempts to put on his leash.

"Sit boy!"

Jackson stops, sits up tall, and pants with saliva dripping on Dan's sneakers. He struggles to contain himself as Dan slips on his leash.

"Good boy! Let's go! Bye honey," not turning back as he runs out the front door with Jackson and closes it behind him.

A beautiful early spring day, the sun beats down hard as they walk the treelined streets. He notices it feels more like the middle of August rather than the end of March. Neighbors, having come out of winter hibernation, wave, saying "Hello." The cloudless sky is bright azure blue, and the green grass looks too perfect to be real. Jackson gallops alongside Dan like a champion show dog at Westminster as the two make their way to the park just four blocks down the street.

The unseasonable weather has attracted a large crowd. A group of teenagers play frisbee and a young couple stretch out on a blanket holding hands. A family gathers at a picnic table with the dad cooking burgers on a small grill.

Dan and Jackson walk around the lake, teaming with ducks, as a heron flies overhead and lands on the opposite side. Several people stationed at different points at the water's edge enjoy the picturesque day, including a woman in a large, flowery floppy hat lounging on a beach chair with a fishing rod by her side.

The two walk a half-a-dozen laps around the half-mile trail at the perimeter of the lake. When they have both had enough, they land on their usual bench several yards from the picnicking family. Dan bends down on the ground and ties Jackson's leash to the bench leg, near an overgrowth of mint leaves. He sniffs their aromatic cool scent while he secures the leash end. He sits, clasps his hands together, and places them behind his head. He leans back, takes in the bucolic scene, and closes his eyes.

Jackson finishes lapping up the water from the portable bowl Dan has laid before him and now pants as he scoots his body down into the bushes and under the bench by Dan's feet. The strong mint scent lingers in Dan's nostrils, joined by the smell of the sizzling burgers. The unmistakable mixture of the two odors paints a childhood memory in Dan's mind, which transports him to a scene he has long forgotten.

It is his last season playing Little League Baseball. He is eleven. In the three years he had played, he had established himself as one of the better players. Unfortunately, at the end of every season his team was in last place.

On this August Saturday afternoon, the sweltering heat was oppressive, and moms in the stands held umbrellas and sucked on multi-colored ice pops, sharing them with younger siblings in attendance. The humidity caused his long hair to curl up from under his cap while sweat dribbled down his back.

His team, the Braves, were losing again, this time 14-3. Although, it was not a bad score for the team, considering it was already the top of the ninth inning. He didn't like losing each Saturday, but he accepted it in exchange for the electronic scoreboard, the professional-looking built-into-the-ground dugout, and hearing his name called over the PA system as he stepped up to the plate. Of course, he also loved buttoning his wool baseball jersey with the name Braves embossed in script across his chest before each game, and wearing the blue stirrups high on his legs like the guys in the pros. He kept them up with rubber bands, which left a red mark when he took them off.

He stood on first base at his usual station. He was talking to the sixteen-year-old umpire who was pointing out the cute blonde girl in the bleachers who was in Dan's class at school. He blushed, turned the other way, and noticed a swarm of little kids amassed around the square opening at the end of the brick dugout. They were calling down to one of the ballplayers. He remembered when he was the little boy sitting in the dirt around the same opening, trying to get his brother's attention. It was here, surrounded by the mint leaves and the smell of burgers on the grill where he first imagined himself inside the dugout and springing out onto the field taking his position.

Old Man Mercado was on the mound doing his best to console Jimmy Hicks who had just given up four runs and walked the bases loaded. Coach Mercado knew how to get kids to play above their ability, but even in the era before pitch counts and mercy rules, it was apparent Jimmy was cooked. Coach Mercado knew Jimmy's tank was empty and pulling the old "ice cream cone for two more out" inducement was not going to magically infuse Jimmy into securing the last two outs.

At this point catcher Bobby Singer and third basemen Marty Russo had joined the Coach on the mound. Old Man Mercado took the ball from Jimmy and tousled his baseball cap and patted him on the rear. Jimmy ran off into the dugout with his head down low, hiding beneath his cap and running the sleeve of his jersey across his face. The coach held the ball in his hands, rubbing it as if it were a magic lamp ready to release a genie who would grant him three wishes: two outs and a cold beer.

Old Man Mercado scanned the field, searching for the boy who was going to procure him two more outs and no more runs. He pivoted his body toward first base. He pointed his bony finger at Dan and curled it several times, calling him over to join the quorum on the mound. Dan sprinted over and assumed, like Old Man Mercado had done many times before, he wanted to seek his counsel.

"Who're you thinking of coach?"

"Well, I was going to go with Hector, but he can't hit the broad side of a barn, but then it came to me. There's this one kid on our team who's been dying to pitch but has never tried."

"Yeah, who?"

"Hey, what's in your glove?"

Dan turned his glove up and opened it.

47

"What? I don't see anything?"

Coach Mercado dropped the ball in the open mitt.

"Now you do."

It took only a split second for Dan to go from well-seasoned, confident team leader to an inexperienced bundle of nerves with the potential for failure.

"Oh no, no way! I'm not pitching."

"C'mon Dan. Just two outs, and we can survive the inning. You know you've been dying to pitch. You're always pitching to Paul during practice. I've seen you. You can pitch."

"Yeah, but in practice and with no one standing at the plate."

"You know you could be good if you had some confidence. We all know it, right boys?"

Bobby and Marty shook their heads like bobble head dolls.

"Yeah...right. You're pretty good," said Marty.

"You even get it over the plate sometimes," Bobby said.

Old Man Mercado and Marty looked at Bobby and each gave him an odd look.

"Listen coach, there's no way I'm pitching. Yeah, sure I've dreamed of trying it, but I'm not ready yet. Besides, I'm too wild. What if I hit someone?"

"No problem. We rub some dirt on the bruise. C'mon Dan, It's the ninth inning. What's the worst that can happen?"

"I could plunk the next batter in the head. I could walk the bases loaded; I could give up a home run to their worst player—that can happen."

"I'll tell you what, ice cream for two more outs?"

The home umpire then appeared at the mound and joined the growing crowd.

"Gentlemen, are you having a party and you forgot to invite me?"

"Yeah, we're serving ice cream," said Mercado.

"Mercado, we need a pitcher. Let's get moving."

The ump made his way back to home plate.

"Okay, Dan, here's your moment. Your coach is offering you the ball. Are you going to grab it and strike out the next two batters? Or are you going to live with regret for the rest of your life until you die, or live to be a crotchety old man like your coach?"

"Has my mother been giving you lessons in guilt, coach?"

"Dan, someone's got to pitch."

"I'm sorry. I can't. I'm sick to my stomach just thinking about it. I promise, I'll work at it and maybe next time when I'm more prepared.'

"Kid?"

"I can't."

"Okay, no sweat, kid. I just thought you really wanted to..."

Coach turns to the dugout and calls, "Hey Pee Wee, you're up!"

He rushes out of the dugout like a small greyhound out of the starting gate and appears on the mound in an instant.

"What took you so long Pee Wee?" coach says as he drops the ball into Pee Wee's wide open glove. He always wanted to pitch but the coach would tell him every time, "Maybe next week, kid." It wasn't because the old man thought he couldn't pitch it was more about his stature, which matched his moniker. Coach was concerned a hard-hit ball back at him would knock him down like a pyramid of bottles at a carnival.

Coach Mercado claps his hands several times and says, "Go get 'em."

The coach walks off the mound with Bobby and Marty running back to their positions. Dan stays on the edge of the grass off the mound while Pee Wee throws some warmup pitches. After the second pitch flies over the catcher's head and hits the backstop, Dan makes a hand motion to the coach, who is looking down and writing something on his clipboard. Dan adjusts his cap with the hand he had raised.

After the third warm up pitch lands over home plate, the umpire walks out in front of the catcher and calls out, "Play ball!"

Sweat pours down the sides of Pee Wee's face, which is ghostly white with tinges of green and yellow throughout. Dan sees the hand holding the ball shaking.

"Hey, you okay Pee Wee?

"Yeah, I'm great. Well, except for this overwhelming feeling I'm going to throw up.

"Okay then, as long as you're okay. You know if you can't pitch..."

"I'm good Dan, I got this."

Dan sprints back to his position and pounds his glove with his fist.

"Just two outs, Pee Wee. You can do it!"

Pee Wee faces the first batter. He gets into position and looks down at home plate and Bobby crouched in front of the umpire. He shakes his head as if agreeing with Bobby to throw the curveball or the fast ball. Pee Wee knows how to throw only two pitches; "over the plate," and "over their heads." He places his foot parallel to the pitching rubber and pushes it snug against it. He winds up in a crazy and uncontrollable motion, and releases the ball, which sails to home plate and whizzes by the batter and into Bobby's glove.

"Strike one!"

In unison the entire team yells, "Yeah!" except Pee Wee, who, stunned by the result, stands still in astonishment. Bobby calls to him to get his attention before he throws the ball back to him. Pee Wee goes into motion again and throws the next pitch, but this time with more confidence, like he's the team's number one pitcher.

The batter swings, reaching out over the plate.

The ball, several inches off the plate, hits the edge of the webbing of Bobby's stretched out glove and trickles to the backstop. As the runners make their way toward the next base, Bobby pounces on the ball and springs up like a rabbit and fakes a throw to Marty at third. All the runners hot tail it back to their bases with great urgency.

Now there are two strikes on the batter.

The crowd's making noise. Kids in the stands scream, "Let's Go Pee Wee!" Pee Wee's mom yells, "You can do it sweetheart!" as chants of "swing batta, batta" call out from the infield. Pee Wee circles the mound and grabs some dirt from the ground like they do in the big leagues. He pushes his foot back up against the rubber and winds up in his tumultuous motion and flings the ball toward home plate…where it meets the batter's bat and makes a loud "Crack!"

The ball jumps high in the air. Everyone in the bleachers stands and turn toward the flight of the ball. Fans gasp while Pee Wee's mom squeals. The ball drops like a can of corn in mid-air and sours down into Marty's glove at third base.

The umpire yells, "Out!"

The crowd cheers and jumps up and down with exuberance as if Seaver had struck out Pete Rose in game one of the 1973 playoffs.

The next batter makes his way to the plate as the clamor of the crowd grows louder.

"Just one more!" yells one of the kids congregated around the square opening at the side of the dugout. Pee Wee throws the pitches, the umpire calls a ball, outside. Another, and it's a ball, this one in the dirt.

He then throws a ball over the plate that the batter rips down the third base line into foul territory. The crowd gasps. He goes into his motion again.

The batter raises his bat high in the air over his head, waving it in a circular motion as he wiggles his knees, waiting for Pee Wee's pitch. He throws the ball as hard as he can, letting out a loud grunt.

The fidgety batter swings his bat in a long uppercut motion. The bottom of his bat grazes the top of the ball. It dribbles to the right of Pee Wee near the third base side. He springs from the mound and grabs the ball and hurls it to Dan at first base for the final out of the inning.

Pee Wee vaults up and down as Dan and the rest of the infield rush to the mound and jump all over him, slapping him on the back and his head.

"Come on guys, just twelve more runs and we can win this thing!" says Marty.

"I knew you could do it; I knew you could!" says Dan.

The crowd bursts into raucous commotion filled with exuberance and elation as the boys run off the field into the dugout. Some parents in the stands rise to leave, hoodwinked into thinking the team had won and the ballgame was over. The sound of an ice cream truck can be heard atop a dog barking. Dan throws his arm over Pee Wee's shoulder.

"I knew you could do it. I knew you could! "

The dog's bark becomes louder and more persistent.

"I knew you could do it; I knew you could do it!" He feels a warm breath on his hand and a wide wet tongue licking it.

"Hey, mister!"

Dan opens his eyes and departs from his daydream as he mumbles, "You can do it, you can do it." Jackson lets out three quick booming barks and jumps on Dan's lap.

"Hey mister, can you throw us our ball?"

One of the boys playing catch nearby is calling out to Dan.

Dan looks around his immediate area, searching for it. It's under the bench—next to his feet. He bends over and grabs it and starts rubbing it like Old Man Mercado. He stands up and signals to the boy he is going to throw a fastball. The boy returns a befuddled look.

Dan winds up and with ease launches the ball straight into the boy's glove. The boy catches it and winces. He removes his hand from his glove and flaps it around, hoping to lessen the sting.

"Nice throw, mister."

"I knew I could do it," Dan whispers.

The two boys turn from Dan and Jackson and go back to playing catch.

Dan drops back on the bench and thinks, *Hmm, that was a pretty good throw.* It has been a long while since he thought about that day on the baseball field and how he missed the opportunity to see what it was like to stare down at the catcher's glove and throw a baseball from a mound past a swinging batter.

He never got another opportunity.

He remembers how impressed he was at the way Pee Wee leaped out of the dugout and charged the mound. He knows Pee Wee was scared too; probably more petrified than he would have been. But despite his fears, Pee Wee took the plunge and swatted aside his trepidations like they were annoying and pesky gnats on an oppressive hot day in the summer. This was no earth-shattering epiphany; it was more an ice-cold splash of water in his face waking him to a reality he already knew.

"Hey Dan!"

He turns and sees Rick waving his hand and sprinting toward him. Rick slows down to a quick walk until he reaches him and Jackson at the bench. Rick pats Jackson on the head.

"What are you doing here?"

"I thought I'd come by, and we could hang out tonight."

"Didn't you have a hot date?"

"Yeah, my date has a cold. Oh, did you hear the news?"

"No, but I have news for you."

"Hanrahan is playing tomorrow night for the Devils."

"Really? But I thought he had a concussion and had popped his shoulder."

"Well, he said he wasn't going to let some injuries get in his way and he was ready to get out on the ice."

"Why am I not surprised? Hanrahan is one tough cookie."

"What's your news?"

"I'm ready too."

"Ready for what?"

"I can do it. I'm going to do it. I'm going to become president."

"What happened? Do you have a concussion too?"

"Nope, I just decided. I'm not letting this opportunity pass without trying it."

Rick puts his arm over Dan's shoulder and says, "I know you can do it; I know you can."

I'll Make Them Say Yes

Fight for the things that you care about but do it in a way that will lead others to join you.
Ruth Bader Ginsburg

Joy and Rick sit on the couch while Jake and Max lie on the floor in front of the TV huddled around a large bowl of popcorn. They toss pieces into Jackson's mouth and giggle as they listen to the sound of him crunching. A box of half-eaten pizza lies on the square coffee table.

"What ya guys want to drink?" Dan calls from the kitchen, "I'm going to have a beer."

"I'll have one of the wine coolers Rick brought." Joy turns to Rick. "Thanks again for bringing them. You know they're my favorite."

"My pleasure. I'll have one too," he shouts."

"You sure you don't want a martini? I can make you one," Dan offers.

"The wine cooler will be fine."

The large screen TV hangs from the wall and broadcasts the hockey game. The New Jersey Devils battle it out against their cross-state rivals, the Philadelphia Flyers. The teams are locked in a scoreless tie halfway through the first period.

"Have you always been a hockey fan like your husband, Joy?" Rick asks.

"Yeah, I grew up in the suburbs of Philadelphia during the 'broad street bullies' days and we lived around the corner from Bernie Parent. I was a kid when they won the Stanley Cup. It was a big part of my childhood and I've always loved the sport.

"Are you a Devils fan or a Flyers fan?"

"The boys and Dan are Devils fans and I now root for them too. Sometimes we make compromises."

Dan enters and hands them their wine coolers and takes a sip of his beer out of a tall glass. He sits on the arm of the couch and puts his arm around Joy.

"Did you always follow hockey growing up or was it Dan that turned you on to it?" asks Joy.

"No, I got into hockey when I was in college. I was also a competitive figure skater in my early teens. I was around the rink a lot."

"I didn't know that about you! I feel like we've been friends for a longtime, but I know nothing about you," Dan says.

"Well, we haven't known each other that long, it's just feels like it's been a long time."

"How'd you get into figure skating?" Joy asks.

"My stepmom was a competitive skater as a child and won a bunch of regional competitions. She had the potential to make it to the Nationals until an injury sidelined her and she never competed again. I think she was hoping I'd find the glory she missed."

"You must have been an excellent skater."

"I was okay, since I love skating. In college, I skated on Penn's ice rink whenever I had the chance. I met my friend Ross there, who was on the hockey team. He was a winger. I used to go to their games and loved watching. He played for a while in the minors and even had a season with the Kings. That's when I got into the sport."

"Are you still in touch with him?" Joy asks.

"Yeah, we talk occasionally. He lives in LA and is married with two kids and works in the Kings' back office."

"Score!" Max and Jake yell, as they leap in the air spilling mouthfuls of popcorn on the floor. Jackson gobbles up as many pieces as he can while the boys jump up and down.

"Yay!" says Rick, Joy, and Dan, each going over and high fiving each of the boys.

They all stand and watch the replay of the goal and revel in the finesse of Elias. Jake pretends he has a hockey stick in his hand and loops around the room like a chipmunk forging for food attempting to perform his own replay. When he finishes his acrobatics, the boys sit back down cross-legged on the floor with Jackson lying between them. The three friends fall back on the couch.

"By the way, I forgot to tell you. Guess who I ran into in the liquor store?"

"I don't know, Greenblatt?"

"No, not Greenblatt. I saw the Rabbi. He was with Jackie."

"What were they doing in a liquor store?"

"They said they were getting wine for the synagogue."

"I thought Ralph, the maintenance guy does that?"

55

Joy gets up off the couch from between the two men and carries the box of pizza back into the kitchen. They move closer, closing the void she has left. They discuss their conspiracies on why the Rabbi and Jackie were together in the liquor store, each one more outlandish than the other until they can't stop laughing.

"What are you hens cracking yourselves up about?" says Joy, who has come back from the kitchen. "There's nothing unusual about the Rabbi and Jackie getting wine for the synagogue."

"I know, it's just that there was something peculiar about the way the Rabbi was acting. He seemed fidgety and nervous. He's usually calm and together."

"Maybe he was just surprised to see you outside of synagogue," says Joy.

"I told them I was coming over here and the Rabbi said he was looking forward to talking with you and allaying your fears about being president."

"The last I told him was I wouldn't do it."

"Well, I think they both just assume they'll convince you. Jackie said she's looking forward to your night at Blanche's."

"Well, I made the decision on my own, no pressure from anyone."

"When are you going to tell them you're in?"

"I'm meeting with the Rabbi Thursday night. I'll tell him then. Rob will be there too."

"Why did you change your mind?"

"Dan realized you and I were right and he could do it," says Joy.

"No, I remembered a time when I was a kid playing baseball and my coach asked me to pitch. I was terrified. Afraid of hitting someone or looking like a fool. My gut said no. I never got the opportunity again."

"...and you think the Rabbi is going to let you pitch? At best he'll let you carry the bats and balls."

"Well, I won't let him do that. I'm determined not to be a ball boy."

Dan gets up from the couch and grabs the bottles of empty wine coolers with one hand, leaving his couch companions behind. In the kitchen, he opens the pantry closet and dumps the hollow bottles in the recycling bin where they make a clang which ring out alongside the buzz from his cellphone in his pocket. He takes it out and reads the text message.

Dear Boy,

You can pick
from anything
off the menu.
See you at
Blanche's

Warm regards,

JG 🍸 🖤

He taps the right-side button, stashes it back into his pocket, and returns to the living room.

"Ya know, I was just kidding about that whole carrying the balls and bats thing. Right?"

He stands for a moment, staring at the TV in a zombie-like state. He drops on the couch on the opposite side of Joy and lifts his empty glass to have a sip.

"Dan?" Joy says.

"No, thanks, honey."

"Rick said something to you!"

"I'm sorry. What did you say, Rick?"

Rick repeats his rhetorical question louder this time just to make certain it is heard.

"Yeah, no problem. I'm good. I know you were kidding."

"You know I'll be there to carry the balls, too. I did promise to be your VP."

"Well, it takes a lot of balls to be my VP. Ha ha ha ha.

The two went back and forth lobbing childish puns at each other about bats and balls as if tossing a water-filled balloon until Rick says, "Oh boy, if these *balls* could talk. "

The two men go from cackling to uproarious laughter.

"Sometimes the two of you are worse than Max and Jake."

In time, their chuckling and snorting become intermittent and slow down. They let out a few quiet sighs and go back to watching the game. There are now just minutes left in the period. The Devils still lead 1-0. Joy calls to the boys to get ready for bed. They protest and negotiate an alternative plan; they will get ready during the second intermission and then they can return to watch the end of the game.

"By the way, Rick, you meant it when you said you'd be my vice president?"

"Of course, I meant it, assuming they'll let me."

"Please, I'm not worried about that. I'm sure they'll be delighted you're willing to do it."

"I wouldn't bet on it."

"Why do you say that?"

"Let's just say it's a hunch."

"Well, you're the only one I want as my vice president."

"What if they say no?"

"I'll make them say yes."

"You can't make the Rabbi do anything he doesn't want to do."

"Then I'll convince him you're the best person for the job. I'll make him see what I see."

"Dan, you're already sounding like a president."

"I suppose I am."

Moses Didn't Want to Lead

To succeed, jump as quickly at opportunities as you do at conclusions.
Benjamin Franklin

Dan peeks in his head from behind the door of the Rabbi's office and sees him sitting behind his large mahogany desk. He waves him into the room and points to the big black leather chair on the left. Rob sits in the identical chair on the other side. As directed, Dan deposits himself into the oversized chair and falls into its luxuriousness.

He places his hands on the soft leather arms and squirms, causing the chair to produce an embarrassing squeaking akin to flatulence as he settles on the opulent furniture. Rob glances over and delivers a smirk before continuing.

"…I just think the hallway looks cluttered."

"I think you're right. We could probably clean up a few things."

"We've three posters promoting our event on the crisis in the Middle East…"

"Rob, I'd be happy to walk with you through the hallway and see what we can clean up."

"Why don't I take down one poster now?"

"But Rob, these posters send an obvious message to our members that we've an undying commitment toward the State of Israel."

"Yes, but one poster sends the same message as three."

"I appreciate your zeal, but we have to be thoughtful in this process; these posters in the hallway show who we are and what's important to us.

"But no matter where you stand in the hallway you can see all three posters."

"Sounds like we're dealing with pressing synagogue business."

"See, now Dan understands."

"I was joking. I just thought I'd bring some levity…"

"We always hang our event flyers in the same three spots in the foyer. Our members expect to see them there. You wouldn't want a member to miss an announcement, would you?"

"I just thought…"

"Rob, how about we walk together through the hallway next Thursday before our meeting and see how we might declutter it?"

"Sure, it's not important anyway. I was just trying to clean things up."

"Let's respect Dan's time and focus on him right now. Also, I have to meet with the Tenenbaums in twenty minutes."

"Of course."

"Oh, before I forget, I'm going to need you to sign a few checks before you go."

"Sure, not a problem, Rabbi."

The large phone on the Rabbi's desk rings. He raises his index finger to show he will just need a minute and then uses it to press in its flashing button.

"Hello, Rabbi Ben Stern."

While he holds the receiver with his shoulder and listens, he hands Rob his green tortoise shell Montblanc pen and a folder with a stack of checks inside. Rob places the folder on the end of the desk and scribbles his name on the check at the top. He flips it over and places it beside the stack and continues this process in quick, rote-like motions.

"I've people in my office right now...I understand...We can discuss it later...I know...yes... of course...I'll call you later, sweetie."

The Rabbi places the receiver back on the phone, turns toward Dan, and folds his hands together.

"Was that your wife? If you needed to talk to her, we could wait outside."

"No...No, that won't be necessary."

"Dan, I hear your meeting with several of our past presidents didn't go as well as you'd have liked and have therefore decided not to accept our thoughtful suggestion."

"Yes, but..."

"Before you go any further, Dan, I just want to remind you, Moses didn't want to lead the children of Israel out of Egypt either. He too was concerned people wouldn't follow him and that he wasn't eloquent."

"Well, that's true, I'm concerned about speaking in public, but..."

"God was with Moses, and I'll be here with you...along with Rob, the entire Board, and your family and friends. I promise you'll succeed."

After the Rabbi's mini sermon, and especially since he compared him to Moses, he didn't have the heart to tell him he had already decided on his own. But this seemed an opportune time to mention his choice for VP. He was confident this would not be the issue Rick thought.

"Rabbi, if I'm not mistaken didn't God offer Aaron to Moses to help him face Pharaoh?

"Yes, that's correct."

"I've thought about it some more and I'd like to take you and Rob up on your offer to be president..."

"Dan, that's wonderful!"

"But...I'd like to choose my VP. You know, my own Aaron."

"It's unconventional, but who were you considering?"

"I choose Rick. He and I work well together, and he could provide me with the support I need. I also think he would make an excellent president after me."

"Hmm, that's an interesting selection, Dan."

See, I knew there'd be no objection, he thinks.

"Do you feel people can relate to Rick?" Rob, pausing as he continues scrawling out the checks.

"Well, there are some in our congregation who question his lifestyle choice, and we would want to consider their perspectives before rushing into something like this," the Rabbi says.

"What lifestyle choice?"

He glares at Rob and then looks at the Rabbi and waits for a response. He continues.

"What? Because he isn't married?"

"There is that...," says Rob.

"There are many in our community who're single. Besides, what does his marital status have to do with anything?"

"Most of them are widows or widowers. They aren't single by choice," says Rob.

"Big deal. Both still wrestle with similar issues like attending services or a synagogue function without a partner when most people are paired up. I think our single members would relate to Rick's situation."

"Of course, I've no issue with this choice. I'm just raising the concerns of others," the Rabbi says.

Rick had warned him they would not be warm to the idea. Still, he was surprised by their reaction. He couldn't imagine why they had reservations. He was always levelheaded during meetings and was the first to volunteer.

All because he was single? There must be something else.

He pushes himself up to the edge of the chair and leans forward.

"Rabbi, I'm glad to hear you've no issues with my choice because I'm not doing this without Rick. If you're concerned about what others think, I'm happy to defend my decision."

"What about Goldman? He'd make a good VP," Rob says.

"No Rob, I think Rick is a fine choice for VP," says the Rabbi. Besides, Rick may be satisfied as Dan's VP and choose not to continue as president."

"Yes, but that'll be Rick's choice."

"See Dan, you're already proving to be a bold leader."

"Thank you."

"Rabbi, what's this check for $1,613 to a P. Gleason?" Rob asks.

"Oh…well…that's…for our USCJ dues. Mr. Gleason is their treasurer. I'll resolve this with our bookkeeper." The Rabbi snatches the check from Rob's hand and slips it into his leather folder.

"First thing in the morning, I'll take care of it. Thank you, Rob."

"What is USCJ?" Dan asks.

"It's the United Synagogue of Conservative Judaism. It's the parent organization of synagogues…"

"That sounds like a lot of money."

Ring-ring-ring-ring. The fifth ring vibrates in the air and joins with the only other sound in the room—the scrawling of the green turquoise pen. The Rabbi picks up the phone this time and quickly turns his chair to face the back of the room. He looks out the window to the trees amid the thick, black darkness outside.

"I promise we will discuss it tonight…I understand…I've got to go; I've got Dan and Rob in the office, and I still have to meet with the Tenenbaums. Okay, sweetie."

The Rabbi drops the phone on the receiver, removes his glasses and then rubs his forehead. He springs from his chair.

"Where were we?"

"You were telling me about our USCJ dues…"

"Yes, USCJ. They provide invaluable services. As a matter of fact, they've a program called Sulam, which is a weekend-long retreat for up-and-coming leaders like yourself."

"What does Sulam stand for? Synagogues united…"

"Dan, have you forgotten your Torah studies? Sulam is the Hebrew word for ladder, like Jacob's ladder. This program will help you ascend into your leadership capacity. It'll help with your fear of public speaking, and you'll learn how to understand a budget. I think you'd benefit from this program."

The Rabbi strolls to the large credenza which matches with his mahogany desk. He pulls out the top drawer and riffles through a few folders until he finds a glossy brochure and offers it to Dan. Rob signs his last check and hands the folder of completed signed checks to the Rabbi. Dan's head is down as he inspects the brochure and devours each word.

"Actually, I think this might be helpful," he says.

"Listen, Dan, you stay here and read through the information. I've got to go meet the Tenenbaums in the chapel."

"Yea, well, I must leave too. It's getting late," Rob says.

"I think you made the right choice, Dan. I'm glad you've reconsidered."

"Yes, I agree with the Rabbi, you've made the right decision."

The Rabbi opens the door to his office. Rob walks out first. Before he closes it behind him, he peeks his head in.

"You'll be surprised at what you can accomplish. And remember, Dan, no one expects you to be anything other than who you are."

He hears the latch click. The room falls silent except for the squeaking from his leather chair as he turns back toward the Rabbi's desk. Outside the window, he glimpses the bright round moon hanging in the black sky. He turns his attention back toward the brochure, which exhibits six individuals embracing their own personal Torahs, looking skyward, amid the backdrop of a large fortress wall made of Jerusalem stone.

He reads from the text how the Sulam program is going to help attendees become effective leaders when the phone lets out a thunderous ring.

He jumps from the noise as if someone snuck up behind him and blasted an air horn. It rings again. He looks over his shoulder half-expecting the Rabbi to enter and answer it. Before the vibration of the ring can disappear, the phone rings again. He stands, looks around the room, reaches over the Rabbi's desk, grabs the phone, and pushes in the flashing button.

"Congregation Beth Emet, Rabbi Stern's office. How may I help you?"

"Hello, I'm looking for Rabbi Stern."

"This is Dan Barkan. The Rabbi is with potential members. Can I help you?"

"Oh, Hi Dan this is Miriam, the Rabbi's wife."

"Hi Mrs. Stern. The Rabbi's meeting with the Tenenbaums. Would you like me to go get him?"

"No, that won't be necessary. I'll see him home later. I was just looking to find what time he'll be leaving. I want to know when to warm up his dinner."

"Well, I can give him a message."

"If you happen to see him before you leave, you can let him know I called."

"I'll most likely see him. I'll be sure to mention it to him."

"I appreciate it, Dan. How are your parents doing? I've been meaning to give your mom a call."

"They're fine. Thank you for asking. You know Dad has good days and bad. By the way, speaking of calling. I'm sorry about earlier when you called. I offered to leave the room to give you privacy."

"Earlier? I didn't call earlier."

"Oh, you know…I just assumed it was you. I'm not sure why I thought that."

"No problem. Thanks again Dan and send my regards to the family."

He hears the click of the Rabbi's wife hanging up.

The bright moon shines in his eyes from the window behind the Rabbi's desk as he lowers the receiver onto the phone. He grabs the brochure and walks out, closing the door behind him. He starts down the hallway toward the chapel and looks inside the large glass windows where he sees the back of the Rabbi's head and who he assumes are the Tenenbaums sitting on the other side of the table. The pace of his walking increases as he scurries past the chapel, down the hall, into the foyer and out the glass doors.

In the cool night air, the moon is high in the expansive sky. He places himself inside the comfort of his car and turns on WRTI to listen to soft jazz. He pulls away from the synagogue building. Glancing in his rear-view mirror, he watches as the red brick building becomes smaller in the distance.

The moon, silent, remains enormous and brilliant and seems to watch him all the way home.

Next Rung on the Ladder

One man's trash is another man's treasure.
English Proverb

In a whirlwind, Dan prepares to take on the role of executive vice president—the position that will immerse him in the workings of Beth Emet and ready him to lead the congregation. During a Friday night service in June, within a crowded sanctuary of his friends, family, and fellow congregants, he agrees to accept the role.

"I affirm I will faithfully execute…." he prepares to declare.

His parents are surrounded by a group of their friends congratulating them on their son's prestigious position. His father agrees.

"Oh, yes, president, of course. We're certainly proud of him," when his long-time friend Barney shouts amid the noisy sanctuary, "Dan!—your son, he's going to be president." His mother, using the Yiddish vernacular, "I'm *kvelling*. We're thrilled. You know, all my sons are active in their synagogues."

Joy stands smiling in her new deep purple dress next to "the girls" as members approach to wish her both congratulations and condolences at the same time, telling her that most of Dan's time will now be devoted to the synagogue—and the Rabbi.

"Don't listen to them. You know how important you and the boys are to Dan," assures Hope.

"I know—by the way, your new boyfriend seems sweet," says Joy.

"And he's cute," reveals Beth.

"Yeah, it's really going well. I can't believe it's been a year since my divorce."

"I can't believe you met him online," continues Beth.

"I know and to think we went to high school together here in West Huntington and we didn't know each other existed."

"I think Drew is glad he's here. It gives him someone to talk to."

"How did you get Drew to come? I only remember him here one other time."

"He wanted to support Dan."

"That's thoughtful of him. I know he doesn't like coming," adds Joy.

"I can't blame him; they're not exactly welcoming," retorts Hope.

Max and Jake run around the temple with their friends oblivious to the implications of the evening. They think it's cool their dad is on his next step to being president.

Sylvia Goldstein smiles and waves to Dan as he walks up to the bima and stands next to Rick, waiting for the ceremony to begin. Just before the Rabbi makes his way to the podium and proceeds with the pomp and circumstance, Rick moves in close to Dan's ear.

"There's no turning back now. After tonight you will be executive vice president and then in two years, well you know...."

"Hey buddy, better you than me..." bellows Harold as he slaps him on the back. His wife, Marcy, glares at him.

"No really, good luck. I wish you all the best."

She nods in approval at her husband.

"Just don't forget about the barbeque equipment..."

Apart from when he takes his oath, there is no mention he will become president two years hence during the ceremony. As he stands at the center of the bima surrounded by other Board members, the Rabbi invites him to repeat the words of commitment:

"I affirm that I will faithfully execute the office of executive vice president of Beth Emet of West Huntington, New Jersey.

"I will, to the best of my ability, act with reverence and respect in accordance with the norms of the community and execute my duties in the sole interests of the Beth Emet members.

"I also understand that with this obligation, and two years from this date, I will automatically be conferred as president of the synagogue...

"with all the rights, privileges, and responsibilities as inscribed in the Beth Emet constitution."

He immediately feels humble and responsible, and with the utterance of those words, the journey he has been both looking forward to and terrified of begins.

***

Four months later, in October, he attends Sulam, the weekend-long retreat the Rabbi had recommended during the meeting he had with him and Rob in his office. He's apprehensive about going and leaving the family for the weekend. However, with a little coaxing from the Rabbi and with support from Joy he takes the next step on the rung toward his ascension to leadership.

Held at a camp-like facility surrounded by sprawling hills, a massive lake, and trees with foliage that the autumn season paints golden yellow, fiery red, and carnelian orange, the milieu is uplifting. He coerces Rick into joining him after he promises they will learn together and have a great time. They travel in his hybrid down Interstate 95 to the quaint town in Maryland, just outside of DC where the retreat is being held. They talk and listen to music, which makes the three-and-a-half-hours seem like a quick jaunt instead of an arduous commute.

The two men share one of the twenty cabins nestled in the woods connected to the conference center, offices, and a large cafeteria by way of twisting dirt trails. The amenities are rustic, but they revel in it. The water snake who finds its way into their room one night adds to the "roughing it" atmosphere and provides an entertaining tale.

During the retreat, they learn about all aspects of leading a Jewish community from leaders in management for non-profit organizations. They also meet and socialize with other soon-to-be synagogue presidents from around the country, which they agree is enlightening and fascinating. Dan and Rick soon become popular with the others. Their new colleagues and friends are intrigued by the pair. During free time, the two often find themselves surrounded by five or six interested parties who listen with great intent as they describe how Beth Emet functions.

"Yes, Rabbi Stern attends all budget meetings, oversees the custodial staff, and is the principal of our preschool," Dan tells them.

A future president from a synagogue outside of Montgomery, Alabama, says, "Jeez, our Rabbi only wants to lead services and then go home. We try to get him to greet members as they drop their kids off at Sunday school and he just says, 'I'm a Rabbi, not a politician.'"

The long weekend inspires and motivates him.

He arrives back home around four pm after dropping Rick off at his apartment. Joy greets him with a long kiss and passionate embrace. Jackson wildly circles his feet and the boys run down the stairs to hug him.

He feels a variety of emotions exploding.

Feelings he never anticipated on that wintry Friday night in February.

A great deal has transpired in the year and four months since he was asked that evening's momentous question, and yet he still has a year before becoming president. It's like a glowing energy ball floats over him filled with excitement, hopefulness, trepidation, and happiness.

For the first time, he feels—really feels—he can do this.

He can make a difference.

A Broken Heart

You never really understand a person until you consider things from his point of view...until you climb inside his skin and walk around in it.
Atticus Finch–To Kill a Mockingbird

Monday dawns and he and Rick are scheduled to meet with the Rabbi in the evening. Rob is out of town and the Rabbi needs Dan to sign some checks and go over a few other items. He also wants to hear about their weekend.

After a shower, dinner with the family, and a quick game of toss with Jackson, he starts the hybrid, picking up Rick on his familiar route past the broken lamppost on his way to the synagogue.

They enter the glass doors and walk into the foyer where a man walks around, looking at the event posters near the sanctuary entrance. He doesn't recognize the man who wears a sad expression on his face.

Dan, not accustomed to the silence in the hallway let alone a stranger there, glances over at him and flashes a quick and nervous smile. The man returns the expression. He raises his head, squints, and then opens his eyes wide.

"Is that you Rick?"

"Sandy, is that you? Oh my god, I haven't seen you in years. How are you?"

"Not good Rick."

"Oh no!"

"Yes, Denise passed away yesterday."

"Damn! I just saw her a few weeks ago...That's awful. I'm sorry to hear the news. She was a wonderful person."

"That's nice of you to say. She was always fond of you, too. She told me you spoke on occasion and how much it meant to her. She said you reminisced..."

As the man sobs, Rick approaches him and the two embrace. He buries his face in Rick's shoulder for a few seconds and then regains his composure. He wipes his moist, puffy red eyes with his shirt sleeves and covers his face until he reveals a sorrowful smile that cannot conceal his tremendous grief.

"Rick, it's wonderful to see you," and he turns away, trembling.

Not accustomed to witnessing a grown man in anguish, Dan looks down on the floor and rocks back and forth unsure of what to say. He stands there with a furrowed brow, his eyes welling as he listens to the man talk about his deceased daughter. He winces with each gasp of air the man takes.

"Please let me know if there is anything I can do," Rick says.

"Sure, I'll…do that."

"How is Lisa taking it? She must be devastated."

"She's struggling…she's home with the baby. Having to care for him helps her cope."

"Oh, Sandy, this is my good friend, Dan Barkan. This is Sandy Tenenbaum. Sandy and his family used to be members here. I grew up around the corner from him and I was friends with his kids. I was especially close to his daughter. Dan is going to be our next synagogue president."

Dan reaches for the man's hand and misses his target. Sandy takes his left hand and places it on the back of his and directs it into his own. The warmth of Sandy's hands feels comforting.

His voice trembles and cracks. "I'm sorry for your loss. May your loved one's memory bring solace to you always."

"It's a pleasure to meet you, Dan. I wish you the best of luck as president. It's not an easy job."

Sandy's warm voice and kind face eases his nerves.

"Being synagogue president is simple compared to what you're going through. Please let me know if there's anything I or the Beth Emet community can do to help you during this difficult time."

"Sure, that's kind of you."

"Are you here to see the Rabbi?" Rick asks.

"Yes, he said he'd see me even though we're no longer members."

"Well, we'll let him know you're here. We're on our way to see him now, but we can cancel our meeting with him."

"That's okay, I'm about an hour early. I just wanted to come back and look around a bit."

"I understand."

They say goodbye and leave Sandy alone in the foyer and walk down the hallway toward the Rabbi's office. They reach the enormous glass windows of the chapel, which presents a sparse group of members in attendance at the bi-weekly evening service.

"I can't imagine losing a child. He must be devastated."

70

"Yes, I'm sure. Denise and he were very close."

"How did she die?"

"She had cancer."

"That's horrible. The poor man …Who's Lisa and the baby?'

Rick put his hand in front-of Dan's chest and said, "Wait, how many people are in there? 1...2...3…"

"Yes…If they don't have a minyan, ah, we really need to be in there," Dan exclaims.

"There are only eight people, including Mark, who's leading the service."

"Without ten people, they won't be able to recite the mourner's prayer."

"Yeah, and I see Mrs. Berman is in there and she just lost her husband a few months ago."

Dan looks up and sees Jackie inside the chapel, sitting in a chair facing the window. Her head is bowed as she reads from her prayerbook, exposing her gray roots amidst her bright red hair. However, it is her well-manicured, fire engine red nails holding the prayer book that catches his attention. She looks up and notices him looking over at her. Her eyes open wide, and she displays an enormous smile.

The two men walk toward the chapel's entrance. Standing inside guarding the glass door, is Mr. Chasen. He turns around and sees them coming and raises his hand in a signal to stop. He looks down at his prayerbook and mutters a few words then opens it and peaks his head out. Mr. Chasen is a towering individual with large hands and a head full of dark slicked back black hair. He looks more like a bouncer at a nightclub in the city than a volunteer coordinating prayer services.

"Listen, gentlemen, we're nearly done and if you come in now, we'll have to go back and say extra prayers."

"Dan and I wanted to make sure Mrs. Berman could recite the *mourner's Kaddish.*"

"I know you guys would make it nine and ten and then we'd have a minyan."

"Okay, then what's the problem?"

"Listen, Mark's gotta get outta here and I haven't been home for dinner yet."

"Mrs. Berman just lost her husband. What's a few more minutes…"

"Sorry guys, if you can just wait outside..."

Mr. Chasen closes the door and turns his back toward them to finish his prayers.

"What the hell? Now that's one thing I'll change when I become president," says Dan.

"Listen, let's wait here and apologize to Mrs. Berman and see how she's doing."

"Good idea, Rick."

The service continues four more minutes. Separated only by glass, the two men wait. Dan can hear the muffled sound of the prayers and recognizes the moment in the service when the mourners' prayer would have begun had they just been on the other side of the glass. Without warning or thought, he chants the well-known prayer out loud and by heart in a quiet, soft voice. "Yis-gadal v'yis-kadash sh'may raboh."

Rick looks over at him, bemused. He shakes his head in agreement and forms a soft and solemn grin on his flushed face. Dan continues to chant, keeping his sight fixed on Mrs. Berman. Rick joins him in reciting the prayer, but at a louder volume and then in a deliberate motion looks to the chapel. His voice cracks and a small tear meanders down his cheek.

The two men begin to chant vociferously; just loud enough for Mr. Chasen to hear without disturbing the rest of the congregants. Dan swears he sees Mr. Chasen's head turn a shade to the left as if trying to hear something off in the distance.

When the men finish the prayer, they pat each other on the back, still facing the chapel.

"I guess you knew Denise?...I'm sorry...It's difficult to lose a friend," Dan says.

"Yeah, she was my first girlfriend. We were twelve."

He hears the muddled sound of Mark chanting the remaining words of the last prayer. He cannot make out the words Mark speaks just before he closes his prayerbook and walks around the room shaking hands. Larry and his wife Carol walk out of the chapel and greet the two men first. Behind them comes Mr. Chasen and his hurried friend Mark by his side.

"Sorry guys, we just have to get out of here," Mr. Chasen says.

Jackie walks out with Mrs. Berman and Brian Levinthal, the proprietor of one of two Rabbi-approved catering establishments.

Jackie places her hand on Dan's cheek and then slides it down his face until it drops to her side.

"Hi…dear boy. We need to pick a dinner date at Blanche's."

"Yes, we do Jackie. I promise I'll get something on the calendar."

"You boys here to meet with our spiritual leader? You sure take up a lot of his time."

"I think it might be the reverse Jackie," says Rick.

"I believe you might be right, Rick. Well, I've a few things to catch up in the office. I'll see you boys later."

Dan approaches Mrs. Berman and reaches out his hand. She grasps it and places her other hand on top. She wears a green gingham dress and has stark, thin, white hair. A petite nonagenarian, she looks tired and weathered from the three months of mourning since her husband Harry has passed.

"How are you doing Mrs. Berman?"

"It's difficult, but I'm getting through it thanks to my family and of course my family here at Beth Emet."

"I'm sorry we weren't able to get in there and make a minyan for you, Mrs. Berman," Rick says.

"We're going to do something about that in the future," responds Dan.

"But you boys did provide one. You think God couldn't see you standing on the other side of the glass door? I recited my mourner's prayer for Harry. He heard it and now Mr. Chasen is on his way home for dinner and Mark is off to wherever he needs to go. So. Thank you for being here."

She pats the top of her and Dan's clasped hands, then rubs Rick's shoulder, and gives them both a warm smile before she walks away, leaving them with a brief, "Goodnight."

"Hey, Dan and Rick, you guys have a minute?"

"Sure, what's up, Brian?" replies Dan.

"The Rabbi has been pestering me for weeks about this upcoming 'Lunch and Learn' event with him. He wants me to cater it."

"You don't want to do the event?"

"It's not that. I've got a wedding showcase on the same day."

"Can't you just tell him you can't make it?" Rick questions.

"I wish I could. You know how he is. This is a big showcase for me. I really need to be there."

"How can we help?"

"What's worse is the last time I did a similar event there was sparse attendance, and I had to throw away half the food. Can you talk to him?"

"Sure, we're going to see him now. Let's see what we can do."

"Please, I don't mind doing it, it's just that day is terrible for me."

"I hear ya Brian. I promise. I'll take care of it. Consider it done."

"Thanks guys! I really appreciate it." Brian zips down the hallway and disappears.

"You know you probably shouldn't have promised him..."

"What?" Dan snaps.

"You know the Rabbi...If he wants Brian to do the event, then Brian's gonna do it."

"Oh, come on. You said that about being vice president. The Rabbi gave in on that."

"True, but maybe that's what he wanted?"

The Right Decision

The time is always right to do what is right.
Martin Luther King Jr.

The men make their way toward the Rabbi's office.

The back hallway lights are off, but light streams from his open door. He's hunched over his desk when they enter and does not stand; they do not wait for him to acknowledge or wave them in. Many of the formalities that had existed between clergy and volunteer have slipped away in the months since he has become executive vice president.

On his blotter are a stack of letters to congregants Mrs. Winthrop has typed up. He is signing them using his Montblanc pen applying delicate small strokes like a master calligrapher. After he signs each, he lifts the paper up to his face and checks the signature, blows on it, and then places it in another pile on the side.

The men place themselves in the two leather chairs facing the desk.

"Good evening, Rabbi."

"Gentlemen, how are you? I assume you had a pleasant experience at Sulam?"

They each take turns sharing every detail of their exciting weekend. They are like kids just home from a sleep-away camp gushing out to their parent new and exciting experiences. They tell him how the other participants thought it was fabulous two leaders attended from one synagogue.

"It's a marvelous reflection on the exceptional community at Beth Emet, praised Rabbi Kreitzberg."

He was one of the leaders who organized the retreat and had presented a seminar on "Budget Fundamentals for Non-profit Organizations." Dan adds he found the presentation particularly useful. Rick delivers regards from Rabbi Kreitzberg, and Dan tells him how the other attendees were impressed how our Rabbi has his hands in various aspects of synagogue life.

"I would love to hear all about it gentlemen, but we have an issue we have to deal with tonight and it can't wait for Rob to get back from vacation."

"It sounds important."

"A past congregant has requested I perform a funeral for them…I believe the Tenenbaum's were members for over twenty years before they left."

"We saw Sandy in the hallway, and he told us Denise had passed away," Rick says.

"When is the funeral?" Dan inquires.

"Generally, the body should be interned within twenty-four hours and with Shabbat tomorrow night, we need the funeral to happen tomorrow afternoon.

"Are you sure there's no way we can get a hold of Rob?"

"Yes, he said he wouldn't be available."

"Rabbi, how do you feel about it?"

"I'll do what you tell me to do. You're next in command with Rob out of town."

"Why did the Tenenbaums leave, anyway?"

"They could no longer afford the dues, and when we offered them help, Sandy said he didn't want to take charity."

"If I recall, there was a certain delicate situation that led to them leaving too," adds Rick.

"I've spoken to Sandy frequently, and he assured me finances were the only reason they left."

"Dan, you know what Rob would say."

"Yeah, I know, '…they should've thought about it before they left the community.'"

"You remembered the discussion with Rob and his dues policy, and he likened membership at Beth Emet to a gym membership."

"It's your call Dan," reiterates the Rabbi.

Dan pushes back the soft, comfortable leather chair, gets up, and paces. He takes in a deep breath and lets out a sigh. He rubs his forehead, then brushes back his dark brown hair. *This is it;* he thinks, *this is my moment.* He peruses the book titles on the three sizable and crowded shelves that stretch up to the ceiling. He runs his finger along the spine of a book titled, *When Bad Things Happen to Good People.* He read the book not long after his father was diagnosed with Alzheimer's.

Near it a ceramic *tzedakah* box perches a quarter of an inch off the edge of the shelf. The box, a receptacle for collecting money for the Rabbi's chosen charities, is a beautiful replica of an old Eastern-European synagogue, destroyed during the Holocaust. The irony of an elaborate and expensive box purchased to hold spare change dropped by generous visitors to the Rabbi's office does not go unnoticed. He nudges it back, to keep it secure on the shelf.

Rick's and the Rabbi's eyes track him as he strolls around the office like a supreme court judge contemplating constitutional precedent; or, as he learned the night before on NPR, the principal of stare decisis.

"Dan, what are you thinking?" Rick questions.

"I'm not sure…"

He wanders to the wall of pictures where framed portraits are aligned in a systematic and organized configuration. One is a wedding photo of a young Ben Stern and his bride under the *Chuppah* and a picture of the Rabbi and his eldest son. In another the three smile back at him from a stadium full of cheering fans celebrating the Phillies World Series victory.

"Dan, what would you like me to do?"

He stares at the large B and O scribbled on a glossy photo to his left. This one is of the first African American to be nominated for president by a major political party shaking hands with his clergy.

"We need to decide…"

"You should do the funeral."

"What will you tell Rob?" Rick asks.

"I'll tell him the truth. I was asked to make a decision in his absence, and I did."

"I think you made the right decision Dan," says the Rabbi.

"Beth Emet isn't a gym, there are moral and ethical considerations..." Dan says.

Rick pats Dan on the back. "I'm proud of you, it's the right thing. What's more it's what my friend Dan Barkan would do."

"Also, tell Sandy there is one condition. I want he and his family to be members again."

"But they can't afford it and they won't take financial help."

"Tell him it's not financial assistance; we have a special deal right now. All returning members pay eighteen dollars for dues this year. We'll deal with getting him help next year."

"That's a wonderful idea—eighteen—the numerical value of the Hebrew word Chai, nice touch."

"*L'chaim*, to life! Sandy could use a little life right now and I could use a drink," says Rick.

"I think it would be wise if I talk to Sandy now. We're going to need to make plans," says the Rabbi.

"Yes, we shouldn't make him wait any longer," notes Rick.

"It's getting late, anyway; I'm going to head home. Joy will be waiting, and I have an early meeting at work in the morning. Oh, before I go, I spoke with Brian Leventhal earlier. He is stressed out about catering the 'Lunch and Learn.' He has a previous obligation, and he feels he can't say no to you."

"That's nonsense. I'll call him tomorrow and straighten it out. Now you boys go home, and I'll take care of everything. Oh, and before you leave can you just sign a couple of checks? They're on Mrs. Winthrop's desk in a manila folder."

"Just email us the funeral details. We're going to want to be there."

"Sure, now go tell Sandy to come on back."

The two men retrace their steps down the hallway except this time they stop at the office where Dan goes to sign checks. Rick continues into the foyer where Sandy is still wandering. Rick tells him the Rabbi can see him now, and he asks him for his phone to enter his cell number in it.

He reminds him to call him should he need anything.

Meanwhile, Jackie rummages through a filling cabinet in the office when Dan walks in. Jackie greets him with a gentle and sultry, "Good evening, dear boy," which is followed by a sarcastic comment on the brevity of his meeting with the Rabbi.

Dan sits at Mrs. Winthrop's desk and signs checks. He stops in mid-scribble when he notices the name on one of them.

"Hey Jackie, do you know who P. Gleason is and why we're writing him a check for $1,613?"

"Oh, dear boy, I think Mr. Gleason is the lovely man fixin' that damn blasted air conditioner."

"I thought he was the guy from USCJ?"

"Dear boy, why are you asking me if you know who he is? Mr. Gleason was here earlier this week and was up on the roof tinkering with that awful contraption."

Dan finishes signing the checks and exits the office to meet Rick in the foyer. Rick tells him he sent Sandy to the Rabbi's office and gave him his cell number. Dan shares with Rick his discovery of another check for P. Gleason.

"That seems odd…" Rick says, as he pushes the glass door open.

Outside in the cool night air, a pleasant, musky-sweet smell permeates the fall air. The sound of the light breeze rustling through trees is a needed respite from the night's sobering conversation about the untimely death of Sandy's young daughter, and Rick's childhood friend. The parking lot lights are dim, with the one on the far-left corner flickering. The moonlight in the star-filled evening sky shows them the way to Dan's hybrid. It chirps when Dan points his key fob in its direction. He is about to open the driver's side door, while Rick stands on the passenger side.

"Hey Dan, whaddya say we get a drink at Blanche's? Maybe a little l'chaim for Denise?"

"I can't. I told you, I've got an early morning call. We're still working on another website launch."

"Oh, c'mon just one drink. It won't be a late night."

"It already is."

"It's only ten-thirty."

Rick stares at him with his eyes wide and a frown.

"I guess the boys are asleep and Joy will be absorbed in on one of her romance novels, or almost asleep by now."

"I'll buy the first one."

"I thought you said just one drink?"

"I did. One drink I buy and one drink you buy.

"Hey Rick, you feel like driving to Blanche's?"

"Sure buddy."

Dan tosses his keys over the top of the car and they race around it to the opposite sides and get in. The hybrid zips out of the lot as Rick turns on the radio. The host on NPR is discussing clean-energy vehicles. Rick hits one of the preset buttons, which switches the station to classic rock. He turns up the volume. Bon Jovi's *Livin' on a Prayer* now blares out the speakers. They both begin drumming to the beat, Rick on the steering wheel, Dan on the dashboard. At the corner, Rick turns the car left and pulls out into the main street. He then slams on the brakes.

The car lets out a loud "Screeech!"

He stretches his right arm across Dan's chest, keeping him from jolting forward.

"Where the hell did that car come from?" says Dan.

"I've no idea…are you okay pal?"

Dan looks in the rearview mirror and sees the dancing bears on the bumper of a metallic green Cadillac speeding away from them and into the parking lot.

"I'm fine, how about you?"

"A little shaken, but fine. Who was that lunatic going to the synagogue at this time of night?"

"That was Norm. I recognize his bumper sticker."

Rick pats his chest and then lowers the volume on the radio.

"What an idiot. Sorry about that Dan?"

"No, it wasn't your fault. I wonder what's up with him?"

"Maybe he just misses his darlin' wife."

"Well, you know when things like this happen, it makes me miss my wife and kids. It's like they say…in the blink of an eye."

"It makes me think I need a drink."

I'll Have the Usual

*I'm the one that's got to die when it's time for me to die,
so let me live my life the way I want to.*
Jimi Hendrix

They grab two barstools facing the glass shelves jam-packed with bottles of all shapes and sizes filled with various colors of alcohol and wine. The mirror on the back of the bar, while contributing to an illusion of an infinite amount of beverage choices, also assures Rick and Dan they will not be startled by an uninvited guest.

The man down on the other side of the counter wears a short-sleeved, white buttoned down dress shirt with the name Blanche's embroidered in script on the pocket. His arms are covered in bright tattoos. On his left arm is a drawing of Superman with the large iconic "S" on his chest, which covers most of the man's sizable biceps and triceps. Huge and broad shouldered, he has a square jaw and wavy jet-black hair. He twirls a cocktail napkin at each man.

"Hey Rick, what'll you have?"

"Hi Bruce, how's it going? I'll have the usual."

"What's the usual?" Dan inquires.

The bartender explains, "A vodka martini, very dry, extra olives, and ice cold."

"I like to order it the same way every time. I tell Bruce just place the vermouth bottle next to the glass and then make it so cold that it burns."

"That's a creative way to order. You're like the Jewish James Bond."

"You think that's creative? You should see this guy sew. Thanks again for the costume Rick. The guys loved it."

Dan cocks his head to the left and stares at Rick with an oversized smile.

"Well, I'll have what 007 is having," he tells Bruce while his sight remains fixed on Rick.

Bruce nods and then shuffles off to get their drinks.

"I didn't know you could sew?"

"Yes, I sew. Remember, I grew up with three older sisters."

"Well, I'd love to see your creative work."

"You'd have to go to the Blue Moon on Wednesday nights."

"What?"

"Bruce is an exotic male dancer, and he asked me to sew him a Superman costume for his act."

"You're kidding! This is a side of you I didn't know existed."

"There are a lot of things you don't know about me."

"I may have to get you to sew a big "P" on my shirt for my presidential installation."

Another bartender passes by and drops a full bowl of pretzels in front of them. They each grab a few and start munching. Dan looks up at the mirror and surveys the restaurant behind them. He notices the jovial Harold sitting at a table with his wife, Marcy. The scene seems unusual because he has only seen the two arguing or throwing verbal jabs at each other. In this incarnation, they hold hands and laugh loudly. It appears Harold's wife has at last found one of his witticisms humorous.

"Rick, you never finished telling me. Who's Lisa and the baby?"

"Right. Lisa is Sandy's wife and the baby, who probably is no longer a baby, is Denise's son."

"Oh God, how old is he?"

"I'm guessing around five or six by now."

"Where's the father?"

"No one seems to know who the father is, or at least no one is saying."

"Is that the incident you referred to in the Rabbi's office?"

"Yes."

"And you think that's why they left the synagogue?"

"I know that's why they left. Denise told me."

"She told you who the father is?"

"No, she never did, and I didn't ask. But we talked about him."

"Do you think the Rabbi knows who it is?"

"He might. He was incredibly supportive of the family at the time. He called Sandy every week to see how Denise and the baby were doing."

"And that's why Sandy is fond of him and why he wants him to officiate the funeral. It must be terribly difficult for them."

Bruce returns and places a filled martini glass on each man's napkin. Dan dunks the toothpick with four speared olives three times and then bends his head down and sips to ensure it will not spill over when he lifts it.

"Your friend Greenblatt was here earlier," says Bruce.

"Oh, sorry I missed him."

Dan chuckles, looking at Rick sneering in the mirror.

"Speaking of friends, Bruce, this is my actual friend Dan—Dan this is Bruce. "

The two exchange pleasantries.

"You belong to the same Temple?"

"Dan's going to be our next synagogue president."

"Wow, good for you. We need more people willing to serve their community. "

"Thanks. By the way, I like your tattoos. They're incredible."

Bruce's eyes open wide as he dances in place, pointing out the characters on his arm. He tells him Spiderman was his first tat. He got it at seventeen, and it was well worth it despite his parents' ire. Like a docent at an art museum, he provides Dan with a personal tour of each one painted on his beefy arms and ends with a dissertation on the connection between cartoon superheroes and the Jewish people.

"All the great superheroes were created by Jews, you know, like Stan Lee. Superman's name was Kal-El, which is Hebrew for 'All is God.' Ha, look at me telling you, the president of the temple what it means…"

"Not president yet."

"…And when Superman's parents saved his life by rocketing him to earth in that space pod, it's like Miriam sending Moses in a basket down the Nile. And they were both raised by non-Jewish parents."

"Wow, never thought of it that way. Where'd you learn all this? In Hebrew school?"

"Oh, no I'm not one of God's chosen people. Although, I think working here makes me an honorary one. Well, nice talking to you. I gotta get back to work."

Bruce leaves the men alone and struts to the other end of the bar. They sit there for a long minute in the noisy quiet as they sip. Dan looks up from his glass and catches Rick's reflection staring back at him with a smile. He smiles back.

Dan's pocket vibrates. He pulls out his phone, assuming it is Joy checking up, but is thrown off by Rob's caller id.

Did he hear about Sandy already? Maybe something worse? Maybe he is staying on the island and is calling to let him know he is now president?

"Hey what's up? Everything okay?"

"Sure, just checking up to make sure the synagogue hasn't burned down while I'm gone."

"The synagogue is still here...The Rabbi said you wouldn't be reachable?"

"I told him I might *not* be reachable, but you can try. Why anything up?"

"Nothing we couldn't handle. We have it under control."

"Well, I'm glad to hear everything is good. Jill and I are heading out for a late-night swim, I'll talk to you later. Just let me know if you need anything. "

Dan hangs up and places it back in his pocket. He takes a small drink from his half empty martini glass and now feels its affects.

"Who was that?" Rick asks.

"Rob."

"I thought he wasn't available?"

"Me too."

"Sounds like you didn't mention Sandy."

"Well, like I told him, we have it under control."

He feels uneasy and has a headache. Perhaps it's the drink that makes him feel ill. It had been several hours since dinner and he only ate a few pretzels. He wonders why the Rabbi led him to believe Rob wasn't available. Maybe it was just a misunderstanding. Maybe he should have pushed the Rabbi to call Rob.

After all, Rob is the president, it is his decision.

Still, in the few months since he became vice president, he spent countless nights in the Rabbi's office feeling feckless. Tonight was different. He felt empowered; like he could make a difference. When he told the Rabbi and Rob he would accept the role, this is what he had dreamed it would be like. All the late nights and sacrifices would be worth it if he could just make a difference.

"Hey Rick, I meant to ask you, why were you certain they would oppose you being president?"

"They don't like the people I date."

"Why not?"

"They just don't."

"I know nothing about the people you date. How do they know?"

"They know everything."

"What happened with the blind date from Greenblatt's office?"

"Well, we have been seeing each other."

"Are you getting serious?"

"I'm not sure, but I promise you'll be the first to know; at least if I can help it."

"They can't have a problem with someone Greenblatt introduced you to. What don't they like? They aren't Jewish?"

Buzz, buzz. This time it's Rick's phone. He reaches into his pocket. He flashes his phone in front of Dan's face. It's Sandy.

Dan raises his eyebrows and lets out a "Hmm."

Rick answers.

"Hey Sandy, everything okay?"

Dan can hear the muffled voice but isn't able to make out what he's saying. Rick bobs his head in agreement, throwing out the words, "right," "sure," and "great."

"Okay, well get some sleep. It's going to be a rough day tomorrow. Yes, I'm glad we could help. I'll be sure to tell him. Goodnight."

Rick replaces it on top of the bar and finishes his martini, and then pulls the olives off the toothpick with his front teeth and eats them.

"Everything okay with Sandy? I assume the funeral's tomorrow."

"Yes, it is. He just wanted to thank us."

"Well, that was nice of him."

"He said whatever we said to the Rabbi must've helped because he's agreed to perform the service."

"The Rabbi agreed?"

"Yes, and he said he and Lisa are coming back as members of the synagogue."

"Well, that's good news."

"Apparently, the Rabbi offered him a special rate, and he was grateful."

Dan faces the mirror and sees Rick's reflection. They exchange listless grins, saddened yet a little pleased. In the far distance behind them, he spies Jackie and Norm entering the restaurant. He follows the two as the hostess escorts them to a high-backed booth close to the bar. He gulps down the rest of his martini, hangs his head low and close to the empty glass.

"You know, Rick, it doesn't matter. We did the right thing."

"I know, pal."

"We're not in this for the accolades."

Rick purses his lips, nods and says, "Yeah, we're in it for the money."

The two men laugh, still looking at each other in the bar mirror.

Dan peers over at Jackie and Norm's table, trying not to be conspicuous. A waiter rushes over to Norm and delivers an old-fashioned glass filled with two inches of dark amber liquid. Jackie removes her shaded glasses and scrutinizes herself in a small compact mirror. Her eyes seem puffy and as red as her tousled hair. Norm finishes his drink with two quick swigs and points over to the waiter, signaling a refill.

Bruce dances his way to their side of the bar after seeing their empty martinis. He grabs both glasses and drops them in the sink. He crumples up their cocktail napkins and drags a rag across the bar top in front of them.

"You boys want another?"

In perfect unison, both respond, "Yes!"

Stones Never Die

And in the end the love you take is equal to the love you make.
John Lennon—Paul McCartney

Next morning, Dan's rattled nerves feel soothed by the sound of "crunch, crunch" underfoot as he and Rick stride quietly from the parking lot. The comforting noise ceases once they step onto the sprawling unkempt lawn.

In the distance, he can see the Rabbi clutching a prayer book by his side, standing next to Sandy in front of the large gaping hole in the ground. A familiar odor from the towering evergreens behind the rusty wired fence that surrounds the old-world cemetery wafts its piney scents through the air. Despite his apprehension, a subtle breeze at his back compels him forward.

The two men arrive early, along with the Rabbi and Sandy. There are four others present, one a tall, thin man he does not recognize, wearing tight fitting blue jeans, boots, and a black buttoned-down shirt with a sport jacket of the same color.

A well-dressed older woman with pearls circling her neck clutches a wad of tissues. He presumes this to be Sandy's wife, Lisa.

There is also an attractive younger woman in a black pencil dress, donning a wide brimmed black cloche hat with an enormous bow sitting on the back of it like a present waiting to be opened. She holds the hand of a small boy. He is around six years old with long brown hair and a pageboy haircut. He stands still in his tan suit and wears a stoic gaze as he looks out into the sea of tombstones which rolls up and down a hill stretching out into the somber distance.

The scene evokes memories of Dan's grandmother's funeral, the first one he had ever attended.

He was five and like the young woman with the black hat, his mother grasped his small hand and provided him with comfort amid a frightening and alien experience. He recalls shoveling dirt on to the plain oak box which housed his grandmother's lifeless body. His father helped him with the oversized shovel as he scooped dirt from a mound taller than he and tossed it into the grave.

Until then, digging had been a joyous activity; reserved for the playground or a visit to the beach. The loud sound of the clump of earth landing on the coffin and the image of his grandmother blanketed under layers of wood and dirt haunted his childhood nightmares.

An unknown elderly man in attendance noticed his young uneasiness and walked over to explain the Jewish tradition of each person placing a shovelful of dirt into a grave after the casket had been lowered. In a kind and soothing whisper, he told Dan to be proud of what he had done because such an act is deemed by God to be the highest *mitzvah* one could perform since the recipient could never reciprocate the honor. Those words had a profound impact on young Dan who from then on measured all his future altruistic endeavors based on the lofty standard.

However, today, altruistic perfectionism is not his goal. This is his first time at a funeral as Vice President; therefore, his objective is more realistic.

He told Joy before he left the house, "I just hope I don't do or say anything stupid." He told her about the time he and his brother Evan attended a somber *shiva* service at the house of a friend from school who had lost his mom to cancer. They both kept their heads hung low and refused to make eye contact with each other for fear of breaking into nervous laughter.

He had a momentary lapse and looked up to see his friend, and it triggered a chortle that quickly prompted a response from his brother and set off a chain of chuckles, snorts, and giggles. Mom had to drag the two of them out of the house when people gave them dirty looks.

It took fifteen minutes before they stopped laughing and could go back in.

Since then, he's visited many shiva homes and attended countless funerals, and not once did he break into laughter. He never embarrassed himself or said anything "stupid." Besides, only the Rabbi plays any significant role at a funeral and his role is no different from what it was prior to him becoming vice president.

Yet I feel different now. I have a moral obligation to represent my community with grace and dignity.

On previous occasions, he never felt such pressure. He would let Joy drive any necessary interactions as he stood by her nodding or interjecting, "I'm sorry for your loss."

He admires her confidence and always says she could talk to anyone under any circumstance. He even quips "she can strike up a conversation with a ficus tree." However, now as a leader at the synagogue he can no longer rely on Joy to carry him through uncomfortable situations. Besides, she was not feeling well and stayed home in bed.

Rick and Dan stroll side by side, their strides in unison toward the mourners. It's like a scene out of a western—like partners moseying toward a gunfight in the old West.

"Is the boy Denise's son?" Dan asks.

"Yes, he's gotten big."

"Poor thing—to go through life without a mom. What's his name?"

"Paul."

"Paul? Hmm, you don't hear that name for kids his age. I would've expected Jake or Wyatt."

"Well, Denise was a big Beatles fan…"

"Ah…okay, I guess Ringo wasn't an option?"

The two men chuckle.

They reach a row of tombstones and maneuver their way around them like Olympic slalom skiers. Dan glances at each one, reading the names, dates, and epitaphs. He recognizes many surnames and pictures a current congregant with shared lineage standing beside the grave, weeping. Some headstones have a wife's and husband's name etched side by side; others have just one spouse's name and an adjacent blank space, waiting to be occupied.

He tiptoes around a small marker for Mrs. Berman's husband, nestled between the grave for Edith Garfinkel and Arnold Kaufman. He notes to himself to attend the unveiling of the full-sized gravestone scheduled to take place on the one-year anniversary of Mr. Berman's death.

He marches past headstones for Silverman, Goldman, Marcus, and Schulman. He spots Cohen, Levy, Samuelson, and Roth. He is reading details on Charles Toporovsky when a gust of wind blows in from the trees behind him. He shivers when a tingling sensation ripples down his spine and raises the hair on the back of his neck. It feels as if the souls of the surrounding deceased brush by him in a single prescient moment.

What the hell was that? he thinks.

He stumbles over a tiny flat grave with the name Ally inscribed on it. It reads "Our precious daughter…." He calculates the dash between the birth and death date as eighteen months.

"Rick, I'm not sure I'm ready for this…"

"You'll be fine. Just be yourself. You can do this."

Sandy spots the two of them and waves. He makes his way past the Rabbi, who has his back turned, and hurries to embrace Rick. The thin unidentified man screeches Rick's name and makes a quick dash to him, too. After a moment, Sandy releases Rick and allows the other man to hug him.

After a long embrace, the man grabs Rick's face with his hands and gives him a chaste and loud kiss on each cheek, as if a sophisticated gentleman from a European country.

He smacks him on the chest and exclaims, "How the hell are you, Rick?"

"Besides your sister getting up and dying on us? I'm doing okay, Steve. How about you?"

"Yeah, it was a rotten thing for her to do. I may never forgive her."

"Steve, it's been way too long."

"You look great, Rick. Oh man, my sister had a thing for you."

The men place their arms on each other's shoulders as Steve rummages through a bunch of "do you remember when..." moments. Sandy moves next to the two of them and joins the happier reminiscing. Dan finds himself in front of the three men in this kumbaya moment not sure if he should smile or appear solemn. Sandy looks at Dan with tears in his eyes and a wide grin on his face.

He pokes at Rick's chest with his finger and says, "This man should've been my son-in-law."

"We were twelve when we dated! I didn't know what I was doing. We were young."

"Yes, you were. Both. I always thought...she was young! No man should ever have to bury his own daughter."

Sandy separates himself from the group and covers his face in his hands and sobs out loud. He moans and calls out, "Denise! Denise!"

Hunched over, he teeters on his feet like a bowling pin sideswiped and is about to topple. Rick and Steve jump to either side and grab his elbows, trying to keep him from falling.

The woman Dan presumed to be Sandy's wife snatches a folding chair and places it behind him. They ease his shaking body into the seat, where he places his elbows on his lap and continues to cry into his shaking hands.

Dan stands frozen, not sure what to do amid the emotions.

Sandy raises his head and bellows, "Denise...Denise, Denise!" He wraps his arms around Steve's strong one as if holding onto a tree limb for dear life. His body shakes too as he gasps for air. The woman behind him massages his back as tears roll down her face.

The Rabbi, unaware of the drama unfolding, had walked off just after Rick and Dan arrived. He had moved to the rear of the open hearse parked on the dirt road several yards from the grave and stands over the coffin, talking with a man in a black suit.

The woman holding the little boy's hand has joined the one messaging Sandy's back, leaving the boy on his own as he watches the scene unfold. The boy furrows his brow in a look of puzzlement, walks over to Sandy, and tugs at his jacket.

Sandy looks up.

"Grandpa, it'll be all right. We'll get through this. Mom said we've got to be strong and to know she'll always be with us."

Sandy grabs his grandson and hugs him, crushing his small body. He weeps, stroking the boy's hair until he can cease crying.

He releases him, holds onto his hands, and declares, "You're right, Paul. You are absolutely right!"

He stands up, gains his composure, and clutches the child's hand. He shakily makes his way over to the chairs placed in front of the grave. The rest of the group follows and surrounds him.

Dan, still frozen in his spot, wonders if there is something he should have done. He feels the warmth of the small group gathered around the family's patriarch. He takes a deep breath and walks over to Sandy who introduces him to his wife Lisa, his son Steven, and Denise's younger sister Amy, the pretty young woman in the wide black hat.

"I'm sorry," is all he can muster.

Lisa asks him how he knows Denise, but before he responds, Sandy explains, "He and Rick are best friends."

"And Dan is going to be synagogue president."

"That's wonderful. You know Denise used to volunteer at the synagogue..."

Dan says nothing. He simply listens with great intent to the myriad of stories the family shares. He is mesmerized by the avalanche of anecdotes and tales.

"She was a wonderful older sister, you know? She always gave me the black half of a black and white cookie because she knew I loved chocolate. She would do anything for me," Amy recounts."

"Yeah, my sister was pretty special," agrees Steve.

"I'd say so. What about how she donated her bone marrow to save the life of a complete stranger?" adds Rick.

Dan never met Denise; he never knew she existed until the previous night. However, listening to the family share their memories he is left with this feeling he has known her his whole life.

"Oh, and of course this is my grandson, Paul. As you can see, he is a special young man."

Dan shakes his small hand and says, "I'm sorry for your loss. From all I've heard, it sounds like your mom was a wonderful person."

"Thanks, and yes, she *is* a wonderful person."

As the morning sun rises in the clear blue sky, cars fill the parking lot, and a sea of people make their way toward the green canvas tent sheltering the mourners. The Rabbi now stands in front of the crowd with his back to the coffin which lies on the steel device that will ease it into the grave. The few rows of chairs are occupied by family, close friends, and a woman wrapped in a black sweater holding a cane like a queen presiding over her court. The rest of the crowd spread out from the nucleus of mourners and engulf the nearby tombstones.

The Rabbi looks down and adjusts his notes lying inside his open prayer book, which he holds in his other open hand. As he has done many times before, he clears his throat to signal he is ready to begin.

The quiet whispers and mumbled voices mellow to a hush and transition into silence. He presses his lips together and scans the crowd of forty. The redness on the border of his eyes is exposed when he peers skyward. He lets the silence linger a little longer than usual.

"Losing a loved one is never easy...however, some losses...are more painful than others."

The Rabbi's voice cracks and then morphs into a cough that he covers with his fisted hand. Dan wrinkles his brow and glances over at Rick who mirrors the expression.

The two men are now several feet apart having been separated by the swelling crowd. Rick, on one side, is squeezed next to Harold and Greenblatt. Dan is on the other flanked by "the girls;" Hope and Beth. Mrs. Nusbaum stands in front of him with a small black fascinator hat slanted to the side and decorated with black lace.

A breeze appears and tosses his *kippah* onto the ground. He turns around to pick it up and almost elbows Jackie in the head.

"Excuse me, Jackie, I didn't see you there," he whispers.

"Hello dear boy, when are we having dinner?"

"Sorry. It's just, with everything going on...I'll call you next week and we'll pick a date."

"You promise, dear boy?"

"Yes, I promise."

"You know I'm looking forward to it and you wouldn't want to disappoint me."

"I'm sorry about the delay."

"I don't see your other half?"

"Oh, Joy? She's home, she's not feeling well."

"Not her silly, your partner Rick."

Dan points over toward Rick and says, "He's..."

"Shh!" says the implacable Mrs. Nusbaum at a volume louder than his and Jackie's whispers.

Jackie tosses a mocking smile back at her as Dan pats his kippah onto his head, turns toward the front, and inches his way back in between "the girls."

"Seems like someone has a little crush on you," states Beth in a whisper.

He glances over his shoulder like a spy in a dark alleyway and holds his hand to the side of face. He whispers into Beth's ear, "She's just being nice..."

"You know, women love a man in power," interjects Hope.

Mrs. Nusbaum turns again toward them and throws daggers.

"Truth be told, I think Mrs. Nusbaum is more my type."

"Well, you must be discreet; you know how people talk around here...," says Beth.

"Yeah, in loud whispers!" responds Hope.

The three giggle which, precipitates a round of "shhs" from Mrs. Nusbaum again. This time the three acquiesce and turn their focus toward the service. The Rabbi has settled into his customary well-scripted eulogy, filling in the blanks where necessary.

"She grew up here in West Huntington and was a cheerleader at Fitzgerald High School. After graduating, she attended Rutgers University where she earned a bachelor's degree..."

He pauses. He closes his prayer book like one closes the door to a room where a child is sleeping. He moves a few inches closer to the family, presses his lips together, and nods.

"You know, there was this one night in my office. I was working late and had just gotten off the phone with Miriam who was wondering when I'd be home."

A smattering of chuckles come from the gathering. He smiles back.

"Denise had been volunteering in the office for several months. She was always pleasant. She greeted me every day with a smile and piping hot coffee in my Beth Emet mug. She always asked for more work and no matter what I needed of her it was never too much. She spent one-week organizing the disastrous supply closet, and I think we all know how much work that took."

Another smattering of chuckles….

"She had been going through a difficult period. I assumed it was because of the recent breakup of her long-term relationship. I noticed she stayed later and later each night. It was nearly seven o'clock this one evening when she knocked on my door. I told her to come in and she asked if I needed anything else before she left for the evening.

"I told her I didn't, and that she had done a tremendous amount of work and she should go home and relax. I then asked why she had been working late and if everything was okay. Of course, she responded in typical Denise fashion, and asked me the same question.

"I said, 'touché', thanked her, and told her I was doing 'okay' too. We laughed."

Sandy lets out a chuckle punctuated by a sob. Sniffing and weeping come from the crowd behind him. Hope notices Mrs. Nusbaum crying and offers her some tissues. She grabs them begrudgingly and blows her nose.

"She then said something I will never forget.

"She thanked me for letting her volunteer in the office.

"She thanked me?!

"I told her, 'I should be the one thanking you—the entire congregation should thank you.' She told me the work she did in the office brought her peace and gave her purpose. She said she got more from volunteering than she could ever get back. I remember before she left the office, she smiled and said, 'It's like the Beatles' song, you know, *And in the end the love you take is equal to the love you make.'*

"It was a week later that she was back in my office telling me about her diagnosis. I presumed she must have suspected something prior. She was devastated, as anyone would be. She continued to come in each night and help but was just not the same.

"However, two months later, she was back in my office telling me the wonderful news—she was pregnant with Paul. After that, she was her old self. She swore she was going to beat her cancer for her son.

"And she did, valiantly, for a long time…"

The Rabbi's eyes dim. He steps back, opens his prayerbook and chants the *El Malei Rachmim*, the prayer for the soul of a person who has died. After he finishes it and all the requisite prayers, he nods to the two men standing near the grave in dirty jeans and sweatshirts.

They jump into action, lowering the coffin. Sandy holds onto Paul as he watches his daughter's casket settle into its eternal resting place.

The Rabbi invites mourners to assist in the shoveling of dirt, explaining the significance of the selfless ritual. Long lines form on both ends as they wait their turn. Dan places himself at the back of the line, right behind Mrs. Nusbaum.

"It was a beautiful eulogy, wasn't it Mrs. Nusbaum?"

"It was lovely, and I have to tell you it was a pleasure listening to the Rabbi and not freezing to death."

"Yes, thank God, the weather turned out beautifully today. The weatherman had called for heavy rain."

"Well, perhaps God can help fix the air conditioner at Beth Emet, too."

"Well, all we can do is hope so."

Mrs. Nusbaum responds with a reluctant smile and turns from Dan. She grabs the shovel left standing tall in the mound of dirt by the person in front of her. She lifts a small pile of dirt into the dark grave as her oversized purse dangles from her arm. She then spikes the shovel back into the mound. It falls over as she walks off and disappears into the crowd, now dispersing toward the parking lot.

Dan's alone. He seizes the shovel which lies on its side. He lifts large heaps of soil into the hole; one after another, deliberately, methodically.

He pushes deeper into the mound and raises it up over the yawning hole, tipping the shovel at a slight angle to allow the earth to trickle into the grave in the same way he played with sand at the beach when he was a child.

After repeating this motion several times, he picks up the pace and is now moving in quick spurts, as if trying to fill an enormous chasm. Sweat drips from his brow and he inhales in short shallow breaths like Jackson does after sitting in the hot summer sun for too long. The cemetery workers approach nearer to complete the task.

Dan lets the shovel fall from his hand onto the ground.

There are still several attendees lingering around the family. They exchange hugs, tears, and stories. Rick talks with Steve, laughing like they are at a party rather than a funeral.

Dan looks and notices Paul by himself arranging stones atop a neighboring tombstone. He walks to him, and the boy does not look up, too absorbed in lining up the rocks in a pattern.

"Hey Paul, whatchya doing?"

"Spelling out my Mom's name with these rocks."

"You know we leave stones on a grave to let people know we have visited."

Paul picks up more stones from the ground and places them on the headstone, positioning them to form the letters M-O-M.

"You know why we use stones instead of flowers?"

Dan isn't sure if Paul shakes his head no or if he is just pushing his long hair away from his face.

"While flowers are beautiful, they eventually die. But a stone…well, stones never do. You know, like the memory of your mom."

Dan is startled by a tap on his shoulder.

"Hey Dan, we're heading out," says Beth.

"Tell Joy we said we missed her and hope she feels better," adds Hope.

"I'll tell her. And thanks for being here."

"Hey, what are friends for?"

"And remember, be careful about that Jackie," says Hope.

"I wouldn't trust her any farther than I can throw her," mocks Beth in a feeble attempt at a Texas accent.

"You know people whisper loudly around here…," smirks Hope.

Each of the girls kiss him on his cheek and walk off toward the parking lot. Dan turns back toward Paul, tousles his hair, and leaves him to his handiwork. He goes back to the grave, which is now just a plot of dirt topped off by the grave workers who are now taking down the tent and collecting their tools.

"Dan, are you ready to go?"

"Rick, just give me a few minutes and then we'll head out, okay?"

"Sure, take your time."

Brian Leventhaul, stands with his hands in his pockets amid the sparse crowd and spots Dan. He's close to a few people who are gathered talking, but it doesn't seem like he is taking part in the conversation. He walks to Dan still facing the group he is leaving, and situates himself next to Dan as if he has been there all along.

"It's upsetting about Denise. You know we were in classes together in high school. We weren't close friends or anything, but she was always nice to me."

"I never knew her, but she sounds like a wonderful person. It's a crying shame. And poor Paul."

"Oh, Dan, thanks for reaching out to the Rabbi for me."

"I'm glad I could help, Brian. So, who is the Rabbi going to get to cater the Lunch and Learn?"

"I'm going to cater it for him."

"I thought you couldn't do it. I thought it was going to be a financial burden."

"Yes, but the Rabbi was right, my community needs me; besides, I can't say no to him. It's like turning down God."

"I had spoken with him, and he said he wouldn't push you into it. I told him you were stressed out about it."

"He did tell me you spoke to him, and I appreciate it, but I don't want to disappoint him. I mean he made some good points."

"As long as you're okay with your decision."

"Well, I can't disappoint the Rabbi."

"You ready to go Dan?" Rick calls out.

"I'm ready...Well, under better circumstances, Brian."

They each nod, and Dan meets up with Rick. They retrace their steps, meandering through the tombstones, onto the unkempt lawn, and back to the crunching sound of the nearly deserted parking lot. Dark clouds encroach from the west on the bright sunny day as several remaining cars pull out of the lot. They both get in the car.

Dan slams the passenger-side door.

"You know Brian told me the Rabbi pushed him hard to cater the Lunch and Learn. I told the Rabbi that Brian was stressed about doing it and couldn't say no."

"I'm not surprised."

"He just folded like a cheap camera and said he couldn't disappoint the Rabbi."

"Well, in the scheme of things it's not that big of a deal."

"It pisses me off!"

As Rick waits to pull the car out of the lot and onto the street, Dan watches the family make their way back to the parked cars. Paul now holds his grandmother's hand as they approach their car. Once inside, he looks out at Dan with his small, innocent face pressed against the passenger-side window. He waves, exposing the dirt on his hand which he had accumulated from playing with the rocks.

Dan waves back and smiles. The boy draws his lips back and summons a mournful smile.

"You know Rick, you're right. In the scheme of things, it's not that big of a deal."

As their car pulls out onto the street and zips away, the rain comes down in a sudden burst and bombards it.

Loud Whisperers

The tongue weighs practically nothing, but so few people can hold it.
African Proverb

The formidable wind blusters and blows and the late spring thunderstorm smacks and toys with Dan's blue hybrid on Route 22 like a cat playing with its frightened and helpless small gray prey. Even his familiar lamppost seems to shiver in the gusts.

The strong lemon scent emanating from the translucent blue dolphin dangling from the rearview mirror tingles his nostrils. He knows the harsh smell will dissipate, given time. It was a last-minute purchase at Wawa along with other sundry items Joy asked him to pick up.

He needs to eliminate Rick's musky cologne and Jackie's fragrant perfume, which has coalesced inside the car's compartment. The two of them, having been its primary passengers over the past six months since Denise's funeral, have left their impressions in more ways than one.

His car bounds toward Blanche's as he peers through the clapping windshield wipers and the pounding rain. He's avoided this night for some time, maybe not avoided, but demand after demand kept getting in the way.

Jake had a makeup baseball game one night and then there was the late-night meeting at work, where he and his staff had to triage a major bug on the company's website whereby purchasers of a book called *Behind Glass Doors* was crashing the servers. All just happenstances. Nonetheless, he can understand why Jackie feels he is dodging her. It's been over two years since he agreed to be president and at least six months since they started trying to arrange this evening in earnest.

However, he looks forward to it; not only does he want to discuss his goals as synagogue president, but also genuinely enjoys her company and finds her fascinating.

His car scoots up the incline into Blanche's. The parking lot is packed for a Tuesday night as he darts into an open spot at the back of the restaurant. He jumps out and races through the deluge of drops. He hops past puddles as he makes his way around the side of the 50s retro style building with its large blue and green neon lights guiding his way.

He remembers as a kid his dad telling him to run through the raindrops to avoid getting wet. His dad's advice is often laced in vaudevillian overtones with no practical application. He would grab his and his twin brother's hand and fling them as he sprinted across the street in response to a flashing "Don't walk" sign. He advised the giggling boys they needed to run, since they were prohibited from walking, his way of joking.

Dan finds Jackie inside, sitting alone on a bench in the bar area. She nestles in the corner of the waiting area with her left arm stretched out on the windowsill. Her legs are crossed in her short, tight-fitting red skirt, and her high-heeled black shoes are decorated with sequins. She wears a silk blouse with red roses dancing amid a cream-colored background, offering a view of her generous cleavage. She stands and her perfume reaches him before she responds with, "You're late."

"I'm right on time. It's seven o'clock."

"You're six months late."

"I told you. I'm sorry about that."

"Dear boy, if I didn't know any better, I'd say you've been avoiding having dinner with me."

"Jackie, really, I'm looking forward to this."

"What? Your afraid people will talk?

A tall, slender young woman in a long black dress walks over to the two. "Can I take you to your table now, Mrs. Goldin?"

"Thank you, Kathy."

Grateful for the interruption from the hostess, Dan follows the two women toward a section near the bar area.

"Hey! Mr. President," calls Bruce who is passing by and walking toward the bar carrying a large bucket of ice and a towel over his shoulder.

"Hey Superman, how's it going?"

"Lucky you, having dinner with the lovely Mrs. Goldin."

"Hey handsome. How ya been?"

"Busy as usual. When you coming to my show?"

"You know how Norm gets..."

"Nonsense, bring him along...Hey, can I get you two a drink? Dan, you want the usual?"

"Sure, thanks."

"How about you Jackie?"

"Bourbon, straight up sweetie pie."

"Go sit and I'll bring them over to you."

The hostess escorts them to a table near the side of the bar; the same one Jackie and Norm sat at the night Norm nearly crashed into him and Rick pulling out of the synagogue parking lot. They sit face to face.

"What's the usual?"

"Oh, a vodka martini so dry that Bruce just places the vermouth bottle next to the glass. He gives me extra olives and makes it so cold it burns."

"Well, ain't that a hoot. Where d'ya come up with that?"

"It's actually Rick's brainchild.

"You two are remarkably close."

"Yes, best friends. Without him, I'm not sure I could do this."

Dan rests his elbows on the table and leans forward. He presses his hands together as if praying and folds them to his lips. Jackie moves closer, leaning her left ear toward him, expecting to hear secret and confidential information.

"Rick and I—well, we've some really great ideas. I can't wait to tell you about them. For example, we need to support our interfaith married couples…I also want to get a handle on our finances, like that check we keep writing to P. Gleason… I still haven't been able to get to the bottom of that mystery."

"Whoa, easy cowboy, you've blown out the candle and jumped into bed long before it's gotten dark."

"I know, but there're a lot of things I want to get done and I'm getting more push back than I ever expected.

"I'm sure you are."

"The Rabbi asked me to write up a policy to prohibit hiring synagogue members in professional positions. At first, I thought it was a good idea to avoid any difficult situations. You know, we wouldn't want to have to fire a member. Anyway, he ripped it apart to the point it was unrecognizable. He had me put in a clause to override the policy for 'rare and necessary occasions.' It started out to require a two-thirds vote by the Board until it morphed into something that ostensibly became the purview of the 'clergy.'

"It was aggravating."

"Yeah, that's our Rabbi, but Dan, I just was going to ask you how you and Rick became friends. We've plenty of time for synagogue talk."

Bruce arrives at the table, places a cocktail napkin in front of each of them, and serves their respective drinks.

"Dan, when are you officially inaugurated as president?"

"The installation is in two weeks. I can't believe it's almost here."

"Well, that's exciting…"

"Yeah, I may need a few more drinks before I give my speech. I've been working on it, and just can't get it right."

"Dear boy, you've been working on your speech? Already?"

"Yeah, why?"

"If you recall, our current president gave his speech from a few notes he scribbled the night before on a wrinkled napkin."

"Well, that's not me. I have to be prepared."

"Dan, I'm sure you'll do a great job!"

Bruce leaves them and makes his way back to the bar. Dan dunks the olives skewered by the kelly green plastic sword into his drink and glances around the room. He notices several of Beth Emet's esteemed members sitting at tables throughout the restaurant. Of course, Greenblatt is there with a few of his buddies, cackling at the bar.

Jackie picks up her bourbon glass like a claw crane in one of those arcade games and swirls it around.

"Dear boy, are you gonna tell me how you and your boyfriend met or what?"

He tells her about the night at the fundraiser when they were fortuitously placed next to each other at a table, and how they had barely talked to each other before, but they were always in silent agreement at Board meetings. She smiles and listens, asking many questions, like, "Is Rick seeing anyone?" and "How does Joy feel about you and Rick always together?"

Dan then notices the hostess escorting Mrs. Nusbaum to a table on the other side of the room, presumably to be isolated from any air conditioning vents. She sits down with a fellow member of the "it's too cold in the sanctuary brigade" and two other unknown ladies who are contemporaries. He waves and she waves back with a pleasant smile. She then scowls when Jackie turns to see for whom Dan's wave is intended.

"Jackie, what's with you and Frau Farbissina?"

"Oh, she's just as mean as a mama wasp. I think she's jealous that the gentlemen at Beth Emet prefer my company over hers. Anyway, you know how people talk around here..."

"Yeah, in loud whispers."

"Amen!"

"By the way, remember the day I met with the past-presidents, and we talked in front of the store? You promised to give me more details about the night you and Norm drove to Port Chester in your VW to see the Dead."

Jackie becomes excited and gladly shares with him the quirky details of that magical night with Norm at their concert. She tells him how they met the band backstage after the show and smoked grass. She recounts how she and Norm made love in the parking lot of the concert venue, in the back of the van, shrouded in homemade tie-dye bedsheets amid the aroma of incense and patchouli.

He isn't sure how much of the story is true or just embellishments of a more mundane version which, with time and liquor, becomes more elaborate.

Dan is enthralled regardless of its veracity, and Jackie is frustrated by the waitresses' incessant interruptions.

"Are you ready to order? Would you like an appetizer? Do you have questions?"

Once, the server blushes when she disrupts Jackie while describing one of the more salacious parts of the story. He feels awful as she struggles to take their order.

He finally blurts out, "I'll have the cobb salad," having not opened the menu—a task rendered unnecessary because of his frequent visits. He's thankful his gut reaction was the salad. He wants to make sure he can fit into his favorite suit for the installation. Jackie orders a T-Bone steak, rare, and instructs the waitress to freshen both their drinks.

He covers his drink with his hand and shakes his head.

Ordering dinner causes a break in the conversation. He looks down at his table setting, rearranges his utensils, unfolds the cloth napkin, places it on his lap, and mixes his half-full drink with the short plastic sword. He looks up at Jackie, in mid-swig of her bourbon.

"Hey Jackie, you mind if I ask you a personal question? You don't have to answer. I mean we're friends, right?"

"Of course, we are dear boy. You can ask anything."

"The night I found out about Denise, Rick and I were with the Rabbi."

"I'm still devastated by the tragic loss of that lovely girl—and her poor young son, now without a mother."

"After we met with the Rabbi, we came here for a drink. As we left the synagogue, we were nearly hit by Norm, who was speeding into the parking lot."

"I'm really sorry, I've warned him…he drives as fast as small-town gossip…I'll have a word with him."

"Well, that's not why I'm bringing it up. You know later we saw you and Norm at Blanche's at this exact table and you both seemed upset. I know it's probably none of my business, and you can tell me to shut up, but I was just wondering if everything's okay with you two."

"Oh, that's sweet of you to be concerned. My Norm just gets a little jealous is all."

"Jealous? Jealous of what?"

"Well, Norm sometimes worries that the Rabbi and I are canoodling."

"Ha ha ha, the Rabbi? You must be kidding."

"Dear boy, what you think the Rabbi wouldn't be attracted to me?"

"I'm sorry. It's not that, I just…"

"I spend a lot of time at the synagogue and with the Rabbi…and I think Norm is threatened by a man in power."

"Yeah, but the Rabbi? I mean that's one of the big ten. Besides, I don't see him as the philandering type."

"You'd be surprised at who is and who isn't…"

"Actually, something odd happened with the Rabbi awhile back."

He takes a sip from his drink and fidgets with his silverware. He leans forward and whispers.

"You know, the night I agreed to be president I was in the Rabbi's office. He received a phone call and referred to the person on the other end as sweetie pie. I assumed it was his wife."

"I think that's fair."

"I offered to step outside, and he said it wasn't necessary. Anyway, ten minutes later the Rabbi left to meet with Sandy and the phone rang again. I picked it up, and it was Mrs. Stern. I apologized to her and told her I had offered to leave the room when she called earlier."

"What did she say?"

"She said she hadn't called earlier..."

"Oh dear boy, are you becoming one of those loud whisperers?"

"I know it's awful. I feel bad suggesting it. But I felt like such a fool when she said she hadn't called earlier. Besides, he acted really weird about the call. You know, all secretive about it."

"Maybe you've watched too many late-night thrillers. Besides, I've heard him call his daughter sweetie pie frequently."

With that one statement, his face turns as red as her skirt and his head feels as tight. An awful sensation settles in the pit of his stomach. He swallows the rest of his drink and drops it on the table with a thud. The waitress returns with Jackie's drink and with a big smile and asks him again if he wants a refill.

This time he <u>nods</u> "Yes." She runs off to fulfill his request.

"I'm such an idiot! I just assumed..."

"Oh dear boy, don't beat yourself up...you've been around this place too long, it was bound to happen to you too."

"I hoped to change the environment here. Make it less political and stop all the gossiping, and all I've done is turn into the same demon I'm trying to defeat."

"Well there, now you've told me one of your goals."

Dan lets out a quiet and soft chuckle and shakes his head. He flips his fork in his hand and looks up at the entrance to the bar, longing to have the door open for a quick exit to head back home to Joy and the boys. Part of his wish is granted when the door opens.

However, instead of him leaving, it's Harold and his wife entering.

Harold catches Dan's glance, and before he can turn away, they smile and motion to each other. Harold moves his attention away from him, scanning the other side of the table and his dinner companion who sits with her legs crossed and her sequined covered foot pointing at him. Harold's smile and eyes transform from pleasant to lascivious. He winks at Dan and points his chubby index finger in his direction, letting him know he approves.

Dan rolls his eyes and shakes his head in disgust, and then turns away, focusing his attention on Jackie.

She opens her eyes wide at him with a subtle pout. She reaches across the table and places her hands on his.

"Why don't we talk about something more pleasant? Tell me, how'd you meet your lovely bride?"

"It's kind of a long story. I'm not sure you would find it interesting."

"That may be true, but why don't you tell me, anyway? It breaks my heart to see you this discouraged."

"I guess we technically met on Valentine's Day, 1984. I was a freshman at Temple University. Joy was a high-school senior. I just had a difficult breakup with my high-school sweetheart. I wasn't really interested in a serious relationship. I needed some time to be free and have fun. You know…enjoy college life."

"You mean you were fixin' to ride a new horse?"

"I'm not sure I'd put it that way…"

"What do you mean, technically met her?"

"Well, I was able to snag front row seats to the Billy Joel concert at the Spectrum from this girl I was friends with and who was well-connected with the Philadelphia DJ, Ed Shockey."

"Norm was a close friend with Ed, and we hung out with him back in the day. He was a good guy. Left us too early."

"Well, during the encore Billy played 'Honesty,' followed by 'Only the Good Die Young.' When the encore started, the first few rows rushed up, pushing me up against the stage. Nearly thrown on to it. When they finished, they took their bows, and I called out to his drummer, who tossed me his drumstick, which I caught and still have."

"But how did you meet Joy?"

"Right. I didn't meet her that night, but about a year later I was introduced to her by another girl that I was friends with who had gone to high school with Joy."

"Dear boy, it seems you had a lot of girlfriends in college."

"Yeah, a lot of girls who just wanted to be friends, and I thought that was going to be the case with Joy, too. When I met her, I was wearing my Mets hat and the first thing she said to me was 'My boyfriend is a Mets fan.'"

"What does that have to do with the Billy Joel concert?"

"I'm getting to it…So, the minute I met her, I fell in love with her. I just looked into her big brown eyes and knew this was the person I wanted to spend my life with."

"Well, ain't that sweeter than a baby's breath?"

"A week or two later, I saw Joy at a party, and we spent the entire night talking. Of course, as college students do, we shared the music we liked, and I told her about the Billy Joel concert. She told me she was at the exact same concert with her friends. I told her about the drumstick. Turns out she always had a thing for drummers, and she watched a guy catch the drumstick during the encore. She remembered because her boyfriend is a drummer and said he was jealous of the guy."

"And so, you were that guy?!"

"Yep, no one else got a drumstick that night. I thought this was a sign we were meant to be."

"She dumped her boyfriend, and you've been together ever since?"

"Well, no..."

The waitress appears with their dinners and places the steak in front of Dan, warning him it's sizzling hot. He reminds her he had the salad and Jackie had the steak. Flustered, she apologizes, while Jackie sighs and shakes her head like Max and Jake do when Dan tells them a joke. A busboy scurries to the table and replaces Jackie's empty glass with a brand-new drink, which had ice swimming in it filled three quarters of the way.

"Would you like some ketchup with your steak?" The waitress asks.

It is not clear if Jackie is more annoyed by her interrupting the story or asking her if she wants ketchup on her T-Bone steak; something viewed as an abomination by those from the Lone Star State. She snarls at the waitress like a wolf in the wild protecting her young.

She swirls her fresh drink and listens to the clinking of the ice as if it's a beautiful melody and then pours the burning liquid down her throat. She repeats this custom two more times, devouring a considerable amount of the special Kentucky bourbon that Blanche's carries only for Jackie.

She then tells her to kindly fetch her another drink.

"I want it ready when I finish this one."

"What happened with you and Joy?" Jackie questions.

"She eventually broke up with her boyfriend and we had a two-week fling. However, it never worked out. She gave me the 'she just wants to be friend's speech.' We became close though, and I hoped someday she would change her mind. Unfortunately, a year later, her parents made her transfer to Glassboro State College down in the boonies of South Jersey after she was mugged on the subway."

"After she transferred you realized how much you loved her, went to Glassboro, professed your undying devotion and the two of you have been together ever since?"

"Ah, no..."

The waitress now returns to ask how their meals are. Dan asks for some dressing on the side and a cup of coffee. The busboy comes back just in time with another drink for Jackie. She is happy to get another glass but remains frustrated by the interruptions.

"...and how'd you end up together?"

"Are you sure you want to hear the rest of this? I mean, we're supposed to talk about what I plan to do as president."

"Dear boy, there's only one thing I love more than a bourbon and a good piece of steak, and that's a sappy love story."

"Okay, remember this was before Facebook and texting. Joy and I lost touch. I started dating my roommate's girlfriend's roommate. It started as just a fling and then we got serious. We were dating over a year and my parents were infuriated because she wasn't Jewish. Her name was Mary Smith. She had blond hair and blue eyes. Her dad was William the third, and her mom, Margaret, served him martinis every night. They went to swap meets, belonged to an exclusive country club, and bought their clothes from LL Bean. It was a novel experience for me. In some ways, it was freeing, too. For the first time in my life, I was being myself and doing what I wanted despite disapproval from my family."

"Ah, a real WASP."

"Yes, but because of the religious thing, I felt guilty all the time, and we fought a lot about it. When we weren't ecstatically happy, we were terribly miserable."

"You were too young to worry about such things; you should've been having fun. You know, like making love in a VW bus."

"I know, thinking back I now realize that. I remember her family inviting me to their house for Christmas. I sat in their living room and watched Mary and her brother hang ornaments on the tree. We were drinking eggnog; her mom made the most delicious red velvet cake, and her dad was playing old jazz records. It was a festive and magical night, but I could barely enjoy it. I kept looking over my shoulder half expecting to be struck by lightning."

"No wonder you have this thing about interfaith marriage. But what about Joy? When did you find Joy?"

"Well, I was with Mary one day, and we're sitting on the hood of her brother's blue Dodge outside of a Wawa. We were having lunch and this overwhelming feeling of guilt came over me—more than usual."

"Why?"

"Well, I was eating a ham and cheese sandwich."

"Dear boy you're not the first nice Jewish boy to eat a ham and cheese sandwich with his *shiksa* girlfriend."

"Well, it was during Passover and Lent, and I felt like I was pissing off God from all angles."

Jackie raises her glass of bourbon and winks, "Well, I won't tell the Rabbi if you don't."

"I started thinking about Joy after that day. I couldn't get her out of my mind."

"What'd you do?"

"Nothing, but a month later, she shows up at the dorm to visit her friends and to show off her new engagement ring. She had met someone at Glassboro and was getting married."

"She was engaged!"

"Yes, I figured I had one last chance to tell her how I feel and get her back. I asked her to go to dinner with me, as friends—for old time's sake. She agreed."

"Did you finally tell her how you felt?"

"I was nervous that night. I didn't know how. Our waitress noticed Joy's ring and asked when we were getting married and said we made a cute couple."

"You told her then?"

"No, I couldn't. Joy laughed and looked at me and said, 'Isn't that silly...'"

"I guess things don't always seem like they appear."

"After that night, I beat myself up for not saying anything. I started planning how I was going to win her back. I even broke it off with my girlfriend."

"Did you tell her you were in love with Joy?"

"No, I hid behind the shield of my religion and told her it couldn't work out because she wasn't Jewish. I felt awful about that. It still haunts me to this day. I wasn't completely honest. Needless to say, it didn't go well. It was an ugly scene that lasted several weeks. Six months later, I graduated college, and she transferred to a school on the west coast. A year later, a friend called me to tell me they had found her dead in her bed with an empty bottle of gin and sleeping pills by her side."

"Oh, my Lord!"

"I felt awful. Like maybe I could've done something differently."

"Dear boy, that's dreadful, but you shouldn't blame yourself."

"I felt alone and wanted to talk to Joy, but I had no way of contacting her and assumed she was already married."

"A year later, my brother Evan and I had a party. I hoped that might cheer me up. I invited some friends from college, including the girl who introduced me to Joy. A few days before the party she calls and says, 'Guess who I ran into?'"

"She ran into Joy?"

"Yep, and she invited her to the party, and Joy said she would love to come and see me. So, I licked my wounds and thought it'll be nice to see her and meet the lucky devil."

"That is brave of you."

"Except it turns out she never got married. They broke off the engagement before the wedding. As she put it, something in her heart said it wasn't right."

"Did you tell her how you feel at the party?"

"We talked and danced all night. It was like no one else was there. When it started getting late, I asked her to come to my room to show her a picture of the two of us from college. I was afraid she would leave without me telling her how I felt.

I told her I kept the picture by my bedside and had always dreamed of seeing her again. She went over to my bedroom door, closed it, and shut off the light. She pressed up against me and we kissed. We made love that night. It was a magical evening."

"Oh, dear boy!"

"After that night we were together all the time and a year later she told me we had to get married."

"What, you knocked her up?"

"No! She said we had to get married because it was meant to be, and she loved me."

Jackie takes a swig of bourbon, emptying the glass of all but ice cubes, and then sets it down hard on the table. The ice clinks and Jackie sniffs several times. She takes her napkin and wipes it across her eyes, causing her mascara to smear. She waves to the busboy, without looking at him, to bring her another drink. He is already on

110

his way with Dan's dressing and coffee and a fresh drink for Jackie in anticipation. She places her open hand on her chest.

"Oh, dear boy, my heart...I didn't expect that story from you...you've surprised me, Dan Barkan. You're quite the enigma. I assumed the typical uninteresting boy meets girl story. I just wanted to change the subject. I could tell you were upset about the sweetie pie incident. I thought it would be some boring story like a friend introduced you two.

"Well, technically a friend did introduce us."

Dan places his coffee cup on the saucer and his hands flat on the table. Jackie shoves a piece of steak in her mouth, closes her eyes, and devours it, making a sound which borders on obscene. She takes a swallow from her fourth glass of bourbon and sits back, letting out an enormous sigh. Her eyes look tired and are a comparable color to her messy yet sultry red hair. Her worn face can be seen through her smudged makeup, but she wears the unkempt look well, with an air of serenity and contentment.

"Ready to talk shop now?" he says, knowing full well that even if she agrees, the conversation will most likely be forgotten by tomorrow because of her inebriated state.

"Suuure, dear boy, tell me the great things you're going to do when jewr president."

"Well, I mentioned I want to improve our financial situation."

"I think that's wonderful! We need a better financial sssi-tuu-ation. This way Norm doesn't have to always bail Benny out."

"Oh, Benny, huh. Norm bails out the Rabbi?

"Yeah, who do you think comes to the ressst-que if they can't make payroll?"

"Really, and who is P. Gleason?"

Dan hopes the truth serum Jackie has been consuming well help divulge the nebulous identity.

"Benny says it's the air conditioner man, but I don't b'leaf him. What else ya got? What else we going to do to straighten out ol' Benny?"

"Well, since you're asking, you know my friend Beth? She's one of our most active volunteers, yet she can't be on the Board simply because her husband Drew isn't Jewish! I'm going to change that."

"Ah yes, the interfaith thing again. That's a big one for you, huh? I guess I see why now after you told me about the blonde shiksa."

111

"Well, I have to wonder, what if religion weren't an issue? What if I never met Joy, or she ended up marrying that other guy? Or what if Joy wasn't Jewish? What would I have done?"

"That's an awful lot of 'what ifs', dear boy. You can't worry about 'what ifs.' You gotta focus on 'what is—is.'"

It reminds him of what his father used to say, "...and what if the Pope were Jewish? We'd all be Catholic and walking around with little red yarmulkas."

"Besides, I believe it's the Rabbi's call about letting Beth on the Board."

"Why should it be?"

"I don't know, it's just always been that way."

"I'm going to change that!"

"Good for you dear boy!" Jackie raises her glass and takes another gulp. "You know, I could be on the Board and my husband is a pain in the neck, ha, ha, ha!"

"Hey, I'm going to be president and I've been known to munch on a few cheeseburgers. But it's not just the interfaith thing. I want to make things better for any marginalized group like LGBTQ members or those who come from a more secular background. I'm starting to get why too many people feel disregarded."

"You're right, dear boy, we gotta do something about this! Let's go over to ol' Benny's house and confront him." Jackie raises her hands with enthusiasm and points at him. She takes another sip of bourbon.

"I appreciate your zeal, Jackie, but I'm not sure you're in any condition to storm the castle tonight."

"Nonsense, I'm fiz as a fiddle."

The waitress comes by and asks if they need anything. Jackie says, "Fill'er up." Dan gives the waitress a knowing look and shakes his head, asking her to bring her coffee instead.

"Hey sweetie pie, you have a nice figure. You should wear something more, you know, revealing," Jackie says in a booming voice as she waves her hand and runs her eyes up and down the woman's body, the same way Harold had earlier. She can be heard by a neighboring table. The waitress scurries off like a frightened mouse and goes to another table on the other side of the room.

"Ya know, you're gonna be a great president, you're gonna make things happen."

Dan wishes he could appreciate the accolades, but he knows they are coming from the bottle of the special Kentucky bourbon and not Jackie.

She rambles on with just enough coherency that he can follow her inebriated logic. She goes on about how things need fixin' and not just the "air conditioning."

He shushes her each time her voice becomes amplified. She mimics his shushing and puts her index finger in front of her pursed lips and speaks in a loud whisper. He almost doesn't hear his cellphone vibrate over her voice.

He hunts for it and pulls it out of his jacket pocket, hanging on the back of his seat. He picks up the call without noticing the caller id, in an attempt to get it before it stops ringing.

"Hello?"

"Is that ol' Benny? Lemee talk to'im, I'll give him a what fer."

Jackie swats at the phone like a cat swatting at a ball of yarn. He pulls away and sits back in his chair out of reach.

"Yes, this is he."

"C'mon Danny boy, I wanna talk to him. I'll tellum to let jewr shiksa girlfriend on tzha boardzz."

"Uh huh."

"Hey Benny!" Jackie calls out as she jumps up from her seat with the grace of an elephant dancing the hora and reaches over to confiscate Dan's phone. She misses and inadvertently pours her bourbon on the table. The brown liquid flows from the table and drips onto his lap.

He leaps from his seat and cries out, "Damn it!" Jackie gets up and stumbles over to Dan's side of the table and pats down his lap with her lipstick-stained napkin.

"Oops, sorrry," she says with the innocence of a little girl knocking over her cup of milk.

"Jackie, it's not the Rabbi—Yes, I'm still here…Sorry I wasn't talking to you. Of course, I'll take care of it."

"Who izzz it? Whatcha hiiiding from mey dear boy?"

Falling Down Drunk

Better to be slapped with the truth than kissed with a lie
Russian proverb

"Is zat the little woman?"

Dan pulls the cell phone away from his ear, covers it with his hand, and turns.

"Shushhh!"

"That's right, don't tell the lizzle woman you're here." Jackie responds.

Dan listens to the other person on the phone. "Uh huh, Yes, Sure."

"Tell her you'll be home late…"

"Okay, Tzipora. That's right. Okay, sure thank you. Have a goodnight." Dan ends the call and places his cellphone back in his jacket pocket.

"Whose Tzzzipora?" Jackie asks.

"Moses' wife."

"Wasn't she Moses' shiksa girlfriend? Why' shhe calling you, Moses sick and shhe needs ya to come over and part the Red Sea? Haha!"

"No, the synagogue monitoring company called. The alarm went off; probably related to the storm."

"Why are they calling you?"

"Apparently, the security system is part of the president's portfolio of responsibility, and I guess since Rob's not here, I'm second in command. I have to get there within twenty minutes and reset the alarm or they'll dispatch the police."

"The Rabbi hazzz you doin' that?"

"I don't mind; I just don't like doing it on Shabbat. You'd think the Rabbi would want a *Shabbos goy* to do it, to keep me from breaking any rules."

Dan calls over the waitress, asks for the check, and tells her he's in a rush. When she brings it over, Jackie and he argue for a moment about who is paying. He acquiesces to her insistence, and she signs her name in a wavy and curvy scribble along with a code corresponding to Norm's account at Blanche's. The two gather their things and get up from their seats.

"Dear boy, would you mind holding me up? I'm feeling a little light-headed." He grabs her arm as she toddles.

"You're going to have to come with me over to the synagogue. You're in no condition to drive. I'll take you home afterwards."

"You're a *mensch*, dear boy." She pats him on the chest.

The two sidle out, waving to Greenblatt and Bruce talking at the bar. She wraps her arms around him and leans against his shoulder.

On their way, they pass Mrs. Nusbaum's table. She looks over at Jackie and runs her eyes up and down contemptuously like a kennel show judge displeased with the breed she is inspecting.

"Not feeling well Jackie?" she snickers with a knowing glance.

Jackie flashes a mocking grin, holds her hand by the side of her mouth, tries to whisper, but it's loud enough that the surrounding tables hear, "Stay away from the fish!"

She punctuates her advice with a belch and giggles.

"Hmph! That's not all I'll stay away from…"

"Ah, goodnight Mrs. Nusbaum, ladies," Dan says.

He helps Jackie out to his car. He opens the passenger door and places her on the seat like one would lay a delicate and expensive Lladro on a glass table. Her perfume fights the fresh lemon scent in his car and has help from the stale smell of bourbon she has gained at dinner and his bourbon-stained pants.

She rolls down the window to let the fresh night air enter.

Dan scoots his hybrid out of Blanche's parking lot and down Route 33 past a black SUV lumbering on his right and brandishing one of those ubiquitous bumper stickers spelling out the word "coexist" using symbols of world religions. The highway is serene and well-lit from all the retail stores, which whizz by as they speed down the two-lane road. He salutes his lamppost when he passes by and sings, "Hello lamppost, what'cha knowing…"

Jackie hums the song he began; *Feelin' Groovy,* a familiar tune as he drives into the quiet neighborhood. He can hear the whispering of his tires as he makes his way down the end of the street and turns into the Beth Emet cloister. A mysterious half-moon follows him toward the brick building and the Ten Commandments that stand watch over its congregation. He parks outside the front entrance near the glass doors with a heightened sense of suspense like one feels when a pivotal plot twist in a Hitchcock movie flashes on the screen.

With no other cars there, he parks willy-nilly forgoing the strictness of white lines.

"Jackie, you should wait here while I reset the alarm."

"Don't be silly dear boy, let me join you. The fresh air roused me and I'm fine. I'd like to freshen up and then perhaps you can take me back to my car. I don't want you going out of your way."

He gets out and pauses in front of a puddle which reflects the bright moon suspended in the night sky, eclipsed by the floating gray clouds. He steps around it out of a habit acquired as a child. Not only did he want to avoid his mother's wrath, but he had an inane fear he would step into it and fall into some eternal abyss instead of shattering the moon's reflection on the water.

The storm is gone, the evening cool and calm. He opens the passenger door and Jackie steps out, clumsily groping the car door like one fumbles for a light switch in the dark.

Remembering he doesn't have much time to reset the alarm, he sprints to one of the glass doors and pulls it open while Jackie still gets out. The opening of the door lets out a cacophony of beeps and bells reminiscent of a casino floor in Atlantic City. Sounds blare from all over the building and red and white lights dance around the room, emanating from strobe lights, bathing the hallway in the appearance of a dance floor at a disco. Running to the keypad near the cornerstone plaque from the old temple, he enters the code, taps the keys, and a corresponding chirp rings out.

Jackie walks through the door as he completes entering the code and the commotion ceases.

"Someone must have forgotten to lock the door and the hard wind must have pushed it, setting off the alarm," says Dan.

"All seems quiet now."

"While I'm here, I should probably check and make sure there is no damage from the storm."

"You should also see if there are any checks to sign…"

"Not a bad idea. It could save me a trip tomorrow."

Dan walks over, enters the sanctuary, and peers around to make sure everything is safe. A chill up his spine causes him to jerk, an eerie sensation like the one he felt at Denise's' funeral. Something unsettles him as he stands in the empty sanctuary, shrouded in darkness.

"Is that…"

He thinks he sees the outline of a dark figure at the far end of the room.

But it must have been the shadows dancing on the walls, or from the eternal flame flickering over the ark. Muted colors appear painted on the first few rows of pews from the moon shining through stained-glass windows. The room seems untouched from when the Rabbi would have shut the lights earlier in the evening. He turns back into the hallway and its bright lights illuminate the open space.

Jackie fumbles with keys, attempting to open the office door. He walks over to help and stands behind her as she inserts the correct one into the hole, turns the knob, and enters. She walks into the dark office. Her feet slip out from under, she flies back, and grabs his shirt.

He catches her and holds her in his arms. She feels lighter than expected, but she pulls on him.

He attempts to balance himself while holding on to her and skates on something slippery underfoot.

They both fall to the ground and land hard.

"Thump."

"What the hell?"

"Oh, dear boy, you saved me. You're so gallant."

The two are surrounded by a dozen or more letters apparently tossed in under the locked door, and contributed, along with the bourbon, to the mishap. Jackie's arms, wrapped around his neck, hang on like a baby monkey. He asks her if she is hurt as he sits there holding himself up, bracing his hands on top of strewn letters.

One of them under his left hand catches his attention because of its penmanship, large red ink lettering, and the name P. Gleason written in the top left corner of the envelope.

Before he can grab it, Jackie moves close and says, "Dear boy, you know you have the dreamiest eyes."

She touches his cheek, then slides her hand to the back of his head, pulls him in, and plants a strong wet kiss on his lips.

He jerks away and unclutches her hand from around his neck. "Jackie!"

"What Dan? I just wanted to thank you for saving me. I could've banged my head on this hard floor and been knocked unconscious. I also wanted to thank you for a wonderful evening."

"Dan—Jackie, are you two, okay?"

Dan cocks his head to the right to see Rabbi Ben Stern standing on the threshold of the doorway. The bright lights from the hallway seep in and around his outline. Dan does not know how long he's been there but is sure he saw the kiss. Dan flushes and his cheeks heat up. The back of his neck tingles, but this time not like the feeling in the sanctuary or at Denise's funeral, but how he felt when his camp counselor caught him kissing Marci Kanter in the girls' cabin that summer.

"Rabbi, oh, hi, um, we slipped on the letters on the floor. It was dark, and we didn't see them."

"This dear boy here downright nearly saved my life."

The Rabbi flicks on the lights. The harsh transformation from a shadowy darkness to an intense brightness makes the situation appear more damning. He strolls over nonchalantly to the cubbyholes housing the letters and messages for the staff, clergy, and Board members. He takes a circuitous route to avoid having to step over the two still sitting on the floor. He peruses through the letters and notes with his back turned.

Although not asked for any explanation, Dan proceeds.

"I got a call from the security company and came over to reset the alarm. Jackie and I had our dinner tonight at Blanche's. She came along as she was feeling under the weather…I'm going to take her home after I sign the checks."

You two can get up off the floor now. I assume neither of you are hurt?"

"Oh, I'm just dandy, how about you dear boy?"

"I'm a little shaken, but fine."

Dan rises to his knees and gathers the detritus of letters and places them on the desk. He lifts Jackie to her feet, but she springs up with ease without his help. She brushes her hands on her skirt and blouse and fixes her hair to tidy her disheveled appearance.

"Did you two have a nice evening?"

The Rabbi? When did he come in?

The Rabbi sniffs like a sommelier assessing the aroma of a fine whiskey and adds, "It certainly smells like you had a festive time."

"Oh, ah, you're referring to the alcohol. Yes, well, you see it was an accident. Some bourbon spilled on my lap. I was on the phone with the alarm company—"

"We had the most glorious night. Dan told me all the wonderful things he's going to do when he becomes president. He's going to straighten out our fiscal issues. Isn't that right, dear boy?"

"That is one of many things I hope to accomplish."

"I'm glad to hear that, Dan."

Dan quickly moves to the table where the basket lies with the folder of checks and grabs it. He sits behind the desk with them and wants to make sure he doesn't have to return tomorrow evening. He flips through the small stack, scribbling his signature on each. He hopes there won't be any more questions.

The night's been trying enough.

He continues to flip through the folder signing checks for the typical bills: electricity, gas, the mortgage, some payroll checks. However, the absence of a check for P. Gleason is glaring. Perhaps the check is not ready or had been signed by Rob earlier. It reminds him of the letter from P. Gleason that he saw on the floor.

He peers over at the unruly pile of letters on his left, continuing to flip through the checks feigning a review of them. He spots the letter with the distinctive red handwriting and starts inching his hand toward it.

"Jackie, why don't I take you home. Let Dan get home to Joy and the kids."

"Actually, my car's at Blanche's."

"Oh, that's fine, I can drive you there," the Rabbi says as he wanders over to the desk Dan is behind. He leans up against it in a relaxed and nonchalant manner. He reaches back and snatches the pile of letters beside Dan. He rummages through them until he finds the letter Dan coveted. He places it in the inside coat pocket of his suit jacket, arranges the rest of them in an orderly fashion, and places them back next to Dan.

"Jackie, are you sure you're okay to drive home?" Dan asks.

"Oh, I'm dandy."

"I just want to make sure, because it seemed like you…"

"Oh, please! That's nothin'. I get my drinkin' ability from my daddy. Back in Dallas, they'd say he wasn't born, he was just squeezed out of a bartender's rag."

"Don't worry, Dan, I'll lock up and make sure she gets home safe. I just have one thing I have to do in my office before we go and then we'll be off."

The Rabbi leaves the main office saying goodnight and walks down the hallway toward the dark corridor that leads to his private office. Jackie and Dan are alone again.

"Now go on, skedaddle, I'll be all right. You heard the Rabbi, get on home to your lovely bride."

"Well, if you're okay."

"Oh, I have to get my things from your car."

They walk outside through the glass entrance doors. The night is quiet, and the air no longer still. A slight breeze cuts through the darkness. The Rabbi's car is parked in front of his. He unlocks his hybrid and Jackie takes her things from the passenger side. His head down, he opens the door to get in.

"I'm sorry if you're upset about an innocent kiss. I just wanted to thank you properly for saving me. And for a wonderful dinner. "

"You know I'm a married man—you're married too!"

"Oh, don't take it seriously. I'm old enough to be your mother."

"Humph, my mother…she warned me about women like you."

"Oh, come on, don't be mad. I'm just being playful. It's who I am. Please, don't be mad; I cherish our friendship."

"I'm not mad. It's just been a helluva night and I don't like the way the Rabbi found us."

"Oh, forget ol' Benny. I had a wonderful and adventurous night and you, my dear boy, need to relax. C'mon, give me a hug goodnight."

Hesitant, he relents, the two embrace, and say goodnight.

He gets into his car and drives off, watching the Rabbi's car and the illuminated Ten Commandments on the building fade in his rearview mirror. When he turns onto the neighborhood street, any remnant of the synagogue is gone.

He turns on the radio and pushes the preset button for the jazz station for some quiet music to help him stop thinking about the strange escapade. He doesn't want to contemplate the letter from P.

Gleason or Jackie's kiss or the dismissible look on the Rabbi's face when he found them. He just wants to be home.

The boys will be asleep and with luck, Joy will snore delicately under the covers as Jackson lies at the end of the bed as usual. He vows to slip into the dark bedroom, undress, and crawl into bed to avoid retelling the evening's events.

He clears his mind on the quick jaunt home. The disembodied voice from the radio transitions between songs and presents "the unrivaled John Coltrane." The man with the deep, warm voice helps relax his nerves as he catalogues the performers on the track.

"...Philly Joe Jones on drums..." transports him to the City of Brotherly Love where he first met Joy.

What should I tell her? The truth, of course.

He shakes his head and coerces himself back to the present and the rapidly cascading notes from Coltrane's tenor sax.

On the quiet highway, he passes his old friend the darkened lamppost he can barely see in the dimness. He is thankful the Rabbi offered to return Jackie to her car and escort her home to the safety of Norm. He doesn't want to talk anymore; he just wants to listen to the music and forget all about it.

It was an Innocent Kiss

Things are not always what they seem
Phaedrus

When he arrives home from the synagogue fiasco, he enters the house through the garage and Jackson's wagging tail and wet tongue await. All this talk about how he and Joy met make him long to be upstairs, alone with her, under the covers, holding her as they sleep.

It's dark except for the light emanating from his bedroom door at the top of the stairs.

When he walks into their room, he finds her sitting up, reading another trashy novel. He approaches and kisses her on the lips.

"I love you."

"How was your night? You're later than I expected."

"It was crazy! The alarm system went off again."

"You should really tell the Rabbi someone else needs to do that."

"Well, I was at Blanche's...we were almost done with dinner, anyway. It wasn't that big a deal to go over to reset the alarm."

"Jackie went with you?"

"She had too much to drink. I insisted she come with me. I didn't trust her to drive herself home."

"I don't plain trust her at all...did she hit on you?"

Silence. *Think! What to say?* He doesn't want to lie, but the tone in her voice signals right now might not be the best time for honesty. However, she can read him like the book she is cradling in her lap; it's better to come clean, especially since he has done nothing wrong.

"Your silence tells me she did."

"It was nothing...We went into the office to sign some checks and she slipped on letters that were thrown under the door. She dragged me to the floor with her and fell on me."

"And..."

"She kissed me. It was innocent. She had too much to drink and was out of sorts."

"Are you kidding? And you walked in here and kissed me after you kissed her?"

"I didn't kiss her, she kissed me."

"What the hell…she knows we're married."

"She said she was just thanking me for catching her when she fell, and for dinner."

"I bet she was just thanking you. You know I'm getting sick of these late nights and all the time you spend on synagogue stuff. You might as well be married to it, not me."

"What's worse is the Rabbi walked in and found us on the floor. He didn't say anything. It was weird the way he reacted. Like he wasn't surprised to find us there."

"If I had been there, you really would've seen weird. You need to stop seeing Jackie and going to the synagogue all the time. This is crazy. You have a family. You're a volunteer…"

"I'm just trying to make things better."

"Well, you need to make things better at home. It feels like you're having an affair."

"I told you it was innocent, and she apologized."

"Not Jackie, the whole synagogue thing. You're with the Rabbi, Rick, or at the synagogue. It's like you're never around and the boys miss you terribly, too."

"You knew it would be demanding when I agreed to this. You wanted me to do it."

"Oh no, I didn't say I wanted you to. I said you could do it and I supported your choice, but this is way too much."

"What am I supposed to do now? I'll be installed as president in two weeks."

The conversation gets louder as the two go back and forth, throwing jabs at each other and exchanging barbs, until eventually they are yelling.

"You're not being supportive. They need me!"

"Dan, you care more for the synagogue than your own family. I also hate to see how the Rabbi manipulates you just to get what he wants. He's supposed to be a man of God. He should be better than that."

"I'm trying, but it's difficult to fight city hall."

"Don't be a wimp! Stand up for yourself!"

He doesn't know how to respond. His throat, hoarse from yelling, doesn't want to talk anymore. He holds back tears which want to burst.

Behind him, he hears a squeak from the door and turns around to see Max there. For the second time tonight, he is surprised by someone in the doorway catching him in a situation he is not proud of. Max clutches the stuffed animal he and Joy had bought him during their last visit to the Zoo.

He is pouting, and it looks like he is going to cry.

"Max! What are you doing up this late?" Dan demands.

"I can't sleep."

"What's the matter?"

"I dunno."

"Honey, you need to go back to sleep." Joy says in a soft and gentle voice.

"I want Daddy to tuck me in."

"Okay buddy, let's go back to sleep."

He swoops Max up and throws him over his shoulder. The toy lion in his hand flails around as he gallops Max back to his room and drops him on his bed.

"Can we play Name that Tune?"

"It's late honey."

"Please, Daddy…just for a little."

"Okay, just for a little."

Dan turns on the radio at the side of Max's bed to the local classic rock station to a low volume. He shushes him and whispers, "We don't want to wake up Jake." He scoots Max under the covers where he lays smiling on his Sponge Bob pillow.

"Okay, Daddy, what's this song?"

"Umm, let me see, I'm not sure…"

"Oh, this is easy, you know it."

"Okay, it's *I've seen all good people* by Yes."

"Correct, and remember I get to stay up as long as you keep getting them right."

As the two listen, Max tells him about school and how he has been doing well. He tells him he even did okay on his essay about him and his lion at the Mets game. During the playing of *Brown eyed girl* by Van Morrison, he shares how he and his friend Joey had a fight because Joey said Mike Piazza stinks. Max's eyes are heavy when Dan correctly answers *Cats in the Cradle* by Harry Chapin.

By the time the surrealistic organ intro and melodic baseline is joined by John Lennon's high-pitched vocals, Max struggles to stay awake.

"C'mon Dad, you know this one…" Max mumbles with eyes half shut.

"I've no idea Max, what could this be?"

"You know what it is…you just want me…to go to sleep."

"It sounds familiar. How about you tell me?"

Max could only get out the words, *Lucy in the sky*…before his eyelids close and he drifts off. Dan smiles, kisses him on the forehead, and leaves.

Back in their bedroom he finds Joy reading. He enters, they look at each other, and say, "I'm sorry."

Dan takes off his clothes and jumps under the covers and lies next to her.

"How was Max?"

"Oh, a few rounds of Name that Tune and he was out like a light."

"Did he tell you about the story he wrote about he and his Lion going to the Mets game?"

"Yes, it was adorable."

She puts down her book, turns off her lamp, and scooches under the covers, snuggling on his chest.

"Jackie asked me tonight how we met, and I told her the whole story.

"Well, I think she is after my husband and has no interest in how we met."

"Remember the night we went to dinner when you were engaged, and the waitress asked when we were getting married, and you laughed and said it was silly?"

"I told you I only said that because I didn't think you were interested in being with me anymore."

"Well, sometimes things don't always appear as they seem. Do they?"

"That may be true, but I don't trust her."

"Well, the good thing is you trust me."

Joy sits up and kisses him on the lips.

"Yes, I do."

"We also talked about what happened to Mary and the whole intermarriage thing. I told her Beth should be on the Board even if Drew isn't Jewish. I told her I'm going to change that stupid rule."

"Isn't it the Rabbi's call?"

"She said that too, but I'm not sure why it should be."

Joy places her hand on his chest and caresses it.

"I'm sure if anyone can change the rule it'll be you."

"Tzipora!"

"What, Dan?"

"You know, she was Moses' wife."

"Yes, I'm aware of that."

"She wasn't Jewish. If it's okay for Moses to marry someone who wasn't Jewish, then I'm not sure why Beth shouldn't be able to be on the Board."

"That's a good point."

Talking ceases for a moment. He finds pleasure and peace in the silence in the dark room and the feeling of Joy in his arms and the sound of her breathing. But like the rush of water from a crack in a dam, the events of the night hurry back into his consciousness and transport him to the synagogue office, until he shakes off his distraction and turns back to Joy.

"You know, even if you weren't Jewish, I still would've married you."

"I love you, Mr. Barkan."

"I love you too Mrs. Barkan."

Joy looks up at him.

The light from the bright moon outside seeps through the blinds in the bedroom illuminating his face, allowing her to see into his eyes. She grabs the back of his head and lifts her body up while pulling him closer. She kisses him long and hard, like a paramour from one of those black and white noir films from the forties. They scoot under the covers, keeping their lips locked and their arms in a tight embrace.

"Thank you for trusting me…I'm lucky."

"Yes, you are—now shut up and kiss me."

They make love that night like the night they were reunited at his party.

Afterward, they fall asleep underneath the peace and stillness of their quiet and peaceful room.

Finally, the Day has Come

...being president doesn't change who you are. It reveals who you are.
Michelle Obama

Finally. The auspicious day arrived.

After two years of preparing for his leadership role and ignoring demons whispering in his ear, he is ready to jump out of the proverbial plane like an anxious and nervous first-time skydiver. In his two years as executive vice president, he has experienced resistance and politics greater than he had ever faced during his prior years on the Board. He knows this next phase will prove more challenging.

The transition from follower to leader is just an hour away. Although riddled with self-doubt, when it comes to significant questions, he always feels confident he knows the right course of action. However, this same certainty confronts his long-held belief. He had always thought, *most questions have a straightforward answer—when someone else has to decide them.*

Hopefulness and optimism still burn deep within his marrow. If the country can elect the first African American president two years earlier, then there's hope for positive change in a small congregation in central New Jersey. He reflects on the White House letter, embossed with the Great Seal, which he received from President Obama in response to Joy's unrealistic invitation to his installation. An autographed picture of the smiling president accompanied it and praised him for his selflessness and service to others, referring to it as "life's most sacred responsibility."

His blue hybrid sits alone in the synagogue's empty parking lot on the side of the building in a prime slot, a spot coveted by the early birds for its proximity to the front entrance.

It is next to the presidential one—a spot to be bestowed upon him at evening's end and includes a wooden sign which reads, *Reserved for President.*

The sign shows minor cracks and rotting, stands off-kilter, and leans to the left, rendered this way from time, harsh weather, and a poor installation. But it is destined to be his alone. Of course, the closest spots to the entrance lie directly in front of the building, reserved for handicapped parking and the Rabbi.

He leans back against his car and gazes into the surreal and expansive sky overhead. To the east, ominous black clouds loom in the distance while to the west, he squints at a bright blue sky. The scene, reminiscent of the René Magritte painting hanging on his living room wall, now emanates an earthy pleasant smell that permeates the air and counters the threatening sky.

The local weather report foretold of torrential downpours.

"But I'm not going to allow threats to dampen my spirits."

He waits for Rick to arrive. Joy and the boys will come later. Rick had suggested he practice delivering his installation speech from the bima behind the podium in the sanctuary to help calm his nerves and feel more comfortable. While he has rehearsed the speech ten or twelve times in front of the mirror at home, and with Joy and Rick, he thought the suggestion was a marvelous idea.

After all, he believes one cannot practice too much, at least he hopes.

Dan looks down from the sky just in time to see Rick's shiny cherry red Ford Mustang convertible turn into the synagogue's lot. He pulls in next to his hybrid and jumps out.

"Ready for the big night?"

"As much as I'll ever be. I can almost recite it by heart."

"Good, I'm sure you'll do fine."

"Please, don't call my speech fine. Fine should only be used in the context of dining and wine."

"Don't be nervous buddy, you'll be great!"

"I feel like I'm going to puke."

"Hey Dan, I've been hearing these rumors about you and Jackie."

"Oh jeez, what?"

"People are saying she threw herself at you."

"What! That's nonsense."

"Greenblatt said he heard the Rabbi walked in on you. He said if he'd arrived a few minutes later God knows what Jackie would've done to you."

"What she would've done to me? I can defend myself, thank you very much!"

"Whoa buddy, I just assumed it was all BS. Are you saying it's true?"

"Of course it's not. Jackie didn't throw herself at me. She gave me an innocent kiss."

"Hahaha, see Harold was right; women love a man in power."

"Oh God, this isn't funny. What's worse is the Rabbi walked in and found us on the floor in the dark."

"What? How'd you get into that predicament?"

"The alarm went off the night I had my pre-president dinner with Jackie. She had too many bourbons. I asked her to come with me to reset it; I didn't want her driving. We walked into the dark office and between some slippery letters on the floor and her drinking, she fell and dragged me down with her. She kissed me to thank me for bracing her fall—and then, without warning—the Rabbi was suddenly in the doorway."

"No way! That's funny. He caught you on the floor with Jackie, kissing?"

"I don't think it's funny, and neither did Joy. It was one stupid innocent kiss. It just looked bad."

"I'm sure Joy trusts you and knows it meant nothing."

"Yes, thank God. I'm not sure how the rumor got started since the only ones who knew were me, Joy, the Rabbi, and Jackie. Despite her, ah, outgoing personality, I really believe she loves old Norm. And the last thing she should want is people thinking she threw herself at me."

"You think the Rabbi spread the rumor?"

"I don't know. I'd like to think our clergy is above gossiping."

"Hey, how come you didn't tell me?"

"Honestly? I forgot too. My mind's been preoccupied with tonight. Besides why haven't you told me about your…I'm not sure what to call your new 'friend.'"

"In time pal, I promise. I don't want anyone to know until you're further into your presidency. You'll thank me."

"What does my being president have to do with your relationship? Jackie asked me if you're seeing someone and as your best friend, I felt like an idiot not knowing. Especially since I think she knows something."

"I'm sorry pal, I just think it's best for now. But I promise I'll fill you in soon."

"Can't you at least give me a name or tell me how you met?"

"Bobbie. And Bruce introduced us."

"Bruce knows, and you haven't told me?"

"I want to introduce you, I really do. But let's get through tonight and then we can talk."

They make their way into the building; Dan unlocks the front door with the keys the Rabbi gave him when he was put on call to reset the security system. They walk directly into the sanctuary where Rick sits in the front row in his bespoke suit and crosses his legs. Dan makes his way up the steps to the bima where he stands perched high above Rick and the empty pews.

"Did you decide to keep the part about changing the policy for allowing members with a Jewish spouse to join the Board?" Rick asks.

"Yeah, I went for it."

"You know, the Rabbi will argue that it's his call."

"I'm well aware."

"I also added some historical notes about the synagogue. I gleaned them from the library in an article written a few years back during the synagogue's 100th anniversary.

Dan pulls his speech out of the folder in his briefcase. It is printed in a large font to make sure he can read and follow along. He lines up the pages, straightens his tie, and clutches the sides of the podium like a race car driver gripping a steering wheel.

"Okay, let's hear it."

Dan stumbles through the first two lines. He struggles to enunciate words he uses often, such as community, synagogue, and intermarriage. He picks up the pace, hoping to gain the right rhythm.

His words come out with the quickness of an auctioneer and the clumsiness of a teenage boy asking a girl out on a date. His words merge, making his speech sound like it's being delivered in Klingon.

Rick crinkles his brow, looking up at him laboring through his speech.

Dan bangs on the podium, takes a deep breath, and starts over. He gets through it once, although not with the cadence and finesse hoped for. He begins again. One third of the way through he shakes his head in frustration and stops mid-sentence.

Not pleased. He thinks. *Perhaps that's the problem—this isn't supposed to be a performance.*

He settles down a bit and starts reading again.

"Wait! Stop!" Rick calls out.

"I know it's awful."

"No, it's not awful. The speech is wonderful and I'm not just saying that. But you need to relax and take it slow. Pretend you're at home reading it to me like you did the other night."

Rick makes his way up the stairs to the bima and walks closer.

"I know you're scared and nervous." Rick takes the pages from Dan's hands.

"You've practiced enough. You're going to give a terrific speech and be a great president. Now, when you're up here, just look at me or Joy and ignore everyone else."

Rick, a good foot taller than Dan, places his hands on Dan's head as if he is going to bless him, then kisses his forehead and says, "You'll be a phenomenal president. Now relax; ya know I love ya, man."

At that moment, the Rabbi walks into the sanctuary. He looks at them for a moment.

"Ahem. The congregation is arriving. It's time to start services Let's get you installed as synagogue president."

"Oh, jeez this guy is always around when someone's kissing me," Dan mumbles.

Rick laughs and shouts, "Let's do this," like an umpire exclaiming, "Play ball!"

The sound of raindrops slamming against the roof echoes throughout the sanctuary as members enter. The first person to greet him is June. "Good luck, Dan, and congratulations on the wonderful honor."

131

Joy arrives with the boys and gives him a tight hug and kiss and whispers in his ear, "I love you." He thinks, *Isn't it ironic at the moment the Rabbi is putting on his tallis with his back to us he misses my affectionate moment with my wife?*

Dan, Joy, and the boys along with Rick take their seats, seven rows from the front in the pews on the left. An unusually large and boisterous crowd for a Friday night make their way into the sanctuary. The Rabbi stands in front of the podium waiting for the crowd to settle in. After they do, he starts the prayer service before the installation begins.

The service is a blur. Dan doesn't always remember to stand up when he is supposed to or responds to the Rabbi's readings. He looks around at the packed sanctuary.

When the service concludes, Joy holds his hands, kisses them, and whispers, "Take a deep breath. You'll be great." The new members of the Board are called up to the bima, including Rick who will take on Dan's soon to be vacant role of executive vice president.

The Rabbi thanks the sizeable crowd for attending services, "and this important installation of synagogue officers." With a crash of thunder and the loud pounding of raindrops on the stained-glass windows, he adds, "especially, considering the inclement weather." He begins the formal process of installing the new Board members by asking each of them to repeat the same scripted lines, only changing their name and role. The arduous process continues until six new members, including Rick, are confirmed.

It's now his turn to be appointed president of Beth Emet. The Rabbi calls him up.

He takes a slow walk amid the silence from his seat and trots up the stairs onto the bima. He stands face to face with the Rabbi. He listens with care to the Rabbi's words to ensure he can echo them.

"I pledge to serve our congregation to the best of my ability and to uphold its sacred values with dignity and integrity…." He recites the lines verbatim, which helps calm his nerves. Out of necessity or fear, his attention becomes hyper-focused.

He repeats the Rabbi's next prompt, "I pledge my time and energy to its needs and goals, to serve with vigor, and lead with humility."

With those words, he is now president.

No trumpets blare. No crowds cheer. Nothing indicates anything has changed with the recitation of those last few words. Nonetheless,

Dan's stomach churns with the monumental transition that has now taken place. There is no turning back.

With the ceremony completed, the new members of the Board shake each other's hands like football players at the Super Bowl after the coin toss. The Rabbi directs them all off the bima except for Dan, who he asks to sit in the throne-like chair next to his. Rick pats him on the back before he steps down to join Joy.

The Rabbi stands at the podium while Dan sits on the high-backed chair behind him. He recites a prayer for the officers and then says, "I am excited and optimistic about the new leadership and for the future of the synagogue with leaders like Dan."

He thanks Rob for his years of service, his time as president, and welcomes him to what he describes as the most desirable role on the Board–immediate past president. He clears his throat and pauses.

"Now, it is my honor to call Dan Barkan to the podium for the first time as our synagogue president to share a few words."

Dan steps up onto the small stool behind the podium, usually reserved for bar mitzvah boys who have not yet experienced their first growth spurt. He adjusts the microphone.

His hands shake, his mouth is parched, and he feels sweaty, like on those hot summer days as a child out on the baseball field.

The sounds of the thunderstorm's pounding rain pellets and booming thunder rage outside as it drowns out the silence in the room for a few seconds. He looks out into the packed sanctuary and sees all his friends and family. He is terrified.

They all sit expectant, waiting for him to speak. He sees Mr. Chasen checking his watch and Mrs. Nusbaum looking up at him from the pews with a shawl on her shoulders, keeping herself warm. Harold and his wife sit in the usual spot and Rob relaxes with a serene, "this is no longer my headache" expression on his face.

His parents grin with pride, surrounded by their friends and his brothers, their spouses, and his nieces and nephews. Seeing all these familiar faces should calm his nerves.

But truth be told, he thinks, *I'd feel more comfortable speaking to complete strangers.*

He lays out his printed pages on the podium. As instructed, he looks over at Rick, who's next to Joy and the boys. In the row behind them are Beth and her husband, Drew. He is pleased to see Drew, who generally has only attended services for his daughters' bat mitzvahs. He presumes because he feels marginalized or finds the service boring, having not grown up as a member of the tribe.

Next to them is the other half of the girls, Hope and her boyfriend Adam.

Seeing his friends helps ease the anxiety somewhat. However, only when he looks into Joy's glistening brown eyes, the same ones which told him in college who he would spend the rest of his life with, that he feels an equanimity which gives the necessary courage and strength.

He grasps the sides of the podium as he had done an hour earlier, except this time an unfamiliar powerful force flows through his body unlike anything he has ever felt. An impalpable sensation of commanding authority and confidence filters and flows throughout his being. He imagines it akin to what President Obama must have felt that evening in November 2008, when he delivered his victory speech to a crowd of thousands.

He turns and thanks the Rabbi and clears his throat.

He welcomes everyone.

"I would like to thank you for entrusting me with the awesome responsibility of synagogue president." His voice cracks as he completes the sentence. He looks over at Joy and Rick and back at the congregation and begins talking about his goals and hopes for all of them.

"I also desire that any member can be in a leadership role, regardless of whom they are married to," a quiet murmuring fills the room.

He does not falter and continues. His tone and cadence rise, then ebb, how he had wanted it to be. He pauses at pregnant points to allow his fellow congregants to drink in the sincerity of his honest assertions. The thunderstorm soundtrack in the background also rises and falls with his intensity and passion, punctuating the silence between his carefully chosen words.

As all eyes are on him, he shares a story of his recent visit to the old building on Main Street, which had housed the congregation.

"I thought of our original founding members, who are no longer with us…that was their moment in time, and as I walked around the old sanctuary, I realized…now is our moment in time and history."

He chokes up; finding it hard to speak. He pauses.

He admits to the congregation that Beth Emet is not perfect. The Board is not perfect, and neither is the clergy.

A streak of lightning flashes from behind the stained-glass windows, followed by a loud thunderous boom. Some in the crowd including the Rabbi startle and jump from the loud noise.

Recognizing his conclusion is near, he is taken aback by the bittersweet moment which settles upon him.

"The truth is, we are at our best and the possibilities are infinite, when we work together...

"In that spirit of unity, I stand here confident and excited to take on the challenge of synagogue president.

"Thank you and Shabbat Shalom."

Clapping is not allowed during Sabbath. Nonetheless, a spattering of applause grows into cheers as those who either do not care or are not aware of the prohibition coaxes the more obedient into an ovation.

The Rabbi rises from his chair, shakes Dan's hand, congratulates him, then whispers in his ear, "We can talk about intermarried members joining the Board in the future."

Exaltation and relief shower over him when he lands back in the oversized chair. He looks over at Rick and Joy, who are all smiles and still clap loudly. Rick throws him a thumbs up while Joy tosses a kiss. He does not hear the Rabbi conclude the service but before he knows it, the congregation is filing out. As the Rabbi gathers his belongings, Dan asks if he should join him in the hallway to greet the congregants.

"You know that's a great idea. However, why don't we do that next time? You know you had a long night. Why don't you relax a moment in here and then I will meet you in the social hall. Enjoy the night with your family."

"Really? I'm good, it's not a problem..." getting up from his chair.

"Relax, sit. Don't worry about it. This is clergy work."

He drops back down, basking in the evening's revelry.

He relishes the moment and thinks, *Perhaps the Rabbi is right.*

Financial Secrets

Most questions are clear when someone else has to decide them.
Howard Da Silva as Benjamin Franklin in 1776

The glow of his laptop's screen shines on Dan's resolute and tired face. He sits at Rick's dining room table behind a disheveled pawed-over mess of documents and spreadsheets, an oversized lukewarm cup of coffee, and a half-eaten bagel.

He lifts his head and peers over his screen and sees Rick's shadowy figure, a near mirror image of himself, tapping away at his own laptop in the ill-lit room. Overtaken by nightfall, curtains that had allowed the light to filter in hours earlier are still drawn.

It's the third night this week. They are camped in the identical spot, scouring through bank statements, budgets, and invoices. This scene has played itself out several times in the six months since he was installed as president. There is always something critical that precipitates these all-night sessions, which keeps him away from his family. He promises Joy once this work is completed, he will take a break for a week or two. A promise given often but not always kept.

Exhausted and wired he and Rick want to polish and finish the presentation for the Board to discuss their financial concerns.

"I spoke to the bookkeeper this afternoon, and she said we don't have restricted funds," Rick says.

"What do you mean we don't have restricted funds?"

"All the synagogue's money is in one account that we use for operating expenses."

"But what about the money members donate for specific purposes?"

"You mean like the check we just received from the Fineman's?"

"Yeah, didn't they donate one-hundred-eighty dollars in honor of their fortieth wedding anniversary to the adult education committee?"

"Yes, but apparently, that money went into our general account."

"But according to our books there is fifty-thousand dollars in the adult education restricted fund, Rick."

"From what I can tell, it's just a bookkeeping entry. The money doesn't really exist. It's used to keep the lights on and pay the Rabbi."

"What happens if the chair of the adult education committee wants money for an event?"

"I was told Rob would look at our account and determine what money they could spend."

"Are you telling me members donate money thinking it's going to a particular area such as ritual, or education, but it goes to pay our bills?"

"That's exactly what I'm saying, Dan."

"When did that practice start?"

"Only a couple of years ago when money got really tight."

"How come we never heard about this? We're on the Board."

"I was told it was an executive decision made at the time by the Rabbi and Rob."

"I can't believe this. So, technically, we're in debt for thousands of dollars that members have donated to non-existing restricted funds?"

"And what's worse is no one knows about it—except the Rabbi, Rob, and the bookkeeper—and now you and me. Everyone assumes the Board is handling our finances properly."

"What if people find out? They'll be up in arms. What are we going to do about this?"

Dan gets up from his chair and paces.

"I can't believe it! We don't have enough money to pay back this debt and if we tell people the reality of the situation, we'll be liable for breaking our fiduciary responsibility as Board members."

"We didn't' know about it, Dan."

"Yes, but we were on the Board at the time. It was our obligation to know and our responsibility.

"This is really a big problem."

"They told me, '…the synagogue virtually runs itself.' Damn! I can't believe it."

Dan pounds his fist on the table and slumps down into his seat. He looks at the time on his laptop and it's past midnight. It feels like only minutes ago he hung up with Joy who was going off to sleep and telling him not to stay up late working. He wishes he had listened to her and gone home. He'd be warm and in bed and curled beside her by now.

Six months into his term, and now he is challenged with something far more serious than idle gossip.

"Rick, I wonder why we haven't heard from Jackie. She promised to call after meeting with the Rabbi."

"I'd love to be a fly on the wall for that conversation. She's pissed about the rumors. She swears the Rabbi spread them."

"Yeah, I'm not thrilled either, and neither are Joy and Norm. She said she was going to confront him tonight."

"You know, we don't know how the rumor got started. It might not have been the Rabbi."

"Ha, it might not have been, but after tonight, nothing would surprise me. Regardless, he needs to stop it. Perhaps it's time for a sermon on the sins of spreading gossip."

"Maybe the Rabbi should focus on that rather than worry about who's allowed on the Board or how we solve budget problems?"

"She also said she was going to see what she can find out about the money for P. Gleason, since we now know it comes from the Rabbi's discretionary fund."

"Good luck with that…"

"Well, she has leverage, since Norm helps 'ol' Benny' out."

"I'm not sure I want to know what it's about," Rick says.

Meanwhile, the Rabbi walks through the synagogue turning off lights, checking locked doors, and confirming things are in their proper place, a ritual he performs every night as the last person to exit the building. He even enters the ladies' room to ensure the lights are off and ample supplies are on hand for the next day. Jackie, like a reporter dogging a politician, follows him, hurling questions in the grand tradition of Jewish rhetoric.

"Are you sure you didn't mention the innocent kiss to anyone?" Jackie asks with doubtfulness in her voice.

"Why would I tell anyone?"

"Come on Benny, besides Dan, and I, you were the only one there. Who else could it be?"

"Did Dan tell Rick? Those two are always talking…"

"He's as upset as I am…"

"You know rumors spread like wildfire."

"Yes, but someone had to light the match, and I didn't tell anyone and neither did Dan."

"Why on earth would I want to spread such rumors?"

"I don't know Benny, you tell me. Why would you?"

He turns away and moves down the hallway toward the sanctuary. He stops to adjust the Chagall print hanging on the wall over the rack of communal tallises. It was a gift from one of the synagogue's wealthier supporters on the occasion of his tenth anniversary as spiritual leader of Beth Emet.

Jackie catches up and stands behind him, close. They both study the painting of a bride and groom appearing to float in midair.

To get away, he makes his way into the sanctuary, hoping to find refuge from her incessant questions.

Jackie follows.

"You know, Norm is madder than a wet hen with no coop. He doesn't even want to come to Temple anymore."

"Would you like me to talk to him? I wouldn't want him to feel uncomfortable in synagogue."

"You wouldn't want to lose his financial support or his Phillies season tickets either I'll bet."

"Jackie, I know you're only lashing out because you're upset. Therefore, I'll ignore that comment."

"Come on Benny, what's this all about?"

"It's not about you. You know I cherish your and Norm's friendship."

"Then what is it?"

"It's not about anything!"

They are now up on the bima in front of the ark. The Rabbi opens it and takes an inventory of the seven Torahs sitting on two shelves. He draws the curtains and closes the ark. When he pushes the tall ornate metal doors together, they depict the scene of the children of Israel wandering in the desert, making their way toward Mount Sinai.

The sanctuary is empty and silent. It's pitch black except for the bima, where recessed lights and the dancing eternal flame illuminate the stage on which the clergy preaches.

Jackie notices the Rabbi perspiring under the lights, a rare occurrence. Although, it is hot on the bima with the large hot bulbs glaring down and the air conditioner off at this time of night. However, she knows the weight of her persistent questioning is rattling his otherwise unflappable demeanor.

"Listen, I don't care why these rumors are spreading. I just want them to end. As spiritual leader of this congregation, it's your job."

She continues pressing him as he arranges papers and organizes ritual items that lie on the pulpit. He scurries around, gathering several prayer books laying on the high-backed chairs, kissing each one on its spine and piling them in his arms. The practice of kissing religious objects shows reverence, and the Rabbi performs it with great frequency, in a manner bordering on obsessive-compulsive.

It seems to be done more out of habit than veneration.

He walks down the steps from the bima and places them on the book cart against the wall at the bottom of the steps. He turns and looks up at Jackie, still up on the bima.

"I'll tell you what, perhaps I can write a sermon for Shabbat on the evils of lashon hara."

"Well, that's a start. I might even get Norm to show up for that."

"You know, according to tradition, lashon hara, an evil tongue, is a grave sin in the eyes of God; even if one is being truthful."

"Benny, save it for the sermon…and while you're at it, you might want to discuss the harm it does to innocent victims."

The Rabbi avoids commenting on Jackie's suggestion. He stands there, thinking.

"Perhaps you can help."

"Oh Benny, you don't want my help with your sermon.'"

"No, that's not the help I need."

"Okay, what do you want?"

"Well, Dan and Rick have been pestering me with questions about our finances. I told them to talk to the bookkeeper, but they say she can't answer them."

"Questions? Hmm, what kind of questions have they asked?"

"Well, for one thing, how dollars from my discretionary fund are spent."

"You mean like those checks to P. Gleason?"

"Yes, I do believe they've inquired about them too."

"Well, why don't you just tell them, Benny? I thought it was for the air conditioning?"

"Jackie, you know the discretionary fund is just that. A fund with monies to be spent at my direction, as outlined in my contract. The money often goes to our members who are in difficult situations, and it requires my utmost sensitivity and discretion."

"Dan is president, and the Board has a right to know."

"I think if we could direct the boys to focus their efforts on other important aspects of managing the synagogue for now, I could find more time to work on a sermon about lashon hara.

"Benny, are you suggesting a little quid pro quo?'

"You know, I'm busy. It could free up some of my time. I could even discuss the subject in my adult classes."

"I'm listening..."

"Well, I could also have a few words with those in the synagogue who shall we say, are more prone to such chitchat."

"At some point though, you have to come clean about the checks."

"Jackie..."

"At least with me. Norm is going to want to know where his money goes."

"Well, we can discuss that at a future date, but for now, I'll give the sermon and see if I can tamper down the gossip.

"I'll tell you what Benny. You also write your monthly article on the subject and promise to give me more insight into P. Gleason in the not-too-distant future, and I'll talk to Dan and Rick and see what I can do.

"Have we got a deal?"

Rick gets up from his armchair, leaving an imprint on his seat. He stretches his arms and bends over, reaches his toes and makes a loud groan. Dan continues, undisturbed by his noises, tapping at his laptop keyboard. Rick looks out the window and onto the night enshrouded and quiet street.

A lamppost out front shines on the sidewalk where a small orange cat strolls. The townhomes on the block are all darkened save one across the street. A woman sits at a black piano behind an open bay window. He can hear her playing and recognizes the piece as something from Tchaikovsky. *Perhaps Romeo and Juliet,* he thinks. He listens for a while, enjoying the much-needed respite.

But then he draws the curtains and walks around the dining room table and into the kitchen.

"You want a drink?" Rick calls out.

"No, I gotta drive home soon; although I could use one."

Dan takes a deep breath, clasps his hands behind his head, and yells into the kitchen.

"Besides the restricted funds, we also have to deal with the transparency issue surrounding the tzedakah boxes?"

Rick grabs a short glass from the cabinet, tosses a few ice cubes in, and pours an inch and a half of whiskey. He walks back into the dining room, jingling the ice.

"I can't believe the Board has no say or knowledge of how that money is spent," Rick says, after taking a big sip. "After all, it was collected for a special purpose."

"Apparently, the ritual committee decides."

"The only one from the Board at the meetings where they decide that stuff is the Rabbi, and we know he has them wrapped around his finger."

"According to the books some of the money goes to operating expenses, which in turn pays the Rabbi's salary."

"Were I come from that's considered a conflict of interest."

"I doubt Mrs. Berman thinks that's what the money is going to when she slips a dollar in the tzedakah box, and then says the mourner's Kaddish for her husband."

"I just assumed it goes to some charity, like a soup kitchen or a homeless shelter, and I've been on the Board for how many years?"

Rick takes another sip.

"Well, you know what they say. Charity begins at home."

Meanwhile, Jackie, disappointed she didn't get more details on the mystery surrounding P. Gleason, knows Dan and Rick will not be pleased. But stopping all the gossip was her number one priority and will have to suffice. She makes her way out the building, a task that has already taken fifteen minutes.

"Don't forget to let Norm know I'll be calling him."

"I will Benny."

"We will talk and straighten this whole thing out. I promise."

"I'll hold you to it."

Jackie stands out in the chilly air of the October night, bouncing on her toes, trying to keep warm. She has a thin leather jacket on and shivers. The Rabbi stands in the synagogue's doorway entrance, holding the door open.

"Remember Jackie, you talk to the boys about my discretionary fund, and I'll do my best to resolve this whole rumor thing."

"Yes, that's the plan Benny. I've got to get home to Norm; he'll be furious I'm late."

142

"Of course, give him my regards and apologize to him again for my having kept you here this late."

Jackie jumps in her car before the Rabbi can say anything else. She turns up the heat to get herself warm and to protect against the frigid air. She speeds out of the empty parking lot and at the stop sign at the end of the neighborhood street, grabs her cellphone, taps on Dan's smiling face, and pushes the speaker button.

It rings only once before Dan picks up and says, "Jackie!" She hears him call Rick over.

"I've got you on speakerphone and Rick is here. So, what happened?"

"There's something definitely suspicious, but he isn't willing to say much."

"What makes you think that?" asks Rick.

"I asked him a lot of tough questions and he was nervous, and sweating."

"Sweating? The Rabbi never sweats. I've often wondered if he even has sweat glands." Rick says.

"What about your leverage?" Dan remarks.

"I used that, and he's going to give a sermon and write his monthly article on the evils of gossiping."

"That's something, but what's he going to do to stop it?"

"He said he'll talk to those doing it and have them stop. I sense that's his way of saying he'll call off his attack dogs."

"But why did he release them on us?"

"I'm not sure yet, but it definitely has something to do with P. Gleason."

"Why do you say that?" jumps in Rick.

"Well, he asked me to talk to you boys about easing off on the P. Gleason thing."

"That's ridiculous! It's awfully suspicious. Why can't he just tell us where the checks go?"

"He's claiming Rabbinical discretion and confidentiality."

"Well, as a Board we have fiduciary responsibility and if something is going on that isn't kosher, we need to know about it. Speaking of which…" Rick adds.

"Rick found out that money allocated for restricted funds doesn't really exist."

"Oh yeah, I know all about that. That was your predecessor's brilliant idea."

"You knew about it and said nothing?"

"Oh no, I said something, and Norm did too, but they didn't listen. They said they had no other choice."

"At best all this manipulation and lack of transparency is immoral if not illegal."

"...illegal, immoral, or irresponsible, the Board needs to know about this stuff." Rick chimes in.

"The Board will just do what ol' Benny tells them to do. They're happy to be dumb, fat, and ignorant."

"This is crazy! We're dealing with a lot of crap. We have the Rabbi spreading rumors, lack of transparency into how he spends his discretionary money, the P. Gleason checks, and now the restricted funds mess."

"Well, I told ol' Benny Norm won't be as generous in the future if there isn't more transparency."

"I think for now, we wait. Let's take one issue at a time. We'll get this rumor mill resolved first. Rick and I'll have a talk with him about the restricted fund after he gives the sermon and writes the article. After that, we'll deal with the discretionary fund, and you'll continue to see what you can find out about the P. Gleason checks."

"Okay Dan, that sounds like a plan," Jackie's voice calls out at the other end of the cellphone.

"How about you Rick? You good with that."

"Yes, that works. It may take time, but we'll sort this all out."

"Thanks Jackie, we appreciate your help. You sure you don't want to be on the Board?"

"On that last note, dear boy, I'm going to wish both of you fine gentlemen a successful hero's quest and goodnight."

All three chuckle at her response and say goodbye.

Dan understands why she would balk at joining the Board, considering all she knows, and doesn't know. He is regretting becoming president; yet, at the same time feels empowered and excited to clean up the messes they have found. It is not the good he imagined he would accomplish as president, but it's better than being called to reset the synagogue's security system.

Dan closes his laptop and presses his back into the chair.

"Rick, it's almost one a.m. and I've got to work tomorrow."

"How about you stay for just a little longer? Let's go sit on the couch and talk a bit, but not about the synagogue."

"It's really late and I'm exhausted."

"Me too, but I've interesting news about Bobbie. I thought you might want to hear."

"Okay, a few more minutes."

They make their way to Rick's couch in the living room and sit close. Rick points his remote control at his turntable, the arm lifts, and lands on the vinyl already there. Whooshes and pops come out of the speakers. The melodic sounds of horns and someone tickling piano keys are soon joined by a soulful voice singing a verse on unrequited love.

"Billie Holiday, Rick?"

"Yes, one of my favorites."

"I really like this…anyway, what did you want to tell me about Bobbie?"

"I told you I met Bobbie through Bruce, right?"

"You said she's a choreographer and had worked with Bruce."

"Yes, and she works with local theater companies and playhouses. She's even done some Broadway. She's just starting on an upcoming production of *Footloose,* which will play at the State Theater in New Brunswick."

"That's cool. Maybe we can go to the show, and I can finally meet her."

"Well, that's just part of it. The other day I ran into your brother at Giuseppe's."

"You're going to have to be more specific. Which one? I've got more brothers than Campbell's has soup."

"Evan, he was with his daughters Rachel and Samantha."

"Oh, that's nice."

"Turns out Rachel tried out for a part in *Footloose.*"

"That would be cool if she got a part; then I'd be going anyway, and you'd have to introduce me to this mystery person."

"Well, I have some inside information, but you can't tell anyone."

"I'm certainly not going to tell the Rabbi."

"Rachel is going to play Rusty."

"Wow, that's great news and a fantastic part. She'll be phenomenal as Rusty."

"That's not all. Remember, I told you about Bobbie's Bernese Mountain dog? Samantha told me she started this dog walking business and Bobbie's' been looking for someone to take care of Geneva while she works on the play.

"Therefore, Samantha will be dog sitting for Bobbie?"

"Isn't that cool, Dan?"

"What you're saying is, my nieces are going to meet Bobbie before I do."

"Well, yes, I guess that's true. But I promise I'll introduce her to you and Joy soon. I'll set something up and the four of us can double date."

"I'll believe it when it happens."

"Oh, come on, you know I have my reasons."

"When would you like to tell the Rabbi about Bobbie?"

"How about when he tells us who P. Gleason is?"

It's the Rabbi's Decision

Do what you feel in your heart to be right—for you'll be criticized, anyway.
Eleanor Roosevelt

Dan walks through the glass doors to the entrance to Beth Emet, as he has done many times before. This time however, he carries more weight on his shoulders.

Sure, he has walked through the same doors to be installed as synagogue president, to speak to a packed sanctuary of congregants on the High Holy Days, or to meet with a parent of a child in the Hebrew School concerned about inappropriate behavior by a teacher, but he didn't expect problems like these.

The financial issues he and Rick have uncovered over the last few weeks give rise to challenges he had neither foreseen nor expected to grapple with during his tenure. They have legal and moral ramifications beyond his apprehensions about speaking in public or dealing with disgruntled members.

Adding to his anxieties are the promise he and Rick made to Jackie not to raise any of these concerns at the Board meetings or discuss them with the Rabbi. At least not until rumors have died down and Jackie and the Rabbi have time to talk things out.

In the social hall on this second Wednesday of the month, he stands alone, surrounded by silence. The children of the Hebrew School have created decorations and hung them on the walls in celebration of the upcoming Chanukah holiday, giving the room a festive atmosphere. Childish crayon drawings and lots of blue and white paper-chained decorations stream from the ceiling. Each month, he arrives early to Board meetings out of habit. His father has taught him being early for an appointment is equivalent to arriving on time. Being on time means you are late.

Although, he also likes coming early to acclimate himself before everyone arrives. The table configuration for the monthly Board meeting is already setup by the custodial staff as directed by the Rabbi. There is a large head table where he and the Rabbi will sit. Other tables are placed in a U formation facing the head for the rest of the Board members.

He doesn't like it. He has tried intimate layouts, which he feels are more conducive to open and honest conversations. However, each month the Rabbi continues to direct the custodial staff to set it up in his traditional configuration.

In time, Dan relented. It landed in the category of another battle not worth fighting.

He removes a bunch of copies of the agenda from his briefcase and places them on the table. He pulls out his notebook and the gavel he uses to start each meeting. He places his briefcase on the floor and walks around the empty room, perusing the holiday decorations. He sees Max's drawing scribbled in crayon; a picture of a stick figure boy and his stuffed lion playing dreidel around a bright blue and orange menorah. Colorful flames fly and dance topsy-turvy in red, orange, and yellow.

The first person to arrive, Harold, as usual, storms in with the subtlety of the synagogue's alarm system going off. He takes a copy of the agenda and sits in the corner of the U-shaped tables as far from the Rabbi's seat as possible. He beelines it to the same spot every month. He likes its proximity away from the head table and considers himself like one of those cool kids in high school who sit at the back of the bus. He speaks in loud booms that reverberate in the empty social hall and reaches Dan several feet away.

"Hey Mr. President, how's it going?"

"Doing well, how about you Harold?"

"You know, the usual."

Deb, the VP of membership, arrives and wishes both men a good evening in her low, cool voice. Right behind her follows Ann, the VP of Education.

"Hi Dan, do you have a second before everyone arrives?"

She sits next to him on the chair set aside for the Rabbi and leans close. A tall thin woman in her late fifties with long stringy blonde hair laced with streaks of gray, she has a ton of energy and often runs through the synagogue as if caffeine courses through her veins. She speaks in a child-like, quiet, high-pitched voice, which makes her seem as if she is telling you a secret.

"Dan, you know me. I don't like gossiping. It's lashon hara.

"Yes, I know all about me and Jackie..."

"No, not that. I heard that was an innocent kiss."

"There's another rumor?"

"Well, yes, but of course I've said nothing to anyone. I just think you should know."

"Well, I appreciate that."

"Then is it true?"

"Is what true?"

"About Rick? I heard he's gay."

"What? That's ridiculous!"

"Well, it wouldn't surprise me. Not that there's anything wrong with it."

"Ann, where do you hear this garbage?"

"At the Rabbi's Monday morning class."

"The Rabbi brought this up?"

"No, of course not. You know he's always late, people were just talking…"

"Why do people feel it's necessary to talk about others?"

"Of course, I didn't take part and when the Rabbi arrived, he told everyone it was lashon hara and to stop. He said Rick's private life is none of our business."

"Well, Rick isn't gay and the Rabbi's right…"

"Someone said he's dating a guy name Bobby, a choreographer. They met at the Blue Moon; you know, on Wednesday nights?"

"Bobbie is a woman; I assume her name is Roberta or something."

"Oh, you've met her?"

"Well, no, but I know she is a she. Well, I mean, I assume. It really doesn't matter. You need to tell people to stop gossiping."

"Well, I guess you'd know, since you two are friends."

"Yes, close friends, and I'd know if he's gay. He'd tell me."

"At the ritual meeting they said you two had an affair."

"Ann, tell me you don't think it's true! You know I'm married! Besides, I'm not gay."

"I know. I'm just telling you what Murray said."

"Murray said it?"

"I can't say anymore. It's lashon hara. I've already said way too much, but I thought you should know."

"Well, thank you Ann—I think?"

"Of course. I'll let you know if I hear more. But I'm not sure I'm the right person. I try to keep away from such idle chitchat."

She gets up and finds a seat next to Deb and is whispering in her ear as other Board members arrive. Bernie, the recording secretary, comes into the social hall and sits down in the seat closest to the Rabbi's chair. He pulls out his notebook and pen and writes the date at the top of the first blank page in perfect penmanship.

Rick arrives and pats Dan on the back. Both Deb and Ann look at the gesture, and then at each other with a condescending glance. Rick finds a seat next to Deb and says hello to them both. More people arrive, eventually filling most of the chairs. The one at the head of the U-shaped table beside him is conspicuously vacant.

Dan sits alone at the head table next to the Rabbi's empty seat.

The room, silent and empty when he arrives, has now become crowded and boisterous. The banter of Board members began as whispers when only a few were present, but as more arrive and the seven-thirty start time passes, their voices become louder. There is now a loud clamor. People laugh and raucous conversations overtake the room.

"Can we get started? I don't want to be here all night," Harold yells.

"We need to wait for the Rabbi to show up before we can start," says Bernie.

"Rob is also not here," says Ann.

"You know it's already seven forty-five. I think, out of respect for those of us on time, I'd like to get started," Dan says."

"Bang!" He hits the gavel on the table, which startles those members not paying attention. Before the vibration of the loud boom dissipates in the noisy room, the Rabbi and Rob walk in together.

"Look it's our illustrious past president," bellows Harold.

Rob takes the only chair available, the one next to Harold. The Rabbi sits at the head table next to Dan. Bernie turns to him.

"Hello Rabbi, nice to see you."

Rob drops a paper bag on the table, pulls out a paper plate piled high with French fries, and rips open a packet of ketchup with his teeth.

"Rob, what are you doing?" asks Dan

"I'm eating. This is my dinner. I didn't have time to stop home before coming here from the train station."

"You know, we have to be wary of bringing in outside food."

"It's kosher, it's just fries from Blanche's."

"Blanche's isn't kosher."

"Are those the real crispy kind?" shouts Harold.

"Yeah, they're delicious! You want some?" Rob responds.

"Sure!"

Rob tears the paper bag, places a piece in front of Harold, and puts some fries on the makeshift plate. Dan turns to the Rabbi who is flipping through a small handheld spiral pad jotting notes.

"Rabbi?"

"Fries are fine, but it's your meeting. It's really up to you."

"Okay, well before I get started, as a point of transparency, I want to remind everyone I'm recording this on my phone."

It's a practice he started when he was recording secretary. With his tendency toward attention deficit disorder, he found it helpful to record the meeting for transcribing later. He taps the microphone icon on his cellphone sitting in front of him.

"Well, first on the agenda is the d'var Torah. Rabbi, are you ready to illuminate us with some words of wisdom from the Torah?"

"Ahem."

The Rabbi puts down his notepad and sits tall in his chair facing the U-shape. Bernie readies himself with pen in hand to take notes.

"Yes, thank you Dan. So, in Leviticus 19:16 it says..." reciting words in Hebrew and then translating them.

"You shall not go up and down as a slanderer among your people..."

He proceeds in a singsong voice as he would up on the bima railing against the act of lashon hara. His hands fly in the air as he speaks in a monotone voice. His diatribe goes on for, what seems to Dan, a considerable time. He doesn't want to stop him; glad he's broaching the subject. Also, he's delivering it with such meticulousness and speed he fears any interference would be like getting in front of a runaway train. The words slander, talebearing, and scandalmongering fly off his lips with ease as he compares such actions to stealing, idolatry, and murder.

When he finishes, Bernie bangs on the table several times and cries, "*Yasher koach!*" the Hebrew equivalent of bravo. Other Board members join in and repeat the customary expression of congratulations with much less enthusiasm.

"Thank you, Rabbi. I think that's an important lesson for all of us to learn. Okay, next. Rabbi, you can present your report now."

The Rabbi continues and begins talking about upcoming events, including his new class on the impact of social media in the Jewish World. He asks everyone to make every attempt to show up for the weekday service to ensure mourners are able to recite the Kaddish.

He covers more items listed in his notepad, checking each one off as he presents them. As he talks, members text, check sports scores, and play games on their phones.

When he finishes, Harold raises his hand.

"Excuse me, with all due respect Rabbi—Dan, do we need to do all of this at our meeting? We're nearly forty-five minutes in, and we haven't accomplished anything."

The Rabbi turns and whispers in his ear, "You need to tell Harold this is all necessary; Board members need to be informed of what's going on."

Dan must juggle his words to respond to the Rabbi's urging and also answer Harold's question at the same time.

"Harold, I'll work with the Rabbi to see how we might expedite his report to help move the meeting along. However, it's important as Board members that we're informed of all the goings on at the synagogue."

"This meeting takes way too long, and it's a waste of time."

"Well, in that vein, I'd like to propose something I've been thinking about. I believe a productive use of our time twice a year, instead of meeting, is to volunteer at a soup kitchen or homeless shelter. We can do it during our June and December meetings when things are quieter."

"I think that's a wonderful idea Dan," the Rabbi chimes in.

"Me too," says Bernie.

Harold whispers in Rob's ear. "Good. I can take those nights off."

"Okay, next up, Deb our VP of membership."

Deb starts and rattles off numbers of how many members joined last month and how many resigned. She tells everyone the Richman's are moving to Florida and the Horowitz's are leaving now that their eldest son has been bar mitzvah'd. She passes around two applications for new members.

"The Rabbi has reviewed the applications and has found them acceptable; we just need to vote them in."

After everyone is given a moment to review the applicants, Harold calls a motion to vote. Ann seconds the motion.

Dan says, "All those in favor?"

Everyone raises their hands. He pounds the gavel and declares both applicants new members. After everyone puts their hands down, Harold keeps his up and waves it around like an overanxious student trying to get the teacher's attention.

"What's up Harold?"

"Old man Sid is texting me. He says they don't have enough people at the shiva service tonight."

"Dan turns to the Rabbi, "Isn't Esther sitting shiva tonight for her brother?"

"Who's Esther," says Ann?"

"She's the lady with white hair. She's in the choir," Rob shares.

"Oh yes, a gracious lady. That's a shame she can't recite the mourner's prayer.""

"I'd be happy to leave and go help," says Harold

The Rabbi turns toward Dan and murmurs in his ear, "You need to tell Harold we can't go running each time a Board meeting coincides with a shiva service. We'd never have a meeting or a quorum if people just run off.

"Thank you for offering, but it's too late, anyway."

Rick raises his hand.

"Speaking of that, I'd like to let you all know that Dan and I have committed to attend at least one shiva service for every member who loses a loved one."

"I think that's a wonderful idea," says the Rabbi. "Seven days of shiva gives us all ample opportunity to make sure we attend a service at least once. I think this is a wonderful way for us to be there for our community."

"Didn't the Rabbi finish his d'var torah?" Harold whispers loudly to no one in particular.

"I agree, Rabbi, and I will also commit to attending at least one service," chimes in Bernie.

"I usually do that anyway," says Harold. "Can we continue with the meeting? It's getting late."

"Sure, continue Deb," Dan says.

"Well, we only had three people to help at our new members' breakfast. I think we need our Board members to set an example and attend these functions."

"Who was there?" asks the Rabbi.

"Hope, Joy, and Beth volunteered to serve and clean up, and it was appreciated, but we could use more hands."

"That's the eighty-twenty rule. Twenty percent of us do eighty percent of the work," says Rob".

"I can ask people on my committee, but I know they will say no. They're all overextended as it is," says Ann.

"You don't know unless you ask. People want to be asked. They want to feel needed," says Rick

"Also, we need to prepare for the Volunteer of the Year dinner. Rabbi, can you tell us whom that will be?" Deb continues.

"The President decides. I'll discuss it with Dan at our next Rabbi and President meeting."

"Oh, I didn't know I did that."

"Yes, it's your call. Although I have some suggestions. We can discuss them when we meet next month."

"Well, if I could ask all the Board members here tonight to send me some names of who they think is deserving to receive this, that'd be helpful.".

"Beth is always helping. I swear that woman doesn't know how to say no," Deb chimes in.

Harold elbows Rob and whispers, "I bet she was popular in high school."

"I agree with Deb," says Ann. "She's a spitfire."

"She would be a great volunteer of the year," Rick adds.

"I think Beth is a fine choice, but of course, it's Dan's decision. He and I'll discuss it next month.

"We look forward to hearing your choice," says Bernie.

"One last thing about the Volunteer of the Year dinner…every year our volunteers spend the night working the event. The night is supposed to honor them as well as the volunteer of the year. It's a shame they all have to work at a gathering where they are being honored."

"I agree Deb, that's why this year we're going to raise funds to hire a caterer to serve at the dinner," Dan announces.

"That's a phenomenal idea! We can use money from the membership restricted fund."

"Well, we'll have to see where we get the money from, but I agree, it's a wonderful idea," says the Rabbi.

Everyone nods and smiles. Excitement greets the proposal as they share with each other their experiences with Beth and how helpful she has always been. When Harold declares how he hates working the volunteer of the year dinner, others add their input. Voices grow louder and louder, and chaos ensues.

"Bang!" Dan pounds the gavel on the table.

"Quiet, please."

"Okay, if we all want to get home tonight, let's continue."

Each VP discusses their portfolio as outlined on the agenda. Besides providing a status on each of their committees and announcing upcoming events, they discuss their challenges.

A common theme appears with all the reports. The synagogue lacks funds to accomplish all their goals; they struggle to recruit dedicated volunteers, and they have a hard time enlisting members for leadership roles. Each nod or shares similar experiences in their volunteering roles outside the synagogue, too.

One Board member who bemoans no one wants to help at her daughter's kindergarten class and the school's PTA can't get someone to run their annual fundraiser. Another says he couldn't find anyone to help him coach his son's Little League team.

"It's like that all over," the man finishes as he concludes the final Board report.

"Okay, well, if there isn't anything else, do we have any new business?" Dan asks.

Rick raises his hand.

"Yes, Rick."

"Oh, come on it's getting late." Harold complains.

"I'd like to propose that we allow intermarried members of the synagogue to join the Board of trustees."

"Isn't that the Rabbi's decision?" Deb asks.

The Rabbi turns toward Dan and whispers in his ear for the umpteenth time, "It is my call. That's not the Board's decision."

"I thought that is the Rabbi's decision," Ann says.

"I think it is too," reiterates Bernie.

The moment of truth has arrived.

Dan sits up, places his elbows on the table, and leans forward like the indomitable Santiago readying to arm wrestle Cienfuegos in *The Old Man and the Sea.*

The swirl of debate consumes the room.

"It's the Rabbi's decision!" "No, the Board should decide its members." "But it's always been his decision."

Rick and he have teed it up and are now prepared to go into battle.

Table the Discussion

But man is not made for defeat.
A man can be destroyed but not defeated.
Ernest Hemingway

"Bang, Bang!" Dan bangs the gavel hard to get attention.

"Hold on everyone. I confirmed it with our governing body. The USCJ said it's technically the call of the synagogue Board of Trustees."

"What do you mean, technically?" questions Deb.

"Well, they said at many synagogues, the Rabbi provides his input. However, they also said most synagogues allow intermarried members to be on their boards; many even allow them to be presidents."

"Really?" "I'm surprised." "I'm not." "Maybe…" A booming commotion erupts from the U-shaped tables as people express their varied opinions in a fierce rush of full-throated voices.

"Why shouldn't we allow interfaith members on the Board?"

"There are plenty of things I do that are supposedly against the religion, and I'm allowed on the Board."

"Wasn't Moses in an interfaith marriage?"

"It's hard enough to get people on the Board. Why would we handcuff ourselves with such a rule?"

"We live in a world where intermarriage is widespread and have to adjust, or we're going to alienate more members." Dan says.

"I'm good with whatever the Rabbi thinks," Bernie opines.

The Rabbi clears his throat.

"Thanks Bernie. Marrying outside the religion is a graver situation, and a blatant act. While I don't condone the eating of unkosher food, that transgression doesn't occur inside this building and in public view."

"Yes, Rabbi, but our world is changing, and we risk losing members if we hand down such a stringent and absolute ruling. We need to learn to bend."

The Board breaks out again into a rowdy commotion. People raise their voices trying to be heard. "But," "However," "I agree,"

"Can we?" "It's not that simple," spring out of the din of noisy arguments.

"Dan, this is my call. You can't surprise me like this. We have to discuss these issues alone before we take it to the Board," the Rabbi says out loud, no longer able to keep his voice to a whisper.

"That's fair, we will. Rick and I can meet with you and talk about it at the next president's meeting," as he pounds on the table.

"Wait, the Rabbi's meeting is only supposed to include the president," says Rob.

"Crash!" Dan slams his gavel down hard on the table and the room falls silent.

"This meeting has been going on for almost three hours. Can we discuss this next month?" asks a perturbed Harold.

"Out of respect for all our time and to meet the Rabbi's request, I motion we table this discussion for next month," Dan yells.

"Bang!"

"Meeting adjourned."

Dan taps the recording off button on his phone and saves the sound file which, is two hours, forty-five minutes, and thirty-two seconds long. The Rabbi gets up from his chair and walks away to the corner of the social hall. Bernie follows along. Rick walks over to Dan. Harold darts out of the social hall like a scared jackrabbit chased by a fox. Other members get up and mingle while talking. The Rabbi waves Dan and Rick over.

"We have to discuss this. You cannot just bring this up at a Board meeting. We have to clearly talk this through."

"Sure, Rabbi, we're happy to. We want you to feel comfortable with this decision."

"Good. I look forward to a thoughtful and lively discussion."

Dan and Rick gather their things and walk into the hallway and out of the glass doors and into the dark, chilly night. Harold, who was halfway out of the building when Dan's gavel landed on the table to close the meeting, has already gotten in his car and is speeding out of the parking lot. He slows down after spotting Rick and Dan exiting and rolls down his car window.

"Guys, congratulations on pissing the Rabbi off. I completely support your idea, but it'll never happen. He'll never cave."

"We'll see. I think many of our Board members are supportive," Rick says.

"Dan, better you than me."

Harold cackles loudly and drives off. Members pour out of the synagogue, rushing to their cars wanting to get home. Many accost Rick and Dan and thank them for raising the issue.

"I think we should allow any member on the Board regardless of who they are married to or their level of observance," says Ann.

"I agree. It's an old rule whose time has passed. I have a friend at Beth Shalom in Springtown, and they have a president who's married to someone who isn't Jewish," adds Deb.

Bernie walks out of the synagogue and sprints over to the crowd surrounding Dan and Rick.

"You know, I kinda like the idea too; we just have to figure out how to convince the Rabbi."

The bitter cold air disperses the shivering parking lot crowd quicker than normal. Dan wishes they had raised the issue in the spring where the temperature would allow them time to get more feedback from the other members. One by one, they jump into their cars and drive off, leaving Rick and Dan shivering alone next to the blue hybrid.

The moon above shines on the now empty lot and the men get into the car. Dan drives off, passing the Rabbi's car in front of the glass doors at the entrance and the Ten Commandments on the face of the building, illuminated by a spotlight shining up from the ground.

"I think bringing the idea up at the Board meeting was brilliant."

"Yes, we get to finally hash this out."

"At least we can accomplish something until we can discuss financial issues."

"Yeah, and everyone suggesting Beth as volunteer of the year is sweet cream icing on a controversial cake."

Dan turns the hybrid left out of the parking lot and onto the neighborhood street away from the world of Beth Emet.

The night is now peaceful. Stars flicker above, and trees fly by. Dan feels good, as if something was accomplished. He isn't sure how it will all turnout but is hopeful.

If I could just get this rule changed, then maybe, maybe, I'll feel as if I achieved something during my time, Dan thinks.

If I could just prevent one person from feeling the sharp pain that comes from falling in love with someone others deem unacceptable or want to exclude from the community, then it will all be worthwhile.

He passes the lamppost and the empty concrete slab it sits in front. Its light seems to flicker, although he knows that is impossible. It must have been the reflection of the moon or a twinkling star.

A beat-up early model Dodge is parked a few feet from the old broken streetlamp, perhaps with car trouble or its driver stopped for a rest.

It reminds him of Mary's brother's car and eating his ham and cheese sandwich on it. He thinks of the pain he inflicted on Mary; having told her they couldn't be together because she wasn't Jewish. Perhaps it was better that way as it saved them both the heartache from telling her he was in love with Joy.

However, regardless, it was wrong to say she wasn't acceptable because of her religion.

Throughout time, Jews have been persecuted because of their own religion.

To do the same to someone else feels downright duplicitous.

You Aren't My Type

*It's supposed to be hard. If it wasn't hard, everyone would do it.
The hard is what makes it great. - Jimmy Dugan (A League of their Own)*

When a single raindrop lands on a still and motionless lake at the onset of a spring rainstorm, its effect can be seen as a tiny singular circular wave dispersing out evenly from its source in all directions. As raindrop after raindrop falls, together they combine to cause the once tranquil body of water to surge and pulsate. Similarly, a single voice, when joined with a chorus of voices, can reverberate into the ether as a strong and unified message causing universal change.

No single person, not a Rabbi, a president, a volunteer, or a congregant can, on their own, bring about momentous change. It takes all of us, working together, to drive the necessary changes and move our synagogue forward in a positive direction. I look forward to continuing to work with all of you to discover the wonderful things which we, the community of Beth Emet, can accomplish.

Dan had most of his article written earlier in the evening but wrestled with several endings. The piece rose from a sense of powerlessness, as if destined to swim upstream no matter how hard he tries. It's as if he can achieve nothing of great substance. Even with the help of Rick, pronounced change will not happen without support from other Board members assisting and breaking through entrenched roadblocks.

He conjures his closing paragraphs while putting Max and Jake to bed. They are listening to the radio and playing Name that Tune when the ending materializes. The image of a raindrop landing on a body of water appears to him when the ominous sound of rain and thunder in the intro of the Doors' *Riders on the Storm* plays in the dimly lit bedroom.

After two more songs, the boys drift off to sleep. He kisses them both, rushes to his laptop, and types his closing words. He meditates on the last sentence and punctuates it with a period; yet he taps the key like it is an exclamation point. He knows this is it. He saves the document, prints it out, and snatches it from the printer like it's a news story hot off the press.

160

"Joy! Joy!" he calls out, running downstairs and around the house, searching for her. Jackson jumps off the futon beside the desk in his office and follows him with excitement. They find her in the study where she's devouring another trashy novel. She is comfortable with a blanket around her and her feet on an ottoman. Jackson jumps on the matching chair next to her and curls up in a ball.

"What're you doing in here?" Dan asks.

"I'm trying to find some peace and quiet to read."

"Okay, well can you read this?—please."

"Are the boys asleep?"

"Yes, we played Name that Tune first.

"Which song did you fake not knowing?"

"Lola by the Kinks."

"Did they fall for it?"

"Of course not, but they were drifting off at that point."

"Honey, what do you need me to read?""

"I finished my article!"

As a young boy, he always wanted to be a writer, but he struggled with dyslexia, which prevented him from excelling in academics. In second grade, he wrote an essay on his beloved Mets and treasured the praise he received from his teacher.

Her big smile and the words, "Nice job!" at the top of the page was something he cherished. He continued to write and receive accolades from his teacher, but as he moved up in grades and expectations grew, once smiling faces turned into comments like, "You can do better...."

"You finished it already?" Joy asks.

"Yes."

"Dan, you were terrified about writing your monthly article, and now you're churning them out with ease. What changed?"

"I stopped writing them for others and started writing them for me. I figure no one's reading them, anyway."

"Well, I know for certain people are. Sylvia Goldstein told me she looks forward to it every month."

"Really?"

"Yep, and Rachel Schoenfeld's mom told me the same thing."

"Wow, that's nice to hear. I'm surprised."

"I'm not. You're a damn talented writer, Dan Barkan."

"Well, can you read this one and let me know what you think?"

Dan pushes the printed sheets in front of her. She takes them and places both pages on the side table next to her.

"Sure, let me finish the chapter I'm on, and then I will."

"Okay, thanks. You're my favorite editor."

"You know it's been nice having you around these last few nights."

"I agree. It's been wonderful having dinner with you and the boys and tucking them into bed."

"I appreciate you committing to a weeklong radio silence with the synagogue."

"It's actually been an enjoyable break."

Dan puts his hands on the arms of her chair, faces her, and bends his elbows, lowering himself down to where their lips meet. They kiss for a long time with a passion they have not felt in a while.

Jackson's head pops up from his cozy position. He jumps off the chair and runs to the two and starts licking their faces. They hug, pet, and scratch him affectionately. They giggle as they try to rebuff his long wet tongue with the sound of "thud, thud, thud" accompanying their laughter as his tail smacks the ottoman

"I promised Rick I'd meet him tonight at Blanche's."

"Yes, I know. While you're out, I'll read your article and let you know what I think in the morning. But I'm sure I'll love it."

"Thanks, honey!" He plants a quick kiss on her cheek this time and runs off to the hall closet to get his jacket. Jackson ignores the less passionate exhibit of affection and returns to his original slumbering position.

"What's on the agenda for tonight?" Joy shouts out to the hallway.

He comes back to the room with his jacket on and says, "Nothing special, this is more of a social get together."

"Aw, Rick misses you, doesn't he? I guess he needs his Dan time, too."

"I suppose so."

"You going to ask him?"

"I don't know. You think I should?"

"Well, you want to know, don't you? Also, he should know what Ann said. You guys are best friends. Ask him."

"I guess I'm worried. What if I find out he didn't feel safe to tell me? Like maybe he thought I would judge him."

"Honestly, I doubt that's the case. I think this is just another incident of people spreading untrue rumors. But ask him— remember, honest and open, those are your words."

Dan flies out the front door and down the steps to the sidewalk. It's cold and crisp; a beautiful February evening. The painted night sky with stars twinkles at him as if to say, "Everything will be all right." He stops in front of his trusty car and takes a long, slow, deep breath through his flared nostrils, savoring the smell of wood burning from a fireplace chimney nearby. A nostalgic scent which invokes memories of his childhood and the enormous stone fireplace which had warmed his family's living room.

He can hear the syncopated rhythms of early twenties jazz coming from his neighbor Mr. Armstrong's open window. *Why would anyone leave their window open in the dead of winter?*

He assumes only his older brother, Steven, is crazy enough to do that. His brother would open the window right after he himself closed it regardless of the temperature outside. Perhaps if he could've listened to Mr. Armstrong's old records back then he wouldn't have minded.

The hybrid carries him down the well-known route in the synagogue's direction and Blanche's. Inside the compartment, Jackson Browne sings *Late For the Sky*, his favorite and something he rarely hears on the radio. The melancholy melody and lyrics which depict pain and disillusionment, ironically provide him comfort and warms his heart. He passes the dependable lamppost, which, despite its lack of illumination, like a lighthouse, signals he's closer to his destination. He pats the dashboard.

"I don't need one of those fancy self-driving cars. My baby can make her way to the synagogue or Blanche's on her own."

When he arrives at Blanche's, he welcomes the warmth from the bitter cold air. He hops on the stool and places his cellphone on the bar.

"Hey Superman!"

"Hey Mr. President! The usual?"

"Of course…Is Rick here?"

"No, I haven't seen him. Is he coming tonight?"

"He's supposed to meet me. I guess I'm a little early, though."

"More synagogue business tonight?

"Dan Barkan!"

A voice from two seats over calls out. The man in the well-worn brown RAF leather bomber jacket with sheepskin lining scoots over to the stool next to him. He brings along his half-downed beer and a motorcycle helmet.

"Hey Woo! What are you doing here?"

"I was visiting my grandkids earlier and stopped in for a drink before I head back."

"Are you riding in this godforsaken weather?"

"Oh yeah, I love riding in the cold. The fresh air is invigorating."

"Bruce, this is my good friend Woo—I mean Lou. He and I've worked together for many years."

Lou and Bruce share a firm handshake and greet each other with smiles.

"What's with the name Woo?" Bruce asks.

"Oh, my son Jake couldn't pronounce Lou's name when he was a little boy. All he could muster was Woo and it kinda stuck."

"Nice tats, Bruce. I have similar artwork painted on my bike."

"Thanks! Well, this one…" pointing to his Superman tattoo on his left arm, "was inspired by…" before he finishes, a customer calls out at the other end of the bar.

"Can I buy you a drink?" Dan says to Lou as Bruce runs off, disappointed he couldn't show off.

"No thanks, one's enough for me, besides I've gotta head home soon. But let me ask. So, Mr. President? Very impressive. How's it going?'

Dan grabs at the pretzels from the bowl in front of him and pops two in his mouth. He looks up in the mirror behind the bar and spots Bernie and Harold sitting at a booth in the back corner.

He thinks, *I wonder what that's all about?*

"Well, you warned me… But I'm hopeful."

Lou puts his hand on Dan's shoulder and says, "Yeah, any organization where people are involved, you're always going to have politics."

"It's not just that, it's the gossip and their absolute submissiveness to the Rabbi. I guess I just didn't expect that part. They hand over everything to him; even if it's not what they want."

"That's tough, but at least you get stuff done. On our club Board, no one can agree on anything."

"I guess I didn't expect the Rabbi to take advantage of his power for his own benefit."

164

"People are people Dan; even men of God."

"I think some people think he is God."

"I've been working on this damn website for the club, and no one wants to help—you know the old eighty-twenty rule. And nothing's ever good enough. They forget I'm volunteering my time and expertise. I get paid to do this stuff professionally."

"Well, it's like you always say…"

"No good deed goes unpunished," the two men recite in unison, and laugh. Lou swallows the rest of his beer, lets out an "Aaah," and shakes his head.

"You know, we just found out our treasurer has been skimming off the top."

"Well, I think we might be…"

Bruce walks over and places Dan's drink in front of him, just as Rick appears in the mirror behind the bar.

"Hey Dan, sorry I'm late. Bobbie called as I was walking out of the apartment."

"No problem, I was just sitting here with my old friend Lou, trading war stories."

"Oh yeah? What war were you in?"

"Battling the Lone Star Motorcycle Club, as Secretary. I'm Lou. Nice to meet you."

"Likewise. I'm Rick, Vice President, second in command, Congregation Beth Emet."

"You mean third in command. Don't forget the Rabbi," Dan interjects.

"Listen, I've got to head out, I've got a long ride back and I'll let you two talk shop."

The three men exchange goodbyes and Lou drops a generous number of bills on the bar and waves to Bruce who's talking to someone else. Rick sits down in the seat Lou left vacant and signals to Bruce, indicating he wants the usual.

"I saw Greenblatt in the parking lot. He's acting weird."

"How can you tell? He always acts weird."

"Well more than usual. He gave me this funny smile and then winked at me."

"That is strange…Hey, speaking of weird, did you see Harold and Bernie in the back together?'

"That can't be good."

"Yeah, don't turn around. Just look in the mirror to the right of the bottle of Jose Cuervo."

"Yes, there's the cute couple."

"Apparently, some people say that about us."

"What?"

"Nothing."

"Your friend Lou seems like a nice guy."

"Yeah, he is. He went through a tough divorce two years ago. I guess it makes you realize how stupid all this synagogue squabbling is."

"That's a shame."

Bruce brings over Rick's drink and chats for a few minutes. When Bruce leaves to serve another customer, Rick pulls out a package from under his long charcoal-gray cashmere overcoat. It's dressed in shiny silver wrapping paper and the size of a small picture frame or a novel.

Rick stares into the mirror behind the bar and takes a sip of his martini. He slides it in front of Dan while keeping his eyes fixed straight ahead. Dan looks down at it, furrows his brow, and cocks his head.

Rick does not glance his way or say anything.

"What's this?"

"I saw it and thought of you. I know you are nervous about writing your monthly article…"

"That's thoughtful."

Dan rips open the package and discovers a black leather spiral journal with gold leaf lettering on the cover that reads, "Life is a journey and not a destination." He pushes aside the crumpled wrapping paper and slips off the attached elastic black placeholder. He flips through the cream-colored blank pages where a small epigraph is written at the top of each.

Over the last few months, his fear of the notorious blank page has evaporated without warning. He wasn't sure when it happened or why, but empty pages no longer terrify him. They are inviting, calling him to pick up his pen and scribble his musings on the now alluring bare sheets. The epigraphs are inspirational. Dan washes his hand over the cover.

"Wow, this is really nice."

"You know, your articles have been inspiring, and I thought you might like it."

"And my favorite quote is inscribed on it.'""

"I know, Ralph Waldo Emerson, right?"

"I almost hate to write in it. Thanks!"

Dan looks down at his martini and swirls the plastic sword and the skewered olives.

"Hey Rick, Ann said something to me at the last Board meeting in private. It was curious.

"Yeah, what'd she say?"

"She said she heard you were dating someone named Bobbie."

"I guess it was bound to come out; especially with these gossipers."

Rick grabs some pretzels, tosses a few in his mouth, and peers down the bar in search of Bruce. He taps on the edge of the counter as if playing the drums.

"She said the rumor is that Bobbie is a he."

"Really? That *is* curious," comes out between the sound of "crunch, crunch, crunch" that reminds Dan of Jackson chewing on popcorn tossed in his mouth by the boys.

"Man, I'm starving. You want to get some appetizers?" Rick pulls out his cellphone and looks at it for a moment and places it on the bar.

"She also said when at the Ritual Committee, Murray said you and I had an affair."

"Nonsense, you're not my type."

"I'm not your type?"

"Don't take it personally. Women are my type and I prefer my companions to be unmarried. And you, Dan, are neither."

"I guess, you're not..."

"Did you think I was gay? Trust me, if I were gay, you'd know. You think I wouldn't tell you?"

"No, of course you would. It's just I thought maybe that's why you didn't want anyone to know about Bobbie, and since Bobbie can be a male or female name..."

"First off, her name is Roberta. Second, I already told you, she isn't Jewish, and I didn't want to cause trouble with the Rabbi. You know how he feels about anyone on the Board with a non-Jewish spouse."

"Well, you're not married."

"No, but I don't think he'd be okay with a Board member dating someone who isn't Jewish; especially one who is going to be president."

"True. You know, these people spend too much time blathering on about whether or not you're gay. They don't even ask the right questions. I mean, what if you were? Who the hell cares? And why should it matter?"

"They're all *yentas*."

"As my Mom says, they have nothing else to *fradray their kup* about..."

Rick appears bewildered, tilting his head like Jackson does when he hears a high-pitched sound.

"It's Yiddish. I think it means something like they've got nothing else to worry their head about."

"You know what would be funny? They don't need to know I'm not gay."

"Hahaha, that's true...we could toy with them for a while.

"Buzzzzz...." Dan's phone trembles and dances across the bar. He lifts it up and swipes his thumb up.

"Damn!"

He holds it in his hands like a prayer book and taps on it with both his thumbs in a wild and frantic motion. When finished, he places it back down.

"Everything okay?"

"Oh yeah, Joy was just texting me goodnight; she's going to bed. There's something wrong with my phone, though. The app I use for recording the Board meetings keeps spontaneously popping up and starting."

"It recorded our conversation just now?""

"Yes, by accident, but don't worry, I deleted it."

"I guess I better watch what I say around you."

"At some point I probably should reinstall it."

Dan picks up the journal lying on the bar again, opens it, and glances at the unfilled pages. He leafs through them as if perusing a magazine.

"You know this is great! Thank you, dude."

"Hey, my pleasure."

They stand up and exchange a warm embrace while patting each other's backs.

"Hey guys, get a room," cackles Harold.

Rick lowers himself and places his chin on Dan's shoulder, stares at Harold and says with a playful smile, "We would, but there're no hotels around here that charge by the hour." He winks.

He holds Dan's embrace longer. The hand which had been patting his back is now massaging it in a slow, circular motion. Realizing what the mischievous Rick is up to, Dan separates himself from him and turns around toward the two men.

Bernie and Harold, who have snuck up on the two during their hug, wear puzzled expressions and are now startled.

"Hey guys. What's up?" says Rick.

"Um, good—um, what about you two? How are you?" says Bernie.

"Good too. What are you guys doing here?" asks Dan.

"I feel like I live here. My wife's out tonight." replies Harold.

"We're just having dinner. We didn't discuss synagogue business," says Bernie.

"Guys, don't forget, we have a Board meeting in two weeks. I'm counting on you to be there to vote on the intermarriage policy."

"About that, I was talking with the Rabbi and, while I agree with you, he really is uncomfortable with changing the rule," says Bernie.

Rick raises his voice and says, "Bernie, you can't back out on us now. This is too important."

"Bernie, we're not changing a policy. We're only clarifying a long-standing practice the Rabbi implemented himself. Of course, he'll be uncomfortable. But he'll get used to it. Remember, we have to consider our congregants."

"I know…"

"Come on guys, you know this is the right thing to do."

Dan moves closer and huddles with the two men. In a hushed voice, he explains why they need to vote yes. However, sound and valid arguments, no matter how salient, will not secure yes votes. It becomes apparent the only thing that will garner an affirmative is approval from the Rabbi.

Four years as a Board member, two years as executive vice president, and eight months as president, he is no longer surprised at the Rabbi coercing and badgering Board members into voting the Rabbi's way. He has even ceased being shocked, witnessing him exploiting his perceived power for personal gain.

What baffles him though, is that, unlike most cultish personalities, there is no misinformation, brainwashing, or

169

indoctrination necessary. Members hand over their authority with ease or resignation, for mere morsels of approval or out of sheer exhaustion.

He pleads with Harold and Bernie to vote their conscience. They say they will, but he is not sure if they are sincere or just placating him. All he knows is that without them, he won't get the new rule passed, and Beth won't be allowed on the Board.

"Well, I got to get home to my wife. She'll be home soon and wondering where I am," says Harold.

"Yeah, me too," echoes Bernie.

The men exit as quickly as they had appeared during Rick and Dan's hug.

"Well, it looks like the Rabbi got to them," says Rick.

"You know what's funny? When I first started as president, he said to me he thought we'd agree on everything. I told him perhaps we should disagree on some things, this way, people didn't view me as a sycophant. Of course, I was kidding, but now he throws it in my face every chance he gets, claiming I only disagree with him to puff out my chest and prove I'm not his underling."

"He's a stubborn and inflexible son of a..., well, you know."

"And too, one man's inflexibility is another man's unwavering conviction."

"Who said that?"

"I just did."

"That's good. Maybe you should write that down and put it in your next article."

Dan takes out a pen and scribbles the quote on the napkin under his martini and throws it in his coat pocket. Then remembers the journal Rick gave him. He takes the napkin out of his pocket and places it between two gilt-edged pages.

"You should've seen Harold's face when I started rubbing your back."

"I'm sure it was priceless. Can you imagine if Bobbie really were male? I think the Rabbi would have a conniption."

"Well, my Mom wouldn't care, as long as Bobbie is Jewish---- and it couldn't hurt if he were a doctor."

They laugh and continue to enjoy their drinks and their time together. They hadn't spoken during Dan's blackout; therefore, they have a lot of catching up. They talk about the latest Mets trade rumors and lament the Devils loss to the Kings from the night before. Bruce joins them between serving other patrons, which helps keep their conversation off synagogue business. Rick tells him how he and his team's presentation landed the Budweiser account.

"You're a regular Don Draper, Rick."

"Well, my team did a great job. And the pitch was perfect. It gave me such satisfaction."

"How about spreading some of that magic dust on the Board..."

"I wish I knew how. One expects this kind of backstabbing in my field but to see it in a religious institution and from clergy and toward volunteers and members it's just appalling."

While the gossiping about him and Rick is on the rise, the incident with Jackie has faded into the background.

Both know they are going to have to confront the Rabbi on the financial issues. They can no longer sit back and wait. They need to know who P. Gleason is and why synagogue funds go to this person every month. They have a fiduciary responsibility and an ethical obligation to their members. But that subject is for another night.

When the two leave Blanche's, the parking lot is near empty. Besides their own cars, a few are parked in the back, belonging to the waitstaff still inside counting tips. They stand beside their cars parked next to each other and glance into the foreboding sky. Dan keeps his hands in his coat pockets to protect them from the now bitter cold of night as they talk a little longer.

Clouds float past the moon for a moment and allow its shadowed light to peek through.

"It looks like there's a storm coming, Dan."

"It sure does."

It's None of Your Business

A bird may love a fish, but where would they build a home together.
Tevye (Fiddler on the Roof)

"Bang!" The sound of his clenched fist landing on his mahogany desk cuts through Dan like a long razor-thin-steel knife.

It is like an "Humph!" a gut punch to the pit of his stomach.

He clenches his jaw, and a throbbing, sharp pain settles in his forehead. He feels it for the first time that evening in the Rabbi's office. It's a physical manifestation of a visceral feeling that arises from deep within.

"Dammit, Dan Barkan! This is none of your business! It's no one's business but mine!"

Now I understand why otherwise rational individuals relent to positions they vehemently oppose and commit to obligations they'd normally reject. It's an unconscious reaction. They can't help it. Everyone's programmed to avoid pain, which comes from feeling judged and rejected. They're like broken children at the mercy of a manipulative parent who divvies out their acceptance based on obedience to their will.

However, he is not sure which is worse, irate berating or scornful condescension, swiping away their concerns like annoying flying gnats. It is the first time they've heard the Rabbi yell. He has delivered sermons on the atrocities of the Holocaust and the killing of innocent Jews at the hands of suicide bombers but has never exhibited such enraged passion.

It is reminiscent of how a man interviewed on the local news described being stabbed by a mugger in Central Park. He said, "I didn't feel any pain because of the shock and the adrenaline. I just felt a warm liquid streaming out of my body."

Dan concentrates.

"But Rabbi, we've a fiduciary responsibility...you're asking us to sign checks and we do not know where the money is going..."

"My contract states I have full discretion on how money in my fund is spent! You're just going to have faith. If not, there are others like Rob who are authorized to sign checks and will happily do it without grumbling. Besides, when was the last time you saw a check for P. Gleason?"

"We're not telling you how to spend the money, but we're legally responsible—and morally responsible..."

"And the synagogue's constitution states the president and the Board have full financial responsibility," adds Rick.

"Yes, of course the constitution says that, but it's a guideline, not a hard and fast rule. There are exceptions. It doesn't mean you need to know how I spend my funds—all other presidents understood that."

"Yes, but who determines when we make exceptions and when we stick to the rules?"

"Dan, I think common sense determines."

"Common sense says it's the Board's responsibility and we must have transparency into your fund."

"Being responsible doesn't mean you can see how I spend money from my fund.

"You can't just pick which rules you want to obey."

"Sometimes exceptions have to be made."

"Yes, but it's a problem when the exception is the rule."

"There is no problem and we've never had one until now."

"I need to know who P. Gleason is and why we pay this person $1,613 each month."

"No, you don't! Besides, you're the volunteers. I'm the professional."

"You mean the professional hired by the Board who serves at the pleasure of the members of this congregation?"

"They have all enjoyed the pleasure of my services for over twenty years without complaints. Now, I'm done with this conversation."

The Rabbi turns back to signing the letters on his desk Mrs. Winthrop had typed up. His head is down, absorbed in stopping the conversation he no longer wants to have. Rick, sitting in the twin leather chair next to Dan, turns to him.

"You know, Dan, I believe our clergy feels we are just tools for him to use."

"Yes Rick, I think you're right. We're like..."

He looks around the Rabbi's desk and grabs the first thing he can find; a gold-plated monogrammed letter opener sitting at the edge of his desk. He points it at him in his clenched fist and yells, "...like this damn letter opener!"

The bottom half of the opener had been lying under a pile of mail. When he grabbed it, letters scattered, including one with the name P. Gleason written at the top left corner of the envelope. The Rabbi seizes it, stashes it in his top drawer, and slams it closed. He stands up and places his hands palms down on his desk, faces them and screams, "Gentlemen! We have other business to discuss tonight. We can either move on or end this meeting."

The room falls silent. Dan and Rick look at each other with resignation. They know if they are going to find out who P. Gleason is and why the synagogue is paying him or her sixteen-hundred dollars, it isn't going to come from the Rabbi. Dan hadn't seen or had to sign a check written to P. Gleason for a while, but it doesn't mean the Rabbi isn't having someone else sign them.

"Well, you said you wanted to discuss the intermarriage situation in private before we presented it to the Board," continues Dan.

"I am opposed to allowing anyone on the Board who is married to a non-Jew. But I've considered your points and I'm willing to let the Board decide."

"Well, that was our plan all along. That's what we wanted to do the night of the Board meeting."

"I would also like time during the meeting to present my case. Of course, you can present yours as well."

Dan realizes why the Rabbi asked to postpone the vote. He did it to provide time for him to build a case and lobby the other Board members. Of course, Dan and Rick would have to build a stronger case to have any hope of passing the motion. Most of the members on the Board are for the change, but the Rabbi had something which could erase that advantage—his position as Rabbi.

"Rabbi, why don't you tell us your concerns?" asks Rick.

"As the spiritual and religious leader of this community, I don't like the message it sends."

"And what message is that?" asks Dan.

"...that we condone marriage with someone outside our faith."

"How is this any different from allowing members on the Board who don't eat kosher food or attend services on Shabbat?" Rick says.

"Should they be kicked off of the Board?" adds Dan.

"Having a non-Jewish spouse is much more public. A Board member eating a cheeseburger at a restaurant is not as blatant as bringing their non-Jewish spouse into the synagogue."

"No, unless that restaurant is Blanche's. On some Saturdays, there are more members there than in our own sanctuary," Dan adds.

The Rabbi volleys arguments with the two of them. He throws out a quote from *Fiddler on the Roof*, "A bird may love a fish, but where would they build a home together?"

"Please, you're not going to use Hollywood dialog as an argument against intermarriage!" Rick exclaims.

The rhetorical wrestling continues. They return counterpunches as if it were a boxing match. The Rabbi offers several vague and obtuse points, hoping the men will relent. They do not; instead, they fire back with strong, sound, counterarguments.

"Deuteronomy 7:3 Furthermore, you shall not intermarry with them; you shall not give your daughters to their sons, nor shall you take their daughters for your sons," the Rabbi states.

"The Torah also says adultery is punishable by death," Rick adds. "I'm not sure we'd want to enforce that mandate."

The Rabbi expected a fight but did not expect a salient and well thought out debate. He is accustomed to making well-established or even trite points and having his opponents concede in the face of the title of Rabbi.

However, they had moved past the yelling which preceded this discussion and are now engaged in a passionate and principled exchange as if it were sport between civilized people.

The Rabbi brings out his heavy artillery when his objections don't move Rick or Dan.

"My dearly loved parents, who sacrificed everything, survived the Holocaust and referred to intermarriage as the silent Holocaust.

"When a Jew marries outside the religion, we are shrinking the Jewish population. There is just something unholy about it. I just can't accept it."

"We either accept it or we risk alienating those in our community who have chosen to love someone outside our faith," Dan argues.

"Stop! This argument isn't about if we're for or against intermarriage," Rick says.

"Then what's it about?" Dan questions.

"It's simply about determining if a member married to someone of another faith can serve on our Board of Trustees. We have all agreed that determination will be made by the Board. Let's just stop the fighting and move on."

"Thank you, Rick, for that reminder. So, what else do you have?"

Dan looks at the list on his notepad and crosses off intermarriage and reads from it, "Mrs. Kupferberg's son."

"I ran into Mrs. Kupferberg and she asked me to talk to you about officiating at her son's wedding."

"Her son Marty?"

"Yes."

"I'm sorry, you'll have to tell her I can't do it."

"Rabbi, she said she really wants you. You were at Marty's *bris* and his bar mitzvah.

"Why can't you do it?" Rick asks.

"Well, you see Rick, Marty is gay," Dan answers.

"It's not that I've a problem with anyone who's a homosexual...no offense," turning to Rick. "It's just that the USCJ prohibits me from performing gay marriages."

"...none taken," Rick says, looking at Dan with a smirk.

"But I know Rabbi Millman at Temple L'vchm Shl'v performed a same-sex marriage," Dan notes.

"Yes, that's true because he abides by the ruling that says you can perform gay marriages."

"That means you can technically perform a same-sex marriage?"

"Let me explain. I'm not against gay marriage, but the Torah is clear on the matter. It states in Leviticus 18:22, 'You shall not lie with a man as you would with a woman.' It's an abomination."

"I promise you; a man cannot lie with a man as he does with a woman." Rick comments.

"If I were to perform the marriage, I'd be going against the Torah just because I was in favor of gay marriage."

"Let me get this straight..." Dan says.

"Wait! So, the Torah says *You* shall not lie?" interrupts Rick.

"...you won't perform a same-sex marriage for someone who has been a member of this synagogue their whole life..."

"What if the *You* who is reading the verse is a she?"

"...Someone who you officiated at their bris and bar mitzvah..."

"Does that mean *she* can't lie with a man as she would with a woman?"

"...someone whose parents are long-time members..."

"And what if *she's* never lied with a woman?"

"... although USCJ has a ruling which allows you to..."

"...does that mean *she* has no limit on how she can lie with a man?"

"…and you say you are for same-sex marriage…"

"And what if *she* laid with a woman only once? You know, she experimented in college."

"…and you want to officiate the wedding…"

"Would *she* not be able to lie with a man as she did with a woman just that one time?"

"…simply because of one imprecise sentence in the Torah…"

"And what if a man would never lie with a woman?"

"…translated from an ancient language…"

"Could he then lie with a man?"

"…and interpreted by men thousands of years ago…"

"And what if the Torah just meant literally lie?"

He and Rick pause their logical repartee.

"I'm sorry, this makes no sense," says Dan.

"Can he have sex with a man as long as they don't lie down?"

"It doesn't have to make sense. It's my decision as Rabbi and you'll have to tell Mrs. Kupferberg, I can't do it."

"It sounds like you're hiding behind the Torah."

"I'm not hiding behind anything."

"Rabbi, you once called me a bold leader. Do you remember that?"

"I'm sure I've said it several times."

"It was when I said you should officiate Denise's funeral."

"Your point?"

"If you recall, it was an unpopular decision. Rob was against it as were many vocal members. They said the Tenenbaums shouldn't have the same rights as dues-paying members."

"But I did it because I knew in my heart it was the right thing to do. Maybe you thought it was bold leadership because you wanted to do the funeral. Maybe you don't want to officiate the marriage. Maybe you are hiding behind the Torah. It's easy to sit back and claim you want to do it and let the Torah take the blame."

"Damn it Dan, I want to do it."

"Then do it!"

"I can't! The Torah is clear."

"It's obviously not that clear or the USCJ would prohibit it!"

"Dan, you're unreasonable and stubborn and a real pain in the ass!"

"Gentlemen, we're getting nowhere! Please, you two disagree and are not going to change each other's minds," Rick interjects.

Dan looks at his phone to see if Joy texted him and notices his recording app is on again. It recorded over ten minutes of the conversation. He is tempted to save it. He could use it against the Rabbi. He would have a recording of him yelling at him and calling him an ass. If the Rabbi had evidence like that, he'd use it. He pauses for a moment and thinks.

"Hello Dan!" Rick says, nudging his shoulder.

"Do you have anything else you want to talk about?" the Rabbi asks.

"No, that's it. I'm just checking my list to see if anything is left."

He clicks on the recording and hits the delete button. He swore he would not let the Rabbi's behavior change his own.

"How about you Rabbi?" Rick asks.

"I covered all my items at the beginning, thanks…Oh, there is one more thing. However, I think it's just for me and Dan to discuss in private."

"You want me to leave?"

"If you don't mind."

"Sure."

Rick stands up from his chair. Dan places his hand on his arm and says, "Wait, anything you can tell me, you can tell Rick. He doesn't have to leave."

"I think this would be better said in private, but if you insist."

"I insist."

Rick sits back down.

"Well, I want to discuss Rick's attendance at this meeting. It is my monthly meeting with just the president. You are the president of this synagogue. When Rick becomes president, I will meet with him alone."

"What? There's no reason he can't be in this meeting. Why does it make a difference?"

"The purpose of this meeting is for the Rabbi to discuss synagogue business with just the president."

"Oh, come on…"

Rick stands up and turns to Dan. "It's okay, Dan, I don't have to be here. I don't mind. I actually prefer it. I'll have my time. Don't worry about it."

Dan sits back in his seat and takes a deep breath in and lets out a loud, "Wheeze." In the past, he disagreed with the Rabbi, and a lifetime of discussions and debates with his family had prepared him for it, but he had experienced nothing like this before.

There's something different tonight, he thinks. Hostility, actual hostility, underpinned each dispute. In the past, he could achieve consensus and gain compromise, but this time he couldn't get him to budge.

They hadn't discussed his concerns around the tzedakah and restricted funds money. Those items were still on his notepad and were not crossed off. However, he's exhausted. Those discussions would have to wait for another night. He needs time to go to his corner to rest and recoup before going back out in the ring.

The two men get up from the leather chairs and make their way toward the door. The Rabbi is congenial and amiable with the meeting ended. He asks Dan how his family is, including his parents. He tells Rick he had heard he was dating someone and looks forward to meeting his new friend.

Rick nods with a tight smile. For a moment, Dan feels bad for keeping up the charade, but exhaustion and frustration with the Rabbi outweigh his desire for candor.

Dan and Rick walk together down the dark hallway from the Rabbi's office to the bright open area just in front of the social hall. Weary from the long argumentative meeting, they feel good they expressed their concerns. They didn't acquiesce or sugar coat their feelings.

"The Rabbi is as obstinate as Jake is when he doesn't want to go to sleep," Dan says.

"I think it's clear he won't change his mind."

"On the intermarriage?"

"On anything."

"I agree, we're going to have to drive change through our fellow Board members."

"That's not going to be easy. Most of them are feckless and cave to his every word."

"Maybe we can talk to someone at USCJ?"

The hallway is crowded for a weeknight. The evening service in the chapel is letting out and others roam the halls, getting ready to attend meetings or pick up their teenagers from Hebrew High School. From afar, Mrs. Berman gives Dan a thumbs up, showing she had enough people at the service to say the mourner's prayer.

He sends her back his own thumbs up and a warm smile.

On the other side of the hall near the synagogue store stands Lisa Tenenbaum. She sees Rick and runs over, embraces him, and kisses him on the cheek.

"Hi Rick, how are you? It's wonderful to see you."

"Hi Lisa, great to see you too. You remember Dan?"

"Yes, of course, the president."

The two exchange greetings.

"What brings you here tonight?" Asks Rick.

"I'm here to see the Rabbi."

"He didn't mention you were coming."

"He doesn't know."

"Oh, okay, well he's still back there," says Dan.

"Where's Sandy?" Rick continues.

"Sandy's home with Paul."

"Right, I guess someone has to be with him."

"Actually, Sandy doesn't know I'm here."

"Really? ..."

"Yes, this conversation is just between me and the Rabbi."

"Everything okay?"

"Sort of...but he's been dodging my calls."

"Did you try emailing him?"

"I've tried everything."

"You can't ask Sandy for help?"

"Sandy can't know about this. Besides, how can I say this...I'm not as enamored with our Rabbi as my husband is."

"Many people around here seem to believe he is the know-all, be-all."

"Well, I know for sure he's not, and he's extremely stubborn as well."

"You don't have to tell us. We just spent two hours in his office arguing," says Dan. "Is there anything we can do to help?"

"Maybe, but this is extremely confidential, and I'd prefer to handle it myself. If this doesn't work, I may take you up on your offer."

"Just know we're here for you, and you can trust us."

"Thank you, Rick...and Dan. I know I can. My daughter always loved you, Rick." She looks into Rick's eyes with a sorrowful smile and places her hand on his shoulder. She turns to the ground, takes a deep breath and says, "I guess it's time." She drops her hand from his shoulder, turns from the men, goes down the dark hallway and disappears into the Rabbi's office.

"What the hell was that all about?" asks Dan.

"I've no idea, but I know Lisa. She'll get what she wants."

Dan is interrupted by a familiar smell drifting into his nostrils. It's the floral scent of Jackie's overpowering yet delightful perfume.

"Dear boy, where've you been hiding?" rings out from behind him. He turns and finds himself in front of Jackie's flaming red hair, bright cherry-colored lips, and flirtatious green eyes. She has her hands firmly on her curvy hips and wears an unrestrained grin.

"Hi Jackie, you know where I've been. In the Rabbi's office."

"Have you been a naughty boy?"

"Well, he's not too happy with me."

"Hi Rick, how's Bobbie?"

"*She*...is doing fine. Thanks for asking."

"By the way, I know she's a *she*. Although most of the schmucks around here would disagree."

Feigning ignorance, Rick chuckles. "Well, I'm no expert, but I'm pretty sure she's a she."

"Gentlemen, tell me, how'd your meeting go? Did you get any information on P. Gleason?"

"Getting information from him is as hard as putting socks on a rooster," Dan says with a thick Texas twang.

"My dear boy, bravo! I've taught you well. Now you need to help me with my Hebrew."

"Unfortunately, he's standing strong and not budging. He told us nothing. I think he's hiding something," says Rick.

"We saw another letter from P. Gleason on his desk."

"Interesting. Did you get anything from it?"

"No. As soon as he noticed it, he shoved it in his top drawer."

"We pushed him to tell us who P. Gleason is, but he wouldn't say a thing."

"Methinks the Rabbi doth protest too much," adds Dan.

"Well, I think I'm going to have to have another word with ol' Benny. I'll have to play the Norm card harder this time. My big hulk of a man is always good at that."

"You're going to have to wait your turn because Lisa Tannenbaum is in there now."

"Oh, I'll talk with ol' Benny on another evening, when no one else is here."

"Well, I need to head home, I've had enough for one night," says Dan.

Jackie turns from the men and waves her fingers in the air behind her. "Goodnight, boys."

They turn around to head home and hear yelling coming from the chapel. They walk over to see Beth standing in front of Mr. Chasen wagging her finger. It's quite the sight with Beth standing just under five feet tall and him towering more than a foot taller and weighing two hundred and fifty pounds. Despite the height disparity, Beth holds an unfair advantage with her New York attitude and well-publicized black belt. Mr. Chasen wears an expression like a puppy being scolded for having urinated on the living room carpet.

"I don't care what you or the Rabbi say, my husband will stand on the bima with his daughter during her bat mitzvah. I will make him do it and there is nothing you can do about it."

"Is everything okay?" asks Dan.

"This jerk thinks because Drew is not Jewish, he has no right to be on the bima."

"I just said..."

"That's enough from you..." Beth turns back and points her index finger at his chest again as Mr. Chasen cowers under her withering glare.

"Well, it looks like you have everything under control, Beth."

"Dan, can you tell her to back off?" he pleads.

"Beth, I think Mr. Chasen has gotten the point."

Dan links arms with Beth and backs her away from Mr. Chasen and down the hall with Rick on the other side of her.

"Goodnight, Mr. Chasen," Dan calls out.

"That no-goodnik," Beth says and continues mumbling expletives under her breath.

Dan puts his arm around her and says to Rick, "I think I need Beth at the next president's meeting."

I'll do it, I'm the President

There is no terror in the bang, only in the anticipation of it.
Alfred Hitchcock

"Dan, you need to turn up the heat on the Rabbi! Let him *schvitz* a little."

The irony of these words does not go unnoticed. He had been pressing the Rabbi for months without success, trying to learn the identity of P. Gleason. However, he may have found a clue searching the internet.

"Mrs. Nusbaum, we're working with our HVAC technician to solve the problem," Dan tells her again.

"If you simply lower the air conditioner, it won't be this cold."

"Yes, but our clergy will roast under the spotlights on the bima."

"In the meantime, we're freezing..."

"Let me talk to the Rabbi and see if we can come up with a compromise."

Mrs. Nusbaum trudges off mumbling, "...not sure why members have to suffer...."

Dan noticed early in his tenure as president, the air conditioner blasting down on the bima fighting to keep those near it comfortable under the hot spotlights. This had the opposite effect for those sitting in the first few rows of pews. It was fascinating what he noticed sitting elevated high on the raised platform in the throne-like chair next to the Rabbi.

He never intended to sit on the special chair, but when several congregants approached him, recalling the "good ol' days" when other presidents did, he obliged. He sat on the bima next to the Rabbi each Shabbat with the resigned excitement of a condemned man awaiting execution.

Yet, every week the Rabbi suggested he sit in the pews, asserting he might find the service more meaningful there. He presumed the recommendation was driven out of his desire to be alone in the limelight, rather than motivated to help increase Dan's spirituality. When the Rabbi persisted, he capitulated, moving back down into the pews with Joy, Rick, and the boys.

183

"Goodnight Mrs. Nusbaum! Thanks for coming tonight to help make a minyan."

From outside the chapel, Jackie opens the glass door for Mrs. Nusbaum, returning after leaving earlier to powder her nose when the service concluded. She delivers a sweet smile and a sarcastic southern-style-wink to Mrs. Nusbaum, who purposefully shuns the attention. She marches out of the chapel, passes 'the girls,' and out of the building, mumbling to herself.

It's Thursday night, and Dan scrambles to gather the requisite ten people to recite the mourner's prayer for Elenore Riggleman, a long-time member who passed away earlier in the week. Elenore died at forty-four from what the doctor cited as natural causes.

There is nothing natural about dying alone at such a young age, he thinks. She never had children and her husband, Tom, had died ten years earlier. Her only friends were the few acquaintances she had at Beth Emet. Dan recited the Kaddish. An honor customarily performed by a family member or, when none is available, a close friend.

He looks out the large glass windows of the chapel into the hallway. Joy chats with 'the girls' underneath the monitor hanging on the wall cycling through event announcements, service times, and candid pictures of smiling congregants. The Rabbi darts out after the service ends and retreats to his office. Mr. Chasen stands on the other side of the glass door schmoozing with Mark, who led the service.

Jackie runs in like an investigative reporter with a scoop.

"I just got off the phone with Lisa and she's still not willing to say much. Although, she told me the Rabbi talked to her the other night and promised to do the 'right thing;' whatever that means.

"She said, 'If he doesn't, I'll reach out to you for help.'"

"I wonder what doing the 'right thing' is?"

"I pushed the Rabbi earlier too, but he just kept repeating the same talking points. I told him Norm wasn't happy...I'm not sure how long I can get away with that. Norm keeps telling me to stay out of it; especially since we haven't seen checks for P. Gleason in a couple of months."

"Jackie, it's funny you say that. I thought you ruled the roost."

"Dear boy, of course I do, but my Norm can be a tough nut to crack. Give me time.

"Dan, you said you might have something."

184

"I searched the internet and found a couple of people with the middle initial of P and the last name of Gleason. Unfortunately, I didn't find anyone with a first name starting with P. At least, not nearby."

"That's not much of a clue."

"No, it isn't, but I found an Alexander P. Gleason from Robbinsville. He was a lieutenant colonel in the army who died in the Afghanistan War in 2003."

"Dan, that's interesting, but I still don't see how he could be our P. Gleason," Rick chimes.

"I looked at his Facebook page and he's friends with Denise, Sandy, and Lisa."

"Oh, dear boy, that's creepy. That's two dead people who're friends on Facebook."

"You think Lisa's reason for meeting with the Rabbi has something to do with Alexander P. Gleason?"

"I'm not sure, but it's the only thing we've got."

"The guy's been dead for over eight years. How can he send letters?"

"I don't know. If only we could read the letter from P. Gleason that's sitting in the Rabbi's drawer."

"Dear boy, why don't I just mosey on into ol' Ben's office and grab it?"

"No, you can't do that."

As if on cue, the three of them watch the Rabbi walk down the hall, past the chapel and join Joy and 'the girls' under the monitor.

"Sure I can, dear boy..."

"It's not right. We can't just go into his office and read his letter. Besides being immoral, it's illegal."

"Dear boy, you're bringing a knife to a gunfight."

"I happen to agree with Jackie on this one," Rick joins in. "We're in a bad position. The Rabbi is wrongfully keeping information from us. We have members who struggle to pay dues each month and the Rabbi sends checks for over sixteen hundred dollars to some person named P. Gleason? And now we've stopped seeing the checks and for all we know someone else is signing them? How is that right? And he's the clergy. He's supposed to set an example."

"I know, you're right."

"Dan, I'll go and look at the letter. If I get caught, it's no big deal. The Rabbi doesn't like me, anyway."

"That's only because he thinks you're gay."

"Regardless, we have to do something."

"We're not even sure the letter is still there."

"Dear boy, I will read his letter. He will do nothing to me."

"I appreciate you both offering, but I've got to do it. I'm the president."

Dan pulls his cellphone out of his pocket and types furiously with his thumbs. When he finishes, he looks out the glass windows and smiles.

"OK, I'll go see what's in the letter. Joy and 'the girls' are going to keep him occupied."

Joy, Hope, and Beth congregate under the monitor after the service finishes. They see Dan and Mrs. Nusbaum alone in the chapel talking.

"I wonder why the Rabbi was in such a rush," asks Hope.

"I saw Jackie painting her face in the ladies' room and she asked me the same question," says Beth

"I'm glad Dan could gather ten people so he could say the mourner's prayer for Elenore," Hope offers.

"It's sad about Elenore," Joy confirms.

"She was as quiet as a church mouse. She barely said anything," adds Beth

Hope says, "I think she was friends with Leah."

"She was always here. She showed up for every event and always helped," laments Joy.

The women continue their conversation, watching Jackie exit the ladies' room and enter the chapel, letting Mrs. Nusbaum exit first. Mrs. Nusbaum, mumbling under her breath, passes by them in a hurry to get out of the building like the place was on fire. They try to say goodnight, but she doesn't notice. They turn their attention back to Jackie who's now on the other side of the glass window with her flirtatious smile slinking up to Dan.

"She stands on top of Dan," Hope notes. "Doesn't that bother you?"

"A bit, but I trust him. That's just Jackie. She's actually a wonderful person once you get to know her."

Joy gets up on her tiptoes and peaks around Mr. Chasen and Mark who stand outside the chapel blocking her view of Jackie and her husband.

"I trust Drew too. If he wanted an affair, I'd have to arrange the whole thing."

"Yeah, I could never see Adam do anything like that, either."

Rick comes out of the social hall, rushes into the chapel, and joins Dan and Jackie.

"I think you've got to worry more about Rick than Jackie," says Hope.

Joy laughs, "Yeah, that's true, those two are inseparable."

"I for one don't believe he's gay," says Beth.

"He's not," Joy affirms, "He's got a girlfriend. He's not gay."

"Just because a guy dresses well, is polite, and doesn't hit on women, doesn't make him gay," says Hope.

"Well, the same goes for Jackie. Just because she wears suggestive clothing, is a strong woman, and flirts with men, doesn't mean she wants to sleep with my husband."

"Hey, here comes the Rabbi," says Beth.

The Rabbi joins their circle. He left his office and scampered over so fast, they barely have time to acclimate their conversation and demeanor. Even though it was a weeknight, he was dressed as if it was a large gathering during the High Holidays. He wore a solid blue suit, a red tie, and black polished shoes, which shine like Dan's grandmother's silverware on the holidays. One could see the reflection of the fluorescent lights in them.

However, since the service had concluded, and the evening was ending, he gave himself permission to remove his suit jacket. Mr. Chasen and Mark wave to the Rabbi and say goodnight.

"Goodnight gentleman. Mark, I'll see you at my class tomorrow."

The two men walk out of the building and into the night.

"Good evening, ladies."

"Hello Rabbi."

"Hi Rabbi."

"Good evening."

"Thank you all for coming tonight to help make a minyan."

Joy feels her phone vibrate and pulls it out of her purse. A message from Dan reads:

Keep the Rabbi
occupied, I'm
going into his
office to read
the letter. 😊 -
Dan

Joy looks over at the chapel and sends him a knowing smile.
"Rabbi, isn't that awful about Elenore?"
"Yes, it's a sad situation."
"Can you tell us more about her?"

Dan nudges the door of the chapel open and peaks into the
hallway. With a large glass window and a glass door providing full
transparency out into it, his inexperience with clandestine matters is
obvious.

He looks over at 'the girls' and the Rabbi under the monitor. The
Rabbi's back faces him. He rushes into the hallway and closes the
door behind him just as quietly as he does the boy's door after
tucking them into bed. He runs down the hallway on tiptoes and
makes his way under the red exit sign, into the dark corridor leading
to the Rabbi's office.

The door is closed.

*Is it unlocked? What awaits on the other side? Is the letter from
P. Gleason still there?*

He accounts for everyone at the minyan, confident no one is in
the office, although his hands shake and his heart pounds.

He turns the knob and feels its latch retreat, thankful the Rabbi
didn't lock it. He lifts the doorknob and urges the door open just
enough to allow him into the shadowy room. Light from the moon
hanging high in the night sky seeps through the blinds behind the
desk to help illuminate the area. He jumps in and closes the door
behind him, making sure it does not let out a loud click.

He turns on the light. The bright fluorescent bulbs overhead make
it clear he is alone and there is no turning back from his nefarious
act. His heart pounds harder, like it's trying to break out of his chest
and fly away. It's the same sensation he felt that night as a young

boy, when he stayed up late, alone, to watch *Psycho*. His older brother Alan made a surprise late-night return home from college. Young Dan heard the front door creak open from the living room and screamed, but nothing came out of his wide-open mouth except a wheeze.

He feels short of breath and wonders if he would have the same reaction should the Rabbi somehow escape the girls and walked in on him.

He rushes to the desk, passing the matching mahogany filing cabinet and knocks a framed picture off it. It falls to the floor, making what sounds to him a loud crash.

Oh no!

He picks up the intact frame gingerly. It's of the Rabbi standing next to Hillary Rodham Clinton.

"Phew!" He places it back on the cabinet, angled to face the door, hoping it's in its original position. He knows the Rabbi would notice the slightest variation.

He resumes his quest to the Rabbi's desk and opens the top drawer.

"Where's the letter?"

He fumbles around a notepad, a tiny prayer book, and some pens, but the letter isn't there. He has come this far, going against his better judgment and risking being caught, for naught.

It has to be here, he thinks. He scours the desk and hunts through the other drawers, but no letter from P. Gleason.

He looks around the room. There are no papers on his desk, not even a notepad or pen. The books on the shelves are aligned in height order. Faces in the sparkling framed glossy pictures stare back at him. They are perfectly arranged, not one is askew. His collection of memorabilia pins stands vigilant on one bookcase like soldiers in perfect formation. Nothing out of place. Where could the letter hide?

He notices the Rabbi's suit jacket hanging on the back of his chair behind the desk.

"Maybe?" He thrusts his hand into the inside pocket of the blue suit jacket. Something feels like an envelope.

"Yank," it pops out like a rabbit out of a magician's hat. It's a letter. He holds it in his cupped hands like discovering gold or an ancient artifact. He stares in astonishment at the name P. Gleason written in the top left-hand corner. Not only is it fortuitous that he discovered it, but it's been opened.

He pulls it out and unfolds the single thin paper. He reads the nine-word sentence and takes a snapshot with his phone when he hears a noise coming from the other side of the door. He pushes the letter back into its envelope and shoves it into the jacket pocket. He darts from behind the desk and dashes to the door while the knob turns.

It opens just when he grabs it.

"May I help you, Mr. Barkan?"

Unhealthy Relationship

When someone shows you who they are, believe them the first time.
Maya Angelou

The Rabbi asks Joy and the girls, "How are the plans for the *Purim* carnival going?"

"Oh, I really look forward to the children throwing wet sponges at my face, haha."

Hope comments, "I think the high school students are probably looking forward to it even more."

When the chit chat wanes, to keep the Rabbi preoccupied, Joy raises the last subject in the world she wants to discuss. However, she knows this will keep him talking and besides, she's been disturbed at how he's handling the situation.

"Rabbi, I've been upset about all the gossip around Rick and Jackie."

"Joy, can I give you some advice?"

"Of course, Rabbi."

"Perhaps we should discuss this in my office."

"No! Not there!—I mean, here's fine. Hope and Beth are my best friends. I think they'll support me on this. Okay then Rabbi, what is your advice?"

"I think Dan's relationship with Jackie and Rick is unhealthy."

"I'm not sure what you mean."

"Dan spends a lot of late nights with them. He goes out drinking with Rick at Blanche's."

"Rick's his best friend. Besides, they're mostly working on synagogue business."

"I know, but I'm not sure it's good for Dan, considering Rick's lifestyle choice, although I really don't judge it."

"Rabbi, what do you mean Rick's lifestyle choice?"

"Dan and Rick have been pushing me to perform gay marriages."

"Rabbi, you're aware Rick isn't gay?"

"Joy, I've no issue with him being gay."

"Except he's not."

"The two of them have been relentless. They want me to officiate at Marty Kupferberg's wedding. I wish I could, but I can't. The

191

Torah is explicit. If I officiate at his wedding, then they'll want me to marry Rick and Bobbie. And Rick is going to be president."

"Do you know Bobbie is Roberta?"

"Then why are they pushing me? Why do they care about Marty Kupferberg?"

"You've got to stop listening to the gossip. Did you ever think they believe it's the right thing to do? Dan is passionate about people being treated fairly, regardless who they love."

"Yes, but I still can't do it."

"He also had a horrific experience in college that really affected him. He doesn't talk about it much. Besides me, I'm not sure anyone else knows; not even Rick."

The Rabbi, Hope, and Beth move in closer. Her voice becomes quiet and solemn.

"You see, in college Dan had a close friend named Steve. He and Dan were as close as Rick and Dan are. I knew Steve. The three of us hung out a lot. Steve was gay but had not come out. He was also a guitarist in a heavy metal band named Iridescent Socks."

"That's a cool name," says Beth.

"Back in the eighties, lots of guys had long hair, wore makeup, and earrings; especially those in heavy metal bands."

"I remember. There was a lot of sexual ambiguity back then. There was Boy George and George Michael. It became mainstream," says Beth.

"Except there was a backlash against the gay community with the outbreak of AIDS," adds Hope.

Joy continues, "One night Steve was walking home from a gig in Philly and was jumped by a bunch of guys screaming homophobic curses. He spent two weeks in a comma with broken ribs and a punctured lung. He eventually recovered, but was never the same."

"That's awful!" says the Rabbi.

"As you can imagine, Dan was devastated, as we all were."

"What happened to Steve?" asks Hope.

"He stopped playing music and became super depressed. One night Steve confided in Dan, telling him after the beating he realized he could never live an honest life. He would be forced to marry a woman and have affairs with men on the side."

"Things are better now," says Beth.

"Unfortunately, they found Steve two days later in his apartment, dead on the floor from a self-inflicted gunshot wound."

Beth gasps and wipes moisture from her eyes.

"Oh my God, that's horrific. Poor Dan," says Hope.

"Joy, that's a tragic situation. I wish I had better answers. I wish I could make this right for Dan, but I need to answer to a higher authority."

"I didn't tell you the story to get you to change your mind, Rabbi, just to help you understand where Dan is coming from. Now, what's your issue with Jackie?"

The Rabbi hesitates. He seems unsure if, after the story of Dan's friend Steve, he wants to broach the next uncomfortable subject.

Joy glances over his shoulder and down the dark corridor. She sees a faint light in the hallway, which she presumes comes from under the office door. There is movement in the back of the hallway, some shadowy figure she hopes is Dan returning from his pursuit.

"Joy, as you know, Jackie is a married woman and Dan and she have been seen gallivanting together at Blanche's.

"Gallivanting? Hahaha! I think Dan might hurt himself if he tried to gallivant."

Hope and Beth laugh with Joy at her sarcasm and the absurdity of the Rabbi's insinuations.

"I presume you heard I found them on the floor of the office?"

"Rabbi, are you trying to tell me my husband is having an affair with Jackie? She's old enough to be his mother. Besides, my husband wouldn't do that!"

"Well, maybe he's not having an illicit affair, but the time he spends with her is, in a way, an emotional affair. He should be home with you and the boys. I just think it would be in everyone's best interest if you could get all three of them to spend less time together."

"They're doing nothing wrong."

"Of course not, but you must admit it doesn't look good and as you pointed out, people are talking."

Hope interrupts, "I'm sorry. I'm not sure I understand. Wouldn't the problem be with the people gossiping and not those who are doing nothing wrong?"

"Yes, of course Hope, but it would be helpful if we could not provide the fodder."

"I think the problem isn't the fodder but the crap that comes out after these yentas devour it," adds Beth.

"Dan is a good man, Joy. I just think as his wife, you need to steer him in the right direction."

In the office, the door opens.

"Ahem, may I help you Mr. Barkan?"

"Mrs. Winthrop, what are you doing here?"

In front of Dan stands a tall blonde woman in her late fifties with thin lips and suspicious blue eyes. Her hair is tied tight in a bun, and she wears a long black dress and a white blouse buttoned to her neck. She clutches a stack of papers at her chest. She reminds him of an old-fashioned schoolmarm. The only thing missing is a ruler which, he is sure, she would hit him with if she had one.

"Dan, how may I help you?"

"Oh, I was just looking for the checks to sign."

"Did you try the usual place?"

"No, but that's a good idea."

"What're you doing in here without the Rabbi?"

"I told you, I was looking for checks to sign. What are *you* doing in here?" Dan says in an equally demanding voice, attempting to reverse the questioning along with the balance of power.

"I'm typing letters for the Rabbi."

"Well, then I'll let you continue. I've got to go sign some checks."

Dan runs out the room leaving Mrs. Winthrop and the open door behind him. He scurries down the dark corridor and into the hallway. Joy peers over the Rabbi's shoulder. Her eyes widen and she places her hand on her chest.

"Hi Dan, we were just talking about you," the Rabbi offers.

"That can't be good."

"Nonsense. I was just telling Joy what a good man you are."

The Rabbi updates Dan on the progress of the Purim carnival and then excuses himself to find Mrs. Winthrop to have her finish some letters for him. When he disappears into the corridor Jackie and Rick race out of the chapel to join the group.

"Dear boy, what happened?"

"Did you get the letter?" Rick asks.

"I was able to read it and took a picture. Then Mrs. Winthrop walked in."

"Where'd she come from? I was watching the whole time." asks Joy.

194

"Oh, this is exciting. I love the intrigue," says Beth.

"It wasn't exciting for me. She nearly gave me a heart attack. She must've come from the other end of the building."

"Guys, here she comes now," says Hope.

Mrs. Winthrop strolls from the dark corridor to the group and asks Dan if he signed the checks.

"Oh, no, I got distracted talking to the Rabbi."

"I'll show you where they are."

Dan leaves the group without providing details. He vanishes into the office with Mrs. Winthrop in toe. The group stands around waiting for Dan to return and to find out what he discovered about P. Gleason. After five minutes but what seems like twenty, Dan returns.

Joy says, I hope Mrs. Winthrop doesn't mention to the Rabbi she found you in his office."

"I hope not too. I signed the checks. Now let's discuss this outside in the parking lot."

"Was there a check for P. Gleason?" asks Rick.

"Yes, but I didn't sign it."

Rick darts to the glass door and pushes it open. The five others follow him out the building and assemble under the moonlight near their cars.

"Okay, Dan, we're dying to know. Who's P. Gleason?" asks Jackie

"That mystery hasn't been solved yet."

"What? So, what did the letter say?" asks Rick.

"Just before Mrs. Winthrop walked in, I read it. I found it hidden in the Rabbi's jacket pocket. He must have read it because the envelope was open."

"What did it say?" Beth asks, frustrated by how long it's taking.

"It was a note written on a small piece of paper in the same red ink and penmanship as the address on the envelope. I read it and took a picture with my phone."

Dan pulls out his cellphone and brings up the picture. The group gathers around tighter as if they are using the light emanating from the screen to stay warm in the brisk, chilly night air.

They read the note:

You do the right
thing,
or I'll tell everyone!
-LT

What Are You Trying to Say?

Whatever the present moment contains, accept it as if you had chosen it.
Eckhart Tolle

Dan is alone at a table in the back corner of Blanche's. The waitress sat him there as instructed by the person who made the reservation. He looks over at other tables and the end of the bar, disoriented, seated in an unfamiliar area within the confines of the place he and Rick refer to as the "satellite office of Beth Emet."

The waitress brings his coffee with a small clear glass bottle of creamer and a pocket-sized holder with brightly colored sugar packets.

Dan drinks his black.

"Is there anything else you need right now, honey?"

"No, I'm good, thanks. If you can just let my colleague know I'm back here when he arrives..."

"Right, yes, Bernie, correct Dan?" The waitress smiles.

"Yes, thank you Nina, that'll be great."

He sips his hot coffee and considers why Bernie asked him to dinner. He had sounded nervous on the phone and wouldn't divulge the purpose of the meeting.

He only said, "It's an opportunity for us to get together and talk." Seasoned Board members like Bernie use this tactic to pounce on individuals unprepared for and not suspecting delicate conversations. They also limit the length of a meeting to prevent a prolonged, uncomfortable discussion.

Bernie told Dan he needed to be home by 7:30 pm.

He wonders if this is related to Mrs. Winthrop finding him in the Rabbi's office alone. He's convinced she told the Rabbi. His longtime assistant and confidant, she has been growing weary of all of Dan's questions. She even looks up from her desk at him with suspicious eyes and a glaring stare each time he enters the work area.

Bernie appears with the subtlety of a scared runner, avoiding an all too close bull at Pamplona. He sits down and knocks over the creamer with the coat hanging over his arm.

"I'm such a klutz, sorry."

197

The waitress, who spotted him entering the restaurant and followed him to the table, takes her rag and cleans up the mess.

"Hi Bernie, how's it going?"

"...a crazy day. Sorry I'm late. I feel like I'm hopping from one place to the next like a kangaroo."

"I know how you feel."

Bernie sits down and settles in. He folds his coat over the empty chair next to him and aligns his silverware.

"Would you like to order something now or should I come back?" the waitress asks.

"I'm not hungry...Dan, did you order anything?"

"Just coffee. I'm not hungry either."

"We need to order something..."

"Then I'll have a toasted bagel with cream cheese on the side."

"Bernie turns to the waitress, "Can I get a small garden salad with balsamic vinaigrette? Oh, and a cup of coffee too."

"Sure," she answers and scurries off to the kitchen.

Dan's lack of appetite directly results from his uneasiness about the impending conversation. Not sure what the discussion will include, he knows one thing. It's not the amiable and innocent meet up advertised. He also hopes it will be short and he won't have to commit to an entire meal.

Rick and Dan have always thought Bernie harmless. They view him as part of a group of Board members they call the Borg. Joy coined the title after the Star Trek fictional alien antagonists all of whom, linked by a collective mind, serve a single purpose.

Yeah, he thinks, *to serve the Rabbi's wishes.* He knows Bernie's sole motivation is to avoid confrontation and rejection; so, his only concern is the puppeteer pulling the strings, not the puppet.

Bernie plays with the container of sugar packets on the table. His chewed fingernails always repulsed Dan, and tonight they seem worse. He engages Dan with small talk about the Mets and his family.

Dan indulges him until he feels the banter has gone on too long.

"Bernie, I'm sure you didn't invite me here to talk about the Mets. Tell me. What did you want to discuss?"

Bernie's hand quivers as he moves from playing with the sugar packets to the salt and pepper shakers, circling them like he's playing a shell game.

"Well, you see—the Rabbi feels—well, we feel, I mean I was wondering—there are some people talking about you and Rick…"

"What about me and Rick?" Now he knows which controversial subject he will be fighting.

"Well, some people have questions about Rick, and you guys are close so, ah, naturally people wonder?"

"What are you trying to say, Bernie?"

Dan sits back and folds his arms, waiting for insinuations to fly.

"Well, we feel the way you guys are together; it's not how friends should, well…you know, not the way friends should behave."

"How should friends behave?"

Bernie repeats the line again, slowly, as one does when talking to a person who speaks a foreign language. He also simultaneously raises his head up and down, opens his eyes, and contorts his face in a manner he believes will somehow get his point across.

He is oblivious to the fact Dan already gets his point.

Dan says nothing. He sits forward calmly and takes an extended sip from his coffee.

Bernie continues, "You know, not that there's anything wrong with it. I mean I don't care, but are you two…"

"What Bernie? Are we anarchists?! Fascists?!—or worse, Fanilows?! What are you asking Bernie?"

He leans across the table and flaps around a sugar packet. He clears his throat and gulps a sip of water. He looks past Dan and whispers, "…are you h-o-m-o-s-e-x-u-a-l-s?"

"Are you asking if Rick and I are gay lovers?" He says it loud enough that neighboring tables can hear, both in shock and anger at the question. Bernie looks around with an uncomfortable smile.

"Of course, I don't think so."

"Then why are you asking?"

"Well, you know—people…"

Dan feels the need to be angry with Bernie and his insinuation, but for some reason, the moment passes, and it does not bother him. The cat-and-mouse game, the absurdity of Bernie's line of questioning, and Bernie himself, suddenly amuses him. He considers taunting him by telling him the rumors are true, but he recognizes the cruelty of the jest. Besides, Bernie is gullible enough to believe the ruse and it would likely prolong his evening.

Dan beckons him, gesturing with his curling index finger. He looks to his left and then his right, like an informant in a trench coat standing under a streetlamp. The two move closer to the center of the table.

"I have a secret for you. I'm happily married and I'm not gay. Rick is dating a woman named Roberta, and he's not gay. Besides, Rick's not my type. I think…if I were gay, I'd be more interested in someone with glasses and bald." He's unable to control the dry and witty sarcasm his father bestowed upon him.

He winks and smiles at Bernie who adjusts his glasses and runs his hand over his naked scalp. He maneuvers himself in his chair and knocks over the saltshaker.

"Bernie! I'm just kidding."

Dan's light-heartedness around the subject seems to relax Bernie. The two laugh at the ridiculousness of the matter.

"Well, I'm glad we cleared that up…You know I don't care. It's just people thought so."

"Who thought so?"

"You know people…the Rabbi setup a meeting to discuss the situation after he received a letter from a congregant."

"Wait! Are you telling me there was a letter asking if we're gay and the Rabbi had a meeting about it, and no one told us?"

"I didn't actually see the letter. The Rabbi said it was confidential."

"Did it come from P. Gleason?"

"Who?"

"Never mind…inside joke."

"They didn't want me to tell you about the meeting. Don't tell him I told you."

"Really now." He steams.

"The Rabbi feels you guys are together too much. He wanted me to tell you to sit apart at services and not arrive at meetings together. The Rabbi is trying to cut down on the gossip."

"Oh, did he, and I can't believe the Rabbi had a meeting about us behind our backs."

"Well, no one really thinks you're gay. It's just they think it doesn't look good, and they wanted me to ask you to make things better."

"Let me guess, you pulled the shortest straw?"

"Um…"

"No, I understand. I see."

"Great, then can I let them know you'll take care of it?"

"No!"

"What do you mean, no?"

"Why would I change my behavior?"

"Because the Rabbi asked you to, and it would stop all this gossip."

"Bernie, even if Rick and I were gay, it's no one's business. Besides, changing to meet other's expectations is declaring we're doing something wrong. In any case, what kind of a friend would I be if I just stop hanging out with Rick?"

"Yeah, I guess you're right. Listen, I don't really care what you do. It's not my place to judge. Just, ah, if anyone asks, tell them I talked to you. Okay? Oh, and don't tell them I agreed with you."

"Sure Bernie, no problem."

The waitress comes back with their food and places a dry bagel in front of Dan and a small garden salad in front of Bernie.

"You know, I think I'm kinda hungry for a burger and Blanche's wonderful crispy fries. Hey Dan, how about we order some dinner? Maybe we can get some wings too. I'm also craving some onion rings."

"No thanks, I'll just finish my bagel. My stomach is a bit uneasy."

Bernie orders the excess food anyway and when the waitress asks if he wants cheese on his burger, he exclaims, "Sure!" The waitress confirms Dan doesn't want anything and returns to the kitchen. Bernie glances at Dan's stoic face. Pangs of guilt replace his pangs of hunger.

"I rarely ever have a cheeseburger…I just…"

"I don't care what you eat. It's not my place to judge. Besides, I've been known to enjoy a cheeseburger. I won't tell the Rabbi, if that's what you're worried about…"

After Bernie satisfies his voracious appetite, he orders a slice of Blanche's homemade cheesecake. Dan watches him scarf it down and is glad when he sees the empty plate. While they've been there longer than he wanted, he is going to get home earlier than anticipated. Bernie pays for the dinner and as the two walk out of the restaurant, Dan thanks him for his generosity.

Bernie declares, "No biggie, I'll just have the synagogue reimburse me."

"Why don't I share the cost with you?"

"Why? What's the big deal?"

"Bernie, you've seen our books. We're struggling financially."

"Oh, come on, we say that every year and somehow we manage."

"Please Bernie, let me pay half."

"If you're that concerned, I'll cover it. Don't worry about it. All you had was a bagel and coffee."

"Thanks Bernie."

Dan speeds down the highway like a formula one driver racing past a checkered flag. However, his finish line is getting home and far away from Bernie.

He slows to see his trusty old roadside companion.

A fortuitous maneuver, that most certainly rescues him from a speeding ticket and the attention of the police car sitting beside it. He nods to his lamppost, thanking it for the forewarning.

He turns on the radio and maintains a cautious pace for the rest of his ride home.

The insinuation about him and Rick doesn't really bother him. He is amused by the Rabbi sending his attack dog to separate the two. Especially since Bernie is more a harmless little mutt than a pit bull.

He gets it. He and Rick threaten the status quo.

However, what really irks him is the audacity of the Rabbi to have a meeting about the two of them and exclude them. If indeed a member sent a letter, it should have been shared with them.

Dan pounds his fist on the dashboard.

"Damn, damn, damn, damn!"

That's Not the Way Boys Behave

Don't change the way you are just to make someone happy
Unknown

Dan arrives home from Blanche's and Jackson jumps him, forcing him to put the disturbing evening aside. The two race upstairs. Dan wants to at least see the boys before they're asleep. He finds Joy in the boys' room playing Name that Tune.

Max yells, "Dad's home!"

Jake groans as prepubescent boys do, "Mom isn't good at this game, she got the first song wrong and now she says we've got to turn off the light."

"Hey, those are the rules. Besides, I don't know who sings what, I just know what I like."

"Okay, we can all do a few rounds together, but then close your eyes."

Dan sits on Jake's bed and Joy sits with Jackson on Max's bed. Max turns up the radio and *Fortunate Son* is playing.

Joy announces, "I love this song, but I've no idea who sings it."

"It's Credence, Mom!" says Jake.

The family calls out the names of songs as they play; they laugh, sing, and enjoy each other's company. Jackson barks, getting in on the fun. When "Eleanor Rigby" comes on the radio, Dan and the boys shout out the song title at the same time. Dan educates the boys on how Alfred Hitchcock's terrifying shower scene in *Psycho* inspired Paul McCartney to include the edgy cello sound in the song. He illustrates by acting out the shower scene with Jake, pretending to stab him with an imaginary knife along with the staccato playing of the cello.

He falls on Jake and the two laugh.

About halfway through "Sweet Baby James," Max falls asleep. Jake is still wide awake. Joy kisses Max on the forehead and hops over to Jake's bed. She sits next to Dan and puts her hand on his leg and wipes the hair away from Jake's eyes.

"Are you still upset about today honey?"

"What happened?"

"Jake, you want to tell your father about it?"

"It's no big deal."

"Tell me."

"The Rabbi was kind of a jerk to me and Ethan in Hebrew school tonight."

"What did he do?!" asks Dan.

"Well, me and Ethan were thumb wrestling."

"During class?"

"Sort of..."

"What do you mean sort of?"

"Dan, listen to him," asserts Joy.

"I've got enough issues with the Rabbi; I don't need this!"

"We didn't do anything wrong!"

"Listen to him!"

"You're right, I'm sorry Jake. What happened?"

"The Rabbi came into class to talk with Mrs. Epstein and while we waited, Ethan and I were thumb wrestling. All the kids were playing and talking. We weren't even making a lot of noise just laughing a bit."

"And...?"

"He yelled at us in front of the whole class."

Dan stiffens.

Jake rubs his eyes, his voice cracks, and he sniffles.

"We...were just...playing."

"Why don't you tell daddy what he said," prods Joy.

"He said, 'That's not the way boys should behave!' He said, 'Boys don't hold other boy's hands. Where'd you learn that game? From your father's friend Rick?'"

"What! He said that! You must be kidding! Okay, now I've had enough. I'm going over there and telling him..."

"No, don't say anything. Really, it's no big deal. I don't want to make a thing of it."

"Jake, tell Daddy how the other kids reacted."

"Did they make fun of you?"

"No, actually the opposite. I think they were all surprised at how he reacted. Even Mrs. Epstein seemed surprised."

"Tell him about Moriah."

"Moriah? The Rabbi's daughter?"

"Yeah, she came over to me after class and apologized for her dad. She even said he acted like a jerk."

"Really? That's nice of her."

"Yeah, it made me and Ethan feel better. So, please say nothing to the Rabbi."

"I'll keep quiet, I promise. Listen, I've only got a few more months as president. This will all be over soon, and I promise things will get back to normal."

Jake hugs Dan, and Joy rubs his back.

"I'm glad you told me, Jake."

"Yes, it was very brave of you," Joy adds.

Joy and Dan tuck Jake under the covers tightly, kiss his forehead, and turn out the lights. Jackson follows the couple into their bedroom.

"I can't believe the Rabbi said that about Rick in front of the class! First, he insinuates to you I'm having an affair with Jackie, then he gets his feckless goon to tell me to cut off from Rick, claiming members are writing letters saying we're gay lovers, and now he calls my son out in front of the entire class. '…that's not the way boys behave…' huh." Dan repeats it several times, mocking the Rabbi's comments.

"What feckless goon? What letter? This is getting out of hand; I'll be glad when you're done with this whole mess. It's taking a toll on all of us."

Dan continues mocking the Rabbi, "…that's not the way boys should behave…"

He turns to Joy and bellows, "…that's not the way boys should behave!"

"I heard you Dan."

"No, I told you I met with Bernie."

"Yes, what did he want?"

"The Rabbi made him meet with me to convince me to stop spending time with Rick."

"Oh, God!"

"Bernie quoted the Rabbi, 'that's not the way friends should behave…' He said it several times."

"…and now he said it to Jake."

"Yeah, and Bernie also told me there was a letter from a congregant complaining about us. But apparently no one has seen the letter because it's confidential."

"Dan, I'll be glad when you're done with this whole mess."

"I'm not stepping down. Not with just a few months left in my term and when we're close to finding out who P. Gleason is."

205

"Did you have the call with Rabbi Krietzberg from USCJ?"

"Yes, I had a conference call at lunchtime with him, Rick, and Hope. By the way, honey, it was a brilliant idea to suggest inviting Hope. Her experience in HR really helped. She's not only brilliant, but she gets right to the point."

"I knew she'd be helpful."

Dan shares details of the hour-long conversation with the head of USCJ. He tells her how they outlined the numerous dishonest and unethical incidents that took place over the last year and a half.

"We all shared different events. I forgot a few Rick mentioned, and he forgot some I mentioned."

"A lot has happened..."

"I know, but when you lay it all out it's...well, Rabbi Krietzberg was astonished."

"What did he suggest?"

"Unfortunately, he said there was nothing he could do unless we had evidence of wrongdoing."

"Did you tell him how he manipulates the board?"

"Yes, and that's the sad part. He said most synagogues have the opposite issue. Boards complain about their Rabbi's not being engaged enough. When that happens, they come together and direct the Rabbi's behavior."

"Well, that's not going to happen here."

"He said our synagogue is not the norm, but it happens. A Board may complain about their Rabbi being controlling, but then abdicate all authority to him."

"Well, that's Beth Emet in a nutshell."

"He said unless we can get the Board's support, we might want to, for our own benefit, accept this as the personality of our synagogue."

"Oh, Dan, I'm sorry."

"He even said we might want to consider another synagogue for our spiritual needs."

"But all our friends are here."

"I know. I told him that and he said, 'You may have to look in your hearts for acceptance of what is."

"Dan, you must be devastated."

"I wanted to make a positive impact. I wanted to make things better for our members."

He sits on the end of the bed and lowers his face into his hands.

"I just wanted to make a difference!"

"Dan, you did…You did the best you could. You were working in an impossible situation."

Joy massages his back, puts her arms around him, and kisses him on the head.

"Did you eat anything at Blanche's?"

"I had a plain bagel but don't worry, Bernie ate enough for the two of us."

"Why don't you go downstairs and have a bite? I made the boys their favorite meal tonight, hamburgers and french fries. The leftovers are in the fridge, and you can microwave them. I also went shopping today and got you some Swiss cheese if you want a cheeseburger."

"I think I've lost my appetite for cheeseburgers. I'll just have some cereal."

"Okay honey—we only have a few months to go; it will all be okay."

Dan makes his way to the kitchen and eats his late-night dinner. Jackson joins him and is rewarded with a treat of dry kibble in his bowl. They finish their meals and the two go for Jackson's last walk of the night. The cool air helps his mood as well as Joy's reminder that this will soon be over. They walk in the evening's quiet under the star-filled sky and in the glow of the bright moon.

Dan thinks about the P. Gleason issue and the intermarriage policy. He wants to resolve them before his term concludes. However, he still wants to help Rick do even more when he is president—assuming he doesn't back out. He has sensed a recent reluctance from Rick in discussing his presidency and after the call with Rabbi Krietzberg he wouldn't be surprised or blame him if he decided not to accept the position.

The thought of another two years of what they've been through seems unbearable.

When the two finish their walk, they join Joy in the bedroom. Joy is in bed reading another one of her smutty novels. Dan gets in with her, turns on the TV, and flips through channels. Jackson curls up at the bottom of the bed.

"Whatcha reading? A smutty novel filled with animal urges and heaving breasts? Oh, take me, darling. I want you! I need you!"

Dan acts out the campy love seen mocking Joy's reading habits.

"No. Stop! I'm reading *Outlander*, by Diana Gabaldon. It's a wonderful time-travel story and yes, it is a love story. You would love this book. Since when did you become a cynic?"

"Since I became synagogue president."

"Well, this keeps my mind off work and all the other stresses of raising a family.

"I'm sorry, I know it's a lot on you. It'll be over soon. I hope."

You know, while you're off dealing with mysterious letters and money laundering, I'm taking care of the boys and Jackson. Not to mention the bills, laundry, and making dinner."

"I know I feel awful."

"Look I'm not trying to make you feel bad, but this is stressful for me too."

"I know it is sweetie."

"You know, I still get disapproving glances and patronizing questions. I'm either the neglectful wife who isn't satisfying her man or I'm a scorned woman whose had her husband stollen by the seductress Jackie."

"I know it's not fair. It's weird, like I'm an innocent pawn in this fantasy world. I'm not sure I like the characterization."

"Women are still unfairly branded in marital affairs as vixens while men are victims or virile conquerors. Not to mention what the Rabbi thinks of men who, '...lie with another man'""

"Let's remember, there is no marital affair."

"I know, but for an egalitarian synagogue we are still provincial."

"I'm sorry about bringing all this up again. I just...well, I just am frustrated. I didn't even ask you how your day was or how is work?"

"Work is fine, honey."

"No, tell me..."

"Okay, you know I'm working on that study for Crohn's. Ugh, they sent me all these endoscopy videos of hairy butts and male genitals. I still can't get used to looking at someone's colon."

"See, now this time you brought up the synagogue..."

The two laugh at his comment and embrace.

"It's nice to see you smile Dan."

"I love to see you smile too, honey."

Joy goes back to her novel and Dan resumes flipping through the channels on the TV. When the evening becomes late, Joy closes her book, kisses him, and wishes good night. He turns off the TV and pulls the string of the lamp on the night table beside him.

His Grandmother's clock displays ten minutes past eleven.

He closes his eyes. He pulls himself under his warm covers and lies on his left side. When sleep does not come, he switches to his right. After attempts on both sides, he settles on his back, hoping it will help.

It doesn't.

P. Gleason, Mrs. Winthrop, the Rabbi, Bernie, and Rick flood his brain. He looks over at his Grandmother's clock and sees it is now after midnight. An hour has passed, and yet sleep has not arrived to provide a respite from the whirlwind of thoughts that drift in and out. The word acceptance, which Rabbi Krietzberg used several times on the call today, flashes in his mind like the blinking neon sign from the convenience store across the highway from Blanche's.

He wonders, *How does one know when it is time to let go and accept? Has one done all they can or is acceptance a disguise for the resignation that roadblocks and failures bring? Is there more fight left or is he gnawing, like Jackson does, on a bone with no meat? And the Rabbi. What can he do, should do?*

Dan adjusts his pillows but can't get them into the right position. He sits up and faces them, patting and hugging them to fluff them up. The bed wobbles as he maneuvers left and right. Jackson pops his head up from the commotion. The fluffing quickly develops into forceful prods and pokes.

"Damn it! These stupid pillows. I'll never fall asleep. I can't get them right."

He clenches his fist and thrusts it into the pillow.

"Oomph! I can't believe you had a damn meeting about me behind my back!

"Bam! What are you trying to do…siccing Bernie on me as if I'm gonna kowtow to your will and throw my best friend under the bus!"

He pounds one fist and then the other into his pillow as he recaps each of the Rabbi's crimes as congregants do on Yom Kippur during the confessional. However, unlike worshippers who symbolically and gently thump their chests as they call out transgression such as greed, slander, and deception, he keeps pummeling with all his might.

"Do you think I'm an idiot?

"Wham!

"How dare you falsely tell my wife I'm having an affair!"

"Dan! Are you okay?"

Joy jumps and faces him.

"What's the matter? Did you have a nightmare?"

"Thump! How dare you tell my child how he should behave and call him out in front of his friends? I'm his frickin' father!"

"Honey!"

"Whump! Who the hell do you think you are? Spreading rumors about people."

"Dan, you're going to kill the pillow."

"It's not the pillow I'm after! Slam!"

"Who died and anointed him king…telling me I can't look at the synagogue's finances."

"Honey, it's okay. You have to let it go."

"No, I won't, I can't. We have serious problems. I know we can make things better. He spends his time attacking Rick and a defenseless boy, and he's upset you and Jackie with baseless rumors. If he wants a battle, he's going to have to stop manipulating Board members and spreading rumors behind my back.

"He is going to have to face me."

"I have never seen you like this, Dan Barkan!"

"That's right! I'm Dan Barkan and I AM the president of Beth Emet!"

A Fait Accompli

*Insanity is doing the same thing over and over
and expecting different results.*
Albert Einstein

Dan goes through the motions anyway. Hope had helped him prepare for what he believes is a convincing argument, even if it will be for naught. He concludes his five-minute presentation with the Rabbi sitting beside him at the table looking like a tiger stalking a fatted calf ready to tear into its unsuspecting prey.

"I ask you to look into your hearts and imagine how'd you feel if you or someone here had married someone not Jewish and weren't able to serve on the Board."

"If I'd known those were the rules, I'd have married a blonde-haired, blue-eyed shiksa instead of Marcy," says Harold. A burst of giggles and chuckles, like the laugh track from a 70s sitcom breaks the seriousness of Dan's words.

"Imagine if your sons or daughters marry someone not Jewish and they still want to practice their faith and remain connected to their synagogue. What if their non-Jewish spouse supports and encourages them? How do you think they'd feel if we told them they couldn't serve? Too many of our kids have already lost their connection with Judaism. Let's not push them further.

"If we aren't more tolerant, in time, we will lose them all together."

He sits.

Most Board members look down.

"Thank you, Dan, for those thought-provoking words and salient points. As you know as spiritual leader of this congregation, it is my responsibility to guide our members on the right path..." begins the Rabbi.

Dan does not leave time on the agenda for rebuttals or conversations. He knows a debate would only prolong the inevitable conclusion. He does not limit the Rabbi's speaking time either, knowing it would be ignored. The Rabbi had insisted he present his view last.

Dan lets him take all the time he wants in his arguments to the Board on why they should not allow a member who is intermarried to be installed on the synagogue's "distinguished" governing body. He recites multiple chapters and verses from the Torah. He asserts God "commands us to be fruitful and multiply." He claims, "...marrying outside the religion would make observing this commandment impossible as the offspring of such a union would not be Jewish." He weaves in stories of the atrocities from the Holocaust, just falling short of equating intermarriage to the murder of six million Jews.

Dan can't believe the sanctimonious arguments being made although he knows he should not be surprised. As he did at the president's meeting, and Rick pointed out, the Rabbi doesn't focus on the pros and cons of allowing these supposed transgressors on the Board, he only condemns the act itself.

Rick interjects.

"Rabbi, I'm sorry, I'm confused. Aren't we only here to decide if we should prohibit an intermarried member from serving on the Board? "We aren't here to discuss if they should be whipped or stoned. Clearly, that decision would be yours..."

"I for one, reread our constitution and see nothing that excludes an intermarried member from being on the Board. Nor is there anything that states the decision rests with the clergy."

"Rick, this is a serious and complex situation. I don't appreciate your sarcasm. I'm the mara de-atra of the synagogue and have sole authority of all religious decisions..."

"You're the what?" Asks Bernie.

"Apparently Bernie, you aren't the only one who doesn't know the term."

"I'm the mara de-atra. It means 'master of the house' in Aramaic. As per USCJ guidelines, the Rabbi is the central figure in a conservative synagogue. As Rabbi, I'm not only the spiritual leader, but I have sole authority on all decisions as they relate to Jewish laws. I'm empowered to adopt any positions I feel compelled to, even if my congregation does not approve."

"One could argue, as you have, that all things under this roof are religious, but that doesn't make every decision your province."

"Let me finish my presentation and you'll see how clearly this decision falls under my realm."

Rick looks at Dan knowingly. They have discussed countless times the futility of debating the Rabbi, yet somehow, they uncontrollably drag themselves back into arguments with him.

While the Rabbi's diatribe persists, Dan imagines a time, perhaps early in the Rabbi's tenure, when a Board member first proposed a Board candidate who was intermarried. The Rabbi disapproved of the individual—for unknown personal reasons. He rejected the nominee, stating with a fervent authority that their gentile spouse precluded them from holding the position. The Board member agreed without opposition, bowing to the Rabbi's perceived authority.

In that moment, the long-standing tradition was transformed into the immutable law the Board now debates.

The Rabbi expresses, "...of course, I agree with many of Dan's points and would like to be more open-minded toward some of our younger members' lifestyle choices. However, the Torah is clear and I have to answer to a higher authority..."

During his years on the Board, Dan noticed the Rabbi deploying this self-serving tactic. He reshaped traditions, customs, and interpretations of Jewish rules and presented them as hardened laws to produce his desired outcome. Dan learned as a child in Hebrew school there were six hundred and thirteen mitzvahs. Of course, there are the big ten which include, "Thou shalt not kill," and "Thou shall honor thy mother and father," but when you get past the relatively small number of commandments, the rest are customs and traditions interpreted by rabbis with long beards centuries ago.

Apparently, on Mount Sinai, God did not share with the children of Israel future inventions such as automobiles and the internet. It was left to the rabbis to determine, debate, and provide guidance on how such modern inventions and changing societal mores impacted laws handed down millennia.

And thousands of rabbis have done a commendable job guiding their communities.

But Rabbi Ben Stern rarely states his personal viewpoint on any matter. He hides his opinions and beliefs behind Jewish law regardless of the veracity of opposing legal Jewish assertions. His Rabbinic authority gives him the luxury of providing inaccurate and inconsistent arguments. If he shares his thoughts, they are always aligned with popular belief or what is being articulated by the person standing before him.

He laments with them, "I cannot override cemented law with my personal beliefs."

Dan thinks back to his first Board meeting that foretold of the strategy. The Rabbi said to Harold, "You *can* carry food supplies outdoors during Shabbat to prepare for an event to take place at its conclusion." The prohibition of carrying something outside a building during Shabbat is well known by even the most unobservant member. Dan remembers looking around the room, seeing no one questioning the assertion. When young, he had been chastised by his teacher in Hebrew School for the same act. Then, with trepidation, he had asked, "Rabbi, ah, can you clarify?"

He half-assumed he would say his teacher was incorrect.

With a tinge of anger in his voice, the Rabbi said, "Dan, you misunderstood what I said," and clarified that, "Harold *cannot* carry food supplies outdoors during Shabbat."

No one questioned the blatant reversal, they simply moved on to the next subject.

Dan's focus returns to the Rabbi's monologue when he says with determination, "...regardless, as long as I'm Rabbi of Beth Emet, this rule will not change..."

His voice becomes soft and quiet as he continues, "...of course, these members can volunteer and help support the great work this Board does. It's just...they can't be on the Board."

Dan thinks about his installation speech. He did not have to declare his intention to allow intermarried members to be on the Board. He did not have to grant the Rabbi's request to table the motion at the Board meeting when he raised this issue. He also had no obligation to meet with him separately to discuss his proposal. USCJ had confirmed the decision is the Board's to make, not the Rabbi's.

There is no policy prohibiting a Board member from being married to someone outside the faith. Therefore, there is no need for a policy to state otherwise. It's an unwritten tradition that all accept as if it were gospel. Dan's Grandfather once told him how synagogues in Europe required board members to observe the Sabbath, to keep kosher, and to be well-versed in the Torah. He presumes those same values were present in the European immigrants who founded Beth Emet over one hundred years ago.

Yet, Dan felt compelled to negotiate with the Rabbi and to present it to the Board as a question of the Board's legitimacy to choose whomever they want.

I could have nominated Beth all along. Even if the Rabbi argued against it and bullied the Board members into voting down her nomination, I'd be no worse off.

At least then, he would have grabbed his legitimate authority with confidence and pride. He is angry at this late realization. *Why did he feel compelled to accommodate the Rabbi? Was he no different from the rest of them? Did he too, want the Rabbi to agree with him and to avoid the wrath of his disapproval?*

The Rabbi concludes his presentation.

He whispers in Dan's ear.

"I wish this could end differently. I know you wanted this to pass, and you feel passionately about this, but there are many in our congregation who oppose this change."

In that moment, Dan realizes the universal truth.

We are all the same. We all desire approval and want to avoid disapproval. The Rabbi is stuck between those who want the motion to pass and those who don't. His strategy is a means for him to lay responsibility at the feet of the Torah instead of himself. No different from the rest of the Board members, his only shortcoming is his lack of leadership skills to stand for or against something he believes in, despite what others think.

"Bang!"

Dan lands the gavel down on the table and thinks, *Let's get this over with.*

"The question is on the adoption of the motion that would allow intermarried members of the synagogue to join the Board of trustees. All those in favor, please raise your hand."

In one quick motion, Dan and Rick lift their hands in unison, high in the air.

He waits a moment. He looks around, attempting to make eye contact with Harold, Deb, and Ann. He knew it was futile to make the same effort with Bernie.

"Anyone else? Anyone else have the courage?"

No other hand goes up.

"Two in favor. Those opposed..."

Eight hands go up. He had no illusions the motion had any chance of passing. Regardless, the pain he feels from the inevitable result is sharp and biting. No matter how much he prepared himself for the predictable result, there is still a crack left open in his heart, hoping one brave soul would have found the courage to vote yes.

"All those abstaining…"

Three hands go up.

"Come on people, some of you haven't voted."

Four more hands slowly pop up, one after another, like prairie dogs jutting their heads out of their borrows.

Seeing members of the Board apprehensive about abstaining, pours salt on his open wound. He is sickened by those who struggle to find the courage to provide what is ostensibly a no vote, an act he feels is cowardice. He feels the only time one should abstain from a vote is when one has a conflict of interest. Otherwise, it is important to make a stand, to let one's intentions be known.

The Rabbi keeps his head down and scribbles in his notepad. As an ex officio on the Board, he has no voting rights.

The Board meeting continues as usual. Each VP takes their turn, providing their report on the status of their portfolio of responsibility. Now a calm elation accompanies the tedious delivery of the reports.

Harold makes a joke about his wife's cooking, which triggers an apologetic chortle from the Rabbi. Dan recognizes the mood in the room as an appreciation for the controversial vote having taken place without incident. No one yelled or screamed. No one abruptly left the room. The motion was presented, the points were debated, and the vote was tallied.

All seem to be grateful for this.

All except Dan.

He feels helpless. There is nothing he can do except wallow in defeat. He stares past the members at the tables before him. He gazes out the windows at the back of the social hall. Towering trees sway in the powerful breeze. He does not notice the corners of his mouth turning down as Deb delivers her report.

"We had a successful volunteer of the year dinner. All of them appreciated the accolades and recognition. Dan, many people were particularly moved by your kind words, and all felt your choice of Beth was well deserved."

He appreciates Deb's sentiments, but they are of little consolation since he still cannot allow Beth to serve on the Board.

"Oh, one other thing. The members of the committee didn't like using hired servers for the dinner."

"What?! They asked for the help. You said they complained last year when they had to do all the work on a night they were being honored for volunteering."

"I'm sorry, I don't remember that. They said they missed working the dinner together. They enjoy the camaraderie in the kitchen."

"But you said they didn't want to have to work that night. We raised funds to cover the cost of the servers."

"I don't believe I said that."

"Of course you did. It's in the minutes! I can show you."

"I'm sorry..."

"What is it with you people!"

"Dan, I think perhaps we should table this discussion for another time," says Rick.

"Sure, continue with your damn reports," Dan groans, pushing aside the papers in front of him.

Deb proceeds. When she is done, the room falls silent. They all look at him, waiting for direction. He usually thanks each VP when they have finished and then invites the next person to present.

He says nothing. Ann eventually begins her report as outlined on the agenda and the meeting proceeds. He remains trapped inside the confines of his own debilitating thoughts, detached from the meeting, now moving forward without him.

Thoughts bombard him.

I should've just presented Beth as a candidate for the Board. What the hell is wrong with me? Why do I feel compelled to negotiate with the Rabbi? To do the right thing. Especially since he doesn't do the same for me. Each time I expect him to step up to the plate and act like the man of God he is supposed to be...To forego his own needs for what is right for the community. Each time I'm disappointed. I'm an idiot! Einstein was right, "Insanity is doing the same thing over and over..."

Harold is the last person to present. "...and don't forget to show up for our whiskey tasting event next Thursday night...Okay, that's all I got...I'm done...who's next?"

"I think we are finished," says the Rabbi, "Dan?"

Dan, stirred by the Rabbi calling his name, looks down at his agenda.

"Oh, okay, well, does anyone have anything else they'd like to discuss?"

When no one responds, he raises his gavel and says, "There being no further business, I declare the meeting…"

Harold gathers his things and lifts himself from his chair, waiting for Dan to bring down his gavel. When it does not land on the table, he looks around.

Rick says, "Dan?"

"I'm sorry. I have one more piece of business before we conclude."

"Damn!" Harold calls out, sitting back down.

"It won't take long. It's just an announcement."

"I see nothing else on the agenda Dan," the Rabbi questions.

"I want to let you all know in our role as a fiduciary of the synagogue, we're hiring a professional accountant to audit our books."

"What do you mean audit our books?" inquires the Rabbi. His voice trembles.

"I mean a professional accountant will review our budget, our books, and review all the transactions in our discretionary funds."

"No one can review the Rabbi's discretionary fund. There is confidential information in those books."

"Don't worry, Rabbi, a confidentiality agreement will be signed and no one on this Board, including me, will have access to the information."

"Good, then the information will be kept private."

"Yes."

"As you know, per the synagogue's constitution, I have full control of that fund."

"As per your contract, not the constitution…But that could change based on the accountant's findings."

"What do you mean?"

"Well, if questions are raised or something looks off-kilter, it may require our executive Board to get involved."

"But I don't want anyone looking at the fund."

"Rabbi, I'm sure there is nothing to worry about."

"How are we going to pay for this?" the Rabbi questions.

Harold interjects, "I've a friend who is an accountant. He's excellent and reasonable. He'd probably give us a break, too."

"We can't use anyone from the synagogue," the Rabbi says.

"He doesn't belong...he's not even Jewish."

"We can use the money we'll save on servers for next year's volunteer of the year dinner to cover the cost. Worse comes to worse, I'll be happy to help subsidies a portion of the cost since it's such a worthy endeavor," Dan suggests.

"Me too," calls out Rick

Bernie says, "I will too."

The Rabbi scowls at him. Bernie retreats to his notebook, not having realized the Rabbi's opposition to the suggestion.

Ann says, "I would also help with the cost."

When others offer to assist, Dan says, "When the time comes, I'll reach out to all of you. I appreciate your generosity, but no one should feel obligated. I'll coordinate the donations privately. I don't want anyone to be uncomfortable if they aren't able to give."

"Why don't we table this discussion for the next meeting? We can vote on it then," adds the Rabbi.

"We will not be voting on this. If anyone has questions, they can come and see me."

The Rabbi mumbles, "You are just trying to get back at me for the intermarriage vote."

"No, I'm not. I'm just trying to behave like the leader I should've been all along," Dan says in a loud whisper.

"I think this is all great, but can we just end the meeting?" Harold blurts.

"I declare this meeting adjourned," Dan calls out with a smile as he pounds the gavel on the table with a "Bang".

A few members race out of the building oblivious to the enormity of what just transpired. Their only concern is getting home.

Dan turns to the Rabbi and recognizes his dejected look and slumped posture. Surprised, he receives no satisfaction from it.

The Rabbi gets up and meets in the back corner with several of his minions to plan their next move. Rick runs to Dan and pats him on the back.

"Dan, why didn't you let me know about your brilliant plan?"

"Because I didn't know about it until now."

A Break from the Synagogue

The best laid schemes of mice and men go oft awry
Robert Burns

Joy squeezes his hand.

Her smile lightens his heart as does the rays of yellow-orange sunlight streaking down, illuminating the path ahead. He returns the same and plants a slow and soft kiss. He savors their affection like a cool, refreshing drink on a hot summer's day. On most occasions, their kisses have been a quick peck as he runs out the house to synagogue meetings.

Jackson gallops beside them as they stroll along the forested edges of the vast blue-green lake amid herons, squirrels, and shy rabbits. It's a bright spring mid-afternoon with a blue-sky above the limbs and branches blanketing them overhead.

Before he became active in the synagogue, they frequented this park for short, leisurely walks. It was here they held hands as newlyweds, played toss, went fishing with the boys, and trained Jackson when he was but a little fluff ball of a puppy. As Dan promised and as Joy mandated, they skipped Saturday morning services like a couple of schoolkids playing hooky.

Grandma and Grandpa had picked up the boys earlier in the morning. They are to have a day of fun at the local petting zoo and playing the traditional Rummy-Q numbered tile game popular among Jewish seniors. Only second to mahjong, Grandma taught them how to play at an early age before they could barely count. Later they would feast on blueberry bagels and tuna fish and of course Max's favorite cinnamon Bundt cake with sugary white icing draped over it, which Grandma would have defrosted in anticipation of their arrival.

After the boys had left, he and Joy made love in the silent, near-empty house as Jackson napped at the foot of the bed.

Dan had been looking forward to this day for weeks. Tonight, they will see their niece perform in Ford's Theater's production of *Footloose*. They had watched Rachel act in shows ever since her illustrious debut at the age of six when she convincingly played a tree in the McKinley Grade School production of the *Wizard of Oz*.

220

She was now a professional. The days of off-key singing and runny nosed kids forgetting their lines, is now a thing of the past.

They walk by the bench where he once sat with an uncomfortable big-bellied Joy as they timed her contractions. It is the same bench where, on that infamous day, he had his epiphany with Jackson snoozing at his feet.

Well, less an epiphany than an awakening. It was then when his daydream of that summer day on the little league field, when ol' man Mercado offered him the ball, sparked action. It was the place where he was shaken out of his insecurity and self-doubting slumber. That was the day when he jumped in and unknowingly thrusted himself into contentious debates on intermarriage, money laundering, marital affairs, and homosexual lovers.

"I'm still frustrated with Rick. Why did we have to wait this long to meet Roberta?"

"Dan don't let it bother you. He told you he was concerned about the consequences of him dating someone not Jewish. You can understand that."

"I know, but it seems like everyone has met her. Rachel and Samantha have met her."

"Dan, Roberta is the choreographer for the play, and you know Samantha has been dog sitting for her while they rehearse."

"You're right. I know. I'm going to focus on this gorgeous day and you. It's nice to have a break."

"Well, you only have a few more months. It'll be over soon."

"You know the auditor comes on Tuesday."

"Dan, you promised no synagogue talk today. I want you to relax."

They walk along the trail for some time in silence. He squints and spies two boys playing catch as they turn the bend and face the bright, large yellow sun. A man pulls a flopping shiny trout out of the lake with an excited young boy by his side. A woman wearing a pink helmet whizzes close by on a dirt bike and delivers them a refreshing cool breeze.

He grabs his cellphone from his pocket like he would scratch an itch or wipe away hair from his eyes. Joy places her hand gently on his and flashes her wide-open brown eyes. He returns the phone to his pocket.

"Remember when I was pregnant with Jake, and the doctor suggested we walk to induce labor?"

"I remember. We walked a lot during those few weeks."

"We used to walk more often. We will do it more once this craziness is over."

"Let's take a trip somewhere this summer. Perhaps just the two of us or a family vacation with the boys."

"That would be wonderful."

"You know, while I won't be president. I'll still be on the Board, and I'll want to support Rick as he has me."

"Let's see what happens. You've said yourself you'd be surprised if Rick goes through with it. You know, as my *bubbe* used to say, 'Man plans, and God laughs."

"Yeah, my Grandmother said that, too. It's the Jewish version of, 'best laid plans of mice and men.'"

"Oh honey, it's getting late. We need to hurry for the show."

"Yes, I don't want to be late. I expect it to be an incredible evening!"

It's Almost Over

The people of God want pastors, not clergy acting like bureaucrats or government officials.
Pope Francis

Dan and Joy walk briskly from the parking lot to the theater entrance.

"I've never seen the Rabbi as flustered and red-faced as he was when I told him we were getting an auditor."

"Dan, I told you no synagogue discussions."

"I know...I know, but he was really pissed. His eyes were bulging. I really thought he was going to hit me."

"Other than that, how was the play, Mrs. Lincoln?"

"What's that supposed to mean?"

"You're missing the point. You're focusing on the Rabbi being angry with you instead of why he is."

"I don't get it. Am I supposed to be Lincoln?"

"No! Don't you see? You're rattled because the Rabbi is angry you stood up for yourself—for the synagogue."

"Yes, but what does that have to do with Lincoln?"

"Nothing, it's just an expression. Dan, you hit a nerve. His response was a signal you're getting closer to the truth. He's hiding something...You've got to look at this as a positive move forward."

"I know, you're right."

Dan pulls the door open and holds it for her as she walks in. A smiling woman scans their tickets. After the beeps, she tells them, "Enjoy the show!" They walk along the thick and soft burgundy carpet, guided by gold-plated stanchions and red velvet ropes. Dan spots Rick at the long bar. His brother Evan stands next to Rick, chatting.

Dan searches for his sister-in-law and niece.

"Hey guys. How's it going? Where's Lori and Samantha?"

Evan guesses, "I think they went to the ladies' room."

"I'm going to look for them," Joy responds. She disappears in the crowd into the back corner of the lobby.

"Dan, your brother was just telling me about an awful accident he covered last night."

223

Evan started off driving an ambulance because it was something he always dreamed of doing as a kid. He loved playing with cars and trucks in the backyard by their tall pine trees. His little hand would grasp the cars and run them along the ground as he sang out 'vroom!' Over time, sitting on the sidelines as a driver wasn't enough. He took EMT classes and with time and perseverance became certified despite having no medical background.

"A car driven by a teenage boy jumped the railing near South Lake Drive and flew a hundred feet in the air, slamming headfirst into that small island in the middle of Silver Lake," Rick shares.

"Oh, my god! What happened to him?"

"He was killed instantly. There's an investigation going on. They think it might be suicide. I tend to agree," Evan interjects.

"What makes you think so?"

"Well, the road was dry, and the tire tracks showed he sped up deliberately. No alcohol or drugs were found in his body. A lot was going on with the young man. He and his girlfriend broke up and his parents are going through a nasty divorce."

"That's awful..."

"Yeah, that's not all. Some kids caught him kissing another boy and recorded it. They were going to post the video on the internet."

"He was gay?"

"Yes, apparently no one knew except the girlfriend."

"Did he leave a note?"

"No, but he texted her just before the accident saying, 'I feel trapped, the pain is unbearable.'"

Dan shakes his head and his lips curl inwards. "Damn, damn, damn! And Rick, here we worry about a little embezzlement by our Rabbi."

"How about we talk about something more pleasant," Rick responds.

Evan asks, "Did that update I suggest for your phone fix your problem?"

"No, though actually it was kind of nice. I accidentally recorded a session of Name that Tune with the boys. It was during the playing of "Let It Be."

"I've got one more suggestion that might fix it."

"We can try it another night."

"By the way, Dan, can I buy you a drink?" Rick asks.

"No thanks, I'll save it for later at Blanche's when I finally get to meet your paramour."

"Paramour? What, we're in this beautiful art déco theater, and you think your Humphrey Bogart?"

"You haven't met Roberta?" remarks Evan.

"Don't tell me, you've met her too."

"Well, it was just the one night. She was with Rachel at the theater after rehearsal."

"Tell me, what do you think of this mystery woman?"

"Well, she's really incredible, and Rick, if you don't mind me saying, she's breathtakingly beautiful."

"Evan, are you talking about me again!" Lori chimes in.

Lori, Joy, and Samantha appear suddenly from the crowd and intermingle with the men. Samantha gives Dan a hug and kisses him on the cheek, "Hi Uncle Dano!"

"Hey Samanther! How's the world of dogs treating you?"

"They're all as cute as ever...How's the synagogue world?"

"Well..."

"Ah...no synagogue talk tonight," Joy interjects.

"Sorry Aunt Joy."

"Tonight, we relax and have fun. It'll be an incredible night. We get to see Rachel on stage in *Footloose* and meet Roberta."

"Yes, it's quite the significant evening."

The lobby lights flash several times, which triggers a flow of theatergoers to the open doors that will transport them into the theater.

"I guess that's our cue," says Dan.

The group squeezes their way through the swarm of people. Ushers fervently hand them playbills as they push through the entryway. The crowd carries Dan down the long aisle. He looks up at the painted ceiling of cherubs and flowers that dance amid a sky-blue background with white puffy clouds. Humongous and ornate silver and crystal chandeliers hang from the ceiling overhead. He looks to the left of the stage and spots Jackie and Norm sitting in box seats high above the stage. A feathered and pleated US flag is draped in front of their booth.

He waves to her. She sees him, smiles, and waves back. Her bright ruby red lips cry, "Dear boy!"

Although he cannot hear her, he imagines her clear Texas twang.

The group is seated in two rows of three seats on the left side, eight rows from the stage. Rick is to his left and Joy to his right on the aisle seat. He opens the Playbill and finds Rachel Barkan on the list of cast members, then reads her bio.

The lights fall and the chatter of the crowd dissipates until replaced by loud applauds when the tall velvet curtains open. Dan settles into his seat as the orchestra begins. Performers fly out from all corners singing the title song. He spots the bright red curly hair of his niece as she dances in the air.

For an hour he forgets about the Rabbi and P. Gleason and the looming audit. The respite from synagogue worries remains even during the intermission. He sings under his breath when he rushes back from the bathroom to his seat. He holds Joy's hand on his thigh and taps to the beat of the music as Act II begins. The bright lights from the stage allow him to follow along the scenes listed in the Playbill. Scene 5, "Dancing Is Not a Crime," begins as the play reaches a pivotal moment.

Ren, the lead character, just lobbied the town council, controlled by Reverend Shaw Moore, to reverse the ordinance against dancing to allow him and his high school friends to freely dance at their prom.

He loses his battle. Dan saw the movie when released in 1984, and isn't surprised by the outcome.

But he is enraptured by the scene. Ren and his mom stand alone on the bare stage. The middle-aged woman consoles her teenage son after his defeat.

"Sweetie, you never had a prayer."

"That's not funny, Mom."

Chills flow through Dan's head and down his spine like an electric shock. In hindsight, perhaps he shouldn't have been surprised by this gut reaction.

"Reverend Shaw Moore had those votes locked up before he walked in there tonight."

Bam! A jolt of energy courses through his entire body

"You think he told them how to vote?"

He breathes heavily, his stomach and chest fight each other, rising and plunging.

"You can still sound shocked; I love that about you."

"But he's a man of God, Mom!"

The words are a simultaneous slap to his head and a hard punch to his solar plexus.

"He's a man, Ren. And you got railroaded."

He gasps and covers his mouth to hold back the bellow that wants to escape. Tears stream from his eyes and run down his cheeks. As the scene continues, his emotional reaction grows stronger. Tears now pour, like the rain on the night he had dinner with Jackie at Blanche's and the Rabbi found them in the synagogue.

The night this whole affair began.

Joy hears his sniffles and grunts and turns toward him. She places her free hand on top of his shaking one. She moves closer and whispers only to him.

"It's going to be okay. It's almost over."

She kisses him on the cheek and pulls his head onto her chest. He lays sobbing, attempting to stifle overwhelming emotions of shock, despair, and frustration. With each rise and fall of her peaceful breath, he tries to calm his mind, body, and soul until the racking cries and heaves lessen and stop.

In his thoughts, he repeats her promise, *"It's almost over...It's almost over."*

I Don't Know What I'll Do

When I went to school, they asked me what I wanted to be
when I grew up. I wrote down 'happy.'
John Lennon

Bruce brings their drinks to the table. He places Dan's next to his cellphone, which lies near him beside his dinner knife. Of course, Rick and Dan have the usual. Roberta orders a bourbon neat, and Joy a glass of pinot noir.

"How've you been Bobbie? It's nice to finally see you at my bar," Bruce says.

"Well, your friend has been keeping me locked away in his closet."

"Nice choice of words..." interjects Dan.

"The nerve of him, and after I introduced the two of you."

"Bruce, I can't thank you enough for that. I promise, no more hiding."

"Well, speaking of hiding, I gotta go back behind the bar. I'll talk to you folks later."

Bruce lopes off and leaves the couples with their drinks. Rick puts his hand on Roberta's, and they smile at each other. Dan watches closely as the two interact and can see they are in love. Rick's face beams. He's enraptured by her eyes, her lips, hair, and personality. Every word she speaks he gobbles up like a teenage boy with an insatiable appetite.

Dan is familiar with this surreal and ephemeral feeling. He is transported back to the moment he met Joy.

He delights in seeing the two of them together. They are like a glamorous Hollywood couple from the 40s. Even their names, Rick and Roberta, have a certain ring reminiscent of the celluloid romances of Bogey and Bacall and, Tracy and Hepburn.

Dan's brother is right, she is breathtakingly beautiful. She has luxurious raven-colored hair which flows below her shoulders, silky long eyelashes which accompany her sparkling bright green eyes, and pouty red lips. Her figure is exceptional, even for one in her profession.

"Roberta, Rick says you're going to be working on Broadway soon."

"Dan, call me Bobbie," she says in a soft and inviting voice. With those words and through their mutual deep connection with Rick, they are officially christened close friends.

"Yes, this will be my second show on Broadway. I'm going to choreograph the revival of *West Side Story*."

"Wow! That's great. I love that show—'There's... a place... for us,'" Dan sings.

"Bobbie, did you always know you wanted to be in musical theater?" asks Joy.

"Yes, but my parents wanted me to be a doctor like them."

"Then how'd you break in? It's difficult. I see what my niece goes through. Did you study theater in college like Rachel?"

"Not at first. My parents wouldn't pay for college if I did."

"What did you study?"

"Initially, biology. I was planning on becoming a doctor, too. I figured theater was just a pipe dream, but I loved it. It's all I ever wanted to do."

"Did you eventually change majors?"

"Yes, first I took some classes as electives and tried out for roles in the school's productions. However, I couldn't get cast in anything since I wasn't a theater major."

"How'd you switch?" Dan asks.

"In my sophomore year I told my parents I was going to. If they weren't willing to pay for it, I would. I'd take out loans and work if I had to, but I was going to do it."

"That's marvelous—good for you, going after your dream like that," Joy exclaims.

"Did you have to get a job?" Dan inquires.

"Well, my parents relented and paid my tuition."

"...they let you switch your major? How'd you get them to change their mind?"

Roberta hesitates, "Well...there were special circumstances."

"Really?"

"I don't like talking about it. Rick doesn't even know the story. I think my parents were just happy I was staying in school."

"I'm sorry, I didn't mean to pry," Dan apologizes.

"No, no, don't worry. It's okay, you didn't know."

"Where did you go to school?" Dan changes the subject.

"I went to UCI."

"Where's that?" Joy asks.

"University of California, Irvine," confirms Dan.

"You know the school?"

"I knew someone who went there."

"Well, many people went to UCI..."

"Did you know a Mary Smith?"

"What!" calls out Roberta who stops in mid-motion while about to draw on her glass of bourbon. Dan can't help but notice her shocked expression renders her green eyes stunning.

"Hi! How're you all doing tonight?" interrupts the waitress.

"Oh, hi Brooke," says Rick.

"Hi Rick—Dan, Joy...."

The waitress smiles politely at Roberta who maintains eye contact with Dan.

"Oh, Brooke, this is my girlfriend, Bobbie."

Roberta turns her attention toward the waitress, and they exchange pleasantries. She returns her focus back to Dan while the waitress asks the customary questions.

"Can I get you some appetizers to start? Would you like me to read you the specials?"

"Anyone interested in the cheese board?" Rick asks.

"That sounds nice," Joy responds.

"Sure, the Romeo and Juliet cheese board," the waitress confirms as she jots down notes on her pad.

"Would you like plates for sharing? Can I get some refills on your drinks?"

"I'm going to need a little more time," Dan declares.

"Me too," says Roberta.

"Okay, then let me get you the cheese plate in the meantime."

As soon as she leaves, Roberta asks, "How did you know Mary?"

"Well...she and I..."

"Oh my God, you're Dan! That Dan!" She looks shocked.

"You knew Mary?"

"She was my roommate; I was with her the night she died. She's the reason I switched majors. After that night, I realized life was too short."

"I was told they found her the next morning with an empty bottle of gin and sleeping pills by her side."

"She was in a bad way. I tried to get her help."

"I often thought perhaps there was something I could've done differently."

"Oh, Dan, trust me, it was much bigger than you."

He sips his martini, remembering he and Mary together, happy, for a time.

The colorless and odorless alcohol burns his throat and lands warmly in his belly, a familiar sensation which comforts the dredged-up sorrow he thought he had forgotten.

"Dan, I wanted to talk to you about something important. I've been thinking, and although we've accomplished a lot, I believe the Board and the Rabbi aren't open to dramatic or monumental changes as we had hoped. I..."

Dan's cellphone dances next to his glass, causing his martini to sway. At first, he ignores it, wanting to hear Rick's announcement until Joy suggests it might be his mother or it could be the boys calling to say goodnight.

He picks it up without looking at the caller id with his eyes fixed on the piercing bright green orbs in front of him.

"Hello, uh huh, yes, Tzipora. That's right. Okay, sure...thank you...have a goodnight."

He slams the phone on the table.

"Damn synagogue!"

"You want me to go with you pal?" Rick offers.

"No, I can take care of this; why interrupt your night? I'll run there and be back shortly."

"Honey, this will be over soon, it will," Joy consoles.

"Bobbie, I'm sorry I would love to sit and talk with you more. You probably know Mary and I were close, but I have to take care of something."

"That's okay, is everything all right?"

"Yes, fine. The synagogue alarm system went off again."

"Tzipora is the alarm code; it tells the monitoring company he's on his way," Rick explains.

"I swear, if the alarm interrupts another one of my nights, I will...I don't know what I'll do."

Dead Silence

I will permit no man to narrow and degrade my soul
by making me hate him.
Booker T. Washington

His clenched fists, handcuffed together, land furiously on the desk like a judge's gavel handing down a verdict. He looks up at the detective with his wide-open, pathetic, tear-rimmed eyes desperately straining to get out the words.

"I'm innocent."

Dan wants someone to believe him. Where are Joy and Rick? They would vouch for him; they know he wouldn't kill the Rabbi.

All he had hoped for or wanted was the truth. He didn't want the Rabbi dead. But, his dogged pursuit of the truth exposed a tragic and astounding plot he couldn't have predicted, or any scenario or rumor mill at Beth Emet could have conjured.

Dan is cold yet sweating profusely. He is alarmed and shakes, like his cellphone that vibrated at Blanche's. Now here, at a tragic occurrence that triggered a chain of events which have placed him in this precarious situation.

An anonymous police officer places a blanket over his shoulders.

A sturdy, large black man in a wrinkled tan suit towers over him, revealing a firearm in his shoulder holster. The man's paw-like hands grip the arms of the chair Dan sits in as he imagines he might grip his gun. His badge dangles on a chain in front of Dan's face. He is still in shock from the events that unfolded an hour earlier.

He sits, spent, hands clasped in front of him, handcuffed, in one of the leather chairs facing the desk in the Rabbi's office surrounded by armed police officers and the detective. The scene is something out of the black and white film noir movies he and his brother Evan love watching. He is far removed from the delight of his niece's play and the enjoyable dinner with Rick and Roberta.

Mrs. Winthrop is here too, having been the only other person in the building during what the detective refers to as "a homicide." Detective Wilson points to Mrs. Winthrop in the corner sobbing.

He barks, "Mrs. Winthrop here says she heard someone yell, 'Stop! Don't!' moments before he fell from the roof of the synagogue to his death. Is that true?"

With his self-destructive bent towards honesty, Dan answers, "Yes."

He nervously shuffles his feet on papers and other objects strewn across the floor. These items had occupied the barren desk in front of him until detective Wilson asked, "Why did you kill the Rabbi?"

The query sparked rage in him he had never felt. He jumped, swept everything off the desk like an angry little boy losing a game of checkers. Papers and envelopes, pens and mementoes scattered everywhere.

The outburst forced the detective to shackle his hands.

"You hated him, didn't you?"

"Hates a strong word. But I was angry with him!"

He yells again, "…but I didn't kill him."

"Then how did he fall from the roof?" detective Wilson snaps back.

"I don't know!"

"But you were on the roof with him alone, weren't you?"

"Yes, but I didn't see him fall; maybe he slipped or something?"

"But you said he wasn't near the edge; he was on his knees."

"I don't know! I'm confused. I didn't kill him. I didn't want him to die!"

Dan places his head in his handcuffed hands and sobs. He mourns the loss of the Rabbi who he had once been close with, while digesting the magnitude of the allegations. *How could anyone think I could kill someone?*

However, he inventories all the awful things the Rabbi has done to him….

He realizes history has shown lesser infractions, transforming greater men into ruthless murderers.

Detective Wilson demands, "Tell me again why you and the Rabbi were fighting up there."

"I've told you ten times!"

"Tell me again!"

Dan knew the subject of the argument didn't matter. He and the Rabbi had been cat fighting for two years and while their disagreements varied, the underlying theme was always the same.

The Rabbi believed all synagogue business was his to decide, and the Board was there to serve him.

But what infuriated Dan most was that no one could see it. The Rabbi would prod, prompt, and lobby Board members until they capitulated and regurgitated his positions as if they were their own. Dan tried to expose the charade, but it was like being trapped behind a soundproof glass window, screaming for help.

They could see him, but they couldn't hear him.

It all seems inconsequential now. Had he let things go like everyone else did, the Rabbi would still be alive, and he wouldn't be in this predicament.

"Damn it! Why were you fighting?" The detective roars in Dan's face.

"I hired an auditor to review the synagogue's books, including the Rabbi's discretionary fund."

"...and I presume he didn't like that idea?"

"No, he hated it. He was angry at me for it. I've never seen him that angry."

"Why did you want to hire an auditor?"

"It's my responsibility as president. I knew he was hiding something. I wanted the truth to come out."

"What truth?"

"The truth no one wanted to hear. The Rabbi was using synagogue funds for his own personal benefit."

"Liar!" yells Mrs. Winthrop.

"Shut up Mrs. Winthrop! Let him finish. Do you have evidence he was using synagogue funds?"

"No, but I knew something illegal was going on. I knew an audit would reveal it."

"And you said no one on the Board believed you?"

"Besides Rick, no!"

"And why was that?"

"They're all cowards. None of them had the courage to stand up to him. It was easier for them to give in than to fight."

The detective paces and ponders the situation. He peruses the pictures, framed certificates, and various memorabilia hanging perfectly on the walls. He stops at the mahogany filing cabinet, lifts the picture of the Rabbi and Hillary Clinton, and studies it as if it will reveal a hidden clue. His gaze remains fixed on the man whose body now lay covered under a black sheet in front of the glass doors of the synagogue.

He continues, "But that doesn't explain how you ended up on the roof."

"I told you. She told me to meet him up there."

"Tell me again, from the beginning."

"I was at dinner with my wife, my friend Rick, and his girlfriend."

"Go on."

"I got a call from the synagogue's alarm company. They said the alarm went off, and I needed to check the building."

"You're telling me that's the job of the synagogue president?"

"Ha! The alarm never went off. I was here all night with the Rabbi," shouted Mrs. Winthrop.

"That's because the Rabbi set it off silently to get the company to call me. He wanted me to come to the synagogue!"

"That's a lie!"

"Mrs. Winthrop, let Dan finish!" the detective interjects. "How do you know he did that?"

"He told me up on the roof! He said he did the same thing the night he found me and Jackie right here on the floor." Dan points with his handcuffed hands to the floor where the papers lay strewn in the exact spot where the Rabbi found the two of them.

"That night he knew we were at dinner together. He knew we would both go to the synagogue to check the alarm. He counted on catching us alone. However, even he couldn't have planned to find us on the floor. It was plain dumb luck."

"How did you end up on the floor?"

"The office was dark. We slipped on a pile of loose letters. Jackie landed on top of me.

"Don't forget, the Rabbi also saw Jackie kiss you," interrupts Mrs. Winthrop.

"Yes, an innocent one. When she slipped on the floor, I caught her. She was grateful and gave me a brief peck. It was all innocent!"

"Why would the Rabbi want to catch you and this Jackie person alone?"

"He wanted to blackmail us. Jackie knew something was wrong, too. He wanted us to stop digging into his discretionary fund."

"You didn't stop?"

"No, and his rumors about us spread like wildfire."

"What did you do?"

"Nothing, I didn't care. I knew I did nothing wrong. I wouldn't allow him to manipulate me like everyone else. The bastard had the nerve to talk to my wife privately and try to convince her that Jackie and I were having an affair. However, he didn't count on her not believing him. Jackie's husband didn't believe it either. Some people did, but most didn't. It was just grist for the rumor mill."

"Again, how'd you end up on the roof tonight?"

"When I got here, the parking lot was empty. I unlocked the front door and walked in and saw the light to the Rabbi's office on."

"Who was here?"

"Mrs. Winthrop."

"Mrs. Winthrop where's your car?" asks detective Wilson.

"The Rabbi picked me up, he asked me to come in to help him with some letters."

"You didn't find it strange that he asked you to type up letters late at night."

"No, he often works late hours and asks for my help."

"And you just go…?"

"Well, yes..."

"Where's his car?"

"It's parked in back."

"Why didn't he park by the glass doors at the entrance? I see he has a reserved spot."

"I don't know! His office is in the back."

"Does he park back there often?"

"No, so what!"

"But Mrs. Winthrop," Dan intervenes, "you know the Rabbi was a creature of habit. He always parked in his reserved spot. Always. He hid the car deliberately! He didn't want me to see he was here for fear I would turn around and go home!"

"Enough Dan!"

Detective Wilson asks, "Tell me how you got up on the roof."

"Like I said, Mrs. Winthrop told me he was up there and wanted to see me."

"Didn't that seem unusual?"

"A little, but not really. He was always puttering around in odd places in the synagogue. I've had conversations with him late at night in the ladies' room while I followed him as he checked all the rooms."

236

"Why was he up on the roof?"

"Mrs. Winthrop said he wanted to show me something with the air conditioner unit. We've been having problems with it for years. I assumed it was what triggered the alarm."

"Is that true Mrs. Winthrop?"

"Yes, the Rabbi asked me to send Dan to the roof when he arrived."

"You knew Dan was coming?"

"Yes, the Rabbi told me. I just assumed he called him."

"Dan, you went up to the roof?"

"Yes."

"Don't forget to tell him about the knife you took with you," asserts Mrs. Winthrop.

"Knife! What knife?" asks the detective.

"There was no knife!" fumes Dan. "I grabbed a letter and the Rabbi's letter opener. They were sitting on his desk."

One of the anonymous police officers standing behind Dan places a Ziplock bag containing the Rabbi's letter opener and a letter with P. Gleason's return address on the empty desk.

"Chief, we found these items along with a few others at the scene, and retained them as evidence. There's no blood on the letter opener and there were no stab wounds on the body."

"Thanks Ernie."

"Why'd you take the letter and letter opener with you up on the roof? Did you use the letter opener to threaten the Rabbi? Is that why he fell off the roof?"

"No! I didn't want to harm him!" Dan yells. "I just wanted the truth!"

"I bet he tried to stab the Rabbi with it…" Mrs. Winthrop cries. "He was furious with him!"

"Mrs. Winthrop!" screams detective Wilson.

"Yes, I was furious with him. The damn alarm went off again and interrupted a wonderful evening. I don't know why he insisted it was my responsibility as president to check up on the synagogue every time the damn alarm went off in the middle of the night!"

"Dan, focus. Tell me, how'd the Rabbi fall off the roof?"

The detective waits.

Dan's head hangs low.

After a gasp and two heavy deep breaths, he responds softly, like an errant young boy reprimanded by a parent awaiting his punishment.

"I told you, I don't know...I don't know...I don't know..." He shakes his head with each denial.

He explodes, "But the synagogue has been writing checks for sixteen hundred dollars to P. Gleason for years. I was trying to find out who P. Gleason is. That's why I took the letter. I wanted to confront the Rabbi with it."

"Why did you take the letter opener?"

"To open it—I guess. I don't know, it just happened to be next to it," Dan cries, keeping his head down. Dan also tells the detective about the original letter from P. Gleason he discovered the night the Rabbi found him on the floor with Jackie. As he explains, he points to the mess on the floor in front of him, showing him exactly where he found the letter that night.

"Did you push the Rabbi off the roof?"

"No! I swear!"

"Then how did he fall? You were the only other one there, you must know."

"I don't!"

Dan scans the detritus lying on the floor. He spots a ream of stationery paper spilling out of a cardboard box. Printed at the top of the paper is the synagogue's letterhead and the names of the only two people who know how the Rabbi fell fifty feet from the rooftop to the front entrance of the synagogue at the reserved signs, "Rabbi Ben Stern" and "President Dan Barkan."

The Rabbi's mangled and lifeless body won't return from the dead to reveal any tales. Only I can disclose the truth. Perhaps, someday the irony here will amuse me. Sure, the truth might save me...

But will anyone believe me?

He notices the corner of his cellphone peeking out from underneath the cardboard box. He remembers losing it on the roof. It must have been found by one of the officers and placed on the desk. Later, it made its way to the floor during his tirade.

He reaches down for it with his handcuffed hands. A large black boot appears from nowhere and lands on his cellphone like a giant cartoon foot falling from a cloud in the sky landing with a resounding "PFFT!"

He longs to be laying on the floor of his childhood home, his chin resting in his freed hands, laughing at the dry, witty British humor of Monty Python that was an integral part of his childhood.

"What do you think you're doing?" says the deep voice of an officer standing behind him.

"I was just going to pick up my phone. That's all."

The officer stares at the detective and waits for his signal. Detective Wilson nods "No," and grabs it.

Dan slowly sits back up in his seat with one eye fixed on the officer, scared like a prisoner waiting to be horsewhipped.

"I just want to text my wife!"

"I can't let you have the phone. This is evidence."

"What would I tell her, anyway? I'm at the synagogue being held by the police on suspicion of killing the Rabbi?"

"…continue, you go up on the roof…," the detective asserts.

"I went to the storage closet in the back of the synagogue and climbed the ladder up. I popped my head out of the small opening at the top and spotted the Rabbi on his knees beside the main air conditioner unit. I called out, 'Rabbi!'"

"What did he say?"

"He begged me to cancel the auditor. He pleaded, 'Please don't press the issue.'"

"What did you tell him?"

"I told him there was nothing he could do to stop me from going through with the audit. I said, 'I will not back down. You're not going to manipulate me into getting your way.'"

"What happened next?"

"He threw a large wrench at me."

"Where'd he get a wrench?"

"The air conditioner guy must have left a bunch of tools behind."

"I assume he missed."

"Yes, I froze. I remember hearing it whizz past my head, missing me by inches. I was furious. I threw the only thing in my hand, my cellphone. It landed a few feet in front of him. I must have dropped the letter at the same time."

"What next?"

"He screamed, 'I hate you, Dan Barkan! Go to hell!'"

"Then…"

"Um, ah, I don't remember. I ah, think I ran back to the ladder and quickly climbed down. I don't remember the rest."

"You don't remember!" Detective Wilson slams his hand on the barren desk. "C'mon Dan, you're keeping something from us. What happened!"

"I don't remember!"

"Bullshit!"

"I'm innocent I tell you! I didn't kill him!"

"Dan, that may be true, but if you don't tell us every detail, you will be convicted. There's a preponderance of evidence here. You have a motive. You were the only one up there with him. Mrs. Winthrop confirms it and says you were angry at him and grabbed the letter opener. You've provided us with detailed descriptions leading up to the event. Yet, you somehow forget how he fell?

"Dan, this is the time for the truth."

He clutches his sweaty hands and places his elbows on the empty desk like he is praying. An unexplainable shock runs through his body and causes him to jerk. He shivers. Sweat flows from his brow and mixes with his salty tears. He mumbles, barely coherent, "Please, God, save me."

He cries, "Let nothing happen to Joy or Max and Jake. Don't let the Rabbi get them too!"

"What did you do Dan!"

"Nothing! I swear. He did it!"

"How'd he fall!"

"No one will believe me!"

"Try me Dan, I will."

"No, you won't. No one will! The Rabbi will convince you too…You're all in league against me."

"Dan, the Rabbi is dead, tell me."

"Please, I want to get back to normal. I want to play Name That Tune with the boys."

"Dan, if you just tell me we can work this out."

"No! I can't. He'll pit you all against me and tell lies about me." Tears stream down his face. He rubs his eyes with his fists and wipes his face with his sleeves.

"I want Joy! I want to kiss her lips again. I want to play fetch with Jackson! God, please save me!"

He sobs uncontrollably with his head on the desk.

"Someone, get him a drink of water," the detective calls out.

One officer hands Dan a bottle of water. He guzzles it like a man lost in a desert. He sits back up in the chair, sniffing and wiping his face with his sleeve, attempting to gain composure. He ponders his situation inside his head.

If only I had a recording of what the Rabbi said. They would all find out the truth. They would see I didn't kill him. I could prove...

"Wait! A recording!" he cries out loud.

"No, it can't be possible!"

Detective Wilson, Mrs. Winthrop, and the two officers stare at him.

"Dan, what recording?"

"I don't know, but maybe, just maybe...I need to unlock my phone and look."

"I can't let you have your phone. It's evidence."

"Damn it detective! Open it, it might prove I'm innocent and you'll see for yourself what happened. Please, my code is zero nine one five. Please open it!"

Dan directs the detective to his app. They see a new recording dated today at 10:36 pm around the time he would have been on the roof with the Rabbi. The message is over twenty minutes long.

"This app has been going off slipshod for months now. There's a new saved recording from tonight. Just maybe..."

"Let's hear what you got," Detective Wilson places the phone on the desk and hits play. He puts it on speakerphone. There is a second or two of silence followed by a thump. Dan's heart drops into his stomach like it does when he's with Jake on his favorite rollercoaster.

The silence continues.

He assumes his luck has run out.

The Truth

Truth is stranger than fiction, but it is because fiction is obliged to stick to possibilities; truth isn't.
Mark Twain

Still silence. Dan fidgets.

Then…they hear the Rabbi scream faintly, "I hate you Dan Barkan! Go to hell!"

Everyone in the room moves in closer.

Throwing his phone or when it hit the roof, must have started the recording. They each listen with intense focus for what unfolded as the two men talked.

"What are you hiding, Rabbi?"

"It's none of your business, but you've left me no choice. I'm trapped now."

"What is none of my business?"

"This pain is unbearable. You've ruined it for everyone…"

"What did I ruin? Tell me, I can help. Maybe we can solve this problem together."

"It's too late for that, Dan, Mister President. Unless you cancel the auditor and drop this whole thing."

"You know I can't do that. Why are you up here? What are you doing?"

The Rabbi outlines how he set off the alarm silently and tricked Dan to leave his dinner to get him up there with him. He also admits to having done the same the night he found Dan and Jackie on the floor.

"I needed you to stop prying. All other presidents knew their place. Now you'll see what damage you've caused."

"Does this have to do with P. Gleason? I found another letter on your desk." He picks up the letter which had fallen out of his hand and waves it.

"Who is P. Gleason? And what will he tell if you don't do the right thing?"

"Ah, you read the letter. You're a formidable adversary, Dan."

"Who is he?"

"Paul Gleason...is my son!"

"But you only have a daughter."

"He's my son! You met him at Denise's funeral."

"What! Paul? Little Paul? I don't believe it."

Mrs. Winthrop gasps, "Oh no! Rabbi! No, no, no!"

"Shhhh!" The detective calls out.

The Rabbi's voice continues.

"Denise had been volunteering in the office for months. We were alone, together, every night. She was wonderful. She was funny, smart, and did anything I asked perfectly. I made up stuff for her to do to spend time with her. She was beautiful. I fell in love with her. I didn't tell her or anyone. I kept it to myself and treasured every moment I was with her.

"She was dating a man named Alex Gleason. He was a lieutenant in the army and was fighting in Afghanistan. While he was away, she spent all her time volunteering at the synagogue. She said the work took her mind off Alex and the dangers he faced. She was desperately in love with him."

"What happened?"

"I would fantasize about her coming to me one night and we would—"

"What about your wife and daughter?"

"It was all fantasy. We spent a great deal of time together. I couldn't stop thinking about her. There was one short period when Alex was on leave. He returned home and spent the entire time with her. Of course, I told her to take the week off and be with him. It was the worst week of my life. I missed her terribly. When he deployed back to Afghanistan, I was ecstatic, thrilled just to be with her again."

"Yes..."

"Not long after he returned there, two hundred Taliban fighters attacked his outpost. Alex was one of eight soldiers killed. Denise was devastated. I convinced her to continue her volunteering out of selfishness. I wanted to see her, to make her feel better.

"One late night she came into my office. We were the only ones in the building. I consoled her. I held her in my arms, felt her quivers, and smelled her hair. She turned to me with tears dripping down her face.

243

"She said, 'I can't stand this pain, Rabbi.'"

"I said, 'Call me Ben.'"

"She kissed you?"

"No, I kissed her. At first, we fought back our desires, but it proved too much. I wanted her badly, and she needed someone to relieve the pain of losing Alex. We made love on the leather couch. It was glorious. It was the only time we did. We agreed never to do it again."

"How do you know Paul is yours?"

"Alex and she did not make love the week he was on leave. He told her he wouldn't, for fear something would happen to him in Afghanistan, and she would be left alone with a child."

"But I don't understand. Why is Paul sending you threatening letters? He's just a small boy."

"Those letters are coming from his grandmother, Lisa."

"She knows about Paul?"

"Yes, she, now you and I are the only ones. Denise told her just before she died. Sandy doesn't know. He and Paul think the father is Alex. Sandy doesn't talk about it much because Alex and Denise weren't married."

"I see. So, Lisa is threatening to tell everyone you're the father if you don't continue to support her grandson?"

"Yes, the witch. Out of guilt and wanting to help I started giving them money when this all happened, but she hounded me."

"But from your discretionary fund?"

"I have a right to! When you started snooping around, I was afraid you'd find out. I pushed back on her, but she wouldn't relent. She told me Paul is my son and supporting him is my responsibility. But I don't have that kind of money and I didn't want my wife to find out."

"Lisa sends the letters with Paul's name on it?"

"Yes, she didn't want her name on them, and she figured I couldn't ignore them if I thought they were coming from Paul."

"I see. You are in a tough bind. If you stop sending the money, Lisa tells your secret to the world. Your wife and daughter find out, as does your congregation. Your actions are grounds for dismissal."

"But Dan, if you say nothing, no one knows, and we would continue to support Paul."

"Rabbi, you know I can't do that. It would be wrong of me, us. Anyway, what would I tell Jackie and Rick?"

"Just say I told you it was going to charity, and you're okay with it. It's the truth."

"But Rabbi it's not the truth. I would like to, but I can't allow you to use money donated to the synagogue to help keep your secret. It's like paying blackmail. I will do what I can, but you must start with the truth. You are going to have to tell your family and the Board.

"Now please, let's get off of here. I can call Jackie, Norm, Lisa, and Rick. We can all meet and work this out."

"No! I can't do that. I refuse."

"Come on, Rabbi, let's get down, now."

"No, I wanted to meet you up here for a reason. I assumed your 'holier than thou' attitude wouldn't allow you to keep this secret...."

"No! I can't listen!" Screams Dan. He jumps from the chair and grabs his phone and hits the stop button.

"Dan, give me the phone!" says Detective Wilson.

"Fine! Here, but I can't listen. Please don't make me anymore. I'll tell you what happened. Please! Don't make me play it."

"Okay, what happened?" asks Detective Wilson.

"When I told him I wouldn't change my mind, he stood up and stared right through me. His jaw clenched, his face reddened, and his brows furrowed.

His face turned dark, and he said, "...you'll regret this."

Dan weeps and gasps.

"Now that he's dead, I didn't want anyone to know what he did. I didn't want to hurt his family or Sandy and Paul. Besides, I was afraid they wouldn't believe me. They wouldn't believe he was capable of...I wasn't going to tell anyone."

"Dan, tell me, please, go on."

He collapses back into the chair and describes the Rabbi's last few moments alive.

"It was awful; he dropped to his knees, sobbed, wept, and rocked back and forth. He looked up at me with a bizarre and sad look on his face. He pushed himself up, stood facing me, and gave me a blazing, almost crazy glare. He turned and walked toward the brink of the roof like a soldier marching to battle. He seemed to stare out into the horizon, ignoring his footsteps.

"I screamed, 'Stop! Don't!'

"But he walked until he reached the edge and then...disappeared into the night.

"I didn't think he would kill himself.

"I didn't want it to end this way.

"All I ever wanted was the truth."

Angel Hair

That all the love you've been giving has all been meant for you.
Justin Hayward

If Blanche's is the "official" diner of Beth Emet, then certainly the Shop Rite of West Huntington is the same for supermarkets. Like Blanche's, it's where congregants go to gossip and be seen. They also purchase their weekly groceries using gift cards, part of the women's club fundraising efforts.

The two establishments are frequented by Beth Emet members as often as Mrs. Nusbaum complains about the air conditioner. As a result, Dan and Rick joke, "We should sell them on the idea of advertising during services."

Dan would quip, "Murray could call out, 'This second call to the Torah is sponsored by Shop Rite where a second roasted chicken can be purchased at half price.'"

"You would make a good ad man." Rick would reply.

Dan used to love going food shopping with Joy where he would run into fellow members. It was an opportunity for him to schmooze, get feedback, and hear how he might make things better. He thought it more effective than a suggestion box.

Of course, that all changed after that night. He had avoided their shopping excursions since. They've been to services a handful of times and gone to Blanche's with Rick and Roberta, but not much else.

So, when Joy and Roberta asked the men to rush out to pick up a few items for their Saturday night soiree, he replied, "Guess it's time to go shopping...."

"You know, Rick, this is my first time here since that night."

"I know. It must be hard, even after six months."

"I've been to services and to Blanche's. This would be the obvious next place. Besides, it doesn't matter. That night haunts me wherever I go."

Once there, Rick grabs a cart, and they walk through the self-opening doors.

"I promise, in time it will get better. You'll see."

"The other night *Fiddler on the Roof* was on TV and Joy wanted to watch. Within the first minute, I was thinking about that night. You know how Tevye says, 'Every one of us is a fiddler on the roof, trying to scratch out a pleasant, simple tune without breaking his neck.'? That line shook me. I couldn't sleep all night. I kept seeing the Rabbi holding a fiddle and jumping off the roof."

"What did you expect? You watched a Jewish-themed movie with a guy hanging out on a roof!"

The men reach the produce section and begin picking vegetables for the crudites. Dan rips off a bag from the roll and struggles to open it. "You know, I can't help thinking maybe they're right. No good deed goes unpunished."

"I know what you went through was traumatic and it still haunts you. Jeez, it still haunts me. But you must see the good we accomplished."

"I should've quit. You were smart you did."

"Dan, do you think I quit? You know I made my decision before that night," Rick says, waving a cucumber in the air. "I was going to tell you at Blanche's. But I wasn't quitting. I was accepting the way things were and moving on. There's a difference. Had you resigned before all this, no one would've faulted you.

"You—we—did everything we could, above and beyond."

"I don't understand. I thought they wanted someone to make a difference, to bring about change."

"Don't you get it? That's what they said, like all people say they want, but change can be hard and scary. Sometimes people won't let go from the status quo, you know, like the old saying, 'the devil you know is better...'"

"I just wish…"

"Hey guys! What's shaking?" interrupts Harold as he bumps his cart into theirs. "We all miss you at synagogue."

"Hi Harold, yeah we miss it too. It's just hard to go after all that happened."

"Hey, I don't blame you. It's gotta be tough after what you went through. I guess the entire congregation feels that way, too. Maybe you'll pull out of it if you come more often."

Dan confirms, "You may be right."

"I still don't understand what happened to the Rabbi. It's like he suddenly snapped."

"Snap!" Harold flicks his fingers and shakes his head.

"There was a lot going on with him on a personal level. None of us truly knew."

"...just goes to show, you never know what's going on inside a person's head. By the way Rick, I'm sorry you didn't stay on as president. I think you'd have made a good one. I guess if I had a girlfriend who looked like yours, I wouldn't spend my nights at Board meetings either."

Harold elbows Rick in the arm, winks, and makes a clicking sound with his tongue.

"You are one lucky devil."

"Thanks Harold, but I think the Board's in excellent hands."

"Yeah, Hope is great. She even ends Board meetings on time. She's eliminated all the nonsense. And what a coup getting Beth on the Board. I never thought that would happen."

"Yes, Beth told me. Although she said she's just doing it for one term. Hope is a marvelous leader. I wish I could have done more..." laments Dan.

Harold pats him on the shoulder, "Buddy, you were a damn good president. Don't let anyone tell you otherwise. Well, I gotta get going. Marcy needs me to pick up a few things. She's making my favorite, chicken Fra Diavolo."

Harold steers his cart like a Formula One driver negotiating a hairpin turn and disappears from the produce section.

"Wow, that was nice of Harold to say...it's not like him to compliment," Rick declares.

Dan gazes, mesmerized by the shiny red apples in the large bin nearby.

"Dan, did you hear him say you were a damn good president?"

"Yeah, I guess that was nice."

"You guess?"

"Well, he probably feels bad for what I went through."

"Dan, don't be ridiculous. It's more than that. You were damn good."

"If you say so. What else do we need to get?"

"The girls need some cheese. I know Roberta likes brie."

As the men make their way to that section, Dan thinks about the early days when he and Joy were new members of the synagogue. They'd pass the elaborate cheese display and hold Jake's hand while Max sat in the cart. He could picture his adorable and younger son offended by the aroma crying out "stinky cheese!"

It was a pleasure though, to run into members and feel welcomed. He longs to get the feeling back.

Maybe Harold is right. A visit to services might help and put the awful events of that night behind me.

"Rick, while you do that, I'll get the pasta for the boys and find you when I'm through."

Dan leaves Rick with the cheeses and dashes off. He strides down the pasta aisle and scans each shelf mumbling, "…angel hair, angel hair, angel hair…."

Fixed in his pursuit, he bumps into a smiling man with gray hair.

"Oh, excuse me, I'm sorry. I'm just trying to look for my son's favorite angel hair pasta. He's quite particular."

"Hello Dan."

On his knees searching the bottom shelves, he's taken aback and stumbles.

Regaining balance, he turns.

"Oh my God! Gordon Diamond is that you!"

Gordon was president of Congregation Sons of Israel of East Huntington at around the time Dan was asked to be president. On occasion, Dan confided in him about his fears and concerns. They talked over the phone or met for coffee and discussed the ups and downs of their positions. Gordon, a tall thin, handsome man fifteen years his senior, a psychologist by profession, has the uncanny ability of being one's best friend, father, therapist, and well, for lack of a better expression, one's guardian angel. They'd also run into each other at special interfaith programs such as the Reverend Martin Luther King Jr. community celebration.

"Yes, it's me in the flesh. How are you doing, Dan?"

"Okay, I guess. I assume you've heard what's been going on at Beth Emet?"

"How could one not? It's been all over the news."

"Gordon, you look incredible! I'm sorry I haven't reached out to you lately. How's your battle going? Anymore chemo?"

"Nope, done with all that. I'm doing great now. I'm at peace and happy."

"That's wonderful. I'm thrilled to hear it."

"How are you handling the tragic events?"

"It's been tough dealing with conflicting feelings. You know how he and I butted heads..."

"I remember you calling me after you spoke with USCJ."

"I feel guilty for pushing the Rabbi on the transparency thing. I feel in some way this was all my fault."

"Oh, Dan, whatever you may have done, you have to know that the Rabbi was dealing with his own demons. You shouldn't take responsibility for his struggles. It's like what I tell my patients, 'Just eat off your own plate....'"

"But I keep thinking I should've done something different to convince them all without it coming to this."

"Ah Dan, it's time you accepted your members weren't ready for the change you were offering, or the change they were asking for. It's time you let go."

"I tried to make things better and now the Rabbi's...gone. I feel like I accomplished nothing. The expression, 'No good deed goes unpunished' keeps bouncing through my head."

"I know you don't believe that, and even if you did, it wouldn't change who you are. You're a good person who'll always try to make things better. And you know, even with all the sorrow, a lot of good has come from your experience."

"But Gordon, I..."

"We often build an invisible wall that prevents us from seeing all we've accomplished. It also keeps us from achieving great things. Your wall is non-acceptance and beating yourself up over what you could've done, instead of appreciating what you did do. You know, Dan, things may not have turned out exactly the way you wanted them to, they rarely do. You've got to remember they turned out the way they were supposed to."

Dan smiles at the man whose words, like a heated blanket on a cold wintry night brings him the peace and equanimity he desires and has been searching for these last six months.

Gordon pulls a pen and a small notepad like the one the Rabbi used out of his pants pocket. He scribbles something on it and rips the page out. He folds it in quarters, pushes it into Dan's shirt pocket, and pats his chest. He leaves his hand there for a moment.

Dan notices his own heart beating and feels a warmth emanating from Gordon's hand, which permeates throughout his body.

"The next time you're feeling down about yourself, or you question whether doing a good deed is worth it, unfold this little paper and read it. And remember, I'll always be here for you. Just reach out to me anytime you need help."

Dan grabs Gordon and hugs him tightly.

When they release their embrace, he looks up with glistening eyes and says, "Thank you. Thank you, Gordon. Thanks for talking to me and listening."

"Anytime. I'm always here for you. Well, time for me to go."

Gordon strolls in the opposite direction of Dan who walks off to find Rick. He turns around one more time to see Gordon and wave goodbye. When he does, Gordon has vanished.

He thinks, *That's odd. I guess he really is in better shape.*

Dan trots through the supermarket and looks down each aisle. He spots Rick standing with Mr. Chasen in front of a shelf of the sugary cereals the boys like.

"Hey, look who I found," Rick declares.

Like Harold, Mr. Chasen encourages both of them to return to weekly services.

"I know it was rough, what happened and all. But the synagogue is not about one person. It's the big guy's place. It's where you need to go when things get tough." Mr. Chasen gazes past the men and waves his enormous hand high in the air.

"Hi Mrs. Berman!" The tiny elderly woman scoots her cart over to the men with the vigor of the energizer bunny. Next to the sizeable Mr. Chasen she looks even more diminutive.

"How are you doing, gentlemen?" she inquires.

The three men return her pleasantries.

"Dan, glad to see you. I've been wanting to talk to you. I rarely see you in synagogue. You need to come more often."

"I think you may be right Mrs. Berman. What do you think, Rick? How about we go next weekend?"

"Sure, that sounds nice."

"Well, that's wonderful. I'm happy to hear that."

"Yes, I think it's time…anyway, what did you want to talk to me about?"

"I want to tell you what a wonderful leader you've been for our synagogue. You too Rick." Mrs. Berman places her small, wrinkled hand on Rick's forearm.

"Without the both of you, I'm not sure how we could've gotten through these difficult times. It was just awful about the dear Rabbi. My heart aches for his poor family. When I recite the mourner's prayer for Harry, I recite it for him, too."

"Thank you, Mrs. Berman, that's kind of you."

"Also, I want you to know I've taken some of the money my late husband Harry left me, God rest his soul, and donated it in your honor to that wonderful fund you created."

"You mean the Lieutenant Alexander Gleason Memorial Fund?" Rick chimes in. "Yes, that's Dan's brainchild."

"That's generous of you, and I'm honored."

"It's well deserved."

Mr. Chasen asks, "By the way, who is Alexander Gleason?"

"He was a brave soldier killed in action in 2003 during the Afghanistan war. He and Denise Tenenbaum were planning to marry when he returned from combat."

"Oh dear, you mean Sandy's daughter. The one who passed away from cancer some years back. Tsk-tsk-tsk," utters Mrs. Berman as she bows her head and places her other hand on Dan.

"Yes, the money donated will go to the family members of the fallen."

"Oh, that's marvelous. My Harry would be proud of you. You know he fought in World War II."

"I didn't know that. May God bless him for his service to our country."

After the group chats a little longer, Mrs. Berman and Mr. Chasen disperse and leave Rick and Dan alone.

"Did you hear that? She's donated money in your honor to the fund."

"I heard it. That was good of her. I'm just glad to know Paul, along with other families will be helped."

Rick and Dan continue their shopping, traveling up and down each aisle retrieving the items Joy and Roberta requested. In nearly every aisle, a member of Beth Emet greets them warmly. Each interaction is the same. They are told how much they are missed at services and then praised for their service to the community.

They see Greenblatt who thanks Dan for supporting the "Whisky Jewbilee" event. It was here Greenblatt met Leah Lefkowitz, a quiet shy girl. He informs them the two are now "hot and heavy." By the aisle of soft drinks, they run into Rob who embraces them and sobs, talking about the Rabbi's tragic death. He congratulates himself for having appointed Dan president. They bump into old man Sid and even he praises Dan for his leadership and tells them the past presidents are proud of his leadership.

In the chip aisle snagging a large bag of popcorn, they are cornered by Mrs. Kupferberg who thanks Dan for recommending Rabbi Erlich to officiate her son's wedding.

"I know it wasn't easy finding a conservative Rabbi to perform a same-sex marriage. However, she was wonderful! She really got to know the boys. It made the ceremony special," she exclaims.

"Did you know she is one of two final candidates in our search for a new Rabbi?" Dan asks.

"Oh, that would be terrific!"

"I hear she has the inside track; you might want to reach out to Hope and let her know what you think of her," adds Rick.

"I'll do that!"

They see Mrs. Winthrop, who still holds down office affairs, shopping with her husband in the aisle of pet supplies, standing next to the bags of Jackson's favorite biscuits. She comes over and begs Dan for forgiveness, a scene which has played out several times since that infamous night.

"Of course, Mrs. Winthrop, you couldn't have known..." he assures her.

When they make their way to the freezer section and Dan opens the door and grabs some frozen pigs in a blanket, he hears, "Hello dear boy!"

He turns to find Jackie in a tight blue body-hugging dress and high heels standing behind him.

"How is my favorite past-president?" Jackie and Dan hug and she kisses him on the cheek, leaving a bright red lipstick stain.

"Norm is bringing one of his best bottles of pinot noir tonight. I look forward to a fun evening with you all."

Jackie turns to Rick and asks, "I assume you'll bring that gorgeous girlfriend of yours?"

"Roberta will be there Jackie. She wouldn't miss hanging out with you to hear your wonderful stories."

"This place is brimming with Beth Emet members. You can't swing a dead cat without hitting one...and here's another one. Sandy you handsome man, how are you doing and how is that adorable grandson of yours?"

"Hi Jackie, don't you look nice."

"Oh, Sandy you devil."

He turns to the men and gives them a big hug.

"How are you guys doing?" he says as he pats them on their backs.

"Dan, I can't thank you enough for the fund you created in honor of Alex. The extra money has really made a difference for Paul. He's now taking guitar lessons and playing Little League. He's a pitcher like his Grandpa."

"You can thank Jackie for that. She and Norm gave a generous donation. Also, I just saw Mrs. Berman, and she told us she'll be making a large contribution as well."

"You know how generous my Norm is...."

While Jackie and Sandy talk, Dan crosses to the other side of the aisle and opens the glass door, which sends a blast of cold air in his face. He grabs a carton of Joy's favorite ice cream, vanilla caramel chocolate chip. The door slams closed, and he turns around to find Mrs. Nusbaum standing before him.

"Hi Dan, how are you? Is this where you've been hiding? In the freezer section of Shop Rite?"

"Well, it would be a lot warmer at synagogue, wouldn't it Mrs. Nusbaum?" exclaims Rick.

"Yes, it would be since our wonderful past president finally fixed the air conditioner. So, when are we going to see you rejoin us again?"

"We're planning on coming next weekend Mrs. Nusbaum. I'm looking forward to seeing all of you there."

"Or we can just have services right here. We certainly have enough members present," says Sandy.

They all chuckle. Jackie stares at Dan, noticing a sad smile on his face.

She declares, "I would like to make an announcement in front of all you fine people. I know our illustrious leader has been through the wringer by some in our synagogue who fought him on all the wonderful things he tried to accomplish, and that includes our poor Rabbi. May he rest in peace.

"But I think Dan Barkan is the best president we've had. Dan, if I had a drink with me, I'd toast to you because I want everyone to know that you're worth the whole damn bunch of them put together."

"Hear, Hear!' cries Sandy, Mrs. Nusbaum, and Rick.

"Jackie, thank you, it means a lot! You've all been wonderful to me. This experience has really taught me who my friends are. Seeing all of you today and hearing other supportive members makes me certain the tragic events of six months ago are now past us…past us…pasta!

"Damn it. I forgot the angel hair for Max."

"I thought you got it," says Rick.

"I was going to, but then I got sidetracked and forgot. Oh jeez, I forgot to tell you. Guess who I ran into?"

"The Dalai Lama?" jokes Jackie.

"No, Gordon Diamond."

"Oh, he's a lovely man. How's he doing? I know he's battling cancer," asserts Mrs. Nusbaum.

"That's impossible Dan. You couldn't have run into Gordon," advises Sandy.

"Of course I did, and he looks great. He's fully recovered."

"Dan, ah, Gordon passed away last night. That wasn't him."

"What! But I just saw him. He was in the pasta aisle with me. I was getting angel hair for Max."

"You couldn't have. Really, he passed suddenly last night. He was counseling Lisa. She's really been shaken by what happened to the Rabbi. She got a call from Lilith, his office manager this morning."

"But I just spoke with him…" Dan cries as his eyes well up.

"Are you sure it was him?" asks Rick. "I know you've been going through a lot lately."

"No, I swear, you must believe me. He was there."

"Dan, I'm sorry, he's gone," sighs Sandy.

Jackie places her arm on his shoulder and says, "Oh, dear boy."

"Wait! I have a note from him, from just before he walked away. He stuck a note in my pocket!"

Dan takes out the tiny crumpled piece of paper with shaking hands.

They all crowd round to provide comfort and to get a glimpse of the words from the mysterious apparition Dan thought he saw.

He struggles to open the scrap.

Unfolds it gingerly.

In blue fine ink, they read the scrawled words on the wrinkled paper in astonishment.

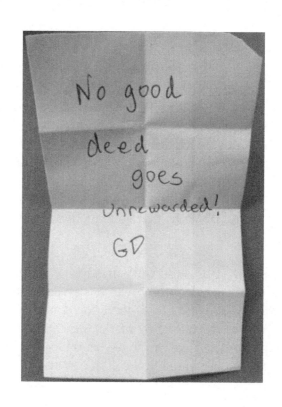

GLOSSARY

While many of these words are commonplace and part of the American lexicon, many may be unknown to some readers.

Ashkenazi. Ashkenazi is an adjective used to refer to the Jewish culture which developed in Germany and Eastern Europe (called Ashkenaz) in contradistinction to Sephardic Judaism, which has its distinctive roots in Spain and the Mediterranean. By extension, it now refers to Jews of Northern and Eastern European background (including Russia) with their distinctive practices and social customs.

Bar Mitzvah. Bar mitzvah means, literally, "son of the commandment": a Jewish boy who has achieved the age of 13 and is consequently obligated to observe the commandments. It is also the ceremony in which the boy marks this important rite of passage by reading from the Torah in the synagogue for the first time. The practice was first instituted in the 20th century.

Bat Mitzvah. Bat mitzvah means, literally, daughter of the commandment: a Jewish girl who has achieved the age of 12 and is consequently obligated to observe the commandments. In non-Orthodox communities, it is also the ceremony in which the girl marks this important rite of passage by reading from the Torah in the synagogue for the first time. The practice was first instituted in the 20th century.

Bima. The bimah is the raised area at the front of an Ashkenazi synagogue where the desk for reading the Torah is located.

B'rit Milah, Bris. B'rit milah is the covenant of circumcision, a ritual in which an eight-day-old male baby or a male convert to Judaism is circumcised. It is frequently referred to as a bris.

Bubbe. Yiddish word for grandmother.

Hanukkah, Chanukah. Hanukkah means, literally, "dedication." It is the eight-day Jewish holiday celebrating the rededication of the Temple in Jerusalem after it was reclaimed from the Seleucid Greeks in 167 BCE. Hanukkah is celebrated with the kindling of the menorah lights and the giving of gifts.

Chuppah. A canopy under which the bride and groom stand during a Jewish wedding ceremony

Dreidel. Dreidel is Yiddish for "spinning top." A dreidel is a pointed, four-sided top which can be made to spin on its pointed base. Dreidels are normally made of plastic or wood, though there are silver or glass "designer dreidels" available on the market, usually intended for display purposes. It is customary to play dreidel games on the holiday of Chanukah.

D'var Torah. A d'var Torah also known as a drasha or drash in Ashkenazic communities, is a talk on topics relating to a parashah (section) of the Torah—typically the weekly Torah portion.

El Malei Rachmim. "El Malei Rachamim", is a Jewish prayer for the soul of a person who has died, usually recited at the graveside during the burial service and at memorial services during the year.

Farbissina. A Yiddish word meaning "embittered"; a farbissiner is an angry, bitter, vocal (male) person, while farbissina is the corresponding female form.

Fradray dein kup. A Yiddish expression that is derived from the word drai meaning to spin, like a dreidel and the word kup meaning head. When someone fardrais their kup, it means they have nothing better to worry their head about.

High Holidays. The festivals of Rosh Hashanah (Jewish New Year) and Yom Kippur (Day of Atonement), the period of repentance in the first ten days of the Jewish new year. Also called Days of Awe or the High Holy Days.

Hora. A Romanian and Israeli folk dance which is performed in a circle. Traditionally danced during a Jewish wedding and other Jewish celebrations.

Kippah. The Hebrew word for a skullcap worn especially by Orthodox and Conservative Jewish males in the synagogue and the home. Yarmulka is the Yiddish word.

Kvells. Yiddish word meaning "to gush" or "swell." To beam with immense pride and pleasure, most commonly over the achievement of a child or grandchild.

Lashon Hara. The Hebrew term for speaking derogatory about a person. The phrase means "evil tongue."

Lag BaOmer. A Jewish religious holiday celebrated on the 33rd day (Lag in Hebrew has the equivalent numeric value of 33) of the counting of the Omer (a sheaf of new barley). It is common to celebrate Lag BaOmer with picnics and bonfires.

L'chaim. Hebrew meaning "To life." The toast offered, with raised glass, before sipping wine or liquor.

Mara De-atra. Means "master of the house" in Aramaic. It is a term associated with the local authority on Jewish law.

Mazel Tov. Literally means "good luck' in Hebrew but is used as a way to express "Congratulations!"

Menorah. A multibranched candelabra, used in the religious rituals of Judaism. The seven-branched menorah was originally found in the wilderness sanctuary and then later in the Temple in Jerusalem. It was a popular motif of religious art in antiquity. An eight-branched menorah modeled after the Temple menorah is used during the eight-day festival of Hanukkah.

Mensch. Comes from the German word for "person" but refers to a person of upright, honorable, and decent person.

Minyan. Hebrew word for "number" or "counting." A quorum of ten men (or in some synagogues, men and women) over the age of 13 required for traditional Jewish public worship.

Mitzvah. Hebrew word for "commandment." A virtuous, kind, considerate, and ethical deed.

Mourner's Kaddish or Mourner's Prayer. A 13th century Aramaic prayer which means 'sanctification' in Aramaic. It is related to the Hebrew word Kadosh, which means 'holy.' Mourners recite it for 11 months and on the anniversary of the death. Traditionally, a mourner is considered someone who has lost a father, mother, sibling, child, or spouse. Often, family or friends may choose to recite it as a sign of love and support.

Purim. The Hebrew word for "lots." Jewish festival held in the spring to commemorate the defeat of Haman's plot to massacre the Jews as recorded in the book of Esther.

Schmaltz. Yiddish for cooking fat, usually chicken fat. It is often used to refer to something that is overly emotional or sentimental.

Schmoozing. Yiddish for "to talk or chat." It is to chat in a friendly and warm manner, also, suggests a discussion for the purpose of gaining something.

Schmucks. From the Yiddish for an "ornament." Often defined as the male genital and is used as a derogatory term for someone who is stupid, foolish, and unlikeable.

Schvitz. Yiddish for sweat.

Shabbat Shalom. Greeting or departing line (hello or goodbye) used on Shabbat. Literally means in Hebrew, "peaceful Sabbath."

Shabbos goy. Yiddish for a non-Jew who is employed by Jews to perform certain types of work that Jewish religious law prohibits a Jew from doing on the Sabbath. Some of the more famous Shabbos goys are Elvis and President Obama.

Shiksa. A term used to refer to a girl or woman who is not Jewish. A sheygets is the male term.

Shul. Yiddish word for synagogue.

Shiva. Hebrew word for "seven." The traditional seven-day period of mourning observed by Jews immediately following the funeral of a parent, sibling, child, or spouse.

Simcha. Hebrew word that means gladness or joy. It is often used to refer to a party or celebration.

Tallit, Tallis. Hebrew word for "prayer shawl." A shawl with a ritually knotted fringe at each corner; worn by Jews in morning prayer.

Torah. Torah in Hebrew means teaching, direction, or guidance and law. The most prominent meaning for Jews is that the Torah constitutes the first five books of Moses traditionally thought to have been composed by him.

Tzedakah. A Hebrew word meaning "righteousness", but commonly used to signify *charity*.

Yasher Koach. The Hebrew words translate literally as "May your strength be firm." The idiom is commonly used in a more orthodox synagogue to congratulate someone on a job well done!

Yenta. It was originally a given Yiddish name for a woman but has since evolved to mean a woman who is a gossip or busybody. It is thought to be derived from the Italian word for gentile.

ACKNOWLEDGMENTS

Thank you to all those people who have helped and supported me and who may be sprinkled in some respects throughout the pages of this story.

To my beautiful and loving wife Helena for all her help with this book and our two wonderful sons Aaron and Alex and their contributions to the audio book. Love to Kate, a special person whose advice and penmanship has been invaluable. Special puppy snacks go to Brodey and Cory, and the late great Boomer all of whom are a part of Jackson.

Love to Mom and Dad. Mom, thanks for reading everything I've ever written and for supporting and promoting my writing. Dad, you gave me my sense of humor and my love of music. May you continue to rest in peace.

To all my brothers, their wives and my nieces and nephews, and their significant others for the love a support they've given through the years. Special thanks to my twin brother Randy, his wife Michele, and my nieces Samantha and Rachel, who inspired characters in the book and who provided counsel for the novel.

To Andy, Robyn, Jake, and Jordan and Uncle Milty, I love and appreciate you all. I can always count on your encouragement.

Special thanks also to Stacey Palant for her incredible support during what was both a difficult and wonderful time. Her strength and intelligence never cease to amaze me. Also, to her husband Adam whose humor and friendship I cherish.

Thanks to Lynne and Stu for being marvelous friends and inspiring and reading my work. Your support and love has always been overwhelming. Keep singing Lynne!

In memory of Gil Gordon, an incredible human being who always gave selflessly to his community.

Love to all my friends and fellow congregants who supported me during my time of community service.

Thank you to Thomas and Jess Bell for their hard work on marketing this novel.

Of course, to my editor Rodney Richards, who helped me fulfill my childhood dream of writing a novel. He has an unbelievable talent to take what I've written, improve on it, and not lose sight of exactly what I want to say.

Last but not least, thank you to my mother-in-law and talented artist Elaine Ivker for her artistic interpretation of *no good deed...* Her tireless effort, love, and support has been wonderful.

https://www.craigshermanwrites.com/artwork

Elaine Ivker
Let the Story Begin... 2022

ABOUT THE AUTHOR

 Craig's fiction, non-fiction, and poetry have appeared in various online and print publications, including Poetica Magazine. He has contributed extensively as a blogger for the Huffington Post, and at one time hosted the classic rock radio program "Connections" on WDDF radio.

Craig received his undergraduate degree in Economics and Finance from Temple University where he worked at the literary magazine, The Journal of Modern Literature. He earned his master's degree in Management Information Systems from St. Peter's University

His successful career in the technology industry has spanned three decades. Craig lives in New Jersey with his family and two rescue dogs.

Contact Me

www.craigshermanwrites.com

craigshermanwrites@gmail.com

You can also find Craig on major social media outlets.

Made in the USA
Middletown, DE
02 April 2022